Allan is an engaging and positive person with an outgoing character; he possesses a fine sense of humour.

Born and raised in Matabeleland, Rhodesia, Allan enjoys the outdoors, wildlife, exploring God's creations and the adventures that these pursuits bring. He has four adult children and five grand-children. Allan is a man of faith and is active pastorally in the local church.

He and his wife, Linda, and their extended family now reside in Mandurah, Western Australia.

To, Lindy, my wife, and my family, for their love and encouragement.

Allan Webb

CANDLES IN AN AFRICAN WIND

AUSTIN MACAULEY PUBLISHERS™
LONDON * CAMBRIDGE * NEW YORK * SHARJAH

Copyright © Allan Webb 2022

The right of Allan Webb to be identified as author of this work has been asserted by the author in accordance with sections 77 and 78 of the Copyright, Designs and Patents Act 1988.

All rights reserved. No part of this publication may be reproduced, stored in a retrieval system, or transmitted in any form or by any means, electronic, mechanical, photocopying, recording, or otherwise, without the prior permission of the publishers.

Any person who commits any unauthorised act in relation to this publication may be liable to criminal prosecution and civil claims for damages.

This is a work of fiction. Names, characters, businesses, places, events, locales, and incidents are either the products of the author's imagination or used in a fictitious manner. Any resemblance to actual persons, living or dead, or actual events is purely coincidental.

A CIP catalogue record for this title is available from the British Library.

ISBN 9781398468054 (Paperback)
ISBN 9781398468061 (ePub e-book)

www.austinmacauley.com

First Published 2022
Austin Macauley Publishers Ltd®
1 Canada Square
Canary Wharf
London
E14 5AA

Foreword

Sequel to the Rhodesians

David Livingstone, one of the greatest European Missionary Explorers, traversed the vast, wild South Central African continent. He was fascinated by the mighty Zambezi River, upon which he was the first European to witness the spectacular falls, which he named after Queen Victoria.

At the time that Livingstone was exploring this region, he was deeply affected by barbaric and bloodthirsty raids carried out by marauding tribes, migrating from the North to the South, namely the Zulus and Swazi. These tribes eventually settled in Natal South Africa and established themselves as the Great Warrior tribes. The peoples that inhabited the land just south of the Great Zambezi River (which was later to become the northern border of Southern Rhodesia) were the Mashonas. They were used to living in scattered villages situated on the higher points of granite outcrops and hills offering a commanding view of the surrounding country for purposes of early warning of these raiding tribes. After the Zulus and Swazis had settled in South Africa, the Mashona tribes enjoyed a period of relative peace, apart from the occasional raiding gangs of Arab slave traders, which lasted approximately seventy years.

This peace was shattered, first, by a breakaway element of Swazi tribesmen moving back up from the south who butchered their way remorselessly through the Shona nation and finally crossed the Great Zambezi River, going North and settling in Nyasaland (Malawi) and became known as the Angoni people.

Again, the Mashonas began to rebuild their nation. At the same time, the feared Matabele nation was being settled at Gubulawayo by the Rebel Chief Mzilikazi. A Zulu general who had fled the tyrant Zulu King Chaka in Natal and had first moved north to the Transvaal area where his army had been defeated by the Boers in a memorable battle in 1838. Subsequently, Mzilikazi decided to move further north and did so, traveling northwest through Bechuanaland and eventually settling in Gubulawayo ('the place of slaughter') just north of the Mtopo hills. From this locality, the Matabele Impi's ranged far and wide, ravaging local tribes of women, children and cattle. Once again, the Shona's were terrorised, as were other tribes as far afield as Barrotseland. The Matabele were fearsome warriors who knew no mercy and who held the whole region in thrall.

In 1870, a young Englishman of seventeen years, named Cecil John Rhodes, landed in Natal. Within a period of twenty years, he was to become the most powerful man within the four states that comprised South Africa.

Cecil John Rhodes had a dream, and it was to extend the sphere of British influence in Africa. Rhodes became a millionaire on the diamond fields of Kimberly. His money and influence as the Prime Minister of the Cape Colony assisted him in his quest to advance northwards into Africa and he persuaded Queen Victoria to grant him a charter to exploit and administer a new country to the north. With the groundwork thus laid, he organised his Pioneer column to travel north to Mashonaland avoiding the Matabele to the west. The column travelled through Bechuanaland and onto the Mashona plateau at Fort Victoria.

On 12 September 1890, the pioneer column arrived at a site later to become known as Cecil Square where they raised the Union Jack in military style and celebrated with three cheers. The column immediately erected a mud fort and called it Fort Salisbury after the British Prime Minister. Thus was born the fledgling Country of Rhodesia and the Jewel of Africa.

Map of Sub Saharan Africa drawn by Llewellin Jones:

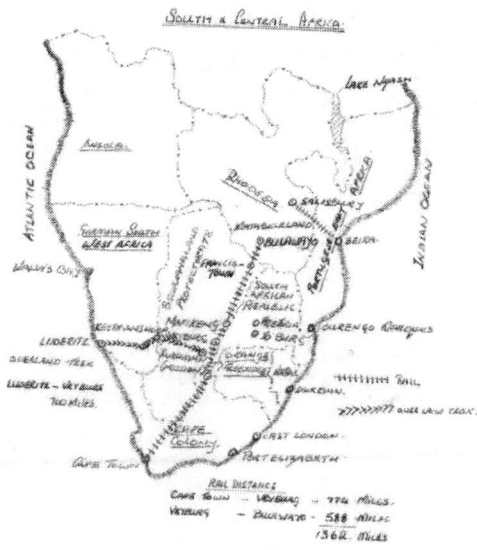

Candles in an African Wind

Exile and a Journey Begins

A blackened and distorted cauldron was chained to a makeshift cart. It contained a tasteless, lukewarm gruel which comprised the one and only meal that would be served to the prisoners today.

The squealing of the cart's wheels was the anticipated signal. An introduction to the hordes of bored and starving hopefuls, a teasing call to a possible meal for those willing and able to fight for the paltry reward.

Hunger-crazed, these dehumanised inmates fought wildly, jostling for position, whilst baying in a frenzy of raucous screaming and growling, desperate in their attempts to achieve the front of the line. Arms were extended through the bars, thrusting and waving their filth encrusted, vitally precious bowls, cups and, indeed, any receptacle that would hold a mouthful of the diluted broth.

Brady was shocked by the scene that unfolded before him. He moved backwards, towards the false sanctuary of a vacant corner within the chronically overcrowded cell. In his attempt to avoid the melee, he almost tripped over a disgusting wooden bucket which overflowed with human waste.

William Brady gagged in utter revulsion but was transfixed and watched on. His sensitivities arrested by the barbaric behaviour of the inmates where, with total disregard, the weak and incapable were cruelly flung to the rear beyond help and hope; although their crime may have been petty, many paid the ultimate price.

One such inmate, an elderly man, already reduced to skin and bone, sat on the floor, his threadbare jacket pulled tightly around his emaciated body. The scum encrusted collar taught around his ears, he leaned against the grimy, mould-covered wall and his feet were wrapped in discarded rags. He stared at the floor. His face was lined with dirt, which clung to his matted white beard. Brady was both appalled and deeply moved by this pathetic vision.

As if he had read William's thoughts, the old man turned his grey head slowly revealing an expressionless face. Wheezing painfully, he coughed softly and then in a cultured but breathless voice he said, "Survival of the fittest is the law in this jungle and that, my son, is the sad truth. Whenever and wherever the human race is devoid of divine order and its principles, we are more wicked and cruel than the beasts and animals over which we have dominion. May God have mercy," he whispered then resumed his blank gazing at the floor.

On the fourth day of September in Queen Victoria's year of 1882, the Crown Court in Reading, South England, had convened and the fate and future of one William Stuart Brady was about to be decided by his Honour Jonathan Doyle Q.C. He was fearfully known as 'Deadly Doyle' by the scores of forgotten inmates now wasting away within the tragic gloom of these disease-ridden, rat-infested, chambers of punishment.

The English Prisons were desperately overcrowded, understaffed and badly administered. A burgeoning problem for the authorities of Her Majesty's Prisons and the Government as a whole. This situation had not been helped by Australia's refusal to accept further shiploads of prisoners onto her seemingly endless shores.

In addition, reforms to the British Penal laws of punishment and servitude resulted in a reduction of public hangings for the less serious crimes. The authorities were leaning towards the modern theory of incarceration and productive punishment and, as a result, English Prison facilities had become grossly inadequate.

A large number of those suffering within these cells had been justly incarcerated but many were innocent, without the means to legal representation.

Many poor souls had descended into criminal acts due to their desperate poverty and the necessity to provide for themselves and their dependents.

Victims of their time!

Today the charge placed against the ragged, but imposing, accused was simple. Poaching on Queen's Land and caught in possession of several rabbits, two brace of pheasant and a flint lock, which bore the mark of H.M. Royal Armoury.

The Magistrate cleared his throat with pompous authority, signalling that the mumbling in the gallery should cease at once.

"Am I to understand that the Accused claims he was employed by the Senior Game Keeper to hunt the before-mentioned game and was also supplied with a weapon by the same Game Keeper, who vehemently denies all knowledge?"

This statement produced loud groans and murmurings from the gallery.

"That is so, Your Honour," replied the Clerk of the Court.

"Hmm, well since there is no evidence to support the accused's claim, and since the senior game keeper has been in the employ of the Royal Estate for many years without prior accusations of this sort, we must assume this incredible story a deceitful fabrication by the accused. Fabricated to subvert the course of justice, and indeed to incriminate a loyal servant of the crown…a serious state of affairs…to be tried under The Game Act of 1831!"

The noise in the gallery now rose further.

One of those in the dock, a poorly spoken individual, clothed in filth encrusted rags, awaiting his own trial, leaned forward and proclaimed his own and Brady's innocence, swearing loudly. His face was covered in ulcerous lesions. His breath was putrid, emanating from a mouth of rotting teeth. His odorous body caused Brady to wretch.

An episode of intense panic gripped the accused. Was this to be his future? Despair overwhelmed him. He had to escape this hellish situation. He grasped the wooden rail before him with such force his entire body trembled. He uttered a prayer and slowly the ensuing pain from his strained muscles calmed him.

"Silence, silence or I will be forced to clear the court," ordered the judge, as he hammered loudly, welding his polished gavel with contemptuous vigour.

Deadly Doyle, turned to face the accused, dramatically holding his silence as he stared at the ashen faced prisoner who stood with huge hands nervously kneading the restraining bar, confining himself and others within the dock.

"William Stuart Brady, you have been tried by the Queen's Court and found to be guilty of being in possession of arms belonging to Her Majesty, as well as holding numerous items of poached game, also belonging to Her Majesty!"

At this point there was a commotion at the door and a tall and well-dressed gentleman entered the court. A man acquainted with the mantle of authority and with a bearing that was unmistakably military. He held a riding crop in his hand which he raised and in a loud and clear voice cut into the proceedings.

"Forgive me, Your Honour, but I have come straight from a crofter's hut on the Royal Estate, within which we discovered many carcasses of poached game and numerous weapons in the care of two villains who swear they, too, were employed by the Game Keeper, Mr Jones."

On hearing this evidence Jones, the chief witness, who only moments before, had sat smugly in the gallery, leaped frantically from his seat, in an attempt to escape through the rear court room doors. This caused further disruption to proceedings but he was easily, though forcibly, subdued by the court police stationed either side of the doors and was dragged pleading and protesting into the bowels of the building.

The bemused judge, now scowling and shaking his head, brought order to the court once more by again hammering vigorously with his gavel.

"And who might you be, sir?" enquired the frustrated judge whilst dabbing at his forehead with a handkerchief.

"I am Colonel Milton-Smythe, Your Honour, and the accused man you have in custody (the colonel indicating Brady with his cane) is from Milton Estate, belonging to my family. Mr Brady has served our family since his youth. A good and trusty worker who was forced to leave our employ by an unscrupulous and corrupt manager who took advantage of his position and replaced our loyal labourers with a horde of his lazy relatives, don't you know? This mischief all transpired whilst I was absent abroad on military operations in the Colonies."

Doyle stared fixedly at the colonel, biting his lower lip in contemplation.

"Well, sir, your Mr Brady has broken the law, and it is common knowledge that to hunt on the Queen's land is forbidden. Although he was misled by a scoundrel, he is still guilty of poaching, and by English law, must be punished.

"My Lord, I beg the Crown's mercy in this case since Brady is a good man fallen on hard times and has shown an uncharacteristic lack of judgment." The judge sat in deep consideration for what seemed an eternity and then he cleared his throat in a most indulgent fashion, enjoying this unusual test of his judicial skill.

"Hmm, most unusual," said the judge to no one in particular. "Very well, sir, may I ask you to approach my bench?"

The judge, Colonel Milton-Smythe, as well as the prosecution were engaged in hushed but, occasionally, animated conversation for some time until there appeared to be unanimous agreement. At this point, the colonel retreated to the rear of the court and the judge regarded the prisoner with undisguised disdain.

"William Stuart Brady, in the eyes of this court you are guilty and, therefore, you are to be taken to the prison at Harwood where you will be incarcerated for a period of five years." A disgruntled moan rippled through the court. Brady felt cold fear grip at his stomach once more.

"Or…" said the judge, enjoying the dramatic moment, "you can be released into the bond of Colonel Milton-Smythe, who has agreed to stand good for your fine of three guineas, payable to the Crown. However, the condition of non-incarceration is that you will remain in the service of the colonel until your bond is paid in full. In addition, you will be required to accompany the colonel to South Africa when he leaves with his regiment in due course. Mr Brady, you will not set foot on English soil for a period of five years, after you leave England. The decision is yours and must be made at once."

The prisoner stared straight at the colonel and said in a loud, but trembling voice, "I will pledge myself into the bond of the good Colonel and accompany him to South Africa, Your Honour."

The passage from Southampton, bound for the Cape of Good Hope, was not an enjoyable one for William Brady. Only a short while into the Bay of Biscay and Brady was in an ever-rolling and plunging world which afflicted him with dreaded seasickness, his heaving gut adding to the greenish bile of many other groaning men. This hunter, a man of the fields and open spaces, was caged "tween" decks, lying helpless within a foul, cramped, miserably cold environment. This was permeated by the stench of human vomit expelled by those trapped and afflicted within this ever-rolling and pitching hell.

William was beyond fear and considered death a reasonable alternative to his present situation. Condensation dripped from every surface. 'As if there isn't enough water outside' thought Brady. He swore to himself that, should he survive this ordeal, he would never again step foot aboard another ship.

As the voyage progressed southwards the weather eased and the seas calmed, ending the terrible rolling and pitching of the troopship, which had now altered to a steady, thrusting sway. The steel hulled 'Penrose' seemed to gain energy from the improved human spirit on board. Many of the soldiers who, for days, had wished to die rather than continue and endure the sea sickness, were now finding their sea legs and were excited by the great power of white sails as they harnessed the fresh winds that powered them towards the warm tropics.

William Brady looked forward to his short periods on deck during this fine weather and from time to time he and others could see the coastline of Africa,

'The dark continent', bringing feelings of excitement and adventure as well as foreboding to William. He was unsure how he would adapt to serving as a batman for five years.

William was certain he could discern a differing, uneasy motion in the ship. Six days had passed since they had crossed the equator and the scuttlebutt through the lower decks was that the ship was to dock at Walvis Bay for provisions. One of the wardroom stewards told Brady that he had heard that the barometer was dropping and that the ship's master was concerned about the forthcoming weather.

Freedom Storm

Every moveable item on board had been lashed or chained down with the storm now grasping at the troopship, 'Penrose'. Mountainous seas preceded the storm's coming, not from the south, but from the northwest. The ship's crew had removed all sails save for a small storm sail. The Master had decided to change course from Walvis Bay and to steer south by west running before the storm, easing to the west away from the notorious reefs and shallows of the southwest coast of Africa. As the full nightmare of the storm enveloped the 'Penrose' in a hell of shrieking winds, pounding waves and deluge of cyclonic rain, it became obvious to the helmsman and the officer of the watch that the seas coming in over the starboard rail would cause untold damage unless the ship steered further to the east. The helmsman tightened the cords that held him at his post.

With a report like that of a small cannon, the storm sail was ripped and shredded by the unbridled power of the gale force winds. Hand over hand, on the storm lines, the captain climbed to the Pilot deck just as another enormous wave came in over the starboard rail pushing the ship downwards and causing her to stagger and groan under the crushing force of furious seas.

The Master had a choice, either he turn the ship into the wind, or run before the storm with a sea anchor. He chose the latter, fearing to chance broaching the ship in these mountainous seas. Below decks William Brady was both terrified and sick. This huge ship was plunging and rising, being tormented and tossed mercilessly by such wild forces the likes of which he had never seen or imagined. He cried out in abject fear, an involuntary wail, lost in the turmoil of the storm. After the previous steep plunge it did not seem possible to Brady that the battered ship would rise again, but she did, corkscrewing upwards only to plunge once more. Seamen were put to the perilous task of fashioning the sea anchor.

Not a soul would realise should I be washed overboard in the next moment, thought a terrified deckhand. He was literally frozen and clutching to his frail lifeline. Cringing in mortal fear beneath the withering gaze of the first officer, who himself clung to the railings with all his strength, praying inwardly for God's mercy.

During all his sailing days, he had never witnessed a sea so angry, so tumultuous as this. With the sea anchor deployed, the ship ran directly before the storm reducing the violent motion. The slight alteration in direction resulted in less water crashing aboard and, though the sea anchor was restraining the 'Penrose', the wind and sea conspired to push her on a convergent course with the treacherous coast. Wishfully, the ship's captain calculated his ship to be well clear of the treacherous reefs along the skeleton coast, but prudently placed additional lookouts on the bow. There seemed little point since the night was as black as a coalers chimney, relieved sporadically by the horrendous flashes of lightening which illuminated the heaving chaos all around.

The scene between decks was just as chaotic. Water sloshed, ebbed and flowed about the compartments, ankle deep and contaminated with every imaginable piece of equipment. This included parcels of food, clothing and other personal paraphernalia rolling or floating across the deck beneath the groaning rows of swaying hammocks. The darkness was probably a blessing to the majority of poor souls now sick beyond caring. The screaming storm seemed, to Bill Brady, to have gone on for an eternity.

He was, firstly, aware that the shrieking of wind had eased before realising that the ships motion was much less violent. He recognised he was able to hear the occasional high pitched shout of a seaman giving soundings. He eased himself from his hammock, still weak from the terrible nausea. Suddenly, gripped by an acute attack of claustrophobia, he had a desperate need to be out in the fresh air above. Against orders, he moved towards the companion way. He was bare foot and wore only an undershirt and trousers. He passed several sailors within the companion way who were focused on maintaining their footing in the dim light and paid him little attention. The motion of the ship was still unpredictable and threatened to throw him from his feet.

Crouching low, William slipped onto the upper deck unnoticed. White crests topped huge seas which the wind ripped away in shredded spume, whistling and shrieking, gusting with a demonic force. To the east the sky was coal black, but Brady could see odd specks of light on the huge back of Africa. William was shocked at how close inshore the ship seemed. He tarried for a short while, shivering with cold and fear. A fear, the like of which, he had never before experienced.

With great determination, he managed to overcome his dread and turned back towards his awful billet. As he moved aft towards the companionway, he was thrown violently to the deck as the entire ship staggered, lifted and staggered again. There was a great rendering crack from above and huge mast heads and tangled rigging rained down from above. The great ship was fast aground, making no headway. A glance around and Brady saw many sailors getting back to their feet. An alarm bell sounded and all manner of personnel were pouring out onto the deck from every portal. It required a musket shot from the marine captain to bring order to the ensuing chaos.

Terrified, the soldiers were forced back below decks by equally distraught marines. As soon as the Master had taken control once more, he ordered two boats to be lowered on the leeward side of the ship. Two platoons were marched up on deck with their personal equipment and ordered into the long boats. Brady had barely found his feet when the bosun's mate had pressed him and two other sailors into the lowering of the first boat. As the bottom of the longboat hit the turbulent sea below, the bosun's mate screamed the  order to 'let go', and the sailors released the ropes on the davits. The long boat bounced and danced on the swells in danger of smashing against the steel hull of the ship.

Amid the thunderous noise of the storm and the crazed shouting of those on deck, Brady plus the two other sailors, were ordered down the side nets to control the boat. William Brady, though strong and agile had no experience in seamanship, especially in such adverse conditions. As the angry ocean boiled and surged beneath he climbed down the nets at half the speed of the other two and dangled helplessly till one of the sailors managed to pull him into the boat. The sea sucked and surged between the hull of the ship and the long boat. Brady lost his balance, desperately lunging for a handhold.

Fortunately, he fell inboard, his hands slipping on the drenched seat, he went headlong striking his jaw and his ribcage catching the edge of the bench with terrific force, which winded and knocked him senseless all at once. He awoke to a press of men crowding into the boat, milling unsteadily about him. He was immediately aware of the metallic taste of blood in his mouth and the chaotic motion of the boat. Oars were locked into the rowlocks and the bosun's mate called out for the long boat to be cast away.

"Talk about out of the bloody pan into the fire," shouted an unknown soldier next to Brady. William did not reply as he was struggling to breathe through his bloodied mouth and each plunge of the longboat brought stabs of intense pain to his ribs. His view of the sea was obscured by those bunched around him and, for this, he was grateful.

He sat on the floor between two benches. He noted that the sky above was obscured and seemed low, with clouds scudding not too high above his head. There was a good deal of water thrashing about in the bottom of the boat and it was ice cold. The barrier of bodies around him reduced the impact of the freezing wind and spray, but he was chilled to the bone and shaking uncontrollably. He wished he had taken the time to don his tunic and boots. Above the wind he could hear the roar of the surf and, for a moment, he caught the scent of rotting fish. Lurching and bucking, the boat entered the surf.

The bosun's mate ordered the sailors to ship oars as he controlled the boat into the shallows. When the boat had been steadied within the wind driven surf, now closer into the beach, the excited soldiers almost capsized the boat in their anxiety and relief to disembark onto solid ground. William Brady, although desperate to gain the shore, was unable to stand. His ribs must be cracked, he thought. He groaned in agony when the two sailors dragged him off the boat and deposited him, somewhat roughly, into the shallow but rampant surf, in their haste to return to the ill-fated ship.

"We must return and remove more people from the ship before high tide so that the Master can re-float her. That's if she hasn't broken up in the meantime. You'd be better off here, rather than trying to climb back aboard the ship in these seas and in your condition, mate," shouted the leading seaman.

And with that they turned their lurching craft seawards and urged the boat towards the roaring waves and howling wind. They were soon out of sight and hearing, swallowed by the blanket of darkness and the roar of the rampant surf.

The troops had moved higher up the beach, now drummed into orderly fashion, and the commander gave orders for the formation of a defensive position, none of which was heard by Brady being buffeted and rolled, unseen and injured in the tormented surf. He was about to shout for assistance when suddenly he decided to remain silent.

Fear and excitement gripped him. What was he thinking? He had no water, no food, no weapon, no identification papers, not even a pair of boots, but no one was aware of his presence. Those who had taken him off the boat would report he was injured and deposited by them in the shallow, but rampant, surf. He quickly reasoned that, if ever there was a chance to disappear and slip the weight of his bondage, this was it. He would rather die here on solid ground in this unknown land, than reboard and endure the living hell of that ship.

William Brady began a slow and painful crawl. Half-drowned and dizzy with pain and exhaustion, he pulled himself out of the surf and turned southwards along the beach into the unknown, but beckoning darkness and possible death…or freedom.

Divine Water

Fritz Grueber and his young fiancée, Anna, had left the horse and trap in the care of a coloured servant. They had followed the track that ran north from the small fishing village at Luderitz, formerly Robert Bay. The couple's intention was of picnicking whilst Fritz continued with his painting. He was busy with a seascape of Shark Island looking from a point north on the cliff top, southwards, thus capturing the Island and the beautiful bay in the background.

Anna carried a basket whilst her future husband carried his easel and canvas. She thought he looked dashing. He had his rifle strapped to his back and a water bottle hung on his belt. A picture of a modern pioneer! She hoped the outdoors would improve his dark moods of late. The day was indeed beautiful with blue sea and an almost cloudless sky, although there was a brisk sea breeze. There was little evidence of the storm which had passed four days previously, other than the dampness underfoot on a usually dry ground.

The British troop carrier had re-floated herself and had sailed south to anchor out in the roads off Robert Bay. Her captain had despatched the first officer and a small crew to obtain tar and additional materials to assist with repairs. The British sailors did not receive a warm welcome, but were adequately supplied with their required materials. The 'Penrose' had sailed the previous evening en route to Cape of Good Hope. Many of the local fishermen were amazed at the British ship's survival as not many ships were known to sail away from this treacherous coast once having floundered in its deadly grip. No doubt the steel hull had been a huge asset in this circumstance.

Sea birds of all types screamed and squabbled on the cliffs and ledges. A slender golden ribbon of beach hugged the rugged base of the dark rock and then gave way to the white froth tipped waves which danced in the morning sun. Anna laid a small blanket on the rocky surface in the lee of a large boulder. Fritz erected the easel using rocks to anchor the feet. He then sat down on the blanket with his back to the rock and had the warm sun shining on his face. Anna leaned her head on his shoulder and purred with contentment. They had a breakfast of cheese, sauerkraut and boiled eggs and drank fresh buttermilk. When satisfied, Fritz placed his canvas on the easel and began his work. Anna walked towards the cliff edge.

"Not too close to the edge, my angel," Fritz warned her. "The rock is slippery and unstable."

"I will be fine," she assured him, as she wandered off to look down on this wild and fascinating coastline notorious for the number of ships it had wrecked. Anna gave in to an involuntary shiver as she gazed out over the cold Atlantic. The wind tugged at her bonnet as if nature was warning her back from the cliff edge. The scent of the sea was strong and invigorating. Shading her eyes, she gazed southeast taking in the panorama of Shark Island. Huge seas crashed against its seaward shore.

She could see the colony of seals on the beach of the mainland like so many humans enjoying the sun on some European Riviera. Fritz had told her that the seals ran a daily gauntlet between the Island and the open sea as the Great White tipped sharks were in abundance and hence the name of the island. She drew her gaze slowly back along the beach and cliff. A boat was anchored close to the shore harvesting guano from the thousands of birds nesting on the cliff ledges and crags. Further out to sea she could see fishing boats heading into shore. What a spectacular day, she thought.

Anna turned to look to the north though her vision of the coast line was obscured as the cliffs moved out to the west and then continued north, invisible from where Anna stood. Sea birds of every description swooped and soared about the cliffs with an accompanying cacophony of screams and cries, continually resounding in the background.

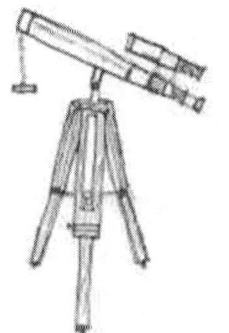

Occasionally, she would see a bird dive with amazing speed towards the sea and disappear under the water only to reappear with a sardine in its bill. She could see a rivulet of rain water cascading down from a point high up on the cliff face across from where she stood. The water glistened and sparkled in the sun as it fell to a ledge just above the thin strip of beach at the base of the rocks. This waterfall was an unusual sight since this was such a dry and waterless part of the world and was obviously a result of the recent storm. Anna wondered what birds and, indeed, other wildlife would enjoy this provision of fresh water. That's strange she thought as there were no birds on that ledge, just a collection of rocks, unusually light in colour when compared to those all around. The rocks moved! Anna was sure the rocks had moved! She watched for a while…no movement. Her interest aroused, she scampered back to Fritz. He had set up his telescope close to where he worked. Anna asked if she might borrow it for a few minutes. She unclipped the ornate instrument from its stand and hurried back to her vantage point. She aimed the telescope at the ledge and focused the optic. Her heart jumped. In the visor was a bedraggled man lying crumpled and half naked on the ledge obviously in some distress. Fritz came running in response to her anxious call. She handed him the glass and pointed to the ledge.

"I can see him," Fritz said. "I think he may be dead."

"No, no," said Anna, "I saw him move earlier."

"He may be a deserter, a pirate or a criminal," said Fritz.

Clearly her escort was reluctant to get involved in this strangers misfortune. Anna was astounded.

"Fritz Grueber," she exclaimed. "I cannot believe you are standing here passing judgement on a fellow human being whom you don't know and who may be dying before your very eyes. If you will not do anything to help him, I will do it myself," she fumed. He held her shoulder.

"Anna, Anna," he moved to calm her, "This is Africa and not Hamburg. Here we need to be most careful."

"Hamburg or Luderitz, he is still our neighbour and he needs our help!" she stated emphatically. Shrugging his hand from her shoulder she spun around and moved off at a trot towards where they had left Luka, the servant with horse and trap. Anna was right of course, but this was just so inconvenient thought Fritz as he hastily, though reluctantly, collected his equipment, leaving the blanket and basket where they lay. Luka, the servant, was already placing the gelding into harness when Fritz reached Anna.

"I am sorry Anna. Of course you are right, we will have to return to town where I will saddle a horse and ride up the beach and see to this man. If your brother Johan is available I will ask him to accompany me." Fritz then turned and instructed Luka to go and collect the items left behind.

Anna's face remained red with anger and disappointment. She had witnessed this lack of compassion before in her husband to be, especially towards the local tribes people. He tended to dismiss anyone or situation where no personal gain was in the offing. Anna prayed she was wrong. She had tried so hard to please Fritz since she had arrived in this remote outpost and he was so handsome and had been charming from their first meeting on the ship that had brought her from Hamburg. Anna had come out from Hamburg to assist her brother Johann at Luderitz. Also her brother and father had persuaded her that her health was sure to improve in the dry coastal region. A visit would also be beneficial for Johann as he dearly missed his younger sister. Johan Scholtz had trained as a Medical Doctor in Hamburg and had come out to South West Africa after reading an article written by Heinrich Vogelsang. The article was printed in the Hamburg Weekly, which reported that a new settlement had been planted in Robert Harbour, South West Africa where a Hanseat from Bremen, named Adolph Luderitz, had purchased land from a local Nhama Chief and set up a trading post. The article promised new horizons and prosperity to those pioneers who would take the challenge to open up new lands for the Father Land. Johann and his family were vibrant members of the Hamburg Missionary Society, Anna included, and Johann felt a strong call to go and set up a practice at Luderitz, now the name of the settlement. From there he could reach the native tribes with the Gospel and also be useful in this isolated new community. Johann met with Heinrich Vogelsang in the winter of 1884 and was warmly received in his intentions by both Luderitz and Vogelsang. By the following spring Johan had embarked to Luderitz, South West Africa.

Johann and Fritz arrived at a point on the beach below the ledge which slopped upwards at a gradual angle. The beach below the ledge was wet, caused by the run off from above. Indentations in the wet sand described where the unfortunate person above had crawled up the rock, perhaps to trace a better source of the water. Johan did not hesitate. He scrambled up the rock, slipping on the wet surface as he went. Will Brady lay with his head near a bowl like depression in the black rock which was full of water being perpetually replenished from the cliff above. His face was covered with dark stubble in contrast to his fair hair. A huge purple bruise ran from the base of his left jaw to below his eye. This whole area was swollen and blistered from the sun. Johan shook him gently. The victim's eyes opened. He weakly scooped water into his mouth without moving his head. Most of the water dribbled back into the pool. His eyes moved slowly around, not focusing. A barely audible croak escaped the cracked and unmoving lips. Johan got down lower with his ear close to Brady's mouth.

"What did you say?" he asked the stricken man.

Brady croaked and hissed. Johan listened.

"What is he saying?" asked Fritz.

"I think he said 'this water's mine'." The prone figure shook his head slightly and Johann listened once more.

"This water is divine," croaked Brady, as he closed his eyes slipping back into oblivion.

Johann smiled as the divine placement of the freshwater had surely saved the stranger's life.

The Trader

"Boris! Borrrris!" Fritz Grueber stood at the office window looking down at the yard below.

"I want my consignment off loaded as soon as possible. Why are these stevedores milling about the yard and not waiting at the wharf? I want those guns on the wagons ready to go overland to the Boers. I told you the rains will soon make the rivers impassable. No more delays 'Schnell! Schnell!" (Hurry! Hurry!) The Arms trader was shouting unnecessarily loudly as Boris occupied the very next cubby hole adjacent to the lavish office of his irritated employer.

'There was always a reason to hurry,' thought Boris. The ship has only just been sighted and would take another two hours to dock. His cousin, Fritz Grueber, was in charge of the business on this side of the Atlantic and only one thing mattered. The Deutschmark or, more recently, the Boer Gold!

Tension between the British and the Boers was increasing daily in South Africa. War was imminent. The British administration had already placed an embargo on arms arriving at ports in Natal and the Cape Province destined for the Northern Boer held territories of Transvaal and the Orange Free State.

The Boers had wrestled against the British influence since 1815, when the British acquired Cape Town at the Congress of Vienna. The British extended their control into the Cape Province and into Natal pushing the Boers further north into the interior of Southern Africa, effectively stealing the Boers access to the seaports. The embittered Boers continued to trek north, crossed the Vaal River and founded the two 'British Free States' namely the Transvaal and the Orange Free State. This became the Boer Republic. A fragile patina of peace followed until 1861 when diamonds were discovered in Kimberly in the Orange Free State. Up until this point the British Administration had been disinterested in the arid, wild Boer regions of the north. However, directly after the diamond discovery the British insisted on a Border recertification which included Kimberly into the Cape Province. The Boers were rudely pushed aside and Cecil

John Rhodes and Alfred Beit formed the Famous De Beers Company. This infuriated the Boers and, when shortly afterwards, in 1886 the Great Gold Strike was made at Wit Waters Rand, where, once again the British were determined to take control, the Boers were equally determined to hold onto the Transvaal and its riches. In addition, since the Germans had annexed the coast of South West Africa in 1884 the relationship between the Boers and the Kaiser had strengthened. Initially through the purchase of mining technology, and later, through the building of the rail link from Nelspruit in the North Eastern Transvaal to Lorenzo Marques on the East coast of Africa.

The British were keenly aware that an accord between these two adversaries would threaten their ability to hold dominance in the mineral rich South and Central Africa. President Paul Kruger, the leader of the Boers, had already confirmed a pledge of assistance from Germany. This included sales of urgently required armaments through his connections with the Kaiser. It was within these winds of war that Grueber had grasped his opportunity and was supplying arms from both Luderitz, on the West Coast of Africa; then overland to Vryburg in the Free State and by ship through Lorenzo Marques on the East Coast of Africa and finally overland to Nelspruit in the Transvaal, thus avoiding the British embargo. In just a few months Grueber had made a fortune from this vital and historic arms trade and was known to the Boer hierarchy simply as 'the Trader'. Fritz Grueber was as shrewd as he was greedy, however, he was efficient and his merchandise was of the highest German quality.

Within the manifesto for delivery to the Boers, were Krupp Cannons 12 and 15 pounders; Creusot 115 mm field guns, fondly known as 'long Toms' (capable of projecting an 88 pound shell 11 000 yards); Maxim machine guns and Maxim pom poms. These guns were used to fire continuous bursts of 1lb percussion fused shells and were highly effective against armoured trains and other fortified positions. Perhaps most importantly, Fritz was able to supply Mauser rifles. The Mauser was an outstanding small arms weapon having a ten round magazine and graded sites to 2 000 meters. This rifle was highly sought after, although the Boers would also purchase Martini Henri and Kraff Jorgenson rifles. A mountain of ammunition was to accompany each shipment of arms. The Trader had become so engrossed in amassing his fortune he had lost perspective, even within his personal life. He had discovered a rare and wonderful woman in Anna Scholtz. Apart from her undeniable beauty, Anna was an accomplished musician and had been well known throughout the environs of Hamburg as a champion for the care of the poor and, in particular, for raising funds for the welfare of orphaned children. She was totally committed to the Hamburg Missionary Society. Anna was able to use the influence of her father and brother within the Medical fraternity to bring medical expertise into the poverty-stricken areas of Hamburg.

Johann, her brother, taught her as much as he could about practical nursing. A science at which she excelled and, when combined with her tender compassion for God's people, she brought hope to many in seemingly hopeless situations.

Grueber had met Anna on the merchant ship upon her outward passage. He had dined at the captain's table the same evening that Anna had been introduced to the Ship's Master. He had been dashing and interesting in his knowledge of Africa. He seemed to know everybody who was important, but, most endearing to Anna was the knowledge that this man was a good friend of Johann's and was able to tell her all about her brother's trials and successes in the past year since she had seen him last. Their relationship had strengthened during the three week voyage to Luderitz and, upon embarking the couple were quite comfortable within each other's company.

Johann had wept with joy when Anna ran down the gangway into his arms. He beamed at her with tears coursing, unashamedly, down his tanned cheeks. They chatted excitedly, simultaneously even, and laughed childlike in their sibling reunion. Grueber came across and shook Johann by the hand. Johann was about to introduce his sister when Grueber placed a familiar hand on Anna's shoulder and said, "I have already had the pleasure of meeting the lovely Anna."

Blushing slightly, Anna looked towards her brother and, just for a split second, saw a fleeting shadow in his eyes. He continued smiling and chatting, but Anna knew him so well and she was both alarmed and slightly annoyed with Johann. But, how she had missed him and he looked so well. Johann had so much to show his sister, so much to tell her.

They went everywhere together over the ensuing three months, but every other day Fritz would come courting Anna. Johann would simply continue with whatever he was doing and leave the couple alone.

Two and a half months after her arrival in Luderitz Fritz had gone to see Johann and made his intentions clear. He had asked Johann if he had any objection to his asking Anna to be his wife. Anna was aware of the reason for the men's meeting behind closed doors, but was concerned at the lengthy duration of the discussion. Although Johann emerged and hugged her, wishing her congratulations and all the very best for the future, she again sensed an indefinable reluctance in her brother. Once Anna had agreed to the engagement she began to notice slight changes in Fritz. Subtle changes in the way he addressed her. Almost as if, after her agreement, he now had complete control of her life, including the manner of her thoughts. He began to disregard what she had to say. Recently he had become annoyed with her because she had insisted on remaining to assist Johann set the fractured leg of a young coloured boy who had fallen from a tree. He had gone into a tirade a few days earlier when Boris, his assistant, had failed to hire an extra driver and wagon for the next trek overland to Vryburg. Boris had explained that he had sent notice to all possible sources, which were limited at best, and could do no more. Fritz had used foul language and slammed his office door. Anna was mortified. Although Grueber had apologised to her shortly afterwards, his words had lacked remorse and his manner was brash, almost indifferent. She had insisted he apologise to poor Boris, but he had refused, asking her not to interfere with his business affairs. These personality swings and black moods were a far cry from the dashing and humorous gentleman that had courted Anna on the ship.

The Englishman

'Dr J A Scholts' was inscribed onto the rectangular brass plate, which was secured onto the granite wall adjacent to the dark, but ornate, wooden door in the front of the small, stone cottage located at the edge of the bustling town of Luderitz. Apart from the grey stone façade, the whitewashed walls with a red iron roof, gave the cottage a neat and orderly appearance. A shaded veranda served as a temporary waiting area whilst Anna occupied the third room within the cottage. Johann utilised the front room as his surgery. He had no provision for bed ridden patients and had appealed, through Fritz Grueber, to the town council several weeks previously, for the building of an infirmary or small hospital to service the town. Previously all patients were interned onto an old whaling ship anchored in the harbour. There was a small livery room or shed which contained all the Doctors livery and horse feed. Johann had partially cleared the room and placed a wooden cot against one wall. He had removed the horse feed as it attracted rats.

His patient from the cliff edge slept soundly on the cot. Grueber had refused to house the man at his spacious and rather opulent house, stating that until he knew the strangers 'history' he could not take the chance of having him at Opel House. Anna had argued that he could be placed into one of the servants rooms, but Fritz had been adamant and had suggested that they take him to the stockade until they were sure who the Englishman was and from whence he had come.

The doctor's sister had demanded that Fritz leave and that she and her brother would see to the man's wellbeing. After a thorough examination Johann concluded that the patient was dehydrated and suffering from exposure. In addition to the swollen face, his ribs on the left of his body were badly bruised, possibly cracked. The doctor judged that the injuries were consistent with a fall since both the injuries were located on one side of the patient's body and there being no other evidence of injury. Johann and Anna washed him down and placed him on the cot. Rest and fluids were the order of the day.

Brady had been awake for much of the time that he was being examined and washed. He had an excruciating headache and was happy to remain dormant. He was not able to understand the foreign language however, the lady had seemed extremely angered and distressed.

He awoke to the whinnying of a horse outside his small and musty room. He sat up slowly. He felt dizzy. Brady eased himself off the cot onto wobbly legs, sat down and immediately drank deeply from a tankard of water near his bed. This was difficult as his face felt three times its normal size. He was trying desperately to orientate himself. He was most pleased to realise that he was still on solid ground. His side hurt and he felt a little dizzy. He heard voices and a knock on his door. William rose stiffly to open the door, but the visitor was already pushing it ajar. It was the lady and she bore a wooden tray upon which there was a bowl of soup and several small bread rolls. She was startled when she saw him up on his feet. She was small and slender with dark hair and huge blue eyes. She said something and smiled nervously.

Brady instinctively raised his hand to his forehead and realised he wasn't wearing a hat…in fact, he wasn't wearing much at all! He said, "Hello Madam," and retreated to the bed covering his underwear with embarrassment. She exited with the tray, much to his disappointment, as he realised that he was ravenously hungry.

Seconds later, the Doctor arrived with the tray and said, "Good morning, I think you are better now, Ja?" (Yes?) he smiled at Brady.

"Yes, thank you," replied the Englishman.

"Good, good, you must eat soup." The exuberant doctor balanced the tray on a small wooden box near the cot. Before Brady could move the Doctor placed a hand on either side of his head and looked into one eye and then the other. "Good, good you are fine, Ja?" and with that he waved to Brady and left the room, still smiling.

Some of the soup dribbled down the swollen side of Brady's mouth. He tilted his head slightly and poured the wonderful life-giving broth from the spoon into the right side of his mouth. Trying to open his jaw any wider was extremely painful. He had to soak the bread in the soup bowl in order to consume it but consume it he did, every last morsel.

The Doctor returned a short while later with a tape measure in his hand. He had knocked on the door and Brady had quickly covered himself once more and bid the visitor to enter. Again was disappointed when the Doctor appeared and not the pretty young lady. Johann walked into the small room and, bringing himself to his full height, he clicked his heels, bowed his head and smiling introduced himself as Doctor Johann Scholtz from Hamburg, Germany. William Brady felt at a disadvantage which was soon dispelled when Johann added, "Please do not get up."

"William Brady," the patient replied offering his hand and the men shook. The German's handshake was both firm and hearty.

"And where are you from?" the Doctor asked William. Brady hesitated momentarily.

"England," was all he said.

The doctor paused, giving William the chance to continue if he so wished. William remained silent so the doctor produced the tape measure. He said, "I will try to get you some clothes, so I need your sizes. Big sizes," he quipped and laughed. "And perhaps more soup, Ja?"

It took more than a month for Brady to heal completely and in that time a strong friendship had developed between Johann and himself. Johann told him a few days earlier that his face had returned to normal and that now even the horses would find him attractive. The skin on Brady's face had healed remarkably well and he had managed to shave for the first time in weeks. He caught Anna studying his profile whilst he was busy sharpening her scissors, she smiled…embarrassed, but said nothing.

Brady was fascinated by the desert surrounding the town and took advantage of every opportunity to accompany Johann on both medical and mission-oriented journeys. Will Brady had been around horses most of his young life but had done little riding. Johann had insisted that to ride, and ride well, was a pre-requisite in that part of the world. He put Will onto a horse as soon as he could. The first attempt was a disaster. William Brady had to dismount almost immediately due to the pain from his ribs. Anna was wild with her brother for even considering placing Brady on a horse in his condition and, him being a Doctor, he should have known better. Johann's excuse was that the ribs were only bruised and the pain would induce Brady to grip more tightly with his legs and thus he would become a better horseman and learn his skills more quickly, which is exactly what transpired. Brady and the horse became one in a very short space of time.

Brady loved to sing and was a natural baritone. Anna played her piano in the evening and practiced for the Sunday services. Brady would sit on the wide Veranda finding it melancholic to listen to the heavenly music, which brought memories of his home and in particular of his late grandmother, a tender and Godly woman.

Brady would sing along to his favourite hymns and was amazed that the Germans sang so many English hymns. Anna reminded him that they were God's Hymns and should not just be enjoyed by the English. As his friendship grew with Johann, Will Brady realised that he was falling in love with Anna. At first, he rationalised that she was a beautiful, educated and Godly lady and that any man, especially in this remote and predominantly male environment, would be attracted to such a creature.

It seemed that he and Anna would spend more and more time together, particularly where there was hard or heavy physical work required. William Brady was not only strong and capable but also ingenious.

Johann and Anna were continually bartering and expressing reasons why Brady's assistance was more important to their individual tasks until one day in frustration Johann told Brady, in Anna's presence, that he had become so beneficial to assisting his Practice that he was now going to offer him permanent employment. Anna tried to show her enthusiasm for Brady's sake, but she was obviously extremely miffed with her brothers plan to monopolise William, a point that Brady didn't miss and found exciting. Will Brady told Johann that he was still indebted to both him and his sister for all that they had done for him and that granting him board and lodgings and friendship was payment enough for the present. Johan had insisted that he and Anna would pay Brady a small salary for his services, which he did the following day and the first item Brady purchased was a pair of leather boots from one of the traders, hand-made and large enough for him to walk in comfort. 'Life changing', thought Brady as he strolled back to the surgery.

Although the reason for his being stranded on the beach had never been approached by either Johann or Anna, Brady was sure that they were curious and Johann had enquired of him on their last ride out to a nearby Nhama village, what his plans were for the future. Johann had suggested that if he was not intending to remain in Luderitz then perhaps a ship to Cape of Good Hope or Europe may be possible. After some consideration Will had said he was content to remain in Luderitz for the present time.

Johann had observed Will's competence when out in the bush. He was always locating spoor and often stopped and studied animal tracks, most of which were new to him. He would spend hours with Luka, the Nhama guide, riding and walking the surrounding environs identifying animals, birds and reptiles and their spoor. Luka was not a pure bred Nhama but the offspring of a bushman woman who had been captured and taken into slavery by a clan of Nhama people.

Brady was enjoying his new found freedom and the challenge of this new and exciting land. His one and only fear was being discovered and handed over to the next British ship that docked at Luderitz.

Will Brady was convinced that the person that would be only too pleased to make this happen was Anna's fiancé, Fritz Grueber. The latter visited Anna on a regular basis and did little to hide his contempt for Brady. He was visibly irritated when he arrived at the house and found Anna and Brady working together with the horses or manufacturing pews for the church. He was becoming exceedingly rude and condescending in his attitude towards Brady on their every encounter. Anna always apologised and was genuinely embarrassed on these occasions. There were only two reasons why Brady had not, as yet, challenged this arrogant German. One being that he did not want to hurt Anna and, secondly, and more importantly, he did not want to encourage Grueber to establish contact with the British authorities regarding his origins. Brady felt a pressure building within, however, and was barely able to control his anger. Things were not made easier by the jealousy that William felt for this pompous and belligerent man's engagement to Anna. It was more than just an envious anger it was also a protective concern that such a wonderful person would be smothered by the self-centred, egotistical prig. Brady decided that the best resolution to the situation would be for him to leave Luderitz. William Brady was also aware that his social standing, or lack of, and lack of education could be huge barriers to a relationship with Anna. Anyway, he was dreaming to think otherwise.

William Brady was a man of the outdoors, a skilled tracker. He was a natural with a bow or a firearm and was strong and able to out walk most men. He would always be a woodsman and now, in Africa, perhaps a bushman. This was the life he loved. Open spaces and adventure. But how and where would he go? Brady decided to take Johann into his confidence and tell him his complete story, including that of his fondness for Anna. Perhaps Johann would have a solution.

The Admission

One evening when Anna was away tending a woman who had given birth, Brady and the Doctor were sipping schnapps whilst watching the sun descend over the sea. It cast pink, red and orange hues across the white washed walls of the town cottages and an explosion of champagne pastels across an endless purple ocean.

"Every sunset is different in Luderitz," the Doctor had told William shortly after his arrival, but in everything you can see beauty in the creative hand of Our father. Brady greatly admired this gentle, brave and profoundly deep thinking man who had chosen to give his life to spreading the Gospel and serving his fellow human beings. Brady broke the silence quite unexpectedly by saying, "Johann, I am an escaped convict."

Johann looked at Brady, leaned across with the bottle of schnapps, and filled the two half empty glasses. He smiled at Brady and said, "I had already come to this conclusion. I thought you were either a deserter or an escaped convict. You have slept under my roof, well close enough, for six weeks and not even a crust of bread has gone missing. You do the work of two men even when you are injured. I have watched you with my patients. You are blessed with nearly as much compassion as Anna and you are even more gentle with the horses and dogs than I. What is it that you could possibly have done that has made you a convict?"

When Brady had related his story as completely and truthfully as he could and revealed his fear of being delivered into the hands of the British by Fritz Grueber.

"William, my good friend, I believe that Col. Smythe undertook to have you released from prison because he knew you to be a good man. I have no doubt that once in South Africa he would have offered you your freedom. As to the intensions of Frits, well he has made comment to me on numerous occasions querying why I have not taken you to the Commissar and demanded an explanation for your presence in South West Africa. Have no allusions about Grueber's dislike for the British and I believe he sees you as a threat."

"How could I possibly be a threat to a man as established as Frits Grueber?" asked Brady.

"William, your fondness for Anna is obvious and, more to the point, her respect and liking for yourself has not gone unnoticed by Grueber. Frankly William, if it were not for Anna's intervention, Grueber would have had you imprisoned the day you were rescued and he is anxiously awaiting an explanation. He would be extremely happy to see you away from Anna and Luderitz." Johann continued, "I am touched by your honesty and openness towards me, William. My advice to you at present is not completely thought through. There are many situations that you must consider. The winds of war are blowing throughout the world. The English are sending armies to South Africa to quell the sabre rattling of the Boers. Your countrymen think that if they have a show of strength the Boers will back down. From the reports we receive, and the urgency the Boers have placed on Grueber's arms shipments, I think war is imminent.

"And what of you, Will Brady? Where do your loyalties lie? If you travel to South Africa will you join your brothers in arms or continue to elude the British authorities. Become a Boer perhaps? Will you remain here in Luderitz? The Kaiser has an allegiance with Paul Kruger the Boer General. Things are not well within the Royal courts of Europe. If you remain in Luderitz as an Englishman you may be called to fight against Germany. Will the community trust an Englishman if you remain here? These are troubled times indeed, my friend. Let us sleep and ponder on these issues. I will pray that God will give us wisdom and I am sure that things will become clear soon."

Brady decided he would do some praying of his own.

The following weeks were extremely busy. The Town Council had agreed to hold a Fete in order to raise money for a new Hospital. Anna had harnessed Will Brady's leadership and organisational skills to set up stalls and facilities at the ground allocated to the fete. Initially the volunteers were reluctant to follow Brady, him being an Englishman, but his ingenuity and enthusiasm were contagious and soon the volunteers were wholeheartedly completing their allocated tasks.

The Fete was a huge success with craft and cooking competitions, horse races, jumping and dressage. The highlight of the day for Brady had been the shooting competition, but little did he realise the impact that this contest would have on the rest of his life. The winner's prize was a Mouser, ten shot magazine rifle donated by Fritz Grueber.

Each contestant had to supply his own horse, weapon and ammunition and was required to compete in three separate disciplines. Five shots fired at a stationary target from fifty yards whilst mounted on a horse. Five shots fired at a stationary target from 100 yards standing and five shots fired at a stationary target from 300 yards whilst in the prone position. Each contestant had to complete firing each set of five rounds in 60 seconds or less.

The doctor had agreed to loan Brady his rifle and a grey gelding called Max, a hunter that was used to the sound of gunfire. Two days before the Fete Johann and Brady located a position on the dry river bed where they could practice their shooting.

"Doctor, perhaps I have misjudged Mr Grueber. He has been extremely generous in donating such a magnificent prize for the shooting competition," said Brady.

"Ja, Ja. Well don't be too magnanimous, William. Fritz would not have donated such a prize if he was not sure he would win it himself!"

'The hypercritical goat', thought Brady. Now even more determined to give it a go.

Will Brady was both nervous and excited. He had admired Johann's rifle, a five shot Martini Henri 9mm, on many occasions, but had never held it. Brady loved shooting and had been well known as an accurate shot with a musket in his village. This modern weapon was a new experience. The Doctor placed a large pumpkin, one hundred steps away from their firing position. He lodged it against the riverbank in the interests of safety. Johann returned and loaded the first clip of five rounds. He fired five deliberate shots with an interval of about fifteen seconds between each shot. Brady could see the fall of shot which seemed high and to the left. The pair confirmed this when walking over and inspecting the pumpkin. Johann had missed the target but only by inches and with a consistent grouping to the left and high. He explained to Brady that he would have to adjust the rear sight slightly, but would let Brady try first. Now it was Brady's turn. He had observed the Doctor's loading technique and required no assistance. The weapon felt light and comfortable in his hands. He pulled it into the shoulder and, after sighting for only a few seconds, fired. The pumpkin exploded, he worked the bolt and fired a second time. Again, the largest remnant of pumpkin disintegrated.

"Bullseye!" shouted the Doctor and slapped Brady on the back. The doctor left the sight unaltered. They fired many rounds over selected distances, including shooting from the back of a horse. This being another first for the Englishman, he found it difficult and his accuracy was inconsistent, but all in all he was extremely pleased with his performance. The Doctor smiled and said he was going to place his money on the Englishman.

The Shipment

Grueber was most anxious to get his next shipment under way. His best route would have been southwest through Grunaw and then on to Karasburg and into South Africa making delivery at Upington on the Orange River. This was presently impossible due to a simmering unrest in the surrounding area which had continued even after the Korana wars of 1879. The Koranas, Griqua Basters and some Nhama from the north had resorted to stock stealing, gun running and river pirating. The British Government had, in conjunction with settlers in the area, formed a special 'Camel Mounted' border patrol unit. The Trader and the Boers had agreed that there was too much at risk to utilise this route since the arms would be extremely attractive to the Korana's or the British. The alternative route was directly east through the mission stations at Keetmanshoop and then on to the waterholes at Aroab, continuing east across the South African border and following the Kuruman river bed to Hotazel and, finally, northeast to Vryburg. This trip of some 650 miles across desert scrub, with very few watering holes, inhabited by raiding tribes and containing Africa's wildest animals was still an ambitious trek. The Boers had agreed to meet the wagons at Aroab with a number of armed men to guide and protect the shipment once within South Africa.

The German Military Commander garrisoned at Luderitz had agreed to dispatch one half section of the cavalry to escort the wagons as far as Aroab.

This comprised four mounted men led by an NCO. Grueber needed as many able bodied men as possible, especially those able to use a weapon and willing to take a risk for good money. Two shipments had gone through to Vryburg without significant incident. The leader of the following shipment had led the very first shipments and was now a well trusted steward of Grueber's team. Frans Becker was the product of a white father and a Griqua mother. He had been trading in the area for many years and had excellent knowledge of the desert, plus he could speak most local dialects. Becker was a superb tracker and had assisted the local authority many times in the tracking of lost persons, fugitives and stock thieves from the south. He had been contracted by Grueber to escort the shipments as far as Aroab where he would hand over the shipment to the Boers. He would receive part payment for the munitions in gold and also wagons full of produce from the Boer Hinterland. A number of drivers and escorts would continue on to trade with the Boers in South Africa and return with loaded wagons enjoying the protection of both Grueber's escorts and the military from Aroab and the west to Luderitz.

Franz Becker selected who would ride with him and who would not. Since Becker was doing his own trading as well as charging a handsome sum for the protection and handling of Grueber's merchandise he was extremely cautious about whom he employed. He varied his route slightly each trip and also travelled utilising native scouts who ranged both ahead and behind giving early warning of unwanted visitors. Becker utilised large red, ridge-back dogs. These were fearless animals and were secured to the wagons at night as sentries against man and beast.

The Contest

Forty-three contestants entered the competition to win the Mauser. They came from all walks of life Farmers, sailors, the butcher, cavalry officers, soldiers from the fort, shopkeepers, travellers and of course Fritz Grueber.

Each contestant was given a number. Brady was number seven. When each contestant had been allocated a number the excited contestants were addressed by the Range Steward who had great difficulty in bringing the group to order.

The rules of the competition were explained in detail. As the steward explained, the doctor interpreted for William. Johann had decided not to enter the competition and made some obscure excuse however, Brady knew that Johann had dropped out to give him exclusive use of horse and weapon.

Essentially, the competitors would shoot one at time. They would each be summoned by the range steward by number. They would be given clearance to fire two warm up or sighting rounds at a practice target, in their own time. They would then come under the steward's control and be given the order to shoot five rounds within 60 seconds. All competitors were required to shoot, firstly, from the one hundred yard standing position. Failure to comply with any of the instructions meant instant disqualification.

The range comprised a dry estuary looking seawards that was barred by a large sand dune. The targets were placed against the sand dune and a series of red flags used to demarcate the range. A small bunker had been dug well to the left of the dune and the range stewards were safely ensconced within. They had a flag pole up which they would raise a red flag to stop all shooting or a white flag if shooting could continue. This procedure was followed before and after each competitor had completed shooting, his score taken and a new target mounted for the following competitor.

The Competitors awaited their turn under the shade of some stunted trees on the river bank. They formed a collection of small groups talking amiably. The doctor was explaining that, since the breeze was directly onshore and mild,

Brady would not have to make adjustments for the wind when firing from the three hundred yard position, just as Fritz and Anna arrived. Frit greeted Johann warmly and dismissed Brady with a curt nod before launching into a full conversation with Johann in German. Anna greeted her brother and immediately came and stood beside Will Brady.

"How are you feeling today, William?" she asked.

"Oh, I'm a little nervous, Miss Anna," he replied, thankful that she had once again stepped in to ease his anger and embarrassment.

"Johann tells me that you will win this competition, William, and I am hoping that you do."

Brady wasn't quite sure how to respond but glanced across at Grueber who seemed not to have heard.

"There is some very good competition here today, Miss Anna," Brady smiled. "Thank you for your support."

She touched his arm gently and moved towards her fiancé. As she did so she turned towards Brady and said quietly with a smile, "Do not be intimidated by bad manners."

When William Brady had fired his five rounds he was told to unload and wait. The range steward looked through his field glasses. He lowered his glasses, rubbed the grime and dust from his eyes and looked again. He turned, looking at Brady, clapped his hands and smiling he summoned competitor number eight. When Brady returned to the competitor's area he noted the doctor in conversation with a dark-skinned man who wore a wide brimmed leather hat. He was short, but of powerful stature and very broad in the shoulder. His clothes were worn but clean and his rifle hung casually in the crook of his arm. He was smoking a pipe. As Brady approached the men ended their conversation.

"Well, William how did you go?"

"It's hard to say, Doctor. They are counting my score now."

"Good, gooood," said the doctor.

Turning towards the third man, he said, "William, this is Mr Franz Becker. Herr Becker has a company which is involved in overland freighting of goods in and out of Luderitz."

"Herr Becker, this is Mr William Brady, who presently assists me in my Practice."

The men shook hands. Brady felt the hard calloused hand and the strong grip. He noted that the man's eyes were the most unusual colour. Almost green, but flecked with yellow. Franz said, "Welcome to Luderitz," in fluent but accented English.

"Thank you," said Brady.

"Mr Becker is highly regarded as one of the best Bushmen in the district. He is also a fine hunter and will be hard to beat in this competition," said Johann.

"My eyes are not as good as they used to be," said Becker, "but I intend to win!"

"I wish you the best," said Brady with a sincere smile. "Good to meet you, Mr Becker."

Franz Becker removed his pipe and said, "Perhaps we can share a quart of beer after the competition?"

"I will look forward to that," replied Brady.

The doctor smiled, looking happy with the world.

The mouth-watering aroma of German sausages and various meats being cooked on the open fire grills were a magnet to the hungry and thirsty crowd.

It was some time before Brady and the competitors were called for the second section of the competition which involved mounting a horse, trotting down to the firing position, halting before a barrel and firing at the target 50 meters away. Again the five rounds must be fired in under 60 seconds.

Sweat ran from beneath the brim of his bush hat. Brady pulled the hat from his head and used his sleeve to wipe the irritating perspiration from his brow. He was amid a 'shoot out' for the win against Franz Becker. There was no sound from the crowd behind him. He leaned down to pat the neck of the big gelding. "You will have to help me now, Max," he whispered into the ear of the big Hunter. The steward signalled for him to trot forward. He arrived at the barrel, removed the rifle from its boot and took aim in one fluid motion. Some of those watching would assume that he had been doing the same all his life, not just with a few days practice. A few moments earlier Fritz Grueber had been eliminated and had argued with the officials, finally storming off to have a word with the council. This had been extremely embarrassing for everyone. Brady's heart had gone out to Anna as she stood shocked at her fiancé's childish behaviour. When the previous tally of the scores were announced Franz Becker had beaten Brady in the mounted shoot but Brady had been better at the prone shoot. They had finished equal overall. The last five rounds would decide who would win the Mauser. Brady gripped the horse with his legs, the big animal stood rock still. He held his breath and squeezed the trigger. He repeated the process a further four times. All that moved were the horses ears. Within the tension, Brady knew he had done the best he could possibly expect to do and he also knew that he owed much to Johann and this magnificent horse. To a short round of applause, Brady returned to the competitors circle to await the final count. The targets were brought to the competitor's tent where they were displayed.

The chief steward called for silence, he cleared his throat and asked if Franz Becker and Brady would come forward. Applause broke out and Brady noticed that Franz Becker received many pats on the back as he made his way, smiling, through the crowd. When he arrived at Brady's side he shook his hand.

"Good shooting Wilem," he said. Using the Dutch form of William.

The steward called order once more. Speaking in German, Brady missed a lot of what was said, but the steward finally announced that Franz had come a close second and that the Englishman had won. The crowd clapped, the atmosphere was both loud and dusty within the tent. Franz was the first to congratulate Brady, followed by Johann with Anna close behind. The steward quieted the crowd and called upon Herr Grueber to present the prize.

Grueber moved with arrogant distain to the centre of the tent. He carried the prize in his left hand and, with a thunderous look on his ruddy face, he addressed the crowd. All the while he focused on Brady and spoke out angrily with undisguised venom in his voice and pointing an accusing finger at Brady. He then changed to English.

"You have been disqualified. This competition called for each citizen to produce his own weapon and his own horse. You do not qualify for any of these things. We do not know who you are, where you are from. You are not a citizen. I believe you are a criminal. You own no rifle or horse. You are an impostor. I have made an official report to the Commissar and you will be investigated and in due course, arrested I think."

"Fritz, don't do this," said Johann, "this is not right."

Grueber disregarded the advice with dismissive wave of his hand.

There was a shocked silence. Grueber turned to Franz Becker.

"Herr Becker, it gives me much pleasure to present this beautiful weapon to you and congratulate you on your skill." Smiling now, Grueber held the weapon out to Franz Becker.

Becker removed the unlit pipe from his mouth. He shook his head and smiled sadly.

"Herr Grueber, you know I am a simple man of the bushveld. There are many things of this great world that I do not know or understand, but I know this. Today this Englishman was better than I and no matter where he comes from, or goes to, that will be the truth, and therefore, I cannot take what belongs to another man. Also, Herr Grueber, it seems to me that since the rifle and the horse were borrowed for the competition only, and therefore perhaps the Englishman is even more skilled, since these items were unfamiliar to him. We speak of honour, but in Luderitz today, I think perhaps there is no honour."

With that he turned to Brady, bowed his head slightly and walked away followed by almost all that were in the tent. Johann took one look at William Brady's expression, collected his jacket and pulled Brady by the arm towards the bright sunshine.

"Come William. Don't do something you will regret. We have work to do. Only two people remained in the competitor's tent and they were Fritz Grueber and Anna Scholtz."

Becker's Trek

Once outside the tent, Johann urged Brady to ride back to the surgery on Max where he would meet him shortly. William did as he was told, although his anger and frustration with Grueber were only just under control. News of the debacle must have circulated quickly, as many persons stared after Brady as he rode through the town towards the surgery. He was comforted though by the handful of friendly waves he received on the journey.

When Johann arrived at his cottage, he had Anna with him. It was obvious from her red rimmed eyes that she had been weeping. She alighted from the trap and made to enter the cottage. She suddenly halted, turned and approached Johann and Brady.

"William," she said, "I am terribly sorry that you have been treated so badly by the man that was to be my husband. His actions today were despicable and inexcusable. I have annulled our engagement and I thank God that you came here to help me see the real Fritz Grueber!"

William did not know how to respond. He felt such an urge to take this beautiful, but broken, lady into his arms and comfort her, but knew this was not the time, nor place.

"I wish only God's very best for you, Miss Anna," said William.

She lowered her head and walked quickly towards the cottage.

Just at this point, Franz Becker and one of his men arrived. Franz handed his reigns to his companion and joined Johann and Brady.

"I received your message," he said to Johann.

"Ja, well Franz, things have happened a little sooner than expected. It seems we may have to get William away from Luderitz a little sooner than I thought."

"After meeting him and observing him shoot I would be only too pleased to have him with me on my next trek," said Franz. "However, I do not want any trouble with the authorities." Johann looked at William and then explained that there was little chance of that since Brady would be presumed lost at sea at this time. Johann then proceeded to explain to Brady that he had enquired of Franz the possibility of William accompanying him on one of his trips in order to get him away from the unpredictable Fritz for a period at least. Franz scratched his bearded face with the stem of his unlit pipe.

"I can offer you passage as a traveller only as far as the Boer boarder. From there you would need to negotiate with the Boers. Since you are English this could be a problem. They may think you are a spy. If you chose to work for me then you could continue as an escort to Vryburg. William, the terms of employment are that you are under my instruction and if we are attacked you will be expected to protect the shipment. You will be paid at the end of your journey in Vryburg. Daily rations will be supplied for you and your horse. If you come as an escort you must provide your own horse and equipment. We are due to leave in two days. There is a hostel for employees on my farm which is also the assembly point for all the wagons."

Brady was a bit overwhelmed by the speed at which his life was having to change. He was still contemplating returning to the fete and seeking out Fritz to give him a real hiding. He had never been so humiliated in all his life. He knew that this would be unwise as he would then surely end up in the stockade. He was reluctant to leave Luderitz. Why? cause he was in love with Anna. He turned to Franz.

"You are very kind and I thank you for your offer. I will confirm my position with you by morning. I need to think this through rationally. I have no equipment and must consider the long term outcomes."

"Ja ok," said Frans Becker, "but one thing is for sure and that is you will be safe from the British on my trek because Fritz has too much money invested to tell them where you are and the Boers will make sure those wagons go nowhere near the British. Let us know, William. You will be welcome." He lit his pipe, shook hands with the doctor and walked towards his horse.

Johann patted William's arm and said, "Alright William, I think we need a drink. Let us go and discuss the way forward in all these things." William Brady was eternally grateful to have such a friend as Dr Johann Scholtz.

Seated on the cool veranda, Brady felt exposed. He anticipated the town militia would arrive at any moment seeking to make an arrest. Johann was aware of his friend's agitation and assured him that if the police did arrive they had no grounds to make an arrest.

"What do you want to do, William?" asked the Doctor.

"I have no doubt that, after today's events, Grueber will pursue your true identity and situation with the British authorities. I do not know how long before action is taken but have no doubt it will happen."

"I think my best course of action would be to accept the offer of employment from Franz, but there are some practical problems," replied William.

"Yes. There are a few practical problems but nothing that we cannot overcome," replied the doctor.

"I do not have a horse. I do not have a weapon. I do not have a bed roll or even a cup and spoon," Brady stated.

"Yes. But you have faith and friends, William, and with these you can move mountains."

Brady smiled at the doctor and marvelled at the spirit and character of this man.

Anna came out onto the veranda. Both Brady and Johann rose from their seats. She held a tray upon which were a flask of lemonade, schnapps and glasses. She placed the tray on a wooden box which Johann used as a table. Her eyes were still red-rimmed but she seemed more composed than she had been earlier.

Anna couldn't bear to be on her own at a time like this. She wished she were at home with her mother. Things seemed to be falling apart. Her breaking off with Fritz, although painful, she knew to be the right decision. She had known for some time that his interests, beliefs and life philosophies were very different from her own and would only cause discontent in the future. She was also confused by the effect this big Englishman had on her. She had grown so fond of his gentle and enthusiastic manner and the fact that he appreciated even the smallest gesture. He had little interest in money and wealth but was happy to work all day if there was benefit to others and, most endearing of all, was his delight in creation and in particular wildlife. Sometimes he was almost childlike in his response to a new species or an animal antic. Indeed life for William Brady was an adventure. Now he was leaving. Anna needed to be a part of this discussion.

"William, what will you do?" she asked.

"Well Miss Anna, I will need to leave Luderitz. I don't know whether the Doctor has told you, but I was a prisoner in bond to an English soldier bound for South Africa. I was taken to shore when the ship ran aground and escaped during the dark hours. Well, you know the rest Miss Anna."

"Why did you escape William?" she asked.

"The truth is I was too afraid to get back on that ship."

"Franz Becker has offered William a position as an escort on the next delivery to Vryburg. This is a good option since Fritz is not going to alert the British as to where William is if he knows it will compromise his own arms shipment to the Boers," said Johann.

"When will he leave?" asked Anna anxiously.

"The trek departs day after tomorrow," said Brady.

Anna sank slowly into a vacant chair. "So soon?" she asked anxiously.

"We need to make urgent preparations," said the doctor.

"Anna, William will need a bed roll and messing implements. He will need a warm coat and gauntlets for his hands in the cold. He will need soap and a razor, socks and a spare pair of boots. What we don't have with us we will have to buy from the store tomorrow. William you will take Max and my rifle."

"Oh no, I couldn't," said Brady. "This is too much. I can't accept all this charity!"

"Who said anything about charity. You can send me the money from Vryburg when you get paid."

"Yes, but Johann, I won't have enough to pay for Max."

"William, Max is wasted here with me. I use the trap most of the time. And I have Bella and Zeus."

"Let me take Zeus. I know how much you love Max," Brady bargained.

"Zeus will throw you off his back the first time he hears a rifle or sees even a little springbok. He is a Stallion and too highly strung. He needs training."

"Ok, what about Bella?"

"William, Bella is my breeding mare. Please you are being difficult now, Ja? You know Max, he trusts you. And don't worry about the rifle. I will get from Fritz the weapon that should be yours, so there will be no charge for the rifle but you can pay me for the ammunition."

With that the Doctor vanished into the cottage.

Anna sat motionless on the rawhide chair. She looked up at William, now standing and who was inwardly overwhelmed by the kindness of these people.

"I will miss you very much, William," she said. "Will you ever return?"

"God knows I don't want to leave, Miss Anna."

"I envy you being able to leave here and start afresh. Things will be unbearable here for me now with Fritz Grueber and the Council working alongside Johann."

"Come with me, Miss Anna," said Brady. The words were out before he realised what he had said. She gazed up at the big English man with so much warmth and affection in her big blue eyes and suddenly burst into tears.

She stood, taking William's big hand in hers and said, between sobs, "Oh, William! If only life was so simple." Then she turned and walked back into the house.

Brady stood for a while looking after her, feeling devastated and desperately alone, what had just happened? Had he been rejected or was she saying she was trapped and would go with him under different circumstances? Brady felt an inexplicable panic rise within his chest as if he would suffer great loss if he were to leave things as they were. He was about to knock on the door when Anna reappeared.

"What did you mean, William, when you asked me to come with you?"

"I meant, well…I meant…"

"Speak man," said Johann, who was standing just inside the door.

"Miss Anna, my fondness for you grows by the minute and I could not bear to leave you like this. Any man in his right mind can see you are beautiful in spirit, body and soul, and I would give my very life to give you happiness. I would gladly accompany you and protect you wherever the Good Lord should lead us. Just having you near me brings me peace and contentment. Perhaps, in time, you would consider becoming my wife?"

"Are you asking me to marry you, William?"

"That I am, Miss Anna."

Karl and Mildred

Karl Kraus and his wife Mildred had been in Luderitz for a month and a half and were now bound overland to Kuruman, situated hundreds of miles inland and directly east of Luderitz. Kuruman is where the famous English Missionary, Robert Moffat, had planted his Mission station in the 1820's and had gained tremendous influence on the Bantu people far and wide. In particular with the Bechuana people. Moffat printed his first translated Bible in Sechuana, the language of the Bechuana people, as early as 1840.

Karl and Mildred had listened and been inspired by Paul Edwards and his account of the tireless and selfless work done by Moffat and other Missionaries, including David Livingstone, who had married Moffat's oldest daughter, Mary. Edwards delivered a moving account of the bravery, determination and dedication of those called to do God's work and, when he gave his heart-wrenching appeal for people to go and win the hearts and souls of those lost in this troubled and primitive land of Africa, both Karl and Mildred felt a stirring within. They had no children of their own. Mildred was a teacher of languages and had met Karl whilst working for the Missionary Society, for who Kraus did a great deal of printing. They were both in their fifties and had been happily married for eight years. They had packed a small, but modern, printing press and taken the majority of their savings and, with the blessing of the Missionary Society, had left their home in Birmingham to join those at Kuruman to further God's work with their valuable skills and enthusiasm. Karl wished only to visit his brother, a Shipwright who had travelled with his Whaling Company and was now stationed at Luderitz.

Karl was extremely proud of his wagon and sixteen oxen. He had spent many hours with his brother and Mildred rigging the vehicle to afford him and his wife as much comfort as was practical. The precious press was securely packed into a compartment cleverly engineered onto the side of the wagon by Gunter, Karl's brother. The wagon wheels were much wider than normal to reduce sinking into the soft desert sand. They were now ready for their trek and anxious to be on their way. They were to join Franz Becker's wagons that evening at his homestead and the wagon train was due to leave the outskirts of Luderitz at first light the following day.

Karl was plunging grease onto a wheel hub in final preparation when a trap appeared at the gate. Karl recognised the doctor as he quieted a barking dog. He walked over to the gate and, leaning on the top brace, noticing that there was a lady in the trap with the doctor.

Gunter walked out to the grunting of the small dog and recognised the Doctor and his sister. He greeted the doctor and was quite perplexed at the reason for the medical man's presence.

"To what do we owe the pleasure of this visit?" He asked the doctor, whilst assisting Anna from the small cart.

"Actually Gunter, we have come to see your brother and his wife," said Johann.

When all were comfortably seated within the small parlour and Mildred had offered refreshments, all within a very formal atmosphere, Johann cleared his throat and turned to Karl.

"Herr Kraus, you do not know us, but my sister and I live in Luderitz. I am the Doctor here and also work among the peoples for the Church and my dear sister, Anna, has been assisting me here for some months." Johann was finding this difficult, however he continued.

"Due to certain events Anna has found it necessary to travel to Vryburg. We understand that you are travelling to Kuruman and, since it is on the way, we wondered whether you would be kind enough to look after Anna? She will have her own horse to ride and her belongings can travel within one of Franz Becker's wagons but err…she…err…"

Mildred had sensed how fragile Anna was, as only a woman can, and moved towards her. Whilst Johann was explaining, she placed a gentle and motherly hand on Anna's shoulder and said, "My dear child, you will be most welcome to travel with me. It will be a delight and she will bring her belongings with her to our wagon, wont she Karl? It means I will have another lady to talk to and, I think this was God's way to keep me from being lonely in a man's world. Bless you, Anna, come with me and together we can decide how we should fit you in at such short notice. How exciting this is for me!"

The men discussed the practical implications and shortly afterwards Anna returned with Mildred and all was settled.

When Anna and Johann returned William was anxiously waiting. He felt party to all the emotional disruption, but also separated. Not excluded, but outside of the inner circle, so to speak. Since his proposal to Anna they had not spoken on the issue again and, although Brady had captured an expression in her eyes that had riveted his heart and soul, she had not verbalised rejection or acceptance.

Anna smiled weakly, patting his arm gently, as she walked up onto the veranda.

"All is settled, William. I must go and complete my packing." And with that she entered the house. Johann was busy talking to Luka. He then came up onto the cool veranda.

"Anna will travel with Karl and Mildred Kraus as far as Kuruman," said Johan. "Praise God. We will accept the offer from Franz to utilise space at the rear of a stores wagon where Anna will sleep and have some privacy."

Brady spoke anxiously, "Johann, a few weeks ago I arrived in Luderitz a complete stranger, an escaped prisoner, you saved my very life. Now I'm leaving you and taking with me everything you love and value. This is too hard to comprehend! My heart breaks with your pain and, yet, you have only been righteous and honest."

"William, my parents taught me from a young age to hold onto the most precious things lightly, for you never know when the Lord may have need of them. That is why we should cherish every moment we have with loved ones. And, my friend, it was not me who saved your life but Anna. You see, you have given more than you know. I was never happy about Anna's engagement to Fritz."

"Yes! You are right there, Johan! I have never met such an arrogant and self-centred man."

"There is that, William, but it is more than that. As a doctor I never discuss my patients with other people, but in this case, William, I must tell you that I have been worried sick about Anna because I have been treating Fritz for Syphilis. I sent him back to Germany for treatment but I am not sure that, even with today's modern medical miracles, that this terrible disease can be cured. I had insisted that he must tell Anna before she married him but he said that he had been cured. I groaned in prayer and anguish imploring God to intervene in the situation and to send another man for Anna. Don't you see, William? God has sent you to look after our dear Anna. William you too are a gift to my family, a divine answer to prayer and an Englishman! Only God could have arranged this!" William looked on with a shocked expression.

"But Anna has not accepted my proposal!" said William.

"Anna has been in emotional turmoil over the past two days, William. Too much has happened. You will have nearly three months of travelling together, during which time you will know whether you are right for each other. And, William, don't forget…God's timing is perfect," said the doctor.

Luka was dressed in his tattered trousers and wore a red blanket pulled across his left shoulder and belted at his waist by a wide thong of rawhide, leaving his right arm free to hold his stick and short spear. The dappled light indicated that the sun was setting, yielding to the cold wind from the Atlantic that was beginning to strengthen.

The two men sensed Lukas presence at the same moment. They had agreed earlier that when Anna's chests had been loaded, William, being assisted by Luka, would take the chests to the assembly point at Becker's farm, where the Kraus' wagon would be waiting to receive them. Luka held the bridle of the draft horse. Loaded in the trap behind the mare were two sea chests. One contained Anna's personal belongings, the second contained foodstuffs, crockery and kitchen wares. Johann called for Anna who appeared on the veranda holding a leather case which contained her piano accordion. Anna was to spend her final night at home with her brother. William would spend the night at Becker's and Luka would drive the trap back from the assembly point once the chests had been delivered.

William, leaving Johann and Anna alone at the surgery and accompanied by Luka, rode towards Becker's farm in the gathering twilight. He was full of thought. A great deal had transpired in the past day. His excitement about his possible future with Anna was tempered by the enormity of the emotional pain he knew that brother and sister were going to endure with this separation. Although Anna could return to Luderitz at any time in the future, William was sure this would be unlikely. Under normal circumstances this trip into the wilderness, with undoubted adventure, would have been 'a dream come true' for Brady, but the thought of parting with Johann and his wonderful friendship brought great sadness to his heart and a hollow excitement.

William knew that his promise to Johann to do everything he could to protect and care for Anna was a responsibility that he would never shirk and that, every decision he now made, would first have to take Anna's wellbeing into consideration. This was a sobering responsibility and was he ready for this? Suddenly a great anger began to swell up within Brady's chest. He was consumed by the fact that the arrogant, selfish conceit of one man had so affected the lives of good honest people in this way. People forced into making rash decisions that could cause so much pain and discomfort.

Just as this volcano of angry protest was exploding within Brady a rider came trotting out of the chill twilight. Recognition for Brady was instant. Fritz Grueber sat his charger with a military poise, but was leaning slightly forward as he passed the carriage, trying to discern the identity of the occupants.

William could contain himself no longer. As the traveller came level he shouted, "Herr Grueber, a word please." As he pulled the cart horse to a halt. Grueber simply waved his hand in dismissal whilst cursing in German and spitting backwards towards the incensed Brady. By this time Brady had alighted from the wagon and was walking after the departing horseman, now a silhouette against the setting sun.

"So, you are a coward as well as an ill-mannered and arrogant fool?" shouted William Brady in his frustration and anger.

The rider stopped at this taunt. He turned his horse back towards his accuser and, with a charging yell, cantered his horse towards Brady who stood his ground ready for a fight. As the great horse thundered down upon him, Brady swung to the left. The German flayed him across the face with his riding crop, whilst the rider's knee caught Brady on the shoulder and sent him spinning into the scrub alongside the road. Brady had the wind knocked from him and his eye was watering where the leather crop had lashed his face, but he was unaware of these things and was back on his feet like a cat.

Pulling the horse into a tight turn the rider came galloping back towards Brady. Luka jumped from the carriage landing in the middle of the road just as the horse and rider came level with Brady. The sudden movement startled the mount and he lunged, raring to the left. At the same moment, an incensed Brady leapt onto the rider and pulled him from the horse. The startled animal bucked and kicked in fear and raced off with slack stirrups, flaying the night air.

The German had landed on top of William and was now fighting to get to his feet, arms thrashing out at his assailant, William, did not feel the blows.

Trance-like he climbed to his feet and hit the now constantly shouting and windmilling German as hard as he could in the face. Three stupendous blows from the big Englishman and the Trader lay pole-axed in the dust. Luka walked over to where William stood, panting, above the German. The little bushman stealthily kicked the prone man to no response and then Luka's big white teeth glinted in the darkness as he smiled up at William.

Brady felt cheated. He had not been able to speak his mind and the fight was over before it started. He was pleased to see, though, that the German's nose was flattened and that a generous amount of blood flowed freely, black and shiny in the darkness.

Brady checked to see that the German carried no weapon and then he and Luka lifted the now semi-conscious man onto the carriage and continued their journey to Becker's.

When the party arrived at the assembly point Franz was called to attend to Grueber. He asked what had transpired to which Brady suggested he ask Luka in his own language. The young native man smiled, shrugged his shoulders and said, "He must have fallen off his horse!"

"And did you fall out of your cart as well, Brady?" asked Franz, studying his torn shirt and the swelling across his face.

No more was said and a quiet and humbled Grueber was transported back to Luderitz by members of Franz's company.

Leaving Luderitz

The sun was well above the horizon before Franz Becker was happy to depart. He had placed the wagons into their order of march and issued strict instructions to the drivers on how to respond to all situations. Each wagon was inspected for travel-worthiness, tools and spare parts. Overloading was a problem and a large amount of gear had to be left behind, much to the chagrin of its owners but the choice was simple. Comply or leave! Provision for water was paramount and each wagon was to ensure it carried sufficient to last between watering points. Eventually Becker had given the signal to move out.
Johann and Anna had arrived at the assembly point before first light.

Final preparations had kept everyone busy, but the final farewell had been extremely painful for Johann who wept unashamedly. William was relieved when summoned by Becker to ride ahead of the column with one other scout.

The train only covered eight miles the first day. Franz Becker was insisting that the column maintained twelve miles minimum a day. This entailed waking well before first light and leaving before the sun rose. Travelling in the cool of the early morning through to a short mid-morning break, the travellers would have a small meal whilst the draft animals would have a short drink out of wooden buckets. Travel would then resume until early afternoon which brought the killing heat of the day. At this point the scouts would call a halt in a suitable area for setting up camp. It was not long before the drivers and animals accepted the rhythm of the days and the train became more efficient.

William could not believe that he was being paid to do the work to which he was assigned. He loved every minute of every day in the desert and thrived on new knowledge and experience with the flora and fauna of this wild continent.

Amongst his responsibilities was that of hunting fresh meat for the guard dogs and to assist Franz with hunting for the column. He saw little of Anna during the day, but spent many precious hours with her in the evenings. The more he talked to this woman the more he loved her. She had already made friends with everyone on the train and her medical knowledge was proving to be invaluable. Nothing seemed too much trouble for her and when she took out her Piano accordion to play and sing the entire camp came to listen. One of the highlights for Anna was on the second day whilst preparing a meal with Mildred. She looked up to see Luka with a bundle of firewood in his arms.

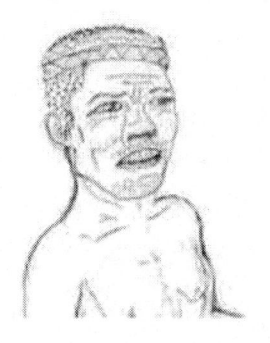

"I have come," was all he said. And he remained.

William continued to learn from Luka, who took great delight in teaching the enthusiastic Englishman. Luka continued to amaze Brady with his attention to minute detail in the bush. This small yellowish brown man had the ability to analyse a patch of sand on the river bank and know what wildlife had visited the river in the past few days. He could tell if the animals were male or female by the spoor the animal left behind. He could discern the age of the young and if an animal were healthy or injured. Luka was a man who could abide in the world of wild animals and simply blend into the tapestry and not upset the balance in any way. This was his world, with which he was one. How William envied his uncomplicated existence, free to come and go, as free as the desert wind.

Franz Becker, was a hard task master and insisted that Brady ride out with his scouts every morning before first light. These hard and experienced men would select a direction out of the camp and then, when a kilometre or so from the wagons, they would do a circular patrol around the wagon train looking for signs of being followed or attacked. When satisfied they would return to the camp and lead the wagons out following the trail left by the pathfinders moving a day ahead of the wagons and leaving markers for the scouts to follow.

An escort of four mounted soldiers had accompanied the wagons but they were ordered to remain with the cargo of arms and the Sergeant-in-charge was reluctant to leave the body of the wagon train. The scouts would range well out ahead of the wagons and from time to time one would be sent to the rear to confirm they were not being followed. The main reason for this activity was to avoid ambushes by Griqwa bandits. Brady struggled in the first few days with the amount of time spent in the saddle, but he was quickly becoming an accomplished bush rider. Max was a magnificent animal with excellent endurance considering his breeding as a sporting horse. Brady couldn't help bristling with pride when the other scouts admired his mount. When Brady was sent to hunt for fresh rations for the guard dogs he would take Luka with him. The little man would trot in front of William's horse for miles and miles following spoor. If the pair were out for a considerable time and had travelled some distance from the wagons then Luka would hold onto a saddle strap and trot alongside Max and, it seemed to William, that Luka could continue to run like this forever.

Franz began loading more and more responsibility onto Brady as his trust in the Englishman grew. Franz was a regular visitor to the wagon of Karl and Mildred where Anna and William spent most of their free time. This wagon was a happy and lively place where the women took great pride in the quality and variety of food they were able to prepare over the open fire. It was an industrious wagon with the mending of clothing for the various men and, when not stitching clothing, Anna would be stitching wounds together, attending burns or removing thorns from the soles of feet.

On the evenings when Franz did visit, he would bring with him a bottle of Brandy or Schnapps and, if William were not on sentry duty, they would sit with Karl and the ladies and relate stories of their very different upbringing and life experiences. Franz, though seemingly serious and focussed, possessed a tremendous humour which resided just below the surface and his ability to relate stories that, though serious in content, were enormously funny. He had laughed like a drain when Brady explained to him that Johann had been summoned to Grueber's house the night he had 'fallen off his horse' to attend Grueber's injuries.

The doctor had told William the following morning that both Grueber's eyes had swollen like plums, almost closed. Both were turning black and his nose looked like a 'vetkoek' (Small shapeless cake fried in oil). When the doctor had questioned Grueber he had reluctantly admitted that the Englishman had thrown a 'lucky punch.' The doctor had said to Grueber, "Well, if that is the damage he did with one punch, you are fortunate he never hit you twice!"

In the beautiful clear and chill mornings Anna would rise well before dawn. She would climb down from the wagon and stoke the fire to warm the coffee pot.

She would give Brady a gentle shake as he slept beneath the wagon. Brady was always awake but would fake sleep just to have the early morning contact with beautiful Anna. The big guard dog, Herman, would whine as soon as he heard Anna as she would give him a small leftover from the previous night's meal. Generally not a friendly dog, Anna had befriended him within the first week. Franz threatened to shoot him as he said he was now becoming soft, and then he would wink at Brady when Anna scolded him for being heartless. The stores wagons had a cable located beneath the wagon bed running the full length. When the wagons stopped for the night the guard dogs were attached to a chain which could run up and down the cable giving the dogs adequate range to intercept any intruder. During the day the dogs either walked beside the wagons or rode within kennels attached to the side of each stores wagon.

Every driver was responsible for his dog and Franz was very attached to each of his big red dogs. Some said he cared more for their welfare than for his men. He claimed that when the men had saved him from as many potential dangers, not only from bandits but also lion and leopards which were attracted by the horses and oxen normally laagered within the circle of wagons, then he would treat them with similar respect!

The days were hot and dusty and the nights clear and cold. Anna could never tell William that she longed for green pastures and a change from the desert scrub since he was completely in his element and came in every evening with an item or experience that had caused him great excitement during the day. They had grown closer in spirit and she looked so forward to him coming back in the evenings. Mildred had become like an older sister to Anna and was just the companion she had needed after her traumatic departure from Luderitz. Mildred never badgered her or gave instruction or advice unless it was asked for and she always had a tender heart and listening ear. This older lady had told Anna that she viewed Brady as a rare and rough diamond, in no way polished, but immensely valuable.

Anna knew that this was a true and honest description of the man she had come to love. She and William had skirted the issue of marriage, both getting used to each other's company. She was amazed at how comfortable she felt with William. It just seemed natural that they should be together. She was reminded of how Johann had told her that William had been sent to her by The Lord. Perhaps he was right.

Bandits

In the third week of travel the wagon train had settled for the night when William was woken by Herman barking furiously, as was another dog further along the train. Suddenly the night air was split with several rifle shots, thunderous in the quiet of the wilderness, followed by the alarmed shouts of men. Brady had exploded from his blankets, located beneath the wagon and, grasping his rifle, he was struggling to pull on his boots. Herman was throwing himself against his tether. Anna stuck her head from the rear canvas awning of the wagon asking anxiously what was afoot. William told her to go back into the vessel until he had established what was going on. He came upon Franz who was quieting the guard dog and trying to find out from one of the men what had transpired. By this time there were several men all armed expectedly awaiting an explanation. The driver had been woken by the agitated barking of his dog. He stated that when he'd looked out of the wagon he saw two figures departing at a run and had fired after them just for good measure. He could not give a description as it was too dark, but he said one was wearing a wide brimmed hat. Franz sent one of his men to inspect all the wagons and see if any cargo or goods had been tampered with or were missing. He reasoned with Benjamin, the Head scout that he thought the intruders had been exposed by the barking dogs before they could really do any damage. He insisted, though, that they would track them first thing in the morning. Benjamin gathered the sentries and instructed them to remain vigilant. He asked Brady if he and Luka would join them before first light to track the visitors. Brady readily agreed, pleased to hear one of the young soldiers volunteer, although he was sure his sergeant would refuse and it was noted that the sergeant had not presented himself at the first sound of gunfire. William returned to the stores wagon where he found Anna had climbed down from the wagon and was petting the big dog, now less agitated but still whining and alert. Anna seemed unusually shaken so Brady placed a comforting arm about her and explained what had happened. The night was crisp and William only wore his vest and trousers. Anna had a blanket around her shoulders. Brady began to shiver and was turning back towards his bed where his jacket was hooked onto the side of the wagon when Anna stopped him. She drew the blanket around behind his back and pulled herself into him gently forcing his face down towards her. She kissed him full on the mouth, passionately, without restraint. William was stirred and responded immediately. His heart was a reservoir bursting with love and passion. This was the first time they had kissed in such a way. Suddenly she pulled back.

"No William, not now," she whispered breathless. "Not yet, but soon. It's true I love you, William, and yes…I will be your wife. I am more certain about this than anything else at this time."

She went up on her toes and kissed him once more then slipped out of his arms, as nimble as a child, and up onto the wagon. William was still shaking though it wasn't from cold but sheer joy and emotion. Her faint lavender fragrance lingered on the night air. Too excited to sleep, he pulled on his jacket, stroked Herman and said, "Did you hear that, my boy? She said yes!" William walked quietly round the camp checking on the wagons but he wanted to scream and shout and dance. He nodded to the sentries and walked to the livestock now settling once more.

Brady found Max and told the horse his good news and the animal nodded his head as if he had prior knowledge of William's good fortune. Brady returned to his bed, close to which the big, red, faithful dog stood looking out towards the desert. Brady's heart was almost bursting with joy and knew his life would never be the same. Sleep finally came and it seemed he had just closed his eyes when Benjamin shook him awake whilst holding the muzzle of William's rifle away from him. He was an experienced bushman and was not about to get himself shot.

"Morning, Villem," he said, "Wake up man. Mr Becker will be ready to ride soon."

The hustle and bustle of a waking camp induced William to jump up just as Anna appeared at his side with a mug of coffee.

"I'm late!" said William, looking startled and disoriented.

"No, you are just in time," said Anna. "I have asked Luka to saddle Max and have packed your bag."

She placed her hand on William's arm.

"Please be careful today," she said. He gave her a gentle hug and rushed off to answer the call of nature. Benjamin arrived back to say that Franz was ready.

"You can't track in the dark," said Anna.

"If that little kerel (fellow) Luka can track with his eyes closed, as everyone tells me, then what is a little darkness to him?" said Benjamin.

Just then Luka arrived out of the gloom from behind the first wagon. He walked boldly into the golden light of the lantern, complete with Max in tow.

"I see you," he said to Benjamin.

"We see you," said Benjamin. "Did you sleep well?"

"I slept well if you slept well," said the little yellow man.

The morning patrol returned just as the first orange streaks of sunrise pierced the silver sky. With oxen in-spanned, the wagon's drivers were eager to get on their way. The Scouts had seen and heard nothing unusual so the wagons began their slow trek to the crack of the rawhide whip and the shrill whistles of the drivers coaxing these bovine beasts of burden ever onwards. Franz re-joined the tracking team, where incredibly, Luka had already identified the spoor of last night's visitors.

"Yes, there were two," the little man indicated. With spear and stick in hand Luka trotted off confidently in the cool morning twilight. The eager trackers mounted their horses in pursuit.

Franz told William that he was not surprised that they were heading north for they were approaching one of the tributaries of the Fish River named Konkiep and that there were several small settlements to the north. He had deliberately travelled to the south to avoid human contact but he knew that the bush telegraph would have sent messages far and wide that the wagons had left Luderitz. He was hoping that, should his visitors from the night before be an advanced party of bandits sent to find the train, he and the trackers would find them before they reached the rest of their gang. Suddenly Luka stopped, he stood statue still, tree like, not moving he lifted his head, turned slowly and retraced his steps. He approached Franz.

"We must be quite now," he said. "There are people ahead. They are cooking."

"How far?" Franz asked.

"Not far. I have seen the smoke from a fire," said Luka. "They are near the water. We must leave the horses for they will smell the water and the people will hear them."

Franz, now off his horse, beckoned the German soldier, William and Benjamin who had quickly dismounted.

"This little chap thinks our friends are just ahead. Apparently he has detected their cooking fire and is also concerned that they have found a small pool of water in the riverbed. He knows this by the type of bird calls he can hear and worries that the horses will smell the water and compromise our approach. He is a slim (clever) little fellow and I think he's right. So, we will leave him here with the horses and go ahead on foot and try to keep surprise on our side.

William you go with Ben. Cross the riverbed and move slowly northwards. Try to keep us in sight. This soldier and I will move along this side of the river. We don't know how many there are and whether or not they are hostile so try to stay out of sight behind the border of stunted trees along the edge of the creek. If shooting starts then Luka will lead the horses towards us but on my side of the riverbed. Only shoot if you think one of us may be in danger. Let me do the talking. I have dealt with these Basters many times. Oh…and William.

Be careful, they will kill you for your boots."

The morning heat was already beginning to bite. William could feel the sun burning the exposed skin on his forearms. As he and Ben had crossed the dry riverbed, William had noted the myriad of animal and fowl tracks on this desert highway. He jerked his concentration back to the task at hand. Ben was slightly ahead of him and, as he looked across the river, he could see Franz's head and shoulders moving along almost abreast of them. They could now hear voices and had instinctively slowed their pace seeking the sparse cover from the dry leafless trees on the river bank. There was a thin spiral of smoke coming from below the bank of the river. Here, the course of the river bent eastwards towards William and Benjamin. A large tree was perched on the bank just to the right of the bend, below which was a patch of green grass. Hanging from the branches were hundreds of weaverbird nests. William now knew how Luka had discerned the presence of water. Moving with great care William and Benjamin crept slowly forward, rifles ready, inching towards the smoke and the lip of the riverbank. They had lost sight of their comrades. William could feel his heart beating, racing, pounding so loudly that surely others could hear it too. Suddenly the talking below the bank stopped. Benjamin went down on one knee, William followed suit. Immediately a coloured man, dirty and roughly dressed climbed the opposite bank, weapon in hand. He had his back to William and Ben. The Bandit was almost at the lip of the bank when he raised his rifle to his shoulder. The sound of a shot rang out and the Bandit fell forward and slid back halfway down the steep bank. He was gone from sight. William suddenly realised it was him who had shot the fellow. A reflex action, as he supposed the bandit was about to shoot one of his two comrades on the opposite bank. A second shot rang out and William and Benjamin skirmished towards the bank, dropping down at the edge to peer below and into the bed of the sandy river. One person was standing up near the cooking fire in similar tattered dress to the inert body lying where it had fallen from William's bullet. Franz was in the river walking towards the small water hole.

Marching in front of him was a prisoner with hands raised. The German soldier was immobile, a pale face, with the shocked expression of a young man who had just stared death in the eye. The German had been twenty yards closer and on top of the opposite bank. He had looked up and straight into the sights of the deceased bandit's Lee Metford rifle, frozen and unable to move, the brain numbing shadow of death caressed him. He heard the shot echo. Brady's bullet exploded into the base of his would-be assassin's skull. The soldier was trying to comprehend the events still thinking that the shot he had heard was his death knoll.

Brady climbed down the bank, his mouth was dry and his legs were shaking. He had never shot a human before. Immediately doubts flooded his mind. What if the bandit wasn't going to shoot. What if he was only checking to see who was approaching?

Benjamin walked over to the body of the dead man and spat, "Kom, Hans!" ("Come, Hans!") he shouted to the soldier still rooted to the same spot, staring at the inert body.

"You are one lucky German. Saved by an Englishman!" said Benjamin, bending down and retrieving the dead man's weapon before walking off towards the two prisoners, who were vigorously shaking their heads in response to Franz' questions.

"Lying thieves," said Benjamin as he approached the two bandits. "You've got two choices," said Franz. "either you tell me the truth or I will shoot you in the knees and leave you for the hyenas." This got their attention!

"No more shoot, pleas' Baas," implored the older of the two bandits.

"Were you at my wagons last night?"

"Ah no," said the older man, his yellow eyes flashing shiftily as he manoeuvred desperate in his fear.

"It was that one," pointing to the body, "and this one," he pointed to his younger colleague.

"No," cried the younger man, "I am not the one!"

Just then they were distracted by the sound of Luka leading the horses into the riverbed. The thirsty animals whinnied and snorted when they smelled the water, just as little Luka had predicted.

"Let them drink," said Benjamin.

Luka released the reins of the horses and took in the scene on the river bed. He skipped down the bank and approached the deceased bandit. Un-erringly he looked up at William. There was no expression of accusation, it was almost as if he was quietly confirming from where the bullet had come. The little man then inspected the rawhide shoes on the dead man's feet. Turning, he came to the group beside the fire. He inspected the footwear of both of the prisoners' and with a satisfied grunt he then indicated to Franz that the older prisoner and the dead man had come to the wagon camp. Franz hit the older prisoner a crushing blow to the forehead with the butt of his weapon and the deceitful bandit fell like a stone. A large wound opened on his head and it bled freely into the dry river sand. Franz ordered the party to collect the two mules and the stunted pony owned by the bandits. He stripped the outlaws of their weapons and ammunition, noting that the Lee Metford rifle carried by the dead man was neatly marked with the initials G.L. He left the young man with a knife and a water skin only.

"Whether he stays with the older one or not is up to him, but whatever he decides, he has a long and dangerous walk back to the nearest point of civilisation. If they survive, perhaps they will think more deeply about what they do for a living," reasoned Franz.

"You should have shot them all and been done with it," snarled Benjamin, scowling angrily at Franz.

"The leopard never changes its spots," he said as he spat at the prone form in the sand.

"You, boy!" called Franz to the young nervous looking bandit.

"Baas!" he replied, in a timid quavering voice.

"If I ever see you near my wagons I will shoot you and anyone accompanying you. Do you understand?"

"Yes Baas, no more steal Baas, sorry Baas."

"Let's go," ordered Franz and the patrol departed towards the wagons all seemingly deep in their own thoughts except for Benjamin, who chewed biltong and hummed a favourite Dutch melody to himself, demonstrating little emotion from the recent events.

Brady was deeply affected by his shooting of the bandit. Around the wagons he was treated as a hero and the German soldiers, in particular, treated him with a new respect.

Anna consoled him by pointing out that if he had not shot the bandit, the young German soldier would most certainly have died at the bandits hand, and in all probability Brady would have shot the bandit, after the fact, and would now be blaming himself for the death of the soldier and wishing he had shot sooner.

"Which would you prefer?" she had asked him. He knew she was correct of course, but, still it bothered him until a week or so later when Franz came for dinner and informed them that the rifle marked G. L had belonged to a well-known hunter, named George Lubbe, who had been shot at his camp and robbed by bandits.

"I think you have done the world a favour, William," said Franz.

Stock Boys

The Stock Boys were recruited from villages close to Franz's ranch. The Nhama had been associated with cattle and livestock for generations where, as nomadic people, they had driven their cattle with them. Those selected to attend to the oxen and camels had been taught by Franz and his deputies, the skills to drive the ox wagons. However, much of their ability to care for the animals was inbred.

The stock boys were scantily dressed much the same as Luka, wearing only a loin cloth and leather sandals but each carried a blanket or a soft tanned cowhide within which they wrapped themselves during the freezing night temperatures. These slight and frail looking men never rode on the wagons. They walked alongside or ahead of their team of oxen with their long rawhide whips, coaxing and speaking, sometimes singing to their oxen and walked for the entire journey. They were extraordinarily adapted for endurance, walking hundreds of miles on each journey and seemingly unaffected by the powerful sun. At every night stop they would remove the oxen from their yokes and traces and place them into hastily erected 'keeps'. These 'keeps' usually comprised of hay wagons driven into a circle and often anthills and rocky outcrops were utilised as natural barriers to augment the size of the keep. The Stock boys would break out the bales of hay and water the beasts from wooden buckets ensuring each one had its ration before they themselves rested.

Karl would spend many hours in the company of the Stock Boys, learning from them how to care for his beloved oxen. The stock boys kept largely to themselves and their lives revolved around ensuring safety and wellness of the stock. Not only did they attend to the oxen but also to camels and horses.

The youngest of the Stock Boys was named Beko. He was an apprentice to one of the older men and, being the youngest, would run errands for the other Stock boys. He appeared always to be on the move, trotting between wagons with his treasured whip in his hands. He soon created a name for himself amongst the travellers as being a bit of a character by the manner in which he would spring into the air, seemingly unfettered by gravity and with a flourish would circle the tail of his long whip up above the heads of all onlookers and, whilst still in the air, bring the short whip handle down with incredible speed causing the tail to come back on itself with a crack like a rifle report. The young man would land in a cloud of dust and shout out the Afrikaans words "Jou Bliksem," (Lightning) which was a mimic of Franz when he was angry, and this would bring a flood of laughter from both black and white alike—even Franz would smile!

Early one morning William was awoken by the gentle but urgent shaking of his shoulder by Luka. He was immediately conscious of the loud and incessant flapping of the wagon canvas. The chill wind was gusting forcibly.

"What is it, Luka?"

"The sand, it comes!" was all Luka said.

William was confused. He could hear the oxen moaning above the wind, but his sleep-addled mind was unable to grasp the significance of Lukas words. The bushman pointed westwards with his spear. The enormous vault of desert sky was crystal clear and studded with bright stars but to the west it was as if a black curtain had been drawn across the sky, completely obliterating all stars. William felt the fingers of fear grasp his gut.

"What is it, Luka?"

"The sand, it comes, Nkosi." William gathered himself.

"Go and wake Benjamin," he instructed Luka as he leapt from his bed.

Benjamin had assembled all the waggoners around the gate of Franz's wagon. The strength of the wind was increasing with moaning gusts. Franz was shouting to be heard above the din of the slapping canvas and the moaning stock.

"Most of you know what to expect when within a sandstorm. Some of you do not, so listen carefully. We will push the wagons against the base of the small hill on the sheltered side. The stock wagons will be used to form an outer perimeter. All our animals will be kept within the circle of wagons. All personnel will take refuge within the wagons and try to limit the amount of sand collecting on the wagon canvas. Take water into the wagons with you, but ensure it is well covered and sealed for this sand will find its way into every nook and cranny, believe me. It's like a living thing. Mothers with small children place the children on the floor of the wagon and then create a tent above them with blankets or sheets so they can breathe. Men, seal the canvas around the wagons as tightly as possible. Everyone should wear a kerchief over their nose and mouth once the sand arrives. Stay in the wagons until the all clear is sounded by the scouts. Are there any questions? Ok, let's move," shouted Franz, "Gou, jong, gou." ("Quick, boy, quick!")

The crowd erupted into frenzied activity, pushing the heavy wagons into position. The animals seemed to sense the oncoming storm and pressed into one another. One by one the wagons were positioned by desperate men frantically lashing down canvas and securing all manner of paraphernalia whilst the wind began to howl eerily announcing the arrival of this sinister and evil veil.

As the final wagon creaked grudgingly into place a desert puff adder moved ponderously towards the shelter of the rocky out crop. The large metal wheel turned slowly and remorselessly on towards the slow moving but deadly snake.

The tremendous weight of the wagon pressed down through the wheel and trapped the tail end of the reptile forcing it into the desert sand. The snake writhed and struck out with fury at the inanimate beast that held it fast, it hissed and puffed its rage into the dust-filled wind that stole its droplets of deadly venom.

For two hours the storm raged and swirled its suffocating veil. William and Anna sat arm in arm in the dark dust-filled wagon, choking in the dusty fog. William was able to stifle the urge to rip the bandana from over his nose and mouth and dive through the claustrophobic canvas only by knowing that there was a worse situation outside. He could not imagine how Max would survive this terrible ordeal. He had no idea where little Luka had gone. Anna sat bravely still by his side with the big dog lying by her feet. Although he could not see or hear her, Brady knew that she would be praying quietly and the peacefulness of her deep faith steadied and calmed him. William dropped off to sleep only to be startled awake by the resounding bark and whining of the big dog, who was in turn responding to Benjamin's shouts of, "All clear".

The weak morning sun barely penetrated the sand-filled atmosphere. To the east, a pink and surreal glow coloured the world in pastel hues. Herman, the dog sneezed loudly and shook his head vigorously with ears flapping in frustrated irritation at the dusty air. Anna stood beside Brady looking out at a strange and alien landscape. Sand seemed to be piled against, over and inside everything. Brady took hold of the eager dog's chain and allowed the agitated animal to spring nimbly to the ground where it took a few steps, lifted its leg and relieved itself against a sand covered boulder. It lifted its nose, sniffed at the air and sneezed once more. Brady turned to Anna, with bandana still in place and said he would go and see if Max had survived the storm. He went with the dog.

Anna was busy sweeping the sand from the front of the wagon when she looked up and saw Beko running from wagon to wagon. He was ensuring that no oxen had passed through the cordon. Anna's had been the last in the line. He waved as he trotted towards the back of the wagon, a huge smile revealing healthy white teeth.

The puff adder camouflaged by sand and shadow and trapped fast beneath the wheel of the wagon sensed the vibrations of the human running towards it. It pulled its broad head backwards into the deadly striking position. As Beko's foot touched the ground, within striking distance, the scaled head shot forward, slightly elevated and vicious jaws ajar. The two hollow fangs, venomous conduits of death, like spears to the fore, the angry viper delivered its venom with dying rage, deep into Beko's lower calf muscle. The boy screamed with terror and surprise, leaping his last and most impressive turn. He landed and, instinctively, crushed the head of the snake with the handle of his beloved whip. He clutched his wounded leg, wailed forlornly as his anger turned to fear and the cold realisation that he was going to die flooded his brain. The primeval and chilling wail permeated through the camp and men came running to assist. Anna was already at the boy's side. She quickly applied a tourniquet above the boys knee, but was completely at a loss as to what else should be done. She had never witnessed a snake bite before. Brady and Benjamin arrived at the same moment. Benjamin walked over to the dead snake and kicked at it in hateful disgust, the reptile was still writhing though dead. He swore bitterly, "Ja William. It's a bloody puff adder and deadly, I'm afraid."

At this news Anna was in tears. Brady gently rolled the now shaking, but quiet boy, onto his stomach in order to study the wound more closely. The puncture marks were quite visible, but already the area around the punctures was becoming inflamed and darkly discoloured. Anna looked up at Benjamin and Franz. Benjamin turned away and Frans shook his head slowly. Brady lifted the boy, as though weightless, and carried him to the wagon. Anna, now crying openly, placed a mattress on the wagon floor upon which Brady lay the boy, still shaking and gazing sightlessly at his surroundings. He appeared small and frail now. Anna endeavoured to make him as comfortable as possible, talking to him all the while, but there was no response. Luka appeared at the wagon gate and peered inside, he had already inspected the snake. He turned to Brady,

"Nkosi," he said, "The snakes body still moves, but the snake, it is dead. So it is with our friend Beko. His body lives, but already his spirit has gone to be with those of his ancestors. The boy is not here, Nkosi."

Beko became comatose by midday and his heart stopped before the red desert sun had set.

A deep rolling dirge announced the arrival of the stock boys. They came as one and claimed the cold stiff body which Luka, and a weeping Anna, had gently wrapped in a blanket. Beko was buried at the foot of the rocky out crop with his beloved whip in his hand.

The Nest Robber

Franz had decided to send a small unit ahead to Aroab to determine the water situation at the mission. The livestock were now showing the effects of the long trek with rationed food and water. The season had been particularly dry and water was in short supply. The wagons had formed a laager and the travellers rested near a water hole dug down into the river bed by the water diviners of the desert; the elephants. A group of eager men from the wagon train had taken shovels and opened up the water source, deepening and widening the well. The camp had been set up far enough from the waterhole to allow the wild animals to drink undisturbed when the travellers were not filling barrels with their noisy hand pumps. After the replenishing of a barrel or two, the source would be abandoned for several hours to allow water to seep into the well.

William and Anna would sit and watch the water hole in the late afternoon from the safety of a rocky outcrop on the dry riverbank. The variety of game was astounding. This arid hot and inhospitable landscape was deceptive in its abundance of life. It seemed to William that the varieties of creatures would never end in Africa. With Franz and Luka to help him, Brady diligently kept a log of sketches of the animals he encountered with a brief description and, when possible, a sketch of the hoof or paw marks. Luka had shown Brady how to treat the hides of animals shot for food and rations and already he had a fine selection of game skins.

It was due to one of these skins that Brady had his first encounter with an elusive, but very dangerous, brown hyena. William had skinned a magnificent gemsbok which he had hung from the branch of a thorny acacia tree. The wagon drivers had come down from the camp and carved meat from the carcass, placing the cuts into a large bin, leaving a few unwanted bits on the hard ground below the tree. Brady had gone for a late breakfast taking with him a couple of choice cuts. Before leaving he had hung the green skin within the thorn tree with the intention of returning to stretch and salt it for curing. When approaching the tree on his return, he heard a distinctive snarling and 'whooping'. He recognised the sound of hyena and, moving slowly upwind, he observed a fully grown brown hyena with two small cubs tearing and devouring his precious skin. Having never seen this particular species before, he felt it was fair reward. He was engrossed in watching the two pups who moved away from their mother embroiled in their tug of war. Brady was jerked back to his senses by the shadow of the mother hyena suddenly appearing in his peripheral vision. Hunched low and slinking towards him, she launched a determined attack. Without consciously thinking, Brady charged towards her shouting loudly, waving his arms wildly. The startled mother broke off the attack and shambled off after her terrorised and yelping pups. Brady knew that this had been a close call. Those crushing hyena jaws could have amputated a limb like a human plucking an apple. You just could not let your concentration slip when in the wild on your own. His legs were shaking as he walked back to the camp from whence two men were running towards him to investigate his shouting.

Franz heard about his encounter and, later, at the crowded fire side said, "William, I heard you shouting today and then I heard the hyenas laughing, so I guessed they had gotten under your skin!" This caused much hilarity and added to the unique bond of friendship formed amongst people who experience both laughter and tears through harsh and dangerous adventures.

On the morning of the fourth day of the laager, William was granted permission to hike out a short distance from the camp on the far side of the river, with Luka, to practice his skills at identifying different animals by their spoor. Luka was the master in the classroom of the veld and would show much pleasure when his student answered correctly, but became quietly annoyed when the Englishman got it wrong. The couple had wandered up a dry shallow gully which meandered away from the river edge and continued around a raised outcrop adorned with a few stunted acacia trees. Luka told William that it was bad practice for them to be walking in the low gully shadowed by high ground onto which they could not see. The pair skirted back and cautiously scaled the out crop, from the top of which they could see for a good distance. There were numerous springbok on the undulating desert scrub and a pair of giraffe that walked with regal step and appeared to look down at the humans even though they were hundreds of yards distant. They stood behind a stand of flat topped acacia trees nibbling at the tasty pods reserved for those browsers with extra-long necks or trunks. Turning, William noted a lone ostrich. He pointed it out to Luka.

"I have seen it, Nkosi," said Luka, "and what can the Nkosi tell me about this volstruis (ostrich)?" Brady studied the large bird. Although it was flecked with the inevitable film of red-brown dust the feathers were magnificent, black with white plumage.

"It's a male," said Brady.

"Yes, Nkosi, and what is it doing?"

Brady watched the huge, flightless bird as it lowered its head and pecked at the earth disinterestedly. It then raised its head searching in all directions. It repeated this manoeuvre several times and then spread its stunted wings as if flexing its muscles.

"I do not know what it is doing," admitted Brady.

"It is guarding its eggs, Nkosi," said Luka. "If you look behind it you will see some grass and small bushes. The nest will be in those bushes." Now that William knew the answer he could see that the bird never wandered from the area and watched every movement close and far.

"If you go near that nest will the ostrich attack?" asked William.

"Yes, Nkosi it will attack! But if you are clever and two of you go, then one will lead the 'volstruis' away from the nest while the other takes the egg."

"A smile moved across Brady's face. I would like to try this," he said to Luka. Luka also smiled.

"Let us try, Nkosi," he said, "but the bird is very strong and will kill you if you are not careful."

"Have you been hurt by the bird before, Luka?"

"Uh, no Nkosi, but I only take one egg and I tell him that I will only take one."

Brady smiled at this. He turned and looked back towards the river and saw that Karl and Mildred were down at the river filling a barrel.

"Karl," he called and waved the couple towards him. Karl took up his rifle and taking his wife's arm the portly couple made their way up to William and Luka, joining them at their vantage point.

Breathless, Mildred asked, "What is it, William?"

"Well, Miss Mildred," said William, pointing to the ostrich strutting again some hundred and fifty yards away. "You see that ostrich? Well, he is guarding a nest and Luka and I are going to outwit him and steal an egg for breakfast!" Said William, extremely proud of his newfound knowledge and presumed ability.

"Das dangerous birds," said Karl.

"Karl, will you hold my rifle? Luka is going to distract the bird whilst I find the nest and take the egg. Please would you watch over us in case another predator should arrive?"

"Jawul Herr Brady," said Karl, "ve vill vatch, but vis my shooting you may be in great danger, ja!" chuckled the German.

The two nest thieves skirted the outcrop and then moved up towards the nest site. Luka in front, hardly noticeable with his sand-coloured skin, and Brady behind, agile…but twice the size of the bushman!

The feathered sentinel did not notice the robbers as they crept closer to his precious horde. When the duo were thirty yards from the ostrich they lay down within a small depression. Luka pulled up a small bush which he held directly in front of himself. He instructed Brady to remain where he was until he called for him and then he was to run to the nest remove only one egg and then make his way back to the rocky outcrop, and safety, as quickly as possible. Simple enough! Luka then moved slowly in short darting runs towards the bird all the while remaining hidden behind the bush which he carried in front of him.

The bird suddenly stood dead still. He watched the small tree that suddenly seemed much closer than before. The tree stood absolutely motionless, the bird looked away and then glanced back again. Still the tree remained unmoving. The Ostrich shook its warlike plumage, stretched its neck then resumed its feeding. No sooner had its head gone down than the tree darted forward another five yards. The bird's head shot up like a rubber periscope, beak slightly open and large made up eyes wide with disbelief. William lay in the depression desperately suppressing the urge to laugh aloud at the antics of Luka and the bird.

Luka, realising that the bird was onto him, placed the bush on his head and stood up straight, this would make him much taller and might intimidate the confused ostrich. The Bushman then mimicked the birds walk stepping out with long legs and head and bush bobbing backwards and forwards with each step. Luka had moved about ten paces in the opposite direction to Brady in his bird walk, when suddenly, the male ostrich decided enough was enough. With stunted wings out and head forward it charged after Luka seemingly furious at the mockery from this half tree, half animal intruder.

"Now, Nkosi, now," shouted Luka, as he fled towards the nearest tree. William was weak with laughter, tears running down his face. He rose and ran towards the patch of dry grass and stunted bushes. He looked around and, at first, could not see the eggs. 'Where, where' he said to himself? Then he saw them. There were three eggs in the clutch. He darted forward and lifted the nearest egg, amazed at the size. He stood for a second forgetting his circumstance as he studied this awesome egg.

"Run, nkosi, Run," he heard Luka shout, which jerked him back to reality. Looking towards Luka, now halfway up an acacia tree, he saw the ostrich coming at full flight towards him. The bird was huge, with dust flying out behind it. Brady ran as he had not run in years, no more laughter, just sheer fright. The bird squawked in anger. It was right behind him. Huge feet pounding at his heels! It stretched its neck…spear-like the beak pecked his hat, snatching it off his head. William swerved to the left gaining slightly as his pursuer was temporarily distracted by the flying headgear. Frantic, William remembered Luka had told him that if he told the bird that he had only taken one egg the bird would leave him alone. Still racing madly towards Karl and Mildred, he shouted at the ostrich, "Only one, I've only got one." Undeterred, the ostrich lunged at his waistcoat ripping it easily.

"Just one, you stupid bird," screamed William in high pitched desperation. He could feel the Ostrich bearing down on him and dived down the gully below the outcrop where Karl and Mildred had stood. Brady was still shouting "Only one", intermingled with several obscenities whilst rolling and kicking at the stamping and pecking monster fowl. Suddenly several shots rang out and shadows appeared through the dust above the bank and the bird was gone.

Brady lay gasping for air. An exhausted dishevelled and dusty heap hardly begins to describe the state in which the bird had left Brady. As more people from the camp lined up along the bank of the gully looking down at William and hearing the tale between fits of hilarity from Mildred and Karl, he began to regain his breath though still panting. He felt as if he had been run over by a heard of wild horses. Every time someone said

"Only one," the crowd above laughed and cajoled him further. Eventually he managed to sit up. The egg that he had risked so much to steal was crushed inside his shirt and the contents oozed disgustingly through his shirt front, mingling with the sweat and dust. He saw Luka standing in the gully with a huge smile on his face.

As Brady began to speak silence fell upon the onlookers.

"Why do you laugh at me, Luka?" Brady asked.

"I do not laugh at you, Nkosi," said Luka. "I only show that I am happy the Big Bird did not kill you." The crowd laughed.

"I told the bird many times that I had taken only one egg, but it still tried to kill me, Luka? Why Luka?" Again the crowd laughed.

"That is because these animals who are from the land of my fathers do not understand English Nkosi," said the wise little man. Again the crowd bellowed and finally Franz climbed down into the gully and assisted the bruised and battered nest robber to his feet, gingerly avoiding the 'broken egg mucus' oozing from every button hole and aperture around William's torso!

Late that night, after an amused, but concerned, Anna had bathed and strapped William's cuts and bruises, they sat arm in arm by the camp fire. They could hear laughter and 'only one' being repeated. Anna snuggled into his shoulder and said

"They are calling you 'Willy just One' and I believe they are correct because, truly, there is no other quite like you!"

The Boer

Benjamin returned with the advance party to report that the Boers had already arrived at the Mission and were anxious to be on their way. Restless after ten days of waiting, the Dutch farmers had not wasted their time. They had drawn water from the Mission well and filled the stock troughs in anticipation of the Luderitz wagons arriving. They had affected repairs to the wagons going on to the West Coast and unloaded fresh hay for the incoming oxen. And, of course, had guarded the bullion carried to pay for the precious guns that would free them from the oppressive demands of the British.

"Who is leading the Boers?" asked Franz.

"Rooi Maritz," replied Benjamin with a smile. "The British have raised the price on his 'red head' but have been unable to catch him and, as long as he remains north of the Vaal River, they never will."

Franz turned to William saying, "Rooi hates the British. The story, as I understand it, is that the Administration confiscated his farm in Natal, paying him half its value and telling him the land was strategic. He refused to move, telling the Governor that the money would not pay for the life lost by his father whilst fighting the Zulu in 1938. Or that of his sister claimed by pneumonia, caught whilst working the freezing slopes of the Drakensburg during winter. When the Bailiff came to throw him off the land a gun fight ensued where one official was wounded. Rooi, already packed, had hurriedly taken his family and fled north with a deep and burning hatred for the British."

"So," said Franz, "he may not like you, William, but you will have something in common."

Although he knew that Franz meant no harm William was offended. He was angry with the sudden realisation that he was now classed as an outlaw. Somehow this truth had eluded him till now. Was this modern justice? He was convicted by a State judge for committing an offence on Queens Land after having been employed to do so by the Royal Trustee. The anger flared and as

Brady turned in his saddle and saw Anna gazing at him from the wagon with a face full of concern, his anger was instantly transformed into thanksgiving.

When the sun was about to set on the 23rd day of the month of September 1883, exactly one year since Brady had been sentenced to five years in exile, the wagons rolled wearily into the mission at Aroab.

A patrol of Boers had met the travellers during their midday stop. They had sat with Franz and exchanged news amicably. Rooi Maritz was noticeable even from a distance, a huge man with red hair and beard, which gave him a wild, menacing appearance.

Later that night, as Brady was completing his duty at sentry, he was approached by Franz.

"William, the Minister from the Mission has requested that Rooi Maritz go, track and shoot a troublesome lion that has killed one elderly Nhama woman. She was with a group of women and children collecting water. The Villager's say the lion is injured. Rooi does not have a tracker and asked if Luka could assist him. Maritz is a Godly man and will do as the Minister has asked but he does not wish to waste time looking for this man eater. He is anxious to get his cargo safely back to Transvaal and believes that, with a good tracker, he would locate and destroy the lion in two days."

"I am sure Luka would relish the challenge," answered Brady, "But he would not be peaceful travelling with men unknown to him."

"I have already suggested that you should travel along with the party, William. I had a feeling you would want to look after the little yellow man." Franz smiled. "I was going to give that small desert pony to Luka as payment for finding those bandits, so he may as well take it tomorrow."

Brady replied, "That's a fine gesture, Franz. Luka will be very proud. I will speak with him now. By the way does Mr Maritz know I'm English?"

"He didn't ask," said Franz with a wicked smile, "but he did say the party would only consist of five people. That would be you, his son, Raabie, Luka, the Mission interpreter and, of course, himself and to please be ready at first light."

"But he hates Englishmen! He may shoot me!" said William aghast?

"You'll be fine, William. Just don't stand near the lion," chuckled Franz as he walked off into the night.

Before dawn William stood in the cold morning air with Max saddled and ready to go. The big gelding had lost some weight on the long journey, but was magnificently lean and muscled. The horse had developed a taste for dried fruit which Anna insisted was good for Brady's digestion. Brady gladly gave it to his horse.

The Boer father and son walked their mounts into the light of the sentry fire where Brady waited.

"More!"(Morning) they greeted William, "Waar's die Bosman," asked Rooi Maritz as he extended a hand to shake William's?

"He's coming," answered William. The Boer's arm froze and then dropped to his side.

"You're English!" he exclaimed in startled, but accented English!

"Yes," answered Brady.

"Nee Man. Waar's Franz?" ("No man. Where's Franz?")

"Ja, ek is hier, Rooi." (Yes, I am here, Rooi) Frans appeared as if by magic with Luka and his small pony behind.

The Boer and Franz entered into a heated discussion. Brady was able to get the gist of what was said. Eventually Raabie joined the conversation speaking earnestly to his father. This seemed to pacify the big Boer.

Rooi Maritz turned to William. The two men were standing eye to eye. Maritz was heavier and older, but they were the same height.

"For many reasons I don't trust or like the English."

"I am not accompanying you because I like or trust you," said Brady. "I am willing to go because Franz has asked me to do this, and also because if I don't go, then nor does the tracker."

"Goed. As long as we understand each other and also understand that I am in charge of this mission."

"We will follow your lead as long as you prove a good and capable leader," said William. The two men continued to stare at each other.

"You had better get going. The sun is already rising," said Franz, skilfully diffusing the tension.

The interpreter for the Mission rode a mule with a hessian saddle and no stirrups. Progress was slow. The Boer and his son rode ahead of Brady and the tracker and although there was muted conversation between the father and son the Englishman was ignored. This suited William as he took in the cool desert morning. They had startled two blue onyx bulls and had seen the inevitable, but graceful herd of springbok. Luka rode his new pony proudly though it seemed stunted alongside Max. The rider and pony suited each other exactly thought William. They were both slim and small. He pondered once more upon the deceased bandit. The pony would hardly feel the weight of Luka after having carried the bulk of the bandit.

Hues of yellow, pink and gold played over the rugged landscape as the sun illuminated the couching shadows of this wild and beautiful land. Two hours after leaving the Mission the five riders arrived at the village. A gathering of sparsely clad women were grouped together in mourning. Wailing and crying due to death of the old lady. This is the custom. The men dismounted a respectful distance from the village and held council with the headman, through the interpreter. Goats were still contained within a ramshackle enclosure. The wretched beasts were hungry and eager to be released for their days foraging. They would be kept within their boma until the marauding lion was eliminated.

Two young men, tall and lithe, dressed only in loin skins and armed with spears agreed to lead the avenging hunters to the area where the lion had attacked the water party. This had been a tragic but natural result, quite within the law of the jungle. When the water party sighted the lion charging, they fled as one, but the older woman was too slow and the lion killed her out right. The slow and the weak pay the price. The rest of the group fled to the village. By the time the men returned to the area the lion had half devoured the woman, but had in turn been chased off the kill by the desert Hyenas. The lion had moved off into the night injured and unable to fend off the scavengers.

The avenging hunters now suitably equipped, left the village on foot following the two Nhama warriors who were now more confident with the inclusion of the fire sticks in the group. After a thirty minute walk the party located, and followed, a waterless tributary which fell steeply towards an ancient river. The leading Nhama gestured with his spear towards a well-used path that ran down the river bank into the wide sun-bleached riverbed. He turned and explained to Luka that the Lion had waited on the path above the river and as the women and children came up from the river with their clay water pots, the lion charged down towards them. Two of the large vessels lay smashed and broken where they had been discarded from the heads of their terrified bearers. The avengers then proceeded down to the riverbed. The Nhama next indicated where the old woman had fallen under the charge of the lion.

Luka, did not come down into the riverbed immediately, but moved about slowly above the river searching for information. Clues left behind by his quarry. Thirty yards back from the river-bank and in the opposite direction to which they had come the bushman squatted down and studied the ground closely. He gathered a pinch of dust and sniffed deeply ascertaining some information that would have been lost to most humans. Seemingly satisfied he moved slowly down the ramped path worn deeply into the hard dry earth by thousands of feet and hooves of every description. The tracker came to the place where the victim had screamed her last and he again squatted in the thick sand. A few small congealed stains were the only evidence of the dreadful episode of a few days before. The scavengers of land and air had done their job well. All eyes were now on Luka.

"Well, what does the Bosman (Bushman) say?" asked Rooi Looking towards Brady as he spoke.

"What have you seen Luka?" asked Brady.

The little man stood. He gazed out towards the muddy pool in the river bed, distorted by the heat waves shimmering and dancing amongst the thirsty warthog and springbok, desperate for the dirty life-giving water. Then he appeared to search the river banks on either side with shaded but intent eyes.

"Nkosi, the lioness is very close, even now she watches us. She will not go far from the water and the animals that drink there, she is also dying. She has one rear leg that is useless and it is rotting. I have smelled her death! Nkosi, we must be very careful. This lioness fears nothing. She is ready to die for it will be easier for her." The tracker pointed back towards the tributary mouth with his lethal spear.

"We will go to her, Nkosi."

Rooi Maritz took charge of the party. He placed himself directly behind Luka and stationed Brady ten meters behind himself, and about fifteen meters to his left. His son Raabie he stationed to his right, also behind and the same distance out, forming an arrow head. He instructed both Brady and Raabie to have their weapons ready to fire, but that when Luka indicated the position of the beast he, Rooi, would do the shooting and only if he missed or was in trouble should they shoot. The two Nhama warriors followed some distance to the rear. No sooner had Luka picked up the spoor and the party gained the riverbank when an alarmed exclamation burst forth from one of the Nhama's.

"Aaiee! Shumba!" (Lion) he screamed.

The man eater came hurtling from behind Raabie. Instinctively the young man turned to face the oncoming lioness, which was almost upon him. He fired frantically and missed in his haste. A second shot rang out immediately followed by a third.

Rabbie's father was directly behind his son and could not see the attacker at first. He watched stricken as he saw the fearsome beast leap onto Rabbie. The little bushman streaked past him and drove his spear into the lioness which now lay dead half enveloping the young Raabie. Both the Boer and Brady arrived at the scene at the same moment and grasping the lion, they hauled it off the young man. The distraught father lifted his son to his feet as if he were weightless, all the while asking if he was alright. The son struggled to reassure the father as he had been winded by the impact with the lion. He quickly regathered himself and quieted his father's concerns.

Luka was examining the lioness. There were two wounds in addition to that left by the spear. One was through the skull just behind the ear, which would have severed the spine causing instant paralysis. Undoubtedly, the shot that had saved the young man's life, whilst the second bullet wound was located just behind the front leg entering the lioness' chest cavity. The big Boer stood with his arm around his sons shoulders. He gazed down at the lioness and the bullet wounds that had killed her. He slowly removed his hat and turned to Brady.

"Maneer," he said, "there is nothing I can say to thank you or repay you for what you have done for me and my family today, for surely you have saved the life of my son and I thank God for you." He held a shaking hand out towards William.

William took the hand and said, "I believe you would have done the same for an Englishman under these circumstances."

"But tell me," said Rooi, "Where did you learn to shoot man?"

"Oh, I'm still learning!" replied William, "that was a very lucky shot!"

The men continued to inspect the carcass of the lioness. She had received a tremendous blow to her rear right hand quarter, dislocating her leg at the hip, but also inflicting a large wound which had become infected. Swelling to three times its normal size and oozing a gangrenous and offensive puss. Luka was unsure of the cause, but thought that it may have been inflicted by a buffalo or a rhino.

The Nhama men skinned the lion, returning to their village hero's for having avenged the death of the woman. Now that the initial frost of mistrust between the Boer and the English man had begun to thaw, the two men found that they had a core of common interests, particularly within their mutual fascination for wildlife.

The Boers, both father and son enthralled Brady with their stories of the abundance of game found in the greener parts of the Transvaal and along the great Limpopo River. When the party arrived back at the mission they were met by the remaining Boers and Franz.

"Well, you are back early. How did the hunt go?" Franz enquired of Rooi Maritz.

"Well, Raabie had the most excitement and learned the true meaning of a 'close encounter'."

Raabie laughed. "You couldn't get much closer," he said sheepishly.

"With some expert help from our English friend, here all went well," said Rooi, leaning forward and giving William a solid pat on the back.

Franz's eyebrows rose at that statement and the other Boers exchanged a glance.

"Ja, man! Don't look so shocked," said the big Dutchman. "Rooi Maritz and William the Rooi-nek…we make a red hot team, hey William?" The Boer laughed heartily at his own wit.

Over the following few days and whilst the wagons were serviced and repaired the story of the lion's shooting circulated through the wagons and became more embellished with each telling. All the Boers now acknowledged William as he passed by and the "them and us" tension that had existed melted away. The oxen were rested and well fed. The Boers had taken responsibility for the wagons loaded with the arms and ammunition and Rooi was happy to escort the east-bound wagons into South Africa. Benjamin, with William to assist, was assigned command of the wagons proceeding to Vryburg with Franz's goods for Trade.

On the night prior to the wagons splitting to go their different ways a social gathering was held and after the Mission Minister prayed for journey's mercies and the safety of the travellers, food and drink was available for all.

Franz sat with William and Anna who had invited Rooi Maritz and Raabie to join them. They reminisced and Anna gave Franz a box of letters to pass on to Johan on his arrival at Luderitz. They also discussed the immediate future in

South Africa, and Rooi informed William that a Railway line was being built from Vryburg, going north through Bechuanaland to Bulawayo in Rhodesia and they were recruiting for scouts and camp guards.

"It may become uncomfortable in the Transvaal for an Englishman in the near future William. Even a good Englishman," said Franz. "It may be worth considering."

Before first light the following day Franz and William shook hands in farewell.

The German soldiers honoured William with a parting salute.

As the sun rose over the Mission the western bound wagons were already out of sight.

Boer Republic

On the night after the wagons had crossed onto Boer soil, Rooi had approached William and quietly inquired as to what Brady would do if the wagons were approached by an English patrol. Maritz said he would need to know if it would be better for the wagons to part company if Brady and Benjamin had no intention of guarding the shipment of arms against confiscation by the British.

Brady had already asked himself the same question and had resolved the answer in his mind. Remaining with Franz's wagons until they arrived at Vryburg was his term of employment. This he was determined to complete and remaining with the Boers meant greater security for Franz' wagons and, of course, the civilian wagons, especially from native attacks. William had decided that he would request when the wagons were at their closest point to Kuruman he should be released to escort Anna and the Kraus wagon to the Mission at Kuruman. Then he would return to complete his escort of the freight to Vryburg.

He answered Rooi Maritz by saying that he was employed by Franz to assist Benjamin to escort the wagons safely to Vryburg. He would, therefore, be under Benjamin's orders and if Benjamin deemed the British a threat to the well-being of Franz's goods then they would take appropriate action. William also explained his plan to escort Anna to Kuruman.

"We will not travel all the way to Vryburg with the guns and ammunition," Rooi explained to William. "But will depart to an undisclosed location which, I'm afraid, is Top Secret. I cannot disclose to you where or when."

As the wagons moved further to the east the Kalahari Desert remained dry and red, but the trees became larger and the variety of shrubs increased. This gave evidence that higher rainfall was apparent.

Finally, after what seemed an eternity to Anna and Mildred, the wagons came to a small settlement called Van Zyl's Rus.

The Boers became increasingly nervous as the party moved closer to civilisation and were, understandably, reluctant to spend any more time in one location than was absolutely necessary. After a thorough search of the surroundings by the scouts, they agreed to rest for one day. Rooi insisted that their wagons would be laagered outside of the settlement. The Boers mounted a vigilant guard with scouts sent out seeking news or reports of British patrols. Rooi Maritz avoided contact with locals, but had several visits from unknown men dressed in similar attire to that worn by himself.

Benjamin had agreed that Brady could escort the Kraus wagon to Kuruman Mission. He estimated that two days travel from Van Zyl's Rus was when they would need to part company with the wagons destined for Vryburg. Luka would accompany William. Benjamin, on William's request, produced a letter of contract confirming his employment with Becker's Transport and, after completing delivery to Kuruman, would travel to Vryburg with his assistant.

Two days travel from Van Zyls Rus, and following the Kuruman River, the Kraus Wagon with Brady and Luka leading the way, turned South East whilst the remaining wagons continued along the alternate branch of the river directly eastwards towards Vryburg.

The previous evening Rooi and his son had joined William and Anna at the Kraus wagon in a farewell supper. This had been a bittersweet occasion as Benjamin, Rooi and Raabie had become close friends. Anna had agreed to play and sing for the group and she sang a haunting melody of war and farewell which was deeply stirring and surreal beneath clear African skies. Rooi told William that it was unlikely they would meet again, but if ever he should find himself in trouble with the Boers he should ask for Rooi, who would, for his own part, spread the story and the name of the Englishman who saved his sons life.

Benjamin accepted letters from Karl to his brother in Luderitz and had wished Anna all the very best. He instructed Brady to simply follow the main river south east and it would lead him to the mission. He told William to meet him at the Devilliers Warehouse in Vryburg within fourteen days. William began to protest that he would only take a few days and then re-join the wagons before they reached Vryburg.

"No my friend, take this opportunity to go to the Mission and get married to the lovely Anna before someone steals her from you! I will see you in Vryburg and pay you your wages. It would be a good opportunity to enquire about the jobs on the Railway to the north. Rooi is certain they will be looking for men with your scouting and shooting skills. This may well be what you and Anna need for a new future free from fear of the past." Brady felt a real affection for this rough and, normally, uncouth man of the desert.

The sight that greeted the Kraus wagon when they neared Kuruman was not what they had expected. The trail climbed steeply up onto a small plateau that looked down into a valley green and rich, totally at variance with the dry surroundings. Anna could hardly believe her eyes after the months of dry red desert.

The oxen seemed to gain energy and moved at an energetic gait as if they could sense the end of their journey. The trail had now become a well-used road and entered a wooded area curving down towards the settlement. Just as the wagons entered the wood the travellers came upon a patrol of Boer cavalry. William was walking Max slightly ahead of the oxen. He felt a jolt of apprehension as the leading officer came into view. The patrol was at platoon strength, moving at a trot. The young officer at the point looked William in the eye, who nodded in greeting. This was curtly returned and then the officer dropped his eyes to take in the magnificent horse ridden by the roughly dressed individual. The young officer then noticed the beautiful Anna on the wagon and instantly the horse was forgotten as he removed his hat and lowered his head in a practiced bow. He replaced his bonnet and waved his troop into a canter, all a flourish of show, obviously for Anna's benefit. Brady was a little shaken. He had half expected the officer to turn and enquire as to where he, a worn and ragged traveller, had acquired such a magnificent horse.

At the settlement they were given directions to Moffatt's Mission. The sun began to set as the weary pilgrims moved slowly up the long entrance to the Mission. Both Mildred and Karl were overcome with relief and gratitude. Husband and wife wept unashamedly, giving praise through thankful tears as Robert Hamilton's beautiful church came into view. Karl pulled the wagon to a halt outside the Kalahari Cathedral, as the Church had been fondly christened by its Parishioners. He hugged his weeping wife, then hugged a weeping Anna, then leapt from his seat on the wagon and proceeded to thank and pet each of his beloved oxen after which he fell to his knees and thanked his father in Heaven.

William was so moved by the scene before him. Karl and Mildred had never once complained on the hard and exhausting journey and now they had arrived strong in faith and more united in their marriage. They had been tested in the desert just as their Saviour had been before His Mission.

Nine weeks of relentless and arduous travel through stretches of Africa's most harsh and remote wilderness had also strengthened William and Anna's love for one another. The trials and tribulations of the trek had tested their relationship by revealing their whole characters. There was very little that they had not shared of their earlier lives on the many nights around the campfire. William had often felt inferior when Anna spoke of her privileged childhood. The places she had travelled and the people she had met. But he was amazed to discover that Anna was just as awed by the tales of growing up in rural England as a farm labourer's son. What Brady did not know was that Anna marvelled at how a person so deprived as a child, and living within abject poverty, could have developed into such a kind and humorous soul untainted with bitterness! In fact, he was thankful for the smallest gesture and exuberant with a great zest for life, including the wellbeing of his fellowman and all God's creatures.

A Mission Wedding and a New Life

The Reverend Timothy Edwards proclaimed them "Man and Wife" before God and the small gathering of witnesses from the Mission staff. Karl and Mildred formed a tearful team of Best Man and Matron of Honour.

Mrs Anna Brady, holding one single yellow rose, wore a plain white dress. Upon her dark tumbling curls was a small netted veil which contrasted with her tanned skin and highlighted her stunning beauty which literally took William's breath away. He stood tall and bronzed looking down at this lovely creature that was to become his wife and was almost overcome with the sense of love and gratitude. This moment would be captured indelibly in his heart and mind forever. This was most certainly the proudest and happiest day of his life and if only, thought William, if only the family…particularly his mother, could have been there to witness and experience this, their most wonderful day.

The couple spent seven happy and passionate days within a sparsely furnished, but comfortable, rondavel in the luscious Mission Gardens. Reluctantly, though expectantly, Brady left the arms of his lovely new wife on the morning of the eighth day to travel with Luka to Vryburg. Anna was to remain with Karl and Mildred at the mission until he returned or sent for her. This suited the Reverend as he was grateful for the medical assistance that Anna was able to bring to the Mission clinic.

Vryburg was a small but busy town…a focal point in the region's development. Brady could have blended easily into the backdrop of agricultural commerce but Luka, riding on his small pony almost naked alongside William, drew unwanted attention. The number of British soldiers and uniformed officials in the town made William decidedly nervous. After receiving directions from a fruit vendor, the travellers located the warehousing site on the eastern edge of the town near the newly completed railway.

Becker's wagons were neatly parked at the corner of the yard in the shade of an elevated water tank. The oxen were nowhere to be seen. Luka took the horses whilst Brady sought information on the whereabouts of Benjamin.

Brady was almost at the office door when he heard a commotion behind him.

"Hey you, Kaffir! Where do you think you are going with those horses you thieving little bastard?"

A heavyset, darkly bearded man appeared at the entrance to a large warehouse and was pointing menacingly at Luka with a shambok. The little bushman turned and looked at the aggressive white man and then turned towards the water troughs with the horses in tow.

"That is my assistant," responded Brady, retracing his steps out into the blinding sunlight from within the small building he had assumed was the office.

"Luka is watering our horses. We have ridden in from Kuruman." The fellow turned and studied William.

"Well, I don't care where you have come from or where you are going. I don't allow kaffirs or English men to walk 'willy-nilly' about my yard. If I did there would be nothing left, so please collect your assistant and wait outside the gate like all the other assistant kaffirs until we decide to deal with you."

"My business here is to locate Benjamin Loods from Luderitz," Brady continued his conversation, trying desperately to remain in control of his rising anger with this crude individual from across the yard. Luka continued to water the horses as if he had misunderstood.

"Stoffel, hou Jou bek!" (Shut up!) came an authoritative voice from within the office.

"Good afternoon, sir. You must be Mr Brady. I have been expecting you."

A short and extremely overweight individual shambled over to where Brady stood. He offered a podgy hand and clasped Brady in a crushing and vigorous hand shake that caused the owners ample double-chin to wobble. He smiled broadly and then said, "Don't take any notice of Stoffel. He is my younger brother and likes to think he is important."

"You must be Mr Devilliers," said William.

"No, no! My name is Jan Pretorius. I bought the place from Devilliers. I am a good friend of Franz Becker," the plump man wheezed.

"Now, Maneer (sir) Benjamin is expecting you. He is buying dried fruit and seed maize from a local farmer and said you should meet him here later this afternoon. The Luderitz men are living in the wagons over there and will be back here by night fall. Please feel free to use our facilities. Mrs Viljoen across the road sells cooked food and there is always coffee on the wood stove near the office," Said Jan Pretorius with a jowl wobbling smile.

Brady thanked him and was about to leave. Stoffel had wandered across from the yard and was leaning against one of the wooden poles supporting the veranda roof. In his right hand, coiled and sinister, was a hippo-hide shambok (whip). Suddenly and with the speed of a striking adder the man's arm jerked and the wicked whip snaked outwards with the resounding crack of a rifle shot. A small rodent scampering along a cross beam was severed in two and ejected in a bloody mass several yards from where it was struck by the scything force of the evil whip.

Brady crouched involuntarily at the unexpected report and was both awed and appalled by what he witnessed and by the still thriving organ that landed on his bare forearm.

"Filthy rats are everywhere stealing our maize and giving us diseases just like the English and the Kaffirs. There is only one way to deal with them, hey, Mr Brady?" taunted Stoffel smiling at William's shocked expression.

The stress of leaving Anna behind, and the constant anxiety of being apprehended by the soldiers and now this loud-mouthed lout and his indifference to all life caused something in Brady to snap. Like a coiled spring the big bushman launched himself at the uncouth and belligerent Stoffel. The first punch caught the dirty and unkempt bully on the side of the head sending his battered hat flying and dropping him to his knees. The second blow came upwards catching him below the chin sending him backwards. No sooner had he collapsed on his back when Brady sprang onto him and, heaving upwards, hauled the half-conscious tormentor across the dusty yard to the horse trough. Brady grasped a handful of the man's greasy hair and plunged his head into the water trough, which he withdrew after a few seconds. He then told him very clearly that he needed his mouth washed out and immediately dunked Stoffel's head below the surface again with murderous force. Retracting the head he demanded of the spluttering and, obviously, petrified thug if his mouth was now clean. He received no response. Stoffel wore only a shocked and bewildered expression. Brady plunged his head into the trough once more and held it below the surface for a little longer. With arms flaying feebly, and half-drowned Stoffel's head was pulled from the water once more.

"Is your mouth clean?" demanded Brady.

Now sobbing, the humbled man cried weakly, "I'm sorry. I'm clean!"

Brady looked at the man in disgust. He released his victim who slumped, coughing and exhausted against the trough. Brady wiped his hands on his trousers and noted that he was still shaking with emotion. William turned to the proprietor.

"I'm afraid I can't apologise for my behaviour, Mr Pretorius," he panted.

"There is no need. Stoffel has been heading for a hiding, or a washing such as this, for a long while. In fact, I am surprised you didn't put all of him into the trough. He is so badly in need of a bath but, then again, perhaps it's just as well you didn't because then the polluted water would kill my bloody horses hey?" He slapped his fat thigh and wheezed a thin laugh. The quip seemed to break the tension and Brady and the fat man chuckled together.

Stoffel rose slowly to his feet, his clothes were sodden and covered with mud from the swill at the base of the trough. Scowling and ruddy faced, he sauntered off towards the warehouse still coughing, his shambok forgotten in the red dust.

"You have won the day, Mr Brady, but I warn you, you have also created a devious and dangerous enemy. Believe me, I know my brother. You will have to watch your back!"

"On some occasions the risk is worth taking, Jan. I am only sorry that it has to be your brother," responded Brady.

When Benjamin and the escorts returned to the wagons that evening there was much jubilation with handshaking and backslapping, wishing Brady and Anna a rich and happy marriage. The celebration began in earnest and out came several bottles of local peach brandy. A cooking grate was thrown over the coals of the fire and the party of men reminisced about their recent trek, whilst the aroma of fresh meat cooking blended with the amiable conversation and the brandy continued to flow late into the clear African night.

Brady awoke to the gentle shaking of his shoulder by Luka. His mouth was dry and as soon as he attempted to move his head he wished the day would go away. He was still fully clothed and lying upon a grass mat near the now dead fire. It was bitterly cold. He noted through one half opened eye a few inert forms lying close by, one of them being the talkative Benjamin. Brady was thankful for his colleague's silence when abruptly Benjamin coughed and then farted loudly. Brady felt ill as he sat up slowly. The spell was broken. He looked at little Luka wrapped in his red blanket now squatting some distance away. William's head throbbed painfully with the slightest of movements. With a tongue like dusty hessian, he asked Luka to bring wood for the fire. The bushman had the flames going in no time, blowing like a bellows onto a lingering ember that flared and caught the bark strips used as tinder. William joined several other men all feeling the effects of the Peach brandy from the night before. Little was said as they washed their faces gingerly in the frosty trough water. As usual Benjamin was the first to speak. He informed Brady that he would pay him once Pretorius had opened the office safe at 0700hrs. He told him that his men were leaving shortly to collect a load of produce purchased the day before and that he would take Brady to the Cape Railway recruitment office.

Benjamin explained that, through Jan Pretorius, he had met with a Mr Headley, who was responsible for Logistics and Supplies for Cecil Rhodes Railway going north into Africa from Cape Town. The new railway was due to push on to Bulawayo through the land of the Tswana's and Bakalanga into the land of the fearsome Matabele.

Benjamin had taken the opportunity to ask if there were vacancies for experienced 'hunter trackers' or 'armed escorts' on the new railway. Mr Headley informed him that the construction personnel were hired by a man named Burns.

The man placed in overall charge of the Cape Railway line from Vryburg to Bulawayo was George Pauling. Pauling undertook to complete the remaining 403 miles of line from Mafeking in the Northern Cape, to Bulawayo in 400 days and Burns was the man to ensure it happened on the ground.

Jock Burns was the Construction Manager with a reputation that preceded him. Burns had been building railways all his adult life. Graduating in 1867 he had studied civil engineering in Glasgow and worked with Scottish Rail. Later in 1880 Burns was recruited by East India Railway and had spent hard years building the vast infrastructure of the Indian Railways network under the renowned Robert Maitland Brereton. Attracted by money and the possibility of running his own construction operation in virgin Africa, Burns accepted the offer made to him by the Cape Railway Company.

Jock Burns worked to a schedule and nothing was allowed to interfere with that schedule. He was a hard task master and ruled with an iron fist. His methods earned remarkable results, especially when operating in extremely remote areas. He was known to be a fair man, but anybody who worked under Jock Burns soon learned that he would earn every penny he received.

Still nursing a throbbing head Brady had managed to force down a breakfast of mielie pap, sour milk and honey.

Feeling more human after the breakfast, William followed the ever talkative Benjamin into the freight office where Jan Pretorius had placed a money bag before himself on a small table that was scattered with papers. Morning pleasantries were exchanged. Ben inquired after Stoffel who was usually settled over a coffee cup in his brother's office first thing in the morning.

"No, no. I haven't seen Stoffel since his bath last night." Jan smiled and looked at Brady, "Perhaps he is still suffering from shock!" Benjamin chuckled whilst he counted out a pile of notes and coins. He then produced a small ledger from his bag and had William sign for his money. It was more money than William had ever seen let alone earned.

"You must have made a mistake, Ben," said William. "That cannot all be mine!"

"No mistake, William. It's correct to the last penny."

Embarrassed, but elated, Brady took the money and shovelled it carefully into his pocket. He was speechless, but thankful. His throbbing head forgotten, he walked across the yard to where Luka had Max saddled and ready.

"Thank you, Luka. Today I will buy you a new komberse (blanket)," he told the bushman.

A delighted smile transformed the yellow face. The bushman answered in a chirpy torrent of clicking sounds that meant nothing to Brady but to which the horse grunted!

Employment

Benjamin led the way to the railway station which was still a hive of construction activity. A gang of men worked on a section of track that linked a huge turntable to an enormous workshop. A wooden fence obscured the area behind a long and elegant building with a raised and spacious veranda. Large brown letters proudly announced, 'Vryburg Railway Station' painted above a Dutch gabled entrance. The building ran parallel to the tracks. At the southern end of the building and, upon the raised deck, was a trestle table at which sat two men. Immediately in front of the table and looking upwards expectantly was a large crowd of men. Three men were upon the deck, one of whom appeared to be signing a large ledger.

The heat of the day was beginning to bite and the shuffling crowd encouraged the dusty atmosphere.

"Man Willie," said Benjamin, "you will be here forever."

"Please take Max back to the warehouse, Ben," requested William, "and I will remain here. I must get work. I will walk back later."

Reluctantly Benjamin left his friend. Taking the horses, he went back to the warehouse. Brady joined the rearmost row determined to wait all day, if necessary, to get work. The gentleman on the left of the table seemed to do all the talking. One by one the jobseekers went before this important man and it seemed that one in every ten climbed the stair up to the ledger. Those rejected moved unhurriedly around the back of the throng, most looking dejected and dispirited with heads hanging amidst their disappointment.

A sudden flurry of movement caused most men to turn, looking to their right. A red whirlwind came barrelling down from the northern end of the building bringing with it paper, leaves and other debris, all caught in its spiralling vortex. The crowd wisely hid their eyes and faces from the invasive dust-devil. Men on the veranda scrambled to secure the official paperwork on the table. Mr Burns, who had been conducting the interviews had half risen from his seat when the twisting devil whipped his fashionable hat from his head. The hat soared into the air twisting and tumbling over and over. It swooped down towards the back of the crowd where, instinctively, Brady's hand shot out snatching the garment from the swirling claws of the thieving wind. There was a rumble of approval from the crowd now busy dusting themselves off as the wind died, rattling defiantly in the rafters of the veranda. With hat in hand, so-to-speak, Brady made his way to the front of the crowd, he being a head taller than most.

A smiling Mr Burns stretched out his hand to receive his hat and, as William extended the hat towards the Railwayman he said, "I need work, sir."

"You and all these other men," answered Burns in a broad Scots accent.

"And what is it you do Mr…er…"

"Brady sir, William Brady. I am a hunter and guide and tracker, sir."

"Weel, because ya fond mae hat doesnae mean you're a tracker, does it, Mr Brady?" Laughter bellowed out from the crowd.

"Besides, we are only looking for Tradesmen today."

He was about to turn away when he hesitated and inquired of his colleague, John. "Do you know if Mr Pervis is still in need of a guide?"

"Yes, sir. He has fired every man we supplied." Burns took a long look at Brady.

"I may have a position for you with the surveyors," he said. "Now, you go back to your place in the line and I will speak to you when your turn comes or I'll have a riot on me hands." With that he dusted his hat off carefully and replaced it jauntily on his head. The manager sat down completely dismissing Brady and the murmured comments from the crowd. Brady was anxious and hopeful as he resumed his position in the line.

After what seemed an eternity, and only after the two railway men had returned from a lengthy lunch, did Brady reach the head of the queue.

"Oh, I see ya found yer wey to the front at last William. Weel, I heard a bit a boot ya from Mr Headly. Just word of mouth mind, but I'll take a chance cause you found me hat. Sign the book and return here at 0800hrs tomorrow morning. Report to the Survey Department and Mr Pervis will be expecting you. Dinnae be late or he'll fire yea on the spot. He will discuss your duties and conditions of service. You have your own horse I take it? Aye good. Next please!"

Brady left the railway yard on foot. Exhilarated by his good fortune, he suddenly realised how hungry and thirsty he was. He patted his tattered jacket pocket within which his pay packet bulged. He would need to find a safe place in which to hide the money.

He was about to turn a corner engrossed in thought when Luka burst round the building almost bowling him over. The little yellow man's face was contorted with anxiety. A state rarely seen in this small brown fellow. He immediately started clicking and clucking frantically whilst tugging William in the direction of the warehouse. William could not understand a word. He lifted Luka from his feet in an attempt to calm the agitated messenger. He finally understood that Max had been taken by some white men from the wagons at the warehouse. Luka bore a large welt on the side of his face and William knew immediately which shambok had made that mark!

William had total disregard for the wide-eyed stares from passers-by as he sprinted behind Luka. One young man thought William was chasing the bushman and launched out to grab Luka who eluded him with ease. They arrived at the warehouse, the office was locked and the yard deserted. Luka called softly to William, turned towards the rear of the yard and began tracking the missing horse. There was a gated rear entrance which was locked. Brady vaulted the gate landing on a disused track. Max's tracks were hidden within the mosaic of tracks of several other horses, but were quite clearly visible to Luka. The group of horses had moved along the track which emerged onto a dusty side street Here Luka stood for some time and then appeared to lead off in the opposite direction to which the group of tracks entered onto the road. Luka shook his head, clicked a comment to himself and then continued in the opposite direction. When it seemed to Brady that they had travelled for some miles and, although he could discern from time to time the particular hoof prints that Luka was following, he began to have doubts that the bushman was on the correct trail since they had entered a suburb of large and solidly built houses within well-established gardens. Luka stopped in front of a white picket fence which separated a beautifully maintained garden from the street. The Bushman simply pointed to a barn at the rear of a newly painted house. William wasted no time he stepped boldly over the fence and walked intently towards the barn. Standing out in front of the barn was a fenced paddock within which stood an expensively dressed man and a few yards from him was Max with a lady mounted on his back exclaiming at his magnificence. Slightly off to one side was Stoffel with two of his cronies.

William called out, "Excuse me, but that would be my horse, Miss," as he vaulted yet another fence. Firstly, a look of shock and then of anger crossed the ugly and still bruised face of Stoffel.

"Nee, Nee vat hom kerels!" ("No, No grab him men!") Stoffel shouted, and the three big men rushed forward to tackle the Englishman. Max bolted off to the side shaking his great head in disgust and trotted off to a safe distance, his rider hanging on for dear life. Brady fought as hard as he could but the trio soon had him pinned to the ground. The well-dressed gentleman now rather shocked and affronted by the brutish behaviour and was demanding after Stoffel what the hell was going on and who was this intruder. The men spoke in fluent Afrikaans.

"This Englishman is a thief and a spy," exclaimed Stoffel.

"We bought this beautiful horse from him this morning." Stoffel searched Brady's pockets and exclaimed gleefully when he pulled the wages from Brady's pocket.

"You see. Here is the money we paid for this magnificent horse. And this English dog is trying to take the horse back, which, we think he stole in the first place. I mean, look at the state of him. Where would a bush jackal like this get a horse like that?" The wealthy farmer looked down at the ragged Englishman and the shadow of contempt began to cloud his grim face. He noticed that a folded piece of paper had fallen from William's jacket. He bent down and scooped up the folded letter, growling at the same time.

"If you are a spy, it will be the gallows for you, my friend."

Stoffel was smiling in triumph and looking at his two accomplices who nodded in admiration at their clever friend's cool deception. The wealthy man finished reading the letter and gazed across at his daughter who had now dismounted and was walking towards him. He noted that the bushman was now holding the horse, Luka stood muttering and clicking his relief to the trusted horse. The farmer turned to Stoffel and smiled.

"Take him into the barn," he ordered Stoffel. "I am going to fetch my rifle."

Stoffel and the two helpers struggled with William who had regained his breath and fought like a man possessed. Stoffel went down holding his crotch whilst the taller of his two companions was bleeding freely from his nose. A shot rang out, thunderous in the confines of the barn, and every one froze in their tracks. Apart from Stoffel, who continued to groan and swear, whilst lying in the foetal position near the barn door, still clutching his bruised manhood! The two bullies fell gratefully to the floor, totally exhausted.

"Shoot this wild English bastard," said one when he saw it was the farmer who had fired the shot. Brady remained on his feet slightly crouched, tense not knowing what to expect.

"Perhaps you would like to come and stand next to me, Mr Brady. My son is on his way to take these three criminals to the stocks."

A stunned silence followed. Even Stoffel had forgotten his pain as everybody, including Brady, endeavoured to grasp what had transpired.

"I read the letter which fell from your pocket from Rooi Maritz, Mr Brady. Rooi is a most respected leader of my Commando and also a very close friend. Not only does he describe in the letter what you did for him and Raabie, but he described your little yellow friend and the horse." Stretching out his hand towards Brady he said, "It is my pleasure to meet you, Mr Brady. I am Johann Duploy. I am sure when Rooi finds out what these three have been up to they will plead for a life in exile rather than face the wrath of Rooi Maritz."

William and Luka were both given refreshments and treated with kindness and respect. William took great delight in retrieving his money from the devastated Stoffel. He also retrieved Rooi's letter from Johann and was assured by the Dutchman that the letter would always be a passport in the Boer territories.

Brady rode Max back to the yard with Luka loping easily at his horses flank whilst holding onto the stirrup.

Cape Railways and Rhodesia

Brady spent the next two months establishing camps, escorting surveyors, collecting water, scouting, guarding and, most enjoyably, for himself and Luka, hunting for camp rations.

The railway route progressed in an almost straight line Northeast to Mafikeng. This was a distance of one hundred miles from Vryburg. The country was relatively flat, dry grassland and desert scrub teeming with game. The nights were typically cold with clear skies and the days warm and mild. Mafikeng marked the border between the Transvaal and Bechuanaland. Water was scarce but the Malopo River and its tributaries formed the main water source.

Brady took to his new job like a duck to water. Raised eyebrows and contempt had been the initial response towards the Englishman and his Bushman assistant. Luka never seemed far from Brady. The eternally caustic Mr Pervis had made a point of informing Brady on several occasions that he was not paying the bushman. William assured Perky that there was no obligation on the Railway to pay the little fellow and that he, William, would take care of Luka. As the days went by and the camp members observed the skills and bush craft of the little yellow man he became an integral part of the team. Pervis began to rely more heavily on advice from Brady and learned to trust his organisational ability. When, after the initial eight weeks, William requested time off, now desperate to see Anna. Pervis was obviously reluctant to let him go. Brady became dangerously agitated until it became clear that Perky Pervis' reluctance was due to a deep apprehension that Brady would not return. Brady reassured him by insisting that Luka would remain at the camp to assist the scouts for the ten days of his absence. Once reassured, Perky provided him with his necessary papers and pay requisition notes to be honoured at the Vryburg office. He also included correspondence to Jock Burns.

The ride back to Vryburg was uneventful although there was a great deal of talk within the last construction camp of pending unrest between the Boer and the British. The town of Vryburg came into being in November 1882 prior to which it had been called Endvogelfontein. The citizens of the town had called themselves Vryburgers or Free Farmers.

When Brady returned to Vryburg the tension within the town was tangible. There were two definite factions. There were those who wished to be totally independent from Britain, mainly the Boers, and those who wished to be included into the Cape Province, which was the determination of Cecil John Rhodes. Those of the latter persuasion were branded Uitlanders (Outlanders) by the Boers.

Brady's arrival back at the Mission found Anna immersed in the children's clinic. When she looked up and saw William standing a few feet away looking down at her, she dissolved into tears of relief and joy. There was much to talk about and the imminent unrest fared at the forefront of topics. Reverend McKenzie was nonplussed as, whatever transpired, the work at the Mission would continue. The Cape Rail link had reached Mafeking and survey was beginning within Bechuanaland. This would continue north into the land of the Matabele. Moffat had already established a strong mission in the area, called Gubulawayo, which means 'Place of Slaughter'.

Many stories of the beautiful lush lands north, teaming with flora and fauna had been brought back to the mission from the travels of David Livingstone and the Moffat family. These tales, and the seemingly endless opportunities, played in the heart of Brady. He felt that, since the Railway was headed in that direction and with the unrest in the Transvaal as well as the Judicial Bond that continued to haunt him, it made good sense for him and Anna to travel north to Matabeleland with other pioneers.

Anna was in full agreement and felt that, from what she had witnessed in this dark-continent thus far, there would always be work for Godly hands and hearts apart from which, as William's wife, she had vowed she would go where Brady led her.

After a blissful week and a heart-wrenching farewell William returned to Vryburg. His journey back to the railway had him preoccupied with an aching heart. Anxious at having to leave Anna once again, and although she never said, William could see that the clinic, with its enormous needs, was beginning to overwhelm his young wife. Dedicated as she was, she was not a doctor. The severity and extent of some of the cases arriving at the clinic were beyond even the most qualified practitioner. Anna, tender hearted as she was, would become too involved and she struggled with the more tragic outcomes. Reverend Mackenzie had counselled her, telling her that she could only do what she was able to and, thereafter, she was to commit all things to God. William was desperately torn between returning to support Anna, and continuing for another eight weeks on the railway. After a sleepless night William prayed for God's guidance and decided that he would assess his immediate future with the railway and if the opportunity for Anna and him to travel north seemed inhibited then he would resign and look for an alternative situation where they could be together. Although now in the employ of the Railway, and with legitimate business in the area, his future was very much an unknown.

When William arrived at the Survey office there was an instruction for him to visit the office of Jock Burns. Apprehensively, Brady knocked on the large wooden door with all manner of thoughts fleeting through his brain.

"Who the devil is wanting me now!" a gruff response greeted his knock.

"It's Brady, sir," said William as he cracked open the door.

"Who? Oh Aye, aye come in lad. I've been expecting you for days. Got lost trying to find yourself, did yea? Ha!" Burns exclaimed at his joke.

"Not exactly, sir. I've been visiting my wife at Kuruman Mission."

"Oh," said Burns. The information seemed to stagger his jovial mood.

"I was nae aware of the fact that you were married. Oh well, that might have a negative effect on why I wanted to see you!"

"What might that be, sir?"

"Well…you must be aware of the growing tension within the region and, therefore, we wish to push on with the line as quickly as possible. In order to do that, I want to speed up the line survey. The report I have received back from Mr Pervis on your abilities and, particularly, organisational savvy is excellent and, therefore, it was my intention to send you north with a forward marking party. I have a young Surveyor arriving from Wales by the name of Jones, would you believe? It was my intention that you would lead Mr Jones…"

Burns bustled to a large wall mounted chart and placed his stubby finger upon a series of convoluted lines and continued, "…Here we are, Mafeking…north to Labotse up to Mochudi. Now from Mochudi the line runs arrow straight to a place called Magalape. It is north from there that we…I, require to mark the best route through to Matabeleland. This will be no easy task, Mr Brady, and will require fortitude and perseverance. Of that, be of no doubt…and dangerous mind, bloody dangerous!"

Embarrassingly, it took Brady some time to orientate himself and Burns had to show him the route up from Mafeking several times before he had fully grasped the strange indications on the chart. Burns grimaced as he estimated that the distance from Mafeking to Magalape was approximately one hundred and eighty miles and at least another two hundred and fifty miles to Matabeleland. Brady couldn't hide his enthusiasm and Burns was delighted.

"I can't deny the dangers, Brady. Marauding Matabele Impis, wild animals, sickness, thirst and who knows what else? But…I'll double your salary and you'll be Camp Boss and run things your way, but you'll report your progress on a monthly basis to me! Any slacking, Brady, and you'll be gone! Do we have an agreement, Brady?"

"Yes, sir. We do, sir. Thank you, sir! I won't let you down, sir!"

Burns was astounded by Brady's enthusiasm. He spoke gruffly to himself, "I've probably just sentenced the poor man to death and he can't stop thanking me. Strange individual this is!"

William spent an enjoyable week preparing for his task whilst awaiting the arrival of Llewellin Jones.

All the information and experience he had gained from his recent overland trip from Luderitz, Brady now employed, beginning with the alteration to his wagons. This work was expertly completed within the huge Vryburg railway workshops. The artificers laughed and joked, at first, at his requests until he explained the reason for each alteration. Their jeers turned to respect. Some of the standard equipment issued to him he chose to discard for items he knew to be far more useful. His wagons were shorter, each with an extra water container. The sides of each vehicle were raised to three foot high with several rifle ports cut into each side. The harnesses were adapted for mules. When the completed party was assembled it consisted of twelve railway police, one coloured cook, two surveying assistants, two scouts, both of whom were Boers much to the distaste of many of the railway police who were comprised mainly of ex British Army.

The team had been assembled for two days awaiting the arrival of Llewellin Jones, the surveyor and all members, including Brady, were becoming restless. A telegram announcing that the Surveyor had left Cape Town the previous day had filled all with the anticipation of leaving the following morning. Two frustrating days later the long-awaited surveyor arrived on the train seemingly at deaths door. Wracked with fever the surveyor was wrapped in a soiled blanket.

He was the colour of damp chalk and reeked of human waste. Burns summoned the local doctor who diagnosed food poisoning. William learned later that the patient's condition was self-inflicted, the result of drinking cheap brandy which, predictably, had ended in alcohol poisoning. Burns, when told that his tardy employee would probably recover after rest and plenty of fluids, gathered the surveyor and his belongings and had them placed, none too carefully, into one of Brady's wagons and instructed William to leave immediately. The ailing Welshman did not care and made it clear that he was happy to die where he was. William refused to have the man travel in one of his prized wagons! That was absolutely unthinkable in his present condition. So, with the help of the two young scouts, William assured the doctor that he would let him have plenty of fluids and they proceeded to extricate the suffering and very odorous fellow from his blanket which was incinerated immediately thereafter. He was then stripped and washed with a mop and repeatedly sluiced under the railways water tank which, under normal circumstances, would have been humiliating in the extreme, especially considering the large crowd of railway workers shouting instruction and insults. But, since the subject was semi-comatose and intent only on dying, no sensitivities were compromised. Once embalmed in a clean railway overall at least three sizes too large the deviant surveyor was laid out in the wagon and the journey to Mafeking and beyond had begun.

Working North

The tension within his small surveying party did, initially, cause William some concern. The two young scouts were excluded completely from the social dinner sessions around the campfire. On the first evening they had joined the assembly only to be snubbed and ignored, after which they chose to eat within the warm kitchen with Cookie, the coloured cook, who always seemed to have a little something extra for the ever hungry young men.

William had selected the scouts himself. They were brothers who had been struggling to make a living on a small holding near Vryburg and had ended up escorting freight wagons for Pretorius in order to survive. The warehouse owner had recommended them to Brady, as he was sending most of his freight south by rail now that the Cape to Vryburg line was in operation, and could no longer justify keeping them.

The Dutch brothers, Dirk and Marty, could have been twins. They both had a shock of unruly blond hair, barely contained within worn and holed straw hats. They wore denim dungarees and woollen shirts. Both were tall and skinny with endless energy and agility. They carried one Martini rifle and a twelve-gauge shot gun between them. Once on a horse they became part of the animal. Their ability to track was acknowledged by Luka, but put into context as 'learning as young lions' by the Bushman. They had been on their own for years and, when together, feared nothing. Dirk was the older of the two and most definitely the leader. Marty had a gentle stutter but a glance into the flinty blue eyes revealed no weakness.

The dawn of the second day presented a fragile but hungry surveyor shuffling around the kitchen looking for food, still clad in the oversized overall. The brothers, already up and drinking coffee with Cookie, looked across at the Welshman and, though trying to control their reaction, both laughed.

"You can laugh as much as you like as long as you feed me," said the Surveyor, with a self-conscious smile on his face. He offered his hand to shake

Marty's but the limb was concealed within the overlarge sleeve. More laughter! A quick glance from Marty and a nod from Dirk and Marty accepted the proffered hand, now half exposed. Marty introduced himself, Dirk and Cookie with the slight stutter and heavy Dutch accent.

Llewellyn accepted the coffee, but studied the 'vetkoek' obliquely that was handed to him by a smiling Cookie.

"What's this strange thing?" he asked.

"Vetkoek," said Cookie, "make you strong."

The surveyor bit it gingerly stating, "No offence. But you can't be too careful about what you eat out here."

"You need to be careful what you drink also!" said Dirk. Laughter followed.

"Yes," replied Llewellyn. He turned to Marty.

"And what do you lads do?"

"W w we wa wa wash the surveyors, Mr Jones," replied Marty with a grin.

"So it was you, you rough-handed people! There are welts all over me!" exclaimed Llewellyn. "And seeing as you now know me intimately…well…you may as well call me Llew'."

The surveyor visited William during the midday stop and both introduced themselves with Llewellyn apologising for the manner in which he had arrived. Llewellyn assured Brady that he would be available to carry out any duties allocated to him until actual surveying engrossed his time. William was polite, but made it quite clear that out here lives depended on full commitment and teamwork, adding that officially the camp was a 'Dry' camp. No alcohol.

William asked if Llewellin had had any training in the use of a weapon.

"Only the Epee at university," was the reply. William frowned with a quizzical stare.

"Oh the duelling sword, Mr Brady."

Brady stressed the importance of being able to shoot a rifle accurately and, in fact, the practise of carrying a weapon with him at all times. Brady was also astounded that Jones knew nothing of the task ahead of him but rested in the fact that Perky Pervis would, in his usual blunt fashion, tell the new employee where he was going, what was expected of him and that, if he was unable to complete the task, would be sacked. How much mettle the Welshman had would soon become evident.

Once the group had set up camp William would insist that an experienced member of the railway Police section take Llew, accompanied by either Marty or Dirk, and give him instruction on firing the Lee Metford rifles as issued to the Railway Police and patrol personnel.

Llew was roughly the same age as Dirk and slightly older than Marty and it was natural that they should become friends. The witty bright-eyed Welshman was not affected by the politics of the land nor was he swayed by the cultural differences amongst them. Marty and the surveyor were continually joking with each other and had a similar sense of humour. Dirk was more serious, but laughed readily at their antics.

It could not be said that Llewellin Jones was a natural shootist. In fact, it was hard to believe that he could accurately measure angles on a straight line. Whilst he was under the instruction of the Policeman, the scout would keep a lookout and ensure that they were not in any danger and that they would find their way back to camp without difficulty.

It was obvious to Dirk, on one particular occasion, that the rifle Officer Deacon was using was totally unsighted and that the officer, whilst more accurate than Llew', was still far off target. The policeman was obviously becoming agitated and losing patience. Dirk decided to wander down and give some helpful advice. Deacon was decidedly rude and ordered Dirk to mind his own business.

Llew' jumped to Dirk's defence and pointed out that the instructor's attempts to improve his ability were going nowhere. The annoyed policeman responded by asking Dirk if he could shoot any better? Dirk's response was to invite the officer to suggest a target.

Up to that point the pair had been shooting at a small anthill, approximately seventy meters away. The policeman challenged Dirk to hit the anthill. Dirk declined and a smile began to cross the face of the instructor which soon faded when Dirk said that it was too close and to choose a worthy target. Dirk climbed onto his horse and cantered over to a large tree. Mid-way up the trunk he placed three strips of white rifle cleaning cloth using thorns from an acacia tree to pin them in place. On his return he asked the policeman if he was able to hit any of the targets. Llewellin estimated the distance to the target to be just over two hundred yards. Dirk agreed. Deacon took careful aim and fired. The fall of shot was way to the right. Dirk stood without the assistance of a rest and fired. The right hand cloth dropped slightly and discoloured. The policeman reddened.

"Excellent shot," cried Llew'. "Bravo!"

The policeman said, "Alright, now try it with a service issue rifle."

"That is your problem!" said Dirk. "You need to adjust the rear sight. The weapon fires consistently to the right for both of you."

The scout took the weapon from the policeman who, reluctantly, released it into Dirk's grasp. Dirk, removing his clasp knife from his dungaree pocket, adjusted the rear sight with one revolution to the right. He handed the rifle back to the policeman and said, "Try it now."

The instructor took careful aim, resting the weapon on a low branch, he fired. Bark flew from the tree just left of the lower target.

"Close," said Dirk, "but it is over-adjusted. Please give me the rifle." Again he adjusted the sight, retracting the screw slightly and taking up the slack with the screw from the alternate side. He then loaded a fresh round and, firing from the shoulder, removed another cloth target from the tree.

"Perfect," said Llew'. The policeman, now excited by his previous success, took the rifle from Dirk. He chambered another round and, after too long an aim, fired once more. Bark exploded from the tree immediately below the cloth target.

The policeman turned and smiled at Llew' and Dirk, "I could begin to enjoy this," he said.

"Mr Deacon, you will enjoy it more when it saves your life," replied Dirk wondering, secretly, if he had lacked wisdom in teaching an Englishman to shoot?

It was well recognised that the English soldier was not necessarily accurate with a firearm as the military tactics of the time relied more on the volume of shot from a section, all firing at once, rather than the accuracy of one killing shot.

On Dirk's advice, Brady instructed the section commander to issue Jones with his own rifle. Dirk and Marty set the rifle up as closely as they could to Llewellin's requirements and taught him the art of controlled breathing and squeezing, rather than jerking the trigger. The brothers encouraged him to practise as often as possible and, within days, he was quite confident of hitting any 'dinner plate' sized target within a hundred and fifty yards.

Tragic Lessons

Ears erect and nostrils twitching the Black rhinoceros snorted loudly. Her calf started and pushed into her flank. Without hesitating she charged up the slope of the pan and straight for the flank of the patrol. When the rear-most rider saw her and shouted a warning, she was already at full speed and only thirty yards away. With an apron of grey dust billowing before and behind her she powered on like a 'juggernaut'. The warning scream caught the six men daydreaming. They had been in the saddle since sunup on a training patrol. Precious seconds were lost in tragic confusion. The enraged beast burst between two horsemen as they spun, attempting to face this terrifying onslaught. Head down, she slashed upwards and to her left, her massive head and huge horn rising with the speed and force of a steam hammer. The brutal granite like horn was driven hard into the stomach cavity of the nearest horse with such force that it lifted the stricken animal into the air. The horn thrust up through the lower rib cage and penetrated the rider's inner thigh, smashing his femur and severing the artery. Momentarily, the doomed horse regained its footing, running several yards before going down disembowelled and dragging bleeding entrails in the grey dust behind. The rhinoceros came around in a tight circle bounding on massive piston-like legs; head down; slashing left and right ready to destroy its next victim. Fortunately, the male rhinoceros remained off to the left of the fray being followed by the bleating calf. The patrol leader now a good distance from the scene of the attack was firing, ineffectively, at the incensed female rhinoceros. The patrol had dispersed apart from the dislodged rider who lay motionless on the sun scorched ground within an ever-increasing pool of his own life-ebbing blood. Since there were no other targets the attacker charged the dead and defenceless horse, once more goring it viciously several times before losing interest. Still blowing and snorting through flared nostrils, she moved off towards her calf, trotting whilst swinging her massive head from side to side in victory.

The whole episode had lasted less than a minute. The prehistoric looking beasts were lost from site having trotted off towards a granite copse topped with a sprinkling of acacia trees. Now only five strong the patrol had regrouped three hundred yards distant.

Sergeant Harrow, quite ashen and visibly shaken, instructed the patrol to form an extended line with at least thirty paces between horsemen. Harrow taking his place in the centre. The patrol would proceed at a walk towards the area of the dead horse, now quite visible, and locate Henderson, the missing rider. When the patrol had reached the deceased horse, birds of carrion were already in the air above them. Henderson's inert and dusty body lay pitifully propped against a small anthill where, in mortal weakness and shock, he had tried to stem the flow of blood from the brutal wound in his shattered thigh. He now stared with sightless eyes into the vast blue African sky. The patrol commander remained on his mount, maintaining a nervous guard whilst facing towards where the rhinoceros had disappeared. Two men attended to Henderson. The remaining members were instructed to retrieve all usable items of equipment from Henderson's dead horse. As they approached the horse a cloud of blue green flies rose from its cavernous wound and the stench of death was already emanating from the carcase.

A stunned and silent patrol returned to camp.

Brady was furious on receiving the patrol commander's report on the death of Henderson. It was only the night before he had issued instructions to the Railway Police sergeant insisting that all patrols were to be accompanied by at least one scout.

The Sergeant tried to argue that even the scout would not have seen the rhinoceros in the pan, but Brady pointed out that now they would never know. But, if the scout had not initially seen the beast, he would still have been far enough ahead of the patrol that the beast would probably have charged the scout who, being vigilant and bush-wise, would have had a far greater chance of avoiding disaster than would a group of newly saddled foot soldiers.

"I haven't even reached Mafeking and I've already lost a man due to your petty racial preferences which swayed you to disobey my orders. You will be relieved of you duties and your rank and confined to camp guard duties until we reach Mafeking where Mr Pervis can deal with you. Your immediate duty will be to bury your comrade in arms. You will do well to accept that, out here in this wild country, Mr Harrow, we must rely on one another always working as a team regardless of our petty likes and dislikes. You are dismissed."

The Wild North

Though it had seemed an eternity, Pervis had finally released Brady and his team to go north. After a week at the main camp now established at Gaborone, Perky Pervis had drummed as much training and information as he possibly could into William and the unfortunate Welshman, Llewellin Jones, who was told endless times that there was no alcohol allowed on the camp and that, as a professional man, he was expected to act the part.

The florid-faced Mr Deacon had continued to take the role of acting Sergeant and was proving to be a worthy leader. He insisted that the scouts join his troop for meals and training sessions and that, henceforth, no group or individual left the confines of the camp without Brady or, at least, one of the brothers at the lead.

Llew loved his work and was pedantic about exact readings. His two assistants soon realised that the jokes and seemingly careless attitude were a front for a meticulous mind couched in a diligent character. What continually thrilled the surveyor was the thought that here, in this part of Africa, he was the first to measure and mark this wild land. Since the beginning of time he, Llewellin Jones, thousands of miles from his civilised home, was the first! Maybe the first human to walk in some of the places he marked. His readings would begin the history of this railway which, hopefully, would last long into the future. He was a pioneer in every sense. The majesty of this vast and ever-changing continent with so many dangers for the unschooled vitalised his soul. Every day brought new experiences, challenges, sights and discoveries.

The exhilaration of new discoveries was tempered by a growing anxiety as the group progressed north. Each member was becoming more vigilant and their bush sense became keener as they were honed by the guidance of the bushman and the scouts. The scouts, including William and Luka, spent hours scouring the veld beyond where Llewellin and the surveyors worked, ensuring there were no surprise attacks from the fearsome and ruthless Matabele impis who were known to be patrolling these parts. Brady had been warned that the impis could travel great distances on foot. As many miles as a mounted troop and, therefore, he must never become complacent, for in this land the moment you lowered your guard you were vulnerable.

One morning when Dirk asked Luka if he had seen any evidence of the Matabele? Lukas' response had been simple and accurate.

"Nkosi, they are here! We will see them!"

Elizabeth

As the weeks turned into months, Anna, now well into her pregnancy, had overcome the nausea. It had been especially bad when entering the clinic where the strong and pungent carbolic scent caused her to wretch.

She had heard no news from William for the previous eight weeks, and, naturally, was becoming anxious. A group of four Sisters had arrived from England a month previously and were destined to leave for Hope Fountain Mission established far to the north in Matabeleland. The London Missionary Society had commissioned the Sisters, under the leadership of Sister Hanna, to travel into the hinterland of Matabeleland where Robert Moffat had planted a church and Mission station.

During his time in Matabeleland Moffat had befriended the Matabele King Lobengula, the son of the great Mzilikazi and had tried to convert him to Christianity. Whilst they became good friends, the King never made the conversion.

The arrival of the Sisters was a God sent opportunity, thought Anna. She could accompany the Sisters to Matabeleland which was where William was headed with the railway. Anna found herself growing angry with the silence from her husband. Surely he must know that she would be worried sick by now. Nine weeks without a word!

Two days later a very tired and travel weary Brady arrived at the Mission. It was late in the afternoon. The journey had taken five days of hard riding. He had left Max in the care of the railway livery and selected a fresh mount at Vryburg to complete the journey. Brady's weariness dropped away immediately he saw his lovely wife. Whilst William was so proud and excited about the prospect of their first child he was also fearful about the unstable world into which the child would arrive. William made two further long trips back to the railway camp before receiving a telegram announcing the arrival of Elizabeth Johanna Brady.

William left the camp immediately for the Mission, full of proud excitement and anticipation of seeing his lovely wife and new daughter he rode harder than ever.

It was late morning when William arrived at the Mission. He had expected a few exuberant welcoming cheers from those working in the gardens, but they simply watched as he rode past. He noted that the Mission was unusually quiet. The curtains of his and Anna's cottage were drawn closed. William felt a terrible foreboding. He looked towards the Chapel where Father Davis stood watching. No wave of welcome just an acknowledging nod. He entered the cottage quietly and saw Anna seated within her darkened room. She was sitting on her bed, leaning slightly forward, hands folded in her lap, gazing at the small cot near the curtained window. She turned slowly on hearing William enter. Her drawn features dissolved into a contorted mask of abject pain and misery and she slipped onto the floor and cried out in moaning agony that came from her innermost being. A wail, that was so intense and disturbing, that William wept instantly, not knowing or understanding the cause for grief.

He lifted her, limp, from the floor and turned to see his baby daughter wrapped carefully in a small pink sheet, pale and still.

For two days Anna hardly spoke, she ate nothing and would only drink black tea when forced to by the pleading of her husband. Either William, or the distressed but motherly Mildred, sat at Anna's bed side for hour upon hour. William, though dealing with his own shock and grief, was intensely concerned for Anna. It seemed she had lost the will to live. The Reverend and Father Hamilton prayed in earnest and visited the cottage frequently.

On the morning of the third day Anna wept loudly and apologised to William for letting their daughter die. She was full of guilt saying that she should have been more cautious, more aware that sickness in the clinic could affect her new born child. William lovingly assured her that he thought no such thing, that there was no blame. He told her how much they now needed each other, how he needed her strength to move on. Anna seemed to respond to William verbalising his absolute dependence on her. Slowly she began to function once more.

William and Father Davis had bonded since the death of their baby, Elizabeth. This mild mannered 'man of the cloth' had a listening ear and was full of wisdom in matters of life and death. He imparted a genuine sense of hope and warmth in this time of crisis…a blessed assurance that Elizabeth was safe in the arms of the Saviour and that the family would be reunited for eternity.

Father Davis was enthralled by the stories related to him by Brady. His particular interest was with the Matabele tribe. There was little that Brady could report from a personal perspective, however, the savage and barbaric cruelty by which this tribe existed was legendary.

William and Anna had discussed her travel to the North extensively, not only with each other but with Reverend Hamilton and the other members at the mission.

William, although limited in his vocabulary, had no difficulty in verbalising the difficulties that would be facing them as a couple and, indeed, all pioneering people. Having engaged in numerous discussions with a variety of peoples, through railway business and information gained from knowledgeable travellers, Brady was able to form a very real understanding of the demands that pioneering these wild lands would place upon them. No matter where he and Anna decided to settle, they would be isolated by hundreds of miles of difficult and hazardous country. Far from any established centre, regular source of supply or civil assistance. Very little could be done to mitigate the ravages of the climate and the trials of the wet season which would often hamper communications for weeks on end. No matter how good their intentions towards the natives might be, they were unwelcome newcomers. Added to this they would be part of a tiny immigrant population, vastly outnumbered by the locals who understood a totally different value system…savage and barbaric, alien in foundation to their own beliefs.

Laws, systems and facilities of Colonial Government would take blood, sweat and tears to implement but, more importantly, time and perseverance. Foundations of stable society would be scarce for all the reasons mentioned above and, undoubtedly, they would be further constrained by the very limited resources available such as medicine, food, money, skills and materials. Added to these trials, William was extremely conscious of Anna's emotional state and felt she should spend more time in the loving care of Mildred and the other members at the Mission.

Anna had been motivated by a deep conviction regarding her work at the Mission but was finding that, living without William, was causing her a great deal of anxiety especially since the loss of Elizabeth. It was also obvious to Anna that as the railway progressed further to the north William's home visits would be less frequent with prolonged intervals in between. Normally calm and full of faith, Anna was unsettled.

She was aware of her agitation and tendency to be short with dearest Mildred and lately, even William. Anna chastised herself being full of remorse after each of her outbursts, which were so beyond the norms of her character, now distorted by the burden of pain and grief which threatened to overwhelm her daily. This was a pain that only a grieving parent can comprehend. She had questioned God many times both in anger and in brokenness, but had not yet found peace. Spiritually, Anna had always had a remarkable faith and a profound understanding of the nature of Godly teachings. The loss of her child had shaken her faith to its roots. She wrestled with the fact that her working in the Mission clinic was where God wanted her to be and yet, with her limited medical knowledge, she was convinced that it was some disease resident in the clinic that had infected and claimed the life of her baby girl.

Due to her conviction that sickness from the clinic had taken her child, Anna found her drive to enter into the building had disappeared and she only entered if requested to do so. She threw herself into operating the Mission printing press, assisting Kurt. Often she was literally pulled from the printing room by Father Hamilton who prayed earnestly for her and William, beseeching the Lord for peace and healing from the disabling cloud of grief.

The constant talk of war and William's safety were ever present in her mind. She knew that if anything should happen to William it would kill her. She desired to be closer to his environment so she would have a greater insight into the threats and risks with which he was dealing. William had assured her that he understood her desires but had countered with the sensible argument that she was safe at the Mission and that this gave him tremendous peace of mind. She also needed the Pastoral care from the Church in order to heal.

Martha

A week after the sad and very private funeral for his baby daughter, it was time for William to return to the Railway. He had decided that he would request from Mr Burns a prolonged absence of leave for compassionate reasons, during which time he would return to the Mission and look after Anna. William had assured Anna that, regardless of Burn's response, he would return within the month.

One evening Anna was alone in the Mission Chapel. She sat quietly praying when she heard the door open. She did not turn, assuming it would be one of the staff. She heard soft foot falls progressing up the aisle towards her pew situated near the altar of the Chapel. She glanced to her right and noted a well-dressed lady kneeling at the end of her pew. The stranger then looked across at Anna and smiled. She rose and moved into the pew and sat next to her. In a quiet voice, she said, "Forgive me for interrupting you, Anna. May I call you Anna?" Martha asked.

Anna nodded in response.

"My name is Martha," said the stranger. She spoke with a foreign accent which Anna could not place.

"We have not met, but I have been wanting to meet you for some time," said Martha.

There was something warm and comforting about this lady, thought Anna, almost motherly.

"All of us that are associated with the Mission have known of your great loss and we want you to know that we all grieve with you in your time of sadness. We are so thankful for the work that you have done in the clinic in the months that you have been resident here. You have brought life to the clinic, literally saving the lives of many ill people, particularly the children."

Anna wept softly.

Just at that moment a gust of wind blew through the open door and the candles on the brass lamp stand began to splutter. Both ladies looked up at the candles. One candle at the far end of the stand spluttered and was extinguished by the wind. Anna turned to Martha and said, "Life in Africa is much like those candles in the African wind. So fragile, burning brightly…here one minute and snuffed out the next."

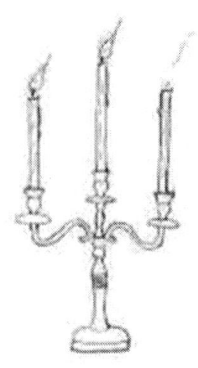

Martha took Anna's hands gently in hers and looked into her eyes and said, "My dear Anna, it is God's Will that we continue to light these fragile candles, in hope, faith and love and let their light shine forth, even if it is only for a very short time, because just a little light in this world's darkness is better than no light at all."

These words, like a healing balm, went straight into Anna's spirit and, for the first time, she felt a release. The pain of her loss remained, but these words in season had initiated the healing of the wound and brought Godly perspective.

The ladies prayed together for a short while after which they hugged warmly and Martha left. The following day Anna returned to her duties in the clinic. She was more like herself and life at the mission began to return to normal. Anna related her meeting with Martha to Father Davis who was most interested, but informed Anna that there was no lady that he knew of in the congregation or, indeed, in the Mission Society named Martha. Anna questioned all the members of staff but none knew of the existence of Martha!

The Impi

The beauty of the African morning was not lost on Dirk. The sun was just clearing the hills to the east tempering the cool of the morning. Turtle doves called softly as if reluctant to break the calm of the breaking day. A troop comprising two scouts and four mounted police moved vigilantly and quietly through the bush, thicker now as they were close to the river. Luka was on foot about thirty yards ahead of the group, moving with his characteristic, but purposeful tracking posture, scanning his surroundings with his every sense. He squatted down, intent, studying the tracks at his feet. A Master tracker, he gazed intently to his left. As he rose once more he turned backwards facing Dirk and the patrol. He placed his hand across his mouth. Dirk halted the patrol without a sound. The men, now well practiced, sat their mounts at the ready, whilst Dirk dismounted and joined the little bushman.

Fresh tracks were unmistakably those of the Matabele. Broad and barefooted, superimposed upon one another leaving a trail of disturbed dew through the grass leading directly towards the Surveyors camp. Dirk swallowed. He felt the hair rise on the back of his neck and fear grip his stomach.

"The Impi goes towards the camp, Luka," said Dirk. It was more of a statement than a question.

"Yebo N'Kosaan!" (Yes, young leader!) agreed the bushman. "The Impi will be there already."

Llewellyn Jones, totally engrossed, carefully and lovingly removed an instrument from its case whilst he quietly whistled a jig. Another beautiful morning, he thought. He blew at a few foreign objects lodged in the lens. This ritual he repeated every morning in preparation for the day's survey duties.

Two hundred yards from where he stood at the tailgate of the stores wagon, an Impi of twenty Matabele warriors stood in full array, but statue-still, watching every movement in the camp and awaiting a command from their leader. The commander was of average height but broad and heavily muscled. He had been ordered to go and investigate the strange actions of the settlers. William Brady's team had been observed a week previously and the report had gone to one of Lobengula's generals based in the Tuli area. Immediately he had dispatched one of his swiftest moving Impi's to investigate. Within this Impi were five new warriors unblooded. They were dangerous to both the Impi and the enemy. They were dangerous to the Impi because they were green and driven by their need to prove their warrior skills and manhood and, therefore, unpredictable and headstrong. Majuba, was in his sixteenth year, but he did not know this. All he knew was that he was ready to quiet the laughter and ridicule of the other young men in the tribe. Majuba was not a true Matabele but a stolen child from Manicaland to the east. He had been taken as spoil during a raid where all the males in the village that did not flee were massacred, all except for suckling babes.

Today he would show all his fellow warriors that he was worthy to be included within this proud Impi and was to be respected. Today he would also win the right to take a wife. 'Namushla!' Today he would have the blood of a settler on his assegai!

'Ukuhlasela' (attack), he said to himself as he broke rank and charged away.

Dube, a seasoned veteran and commander was aware of the thoughts that raced through the green warriors young and immature mind. This was the test of their discipline and maturity. He had specifically ordered the recruits to remain at the rear. To disobey a Matabele Commander was punished instantly by death. However, Dube was not overly surprised when suddenly the insolent Majuba broke rank. With shield to the fore and assegai above his head he charged towards the white man at the rear of the wagon.

Moments before Llewellin had raised the instrument and sighted onto a jagged rock which protruded from the hill side. The image that met his eye was upside down, as was usual but included in that image was the head and shoulders of a fearsome looking black man. Llew', by reflex, immediately focused the lenses which clearly revealed a tall and slender native, almost naked apart from a loin cloth and a black feathered head dress. Around his lower legs he wore beaded thongs. In his hands was a tall shield made of ox hide and a short spear with a broad blade. Matabele warrior! Llew' concluded immediately. Suddenly there was movement to his left and charging down the slight rise towards him was another warrior who ran head long towards him with shield to his front right side and spear raised.

"Bayette! Bayette Ukubulala muntu!" (War cry) Majuba screamed.

Llewellin glanced with despair at his rifle propped against a tree several yards away. Leaning against the wagon at his side were three disconnected legs of a tripod. The surveyor seized one of these rods. It was about four feet long with a pointed brass ferrule at its base. Instinctively Llew' dropped into the stance of a duellist. The warrior was upon him with a blood-curdling scream, "Byette".

Majuba drew back with the assegai and lunged at the settler with all his agile and youthful might. The Welshman held his ground and as the spear was thrust towards him he parried it to the left, knocking spear and shield to his assailant's right and at the same instant his leg shot out catching the front foot of his attacker which sent the young Matabele sprawling head first into the side of the wagon. The warriors head connected with the edge of the wagon bed with a sickening thud. The collision dislodged his headdress ripping skin and hair from his now exposed white skull. He lay limp and bleeding at the Welshman's feet. Llew spun in crouch and retrieved his rifle. He quickly faced towards the Matabele Impi which he now expected to 'follow on.' The war cry had exploded through the still morning air galvanising all railmen into immediate action. They had hastily formed a well-practiced all-round defence.

The Impi slowly ranged outwards, forming a line of warriors with the Induna in the centre. The outermost warriors moved inward slightly to form the infamous 'Zulu buffalo horn' formation. Dube stood statue-still gazing directly at Llew'. By this time all the camp members were armed with rifles. Brady and Marty had flanked Llewellin at either end of the wagon. For what seemed an eternity to Llew', no one moved.

"Why have the rest not charged?" Brady asked of Marty.

"I do not know," replied Marty, "I will ask."

"Hold your fire," commanded Brady loudly.

"I see you, Induna!" shouted Marty, addressing the Commander in his language (n'Dbele)

"I see you young white man," replied the Induna in a gravelly voice.

"Why have the great Matabele come to kill my brothers?"

"We have come only to find out what it is the Settlers are doing in the land of the great Lobengula?"

"It is unfortunate that you come to kill before we can explain what it is we are doing," Marty responded.

"The Manika dog that lies at your feet does not hear the orders of his General and, therefore, deserves to die. If you have not killed him with your white stick I will send my warrior to remove his rebellious heart."

"I believe he is dead Induna," said Marty, hoping to save the life of the young warrior.

Over the hill and behind the Impi the horse patrol came into view. Dirk halted the patrol in extended line behind the warriors. Although there were only six mounted soldiers, plus Luka, it placed the Matabele within a trap. The Induna turned slowly and studied the men to his rear. He turned back towards Marty.

"Since you have done me a good service today in ridding me of the Manyika dog I will not attack. I will inquire as to why you mark a path towards Bulawayo in the north?"

"This is the path for the 'steamela'…the great train that will come from the south. Our father, Cecil John Rhodes, has spoken to the Great King Lobengula and has his permission to do this."

"Of this I do not know, but we will ask the Great King. If this is not the case I will return and kill you all." This was said matter-of-factly.

The Induna then turned once more and surveyed the mounted men to the rear of him. He let his gaze rest on Luka. Turning back to Marty, he said, "Why does the settler walk with a rat by his side? Does the settler not know that the small yellow man does not build a house, but lives in a cave or amongst the rocks or in a tree like a rat? When I was a child, we would hunt and kill such as these for amusement."

"This may be true Induna, but if the settler did not have the rat by his side how would he find food and water in the dry season?"

"We will take the Manika dog and go!" declared the native General.

"Tell the little yellow man not to wander too far from the wagons or one of my children may kill him." Dube gave a harsh and guttural command and three Matabele ran forward to retrieve the inert warrior. Brady and Marty moved from their path, reluctantly, but both knew they would invite confrontation if they interfered with the removal of the disgraced youth. Every person present knew that the young warrior would pay a terrible price for his indiscipline, but this was the way of the most feared native tribe in Africa. A blood chilling wail ending in a crescendo of agonised screams confirmed their fears a short time later and left the whole survey party brooding and perplexed over what wickedly cruel and brutal punishment was dealt to the young warrior before death had brought final relief.

The Journey North

Eleven months had passed since the death of Elizabeth. Time had not removed the pain in Anna but had allowed her to focus more on the future. She had fallen pregnant once more and William was heartened by the positive attitude that was once again flowing from his glowing wife. Travel to the north had been delayed for many reasons, not the least, the passing of Elizabeth. The Mission Society had anticipated that the Sisters would be ensconced at the mission already.

The large ox wrapped his purple, rasp-like tongue around the cabbage leaves in Kurt's hand and pulled them into his huge jaws which macerated the green leaves in a calm side to side motion. Kurt rubbed the barrel like neck and nodded sadly with obvious affection. This same team of faithful animals were in-spanned exactly as they had been all those months previously in Luderitz. Only now they were destined for the north, into the African hinterland, beyond the Vaal River and into the unknown. Kurt was sure he would never lay eyes on his beloved oxen again.

Giving the wagon into the work of the Mission had been easy. Kurt had not given it a second thought when approached by Father Hamilton. However, the oxen were like his children and, heart sore, he had struggled with this decision. The ever sensitive Anna aware of Kurt's love and respect for each of his oxen had insisted that he keep his team. She assured him that they would find an alternate team from somewhere. It had been Mildred's quiet wisdom that had prized the precious beasts from Kurt's loving, but vice like grip. She had simply asked him why, if God had given man oxen as beasts of burden was he, Kurt, keeping them here at the Mission without using them in God's service? She felt sure they were not fulfilling their Godly purpose lazing in the field when everyone was aware there were urgent needs in the Kingdom of God. On pondering these wise truths Kurt had sought Reverend Hamilton and apologised for not having given his animals freely in the beginning. Kurt inspected the wagon once more, everything was in place. Mildred bustled here and there in fake exuberance, purposely avoiding the inevitable heart-wrenching reality of parting with her dearest friend, Anna.

Sister Hanna frowned, scolding two younger Sisters for dithering, as she noted the golden streaks of sunlight appearing over the eastern horizon. The morning chill seemed to bite harder, as if reluctant to retreat with the promise of daylight. Sister Grace, the youngest of the Sisters, had stuttered her apology as she bounced on the top of her small trunk desperately trying to close it. At any other time Sister Hanna might have found the girl's antics amusing, but not this morning. Grace was just seventeen, an orphaned child she had been raised by Sisters at the convent. Grace had required a strong hand as a child. Her unquenchable curiosity and thirst for adventure had seen her in Mother Superior's office on many occasions. There had always been a 'wildness' about young Grace with green eyes that flashed with temper, which emphasised her red hair. When flustered or angry her eyes grew larger and her stutter grew more intense.

Hanna pulled her shawl more tightly about her. She could never have believed she would experience such turmoil and such an acute attack of homesickness such as she was feeling at this moment, and here she was about to venture further into the unknown. She prayed inwardly for God's strength. She knew she would never turn back, yet, at this moment, the agony of missing her family in Ireland was so intense as to cause her a physical pain deep within. Sister Hanna Connor felt no excitement about the forth-coming journey. She felt the burden of responsibility for the three younger Sisters, especially Grace, as though their very wellbeing depended on her.

Reverend Hamilton, followed by Father Hugh Davis, exited from the chapel door. They were talking softly. Hugh was a tall slim man with a pronounced stoop. Bespectacled, he wore a perpetual smile and never seemed to take issues too seriously, but he was totally dedicated to his 'calling' and the saving of lost souls.

Reverend Hamilton turned to Sister Hanna and, as if he had been reading her very thoughts, he said to her, "My dear Sister Hanna, all things are in The Lord's Hands. We have committed the lives of this party to Him, and therefore we must have faith that He will go before us and prepare the way. Release your burdens unto Him that knows all things and rest in Him."

Embarrassed at having revealed her weakness, Hanna wiped the tears from her eyes and said simply, "I will miss you, Father Hamilton."

Laboni of Maasailand 1892

Laboni was the King of the Maasai people, thought to be one of the lost Tribes of Israel. The Maasai were a semi-nomadic people that had resided in an area in the central and eastern woodlands of Africa for thousands of years. They were a tribe of people who relied almost entirely on their cattle for food. Not by the slaughter of the cattle, but on the blood and milk taken from the living cattle.

The Maasai were a proud tribe, tall and lithe in stature with natural athletic ability. The Maasai warriors had proved themselves courageous in battle, thus, this noble tribe had the respect of all other peoples in the region. This included the Arab slave traders who regarded the Maasai as the keepers of the region and paid homage to the Maasai elders when passing through their areas. The name Maasai originates from their language which is the Maa language.

As was happening throughout Africa during the second half of the nineteenth century, colonisation was gathering momentum and bringing with it, not only progress and civilisation, but also the plagues and diseases from the so called 'Modern World'. The tribes of Africa were hardy and resilient people who had lived in a savage harmony with their natural surroundings which the civilised world regarded as 'wilderness'. But, to the Africans, this was home and modernisation would compromise their very existence exacting a terrible price for so-called progress. Breaking their isolation brought a consequence that was immeasurable. Africans had no natural resistance to diseases such as small pox and pneumonia.

The Maasailand Population prior to the introduction of the European settlers was estimated at five hundred thousand spread over the vast area of east central Africa. Small pox and pneumonia decimated the tribe, but the greatest scourge was the arrival of the great plague which killed almost all the Maasai cattle resulting in mass starvation.

Laboni, the Maasai King, who had stood tall and proud just a short while ago, adorned with earrings and ochre coloured hair, had gazed down at the florid-faced white priest who had asked him why the Maasai people left their dead people for the wild animals to devour instead of burying them. Before answering the White man's question the King had asked why the white men contained their farts, which, to the Maasai was quite disgusting. The white Missionary was deeply offended and wasted precious time endeavouring to explain to the African that trousers were essential to modern dress being practical and modest. The King listened with little interest and then explained that it had always been that the spirits of the Noble Maasai people left their bodies before they were devoured by the wild animals. He pointed out that this special gift, the dead body left for the animals to eat, was the basis of a reciprocal profound mutual respect between wild animals and the Maasai. Just a few months later the terrible legacy, imported in the name of progress, would bring many African nations to the point of destruction. This scourge was upon them and both the Maasai and the animals were dying as never before and he, the King, had no answer for his people.

The Great King sat in a dishevelled state, his head was covered in ash and a black cloth was draped over his stooped shoulders. His long arms hung limp at his sides and rivulets of tears formed shinny lines below his dull and hopeless eyes. Why had the ancestors allowed these terrible events, the destruction of all his Kingdoms. Many thousands of his people had died. First the old and the young and now even the strongest warriors were succumbing to disease. The plague now killing the cattle would surely be the end of the great Maasai. The population in the Maasailand was reduced from half a million people to forty five thousand in only a few years.

Zeederberg

The chill morning breeze conveyed the smell of fresh horse manure which coalesced with the strong aroma of the treacle coloured coffee, hot and steaming within the enamelled mug cradled between his work-hardened hands. These were familiar scents, comfortable and reassuring, they had always been there. He raised the chipped enamel mug to his lips, blowing gently on the steaming surface. He then sipped the black liquid, immediately he swore as his tongue was scalded. Andries Pieterse, placed the cup on the veranda railing, he scraped his blistered tongue across his upper teeth. 'Jong, why did he do that so often?' he lamented. He squinted at the sun coming up over the trees. Another long and fruitful day ahead! His Boss, Doul Zeederberg, had left the night before en route for Grooteschuur for a meeting with Cecil John Rhodes. Before leaving he had requested Andries to travel north and meet with the Rail Construction Group based at Magalape in Bechuanaland. There he was to ensure that all was in order with the material deliveries from his Transport Company now preparing for the construction run from Mafikeng, north east, across the great Shashi River to both Fort Victoria to the East and Bulawayo to the West. Rhodes had complained that construction progress was wanning. Momentum seemed to be slowing due to tensions between the British and the Boers. Rhodes' vision for new territories to the wild north was bringing huge opportunity to Zeederberg's business. Doul Zeederberg had ordered two more overland coaches from America to cope with the demand from the seemingly endless number of fortune seekers going north. He had successfully established coach stations every twenty five miles from Mafeking to Tati and beyond, in the west, and up through Tuli from the Transvaal, in the south. Today Pieterse was to travel with one of his mail coaches to Magalape where he would meet with the Railway construction team to discuss the path northwards and understand the logistical requirements for further supply of stores and materials.

Zeederberg was, undoubtedly, one of the most knowledgeable men in the region on the routes to the north, having spent time travelling with pioneers and hunters such as Courtney Selous and Moffat. Rhodes valued Zeederberg's enthusiasm, drive and determination to open up this huge continent. Pieterse considered the brave adventurous people now going north to seek their fortunes in this harsh continent. Some of the more fortunate were able to travel in Zeederberg's wagons and coaches and the majority, who could not afford these fares, were making their way by ox; horse or mule wagon; some on bicycles and, the even less fortunate, on foot. Numerous hopefuls brave and, in many cases, ignorant of the dangers that lay ahead, made their decision to follow a dream, come what may.

The big Dutchman considered the attractive and vibrant young European lady to whom he had spoken the previous day. She was unusual! He couldn't quite put his finger on why. She had said that her husband was working on the rail line going north. She was travelling with four Missionary Sisters and an Anglican priest sponsored by the London Missionary Society. They were bound for Good Hope Mission in Matabeleland, of which Andries Pieterse knew well. The Mission had been established by Moffat and was situated in the heart of Matabele territory.

This could be a daunting and gruelling journey for a team of fit young men, the route being filled with untold dangers, and, undoubtedly, it would be a supreme challenge for a vulnerable young woman. The long journey through the wilds of Bechuanaland and into the brutal lands of the Matabele had left the verges of that trail scattered with stone cairns and lonely crosses that marked the tragic end to some hopeful's journey.

The young lady had come to seek permission for her party to utilise his company's facilities along the notorious route and explore the possibility of travel in the company of other pioneers. Dries, out of concern for her, had told her that Cecil Rhodes had discouraged women from traveling into northern regions until such time as the land was more settled and a suitable Pioneer Force had been assembled and equipped to quell any uprising from the natives. He had assured her that this decree had come from Rhodes himself.

The young lady had looked at him with piercing blue eyes and gently thanked him for his concern but had told him, with quiet conviction, that her party was following the Great Commission of the Lord Jesus Christ, to go and spread the Gospel come what may, and that she was sure that "even Mr Rhodes" would acknowledge that there was no higher authority.

Dries, had coughed softly and had then informed her that Zeederberg Stage Coach service to the north ran regularly at three day intervals. He stressed that each coach completed the twenty five miles between stations at express speed and would travel one hundred miles a day. He informed the young woman there was an armed guard with every coach and that, should the missionaries require assistance, they could count on the services of his men but only if and when they were in the vicinity at that time. The Coach Houses were open to all travellers although small charges would be incurred for meals, lodgings and livery.

The young lady thanked him for his time and left. Dries had watched after her with deep concern, but had thought her remarkable.

'I think she may succeed!' he had said to himself.

Railway

Jock Burns was decidedly irritated since he was of the opinion that the bridge building materials were not arriving at the sites early enough and thus slowing progress. William and Pietersie were pointing out that the area they were now approaching was less accessible and that the threat of Matabele attacks more likely. Burns informed William that he could anticipate a visit from the British army who had agreed to provide a small force to assist in the protection of the railway from attack by both natives and Boers. Burns was about to continue his meeting with William and Dries when Dirk, one of the Scouts, entered the office with an important dispatch from Government House, Cape Town. This was addressed to Andries Pietersie from D. Zeederberg. Dries opened the message and read the content several times, which left him with an expression of deep concern.

"I am instructed, with utmost urgency, to join a 'fact-finding party' that will be traveling north across the Zambesi River in order to establish the nature and extent of a devastating disease that is sweeping southwards from east Africa. This disease is killing both livestock and game with plague like intensity. The party will be led by Courtney Selous and has been commissioned by C J Rhodes.

"I must leave immediately to meet with Selous at Magalape. We will consist of a small force of hand-picked men who know the area." William rose from the conference table and turned to Dirk standing patiently, after having delivered the message.

"Dirk, I would like you to accompany Mr Pietersie on this patrol. Draw the stores that will be needed by the two of you. This will also give you a chance to gather information from the north for our progress."

"Dirk is an excellent bushman and tracker. Trust me, Dries, he will be an asset to your patrol."

Burns turned to Dirk and said, "This is not going to be a holiday I assure you, you will earn your wages!"

Dirk and Dries left immediately. Burns continued to give William instructions and, again, expressed his agitation at sensing that the railway construction was losing momentum.

Military Support

Burns had left the meeting most perplexed and worried at the turn of events. He continually repeated that Brady could not allow outside influences to slow the pace of the survey team, particularly, since they were already behind schedule. Brady knew this to be untrue since Pervis had informed him that Burns had his own personal schedule…influenced by bonus quotas. However, Brady had reasons of his own for reaching the new land of Rhodesia as quickly as possible.

Two days after Burns had left to return to his new office, now in the Western Transvaal town of Zeerust, Brady was summoned by Marty reporting that British Cavalry had arrived at the camp wishing to meet with him at his earliest convenience. Irritated by this interruption, Brady left Llewellin in charge of the team commencing to peg the next section of line.

Brady was unsettled at present as he was consumed by the fear of Anna continuing north without him and, in her very vulnerable condition, with no armed protection of any kind. Although a believer himself, he felt that God valued common sense and he would need to, once again, plead with his expectant wife to remain in Bechuanaland until he himself could escort her and child safely to their new country of choice.

Brady was deep in thought when he arrived at the construction site. He noted the troop of military horses in the shade of the newly constructed water tower and several troopers grouped around Cookies kitchen tent. He dismounted, patted his beloved Max, and handed the reins to Marty. He mounted the roughly hewn steps two at a time and entered his office purposefully.

A tall officer stood facing away from William his hands clasped behind his back. To Brady's left was another person, seated, and wearing well-tailored civilian clothing. Both visitors turned towards Brady as he entered the room.

Recognition was instant and shocking between William and Colonel Milton Smythe. William stared at the colonel in stunned silence, fear and guilt paralysed him. Brady acknowledged the wide-eyed surprise on the sunburned face of the colonel.

The colonel recovered instantly stepping forward he shook William's hand. Introducing himself he then turned and introduced the Senior Government official accompanying him who represented Cecil Rhodes and his Railway.

William dry mouthed and shaken, introduced himself requesting his visitors to be seated. The colonel preferred to stand and William was intensely aware of the incredulous curiosity that must be burning within the Cavalry Officer.

The Government official took the lead by emphasising the importance of the progress of the railway. He was a small man with a balding head, fringed with grey. Not an intimidating or imposing figure until one was engaged by his eyes. Intense; continually searching; demanding complete attention. Burton, the Official, requested information from Brady in regards to sabotage attempts, unusual activity around the camp or on the rail lines etc.

William related the visit from the Matabele patrol and the threat that was made, but otherwise, had experience no other sabotage or disruption attempts to report. Brady was quick to point out that his responsibility was limited to the exploration and survey prior to the line being constructed and not the actual construction. The government official warned that he could expect attempts to slow the rail progress in the future by a faction of Boer detractors and that he and his men should remain vigilant. To this end a section of the colonel's cavalry would be attached to his camp until further notice. Burton stood and requested Brady to indicate, on the map, his planned route and progress north. A short, but accurate, route north towards Murchison Mines and the Matabeleland border was indicated on the map in red wax pen. Brady looked into the brooding face of the official and noted the fatigue behind the intense eyes.

"The road ahead will be challenging of this we can be sure, so go carefully, Mr Brady," said Burton as he shook William's hand.

The colonel collected his gauntlets from the makeshift table and ushered Burton from the office.

"I'll be with you shortly, sir, as I require to confirm arrangements with Brady for the arrival of my section."

"Very well, Colonel, take your time. I wish to stroll a bit and smoke my pipe."

The colonel turned back into the office. He surprised William by placing his hand on William's shoulder and saying, "This has been a wonderful surprise,

Brady. I wrote a letter to your mother explaining your disappearance when we docked at the Cape of Good Hope. I told her I feared for your safety and that there was good chance that you had perished in the rampant seas within that terrible storm. I received a letter back from her some three months later assuring me that you were alive and well living in Luderitz."

"Colonel, sir…I truly regret the trouble I have caused you and I can now repay you the bond I rightfully owe."

"The fact that I find you alive and well is payment enough, man, and the bond was only a means of delivering you out of the hand of the law. It was my intent to release you once in Africa anyway!"

"You are a true gentleman; Colonel sir and I will be indebted to you always. My life is rich, so very much has transpired in the past four years. The Lord has blessed me with the most wonderful lady. We are now married, and we intend to settle in the New Rhodesia."

"Congratulations, Brady! On my next visit I would very much like to hear of your adventures since leaving the Penrose. However, my charge awaits and we should leave as soon as possible. I will return with a section of cavalry within one week." The two men shook hands warmly and walked out into the noon heat.

Anna and the mission party arrived at the rail camp the following day. The joy of the couple's reunion was infectious and Anna was visited by almost all the rail workers whilst William revelled in the numerous reports of how beautiful his wife was.

Brady, Cookie and Luka had spent a few days preparing accommodation for the party which planned to remain at the construction camp for one week.

Anna would share William's quarters which Cookie had upgraded to be luxurious. William told him that he should have made the same efforts in the first place to which Cookie replied, "You are not beautiful, sir."

Luka was always hovering in sight of Anna, clicking and clucking like a mother hen. Anna was now heavy with child. As soon as she attempted to lift anything he appeared out of nowhere shaking his head and dismissing her protests that she was quite capable!

Green Death (Rinderpest)

Captain Frederick Luggard had, as a matter of urgency, reported to the British Colonies Office of a terrible disease that had devastated livestock and wild game in Masai Land. Luggard reported that the disease had migrated south from the Horn of Africa and was continuing southwards and destroying the game and vast cattle herds of Africa with catastrophic impacts on entire communities. Starvation had already reduced populations to the north of the continent.

Rhodes, on receiving the almost unbelievable report, had called an emergency meeting. He and the South African Government had decided to dispatch a patrol post haste. This would be led by Fredrick Courtney Selous to travel north of the great Zambezi River and establish the nature, extent and southward progress of this devastating disease.

The brim of his bush hat drooped, saturated and distorted with sweat. The heat was stifling. He urged his reluctant horse forward into the forgiving shade of a large tree. The handkerchief covering his nose and mouth hung limply, equally drenched with perspiration. The putrid stench of death was overwhelming and seemed to permeate even the water in his canteen. Vultures were so gorged that they waddled about regurgitating their gluttonous excess, unable to take to the air. Hyenas lay sleeping in family groups, so bloated that they hardly acknowledged the riders and porters passing close by. Normally nocturnal and shy, these dangerous beasts showed none of their normal bashful and deceptive mannerisms so evident when forced to find carrion. These hunter-scavengers were almost defiant in this time of such plenty.

As far as Dries could see were the scattered carcasses of, not only cattle, but also a host of other cloven-footed animals. Dries and his party had seen buffalo, gazelle…even giraffe, stricken by this horror sickness. Sheep, goats and even the hardy wildebeest succumbed to this plague. Those still standing, but afflicted, were easily identified by a pale green faeces running freely from their rear ends and their stomach regions appeared to be in a state of continuous convulsion. From their mouths strings of mucus drooled into the dust.

The gravity of this situation numbed Dries's brain. His initial responses had been horror, fear, pity and disbelief. This then changed to an intense anger with God and, finally, enormity of the consequence to the huge herds of Southern Africa, both domestic and wild. It filled him with terrible dread and unspeakable anxiety. This was a nightmare! A vision unimaginable! Surely this was one of the plagues from the Bible being poured out on the continent of Africa.

"God have mercy," he prayed aloud.

To fathom the consequences of this ecological calamity was beyond the capability of this small group. The obvious and immediate impact on livestock and game, being the staple food of the subcontinent, was starkly apparent to Dries and caused him to hyperventilate in his desperation and anxiety.

The significance to the ox wagon, being the backbone of regional transport, was at the forefront of his mind. The effect of this calamity on both human civilisation in the region and the balance of wildlife would be devastating and could it ever recover?

Looking to his left, Dries saw that Courtney Selous had dismounted within the shade of a native tree, beneath which lay several carcasses of animals that had sought shade in their agony and final surrender to this Green Death. As Dries approached this highly respected and renowned hunter and explorer he realised that Selous was weeping unashamedly. Out of respect for this great man, Dries turned his horse and rode slowly away, even more alarmed, after witnessing the profound affect the consequences brought by this plague had on the Great Fredrick Courtney Selous.

Courtney Selous had seen enough. At first light the following day he dispatched Dirk with instructions to 'ride like the wind' carrying a hand penned message for Cecil Rhodes, which was to be telegraphed from the first station that the young Scout could find. This was probably Bulawayo, which was at least six days ride through wild bush country with its many dangers. Dirk departed with three other riders in solemn, but determined, mood.

Dries instructed the messengers to ensure they took no meat products with them south of the Zambezi River and that they should wash all their belongings on the northern Banks of the great river before crossing to the South. It was the hope of Courtney Selous that the great river running west to east across the Continent of Africa, could contain this terrible blight on its northern banks.

The Stutter and the Sister

Dirk's absence from camp automatically elevated Marty to Senior Scout, a task that Marty took very seriously, albeit his genial and infectious sense of humour was never far from the surface. He had been summoned to the carriage office by Brady.

"Morning, Marty."

"Mor-morning M-m-maneer Brady," replied Marty with his normal stumbling speech which was compensated for by the usual beaming smile.

Brady studied the likeable young Dutchman before him. He was amazed at how the skinny youth he had met just a few months previously had filled out with Cookies regular meals and the responsibilities he had undertaken had matured him. Marty was now a reliable and valuable member of Brady's team. The railway issue shirt could not hide the muscled physique beneath. The late parents of these two young scouts would have been extremely proud of the men their two handsome sons had become, thought Brady sadly.

"Marty, the Mission party will be remaining here for two weeks before their long trek north. Please can you and Cookie assist them with the filling of their water drums. Ask Mr Green to please have a look over the wagon wheels and axels. Also, please ensure they have plenty of feed for the oxen in the coming days."

"J-ja M-m-maneer, William," the young man stammered his reply whilst saluting with finger tips to his rawhide hat, which struggled to contain the curly blonde locks beneath.

'Needs a haircut,' thought William. He should speak to Anna.

Marty trotted off towards the Mission wagons. He was met by a stooping Father Hugh Davis, humming a hymnal whilst securing a bit of canvas that flapped annoyingly in the morning breeze, at the rear of his wagon.

"Morning, young man and to what do we owe the pleasure of this visit?" enquired the Missionary.

Marty managed in his faltering speech to explain the instruction received from Brady, and enquired as to when he would be able to collect the wagons in order to fill the water barrels. He also explained that the water would come from the elevated water tank and that, to fill the drums in 'situ' on the wagons, would be the easiest since the water line from the tank could simply be run into the barrel.

"Well, the Sisters have already taken their wagon onto the water tower to be filled young man, and they had Cookie to assist them."

Marty thanked the smiling Reverend and wondered what had amused the Godly man. The Reverend wished he could be a fly on the wall when Marty attempted to converse with Sister Grace who also stuttered. The Lord possesses a colourful sense of humour, thought Hugh Davis, his smile developing into a hearty chuckle.

Marty proceeded towards the water tank. On arrival he observed Cookie standing upon the small operator's platform at the base of the elevated reservoir. One of the Sisters was at the head of the team of oxen whilst Sister Grace stood upon an up-turned bucket and had the end of the rubber hose inserted into the filling aperture, located at the top of the first water casket.

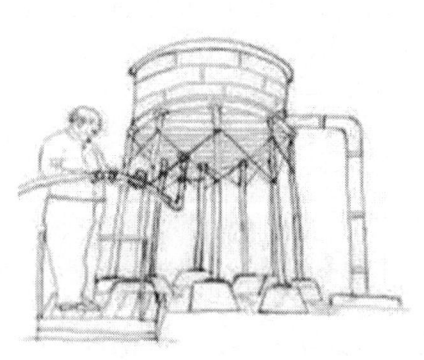

Marty noted immediately that the breather bung was still intact and that there would be nowhere for the pressure to escape whilst filling, which could be dangerous.

Sister Grace assuming all was now ready called across to Cookie to open the valve.

"N-n-n-now, Coo-Coo-Cookie."

This was followed immediately by the authoritative voice of Marty.

"N-n-no, Coo-Coo-Cookie!"

Grace swung her head in absolute disbelief towards Marty, instinctively assuming that this was a low attempt at mimicking her stutter!

"I-I-I b-b-beg your p-pardon, s-s-sir," she demanded, almost losing her footing on the wooden bucket. Cookie, realising what was about to transpire, opened the valve to pour water on the fire 'so to speak'. The resultant pressure in the line caused the hose first to stiffen and then fire upwards with tremendous force. The end shot out of the barrel. It danced about like a serpent possessed, spewing a torrent of water as it thrashed, saturating every item within range including the wide eyed and furious Sister Grace. A jet of high-pressure water shot from the hose catching the Nun in the chest, flashing upwards and into her face with arms grasping frantically at the air the wide-eyed Sister fell backwards toppling the wooden bucket. Cookie, having opened the valve, jumped down from the operating platform. Hearing the scream from Sister Grace as she went over backwards, Cookie immediately turned to re-climb the platform in order to isolate the valve. It was as though the hose realised the closure of the valve would cut short its rampage. It attacked Cookie with determined vengeance, spinning backwards flaying Cookie and drenching him and the platform completely.

The screams and urgent activity, and undoubtedly the thrashing of the hose, upset the oxen which began to swing the wagon towards Sister Grace, now lying on her back in an ever-increasing pool of muddied water, uncomprehending and still furious.

Marty responded immediately sprinting to the aid of Sister Grace in order to extract her from the path of the oncoming wagon wheel which was almost upon her. The Scout dived towards the woman now attempting to sit up. Lunging, he grasped her foot, tugging her towards himself with all his strength, whilst running backwards in the same instant. Her head jerked backwards into the mud once more, but the manoeuvre, undoubtedly, saved her life as her body shot forward out of the path of the wagon.

The Sister was oblivious to the wagon's wheel passing safely behind her as she struggled to cover her exposed and muddied underwear. Marty still had the Nun by the foot, leg elevated and clasped to his chest. He looked down at Grace with huge relief and, instantly, looked away on realising her uncovered condition!

"The-tha-that wa-wa was unbelievable!" Stammered Marty not knowing where to look!

The Sister assumed this Lecherous Lout was referring to her attire and, hearing the mocking stammer, could take no more!

Sister Grace kicked out viciously freeing her foot from the stunned Scout's grip. In a fluid but silent move the agile Nun leaped to her feet, wild green eyes shone defiantly from the muddied mask focusing unerringly on Marty. Lady of the Cloth, perhaps, but vengeance was her only goal. As Cookie remarked later 'it was but a lamb to the slaughter'. For all the Scout's many skills, the young man did not stand a chance.

"Wh-wh what are y-yo-you doing?"

"Wa-wa-wait! N-n-neer, man!" exploded Marty, as he struggled to fend off the blows.

"I-I-I j-j just saved your life, you c-c-crazy g-g girl," wading into the windmill of blows. Marty eventually managed to turn her around and lift her off her feet. She continued to struggle and kick the air for a while and then went limp in his arms in response to Sister Hannah's screamed instruction to, "Cease this barbaric behaviour forthwith."

By this time, both Cookie and Father Davis had arrived. Marty looked at them in desperation.

"C-can I p-put her down?" he asked anxiously. Marty's hat had been dislodged and there were several red welts on his shocked face. He placed her back on her feet, not too gently, and sprang backwards with arms up ready to defend himself once more!

Sister Hannah took Sister Grace by the arm and hurried her away from the scene scolding her all the while. In parting defiance, Sister Grace scowled at Marty and hissed, "I haven't finished with you yet." Her anger left no room for stuttering.

Cookie and Father Davis looked at one another then at the shocked and bewildered Marty. Davis began to speak pious words of wisdom to the stunned young man and then convulsed into fit upon fit of heaving laughter, immediately echoed by Cookie. When Cookie could manage a good breath, he told the red faced Marty that he shouldn't expect too much on a first outing! More laughter!

Two days later Marty was busy assisting Llewellin with the repacking of the survey wagon. News of his altercation with the fiery Nun was now common knowledge around the camp and causing the young man much embarrassment.

He had just related his actions to Llewellyn, who chuckled continuously, whilst the young scout stammered and acted out the turn of events and, eventually, the surveyor suggested that Marty seek audience with the young lady and explain that he too is afflicted by the stutter.

"N-no ch-chance! She will k-k-kill me before I g-get th-the f-first word out," replied Marty with a stricken look.

"Well man, you had better make up your mind to run or speak up, because she is on her way over here right now," said Llewellyn, as he picked up his jacket and slipped away.

Grace marched determinedly up to Marty who had backed up against the wagon. She was holding her long frock up in both hands attempting to keep it out of the mud. She looked up at the handsome, but nervous face. His blonde locks almost covering his wide blue eyes. She released the dress and stepped forward; Marty raised his arms expecting an attack. To his amazement, the girl placed her arms around him and hugged him, laying her head on his chest she said nothing. Slowly he let his arms surround her and they remained in that life-changing embrace for what seemed an eternity. Then she released him, looked up at him and smiled. Turning, she walked quickly back towards the wagons.

Marty stood statue like, quite stunned, when Llewellyn appeared at his side. Placing a friendly hand on his shoulder, he broke the silence by saying, "Marty, sometimes you just don't need words. Actions are far more meaningful and say so much more!"

Something in that embrace awoke in Marty a deep emotion. It was more than a simple desire for a woman…more intense and eternal…the need for a partner, a comforter, a wife. What was more disturbing to Marty was that this amazing and mysterious girl, gentle but wild and unpredictable, hauntingly pretty, was a sister. A nun! May God forgive us!

Lobengula, the Great Ndebele King

Lobengula was a large and powerful man with muscular neck and shoulders. His forehead was large and broad giving the King an intelligent and dominating stare. A large but orderly crowd had gather forming a semi-circle, a respectful distance from the proceedings.

The young warrior standing before Lobengula made no sound. The only indications of his fear were his profuse sweating, which ran in rivulets down his muscular body, and the tremors in his knees when he moved. Clad in an animal skin loin cloth, his regimental headdress had been removed and he carried no weapons. His head hung in resignation. Although a prisoner, he was not bound. The two warriors behind him had their assegais at the ready and the accused man was well aware that he would be dead before he had taken two steps. The young man had been caught in adultery with the youngest wife of a Matabele General.

The King was flanked on either side by the elders of the Tribe. Though they sat a tier lower they had to look up if addressed by the Sovereign. Seated on the ground some distance from the King was the betrayed and disgruntled General.

Lobengula was annoyed with this situation. He knew the accused to be a fine warrior. Well-liked and respected and had been destined for leadership. The General had many wives and, more than likely, hardly knew the young woman who had betrayed him. However, the warrior had broken a trust and had let lust overrule his loyalty and good judgment. All those present knew there could only be one outcome to this situation.

The King stood slowly to his feet, his Elders did likewise. The King then turned his back to the prisoner as did all of the elders.

The executioner came from behind the victim silently and with great speed he brought the club down on the bowed head of the prisoner smashing his skull like a bursting melon. The Sangoma (Witch Doctor, Medium) was draped in a hyena skin and danced around the body, trance like, whilst uttering placations to ancestral spirits.

He drew a mouth full of liquid from a gourd and proceeded to spray the contents of his mouth through pursed lips over the body of the deceased. His helpers plucked the twitching body from the dust and carried it away whilst the adulteress woman was brought forward whimpering, unable to stand without the aid of those supporting her.

The General wanted no mercy shown. He stated that, since she was his wife but had intercourse with another, how could he ever know whether she had produced his children or those of her lovers. Again, the King had little choice but to turn his back on the woman. The adulteress was dragged, unresisting, to the centre of the clearing where she was released by her escorts, dropping trance-like to the ground on her knees. The waiting crowd, led by the General's senior wives, surged forward and mercilessly stoned her to death whilst screaming insults.

After the day's proceedings the King sought the sanctuary of his dwelling. With the aid of a stick, Lobengula limped painfully, whilst panting heavily as he entered his Royal hut. His earlier exploits in the Matabele regiments had proved him to be a capable and brave warrior prior to his installation as King of this great nation. His body had now begun to deteriorate as it accepted the obligated excesses and privileges of sovereignty. The Ndebele King sat heavily upon a pure black ox skin which covered his leather thronged throne. At his side was a gourde of maize beer, partly responsible for his swollen and throbbing foot. Wood smoke with a faint, but discernible, scent of burning cow dung permeated the cool mud hut and kept the mosquitoes at bay. The newly thatched roof was perfectly trimmed and tied and shone with a golden lustre on the outside.

A shaft of late afternoon sunlight illuminated the doorway to the King's lodgings. Misty tendrils of smoke moved ghost like, framed within the shaft of waning sunlight. The King watched and waited, irritated. Lobengula was disagreeable and in an ugly mood. The pain in his foot was not subsiding although it was immersed within a foul scented potion, concocted by the Head Sangoma, or tribal Witch Doctor, and contained in a large clay bowl. The King was desperate for relief from his discomfort. The pills given to him by his White Missionary friend, Moffat, Resident at the Good Hope Mission, had run out. Although they caused his bowels to run like water the pills brought fast relief to his swollen joints. Lobengula had challenged the Sangoma regarding the ineffectiveness of his traditional treatment. The Sangoma had reacted angrily and told the King how the Ancestral Spirits were unhappy that the Great Ndebele King socialised with the White Settlers and discussed the Great Spirit Jesu Cristo. Indeed, the King had also accepted the magic of the white man in the form of the small white pills and this had caused much anger amongst the Ancestral spirits. As a consequence, the power of the Sangoma's 'muti', or medicine, was diminished.

Lobengula attempted to wriggle his toes gently but the resultant pain produced a grimace and a sharp intake of breath from the Great African King. His concubine and servants had scampered at their first opportunity, for when the King was in such an agitated state the smallest of mistakes could result in swift death.

Two handpicked warriors stood guard at the entrance to the Royal Hut. Any attempt to enter or exit without permission would result in death. Three of the King's Impi's, or platoons, comprising the full Guard rested in readiness within a small enclosure nearby. Adjacent to the King's hut were several smaller huts within which the King's wives resided. This Royal area was slightly elevated and within a fenced area. The fence comprised thousands of young tree boughs standing side by side to a height of five feet. Alongside the King's hut a granite copse afforded an additional lookout position, manned continuously by older and more experienced warriors, whose loyalty Lobengula knew was unquestionable. Just to the west of the copse, away from the King's hut, was a magnificent Wild Fig Tree which provided a seemingly custom-made council area where Lobengula would entertain his guests or Induna's to discuss state affairs.

On occasion the King would utilise this venue to arbitrate in quarrels and hearings where the King's decision would be final and justice was usually meted out with prompt precision as had happened earlier that very day. Matabele women were responsible for the bearing of children, cultivating of crops, building of huts, all domestic chores, including preparation of food, and the brewing of opaque maize beer. When the young boys were of age, they would be trained to care for the livestock and, as they reached adolescence, they would learn the art of warfare and train to be included into the King's regiments. This training was extreme and failure to comply could result in severe beatings followed by expulsion from the tribe or, in certain cases, death. Culturally, the Matabele were polygamists and, therefore, most warriors had more than one wife. This increased the labour capability of the family unit. The more senior the husband within the regiment and the more cattle and livestock he owned the more able he was to buy additional wives for his household.

Previously, prior to the first Matabele war, the Matabele nation was situated where the Settler town of Bulawayo now stood. Close to this site is a hill feature that was named 'Hill of the Chiefs' or 'Inthabas Induba'. This important outcrop was loaf-shaped and rose eighty two feet above the surrounding terrain. The feature was flat topped and extended 600 yards north to south and, roughly, two hundred and fifty yards east to west and, apart from two small conical hills to the south, gave a commanding view of the entire area which comprised flat savannah bush land.

It was here that the Matabele were defeated in the first Matabele war, which began when the Matabele attacked a Chieftain in the Fort Victoria area. The disgruntled Manika Chief complained to the Rhodesian authorities that they were incapable of maintaining law and order. The authorities then proceeded to arrest the offenders, which sparked a rebellion and the Matabele went on the rampage, murdering settlers in outlying areas. The rebellion was finally put down when the British South Africa Police mounted two maxim guns on the two conical hills, south of Inthabas Induna, from where the Matabele army attacked. The Matabele forces were caught in a crossfire between the two maxim guns where fifteen hundred warriors were killed for the loss of four British Police officers. Lobengula had not forgotten this terrible loss and devastating fire power of the Maxim machine guns and was, understandably, cautious about a future confrontation. On the previous day the King had been visited by his Spiritual medium, Mlimo, who had entered into several intense séances within which the ancestral spirits spoke through the troop of Tribal mediums. They expressed their utmost displeasure with the King's tolerance of the white settlers that had come into the land of the Ndebele and were stealing their gold and silver, claiming large parcels of land and hunting game indiscriminately.

The Ndebele King was growing more and more disgruntled with the number of settlers that were arriving in his domain. In addition, Lobengula was convinced that the content and extent of agreements reached between himself and the British South Africa Company, were now being grossly flaunted by these settlers.

There was now talk of a terrible plague north of the great Zambezi that was decimating the herds of cattle and many species of wild animals. This was surely caused by white settlers which had angered the African spirits to the north. Now Moffat had warned that, if the sickness crossed south of the Great River, the settlers would slaughter all the cattle in the land to halt the spread of the disease, including the wonderful herds belonging to the Matabele nation.

This could never be allowed to eventuate. The cattle were a symbol of his great wealth, power and regional dominance. The King's health continued to deteriorate. He had contracted small pox and, when he was too weak to function, he was taken to a cave in the Matobo Hills, which was inhabited by the Chief Sangoma. The King was treated, but died shortly afterwards.

Lobengula was never replaced by another King. Rather the Matabele were ruled by a Council of Chiefs amongst which the discontent with the Settlers continued and the great tribe of the Matabele waited for their chance to rebel and push the white settlers out of their land.

The head Sangoma received a report from one of his Impis stating that a large column of soldiers flying the British South Africa Flag, complete with artillery pieces and maxim machine guns, had been sighted heading south towards the Boer Republic. This explained the lack of Settler troops in and around the Bulawayo Settlement. The Sangoma must exercise his wisdom and influence the Tribal Chiefs. This was an opportunity to strike before they lost credibility with the Ndebele Nation. The Sangoma summoned his Generals and Mediums.

It was time for a council of war.

The Massacre

Thandi walked with elegant and fluid motion, essential to accommodate the clay pot balanced on her head. She hardly felt the weight of the empty water pot. She made this journey down to the river twice a day to collect water for her family who were members of a medium-sized Tswana village. She avoided the muddied path leading directly to the water's edge and followed the lesser route which led to an assortment of granite rocks. These projected out into the river from a rocky outcrop which dominated the area. She required the use of her hands to climb up onto the larger smooth granite rocks, but once on top it was an easy series of hops to her favourite water source.

Thandie stretched upwards removing the pot from her head, which she placed upon the sun warmed rock. Kneeling gracefully she scooped water into her hands and drank several times. She lifted the pot and hesitated momentarily as a shoal of small fish, silver flashes, darted in formation past the rock on which she knelt. This was an ideal spot from which to draw water, no mud and the water was crystal clear.

She felt safe here away from the crocodiles which snatched both humans and livestock on a regular basis along this wild river. A pod of hippo grunted contently from the centre of the river as if to remind her that they also owned this part of the river. Thandie scanned the river which was very low, she could see evidence of the flood line on the rocks at least the height of two men above her.

A heart-stopping scream shattered the afternoon peace! Repeated shouts of 'a'Mandebele' and 'byete' caused her blood to run cold. She remained wide-eyed, statue-like, petrified and unable to move for a few seconds. Then frantically, she scooped up the pot and raced towards the base of the outcrop. A massive granite rock hugged by a huge hook-thorn bush obscured a small cave which had been formed by a large fissure at its base. This had been her sanctuary as a child. In her terror she did not feel the ripping of her flesh on the aggressive thorns or notice the stench of the rock rabbit urine as she entered the cave.

The sounds of the horror emanating from the village were slightly muted in the cave, but still audible. Thandie moved towards the back of the small vestibule, holding her hands over her mouth and gasping with fright. She strained her ears and peered through the gaps in the lower branches of the hook thorn. She could see smoke and flames rising above the tree line as huts were incinerated. 'Mai whea', she cried silently. What should she do? Remain where she was or run to the aid of those in the village. She saw movement racing down towards the river. It was one of the young herd boys closely pursued by two warriors. Luyungi, the boy, ran past the edge of the boulder and out of sight. The two fully grown and fierce looking warriors close behind. A loud cry of 'Ukubulala wena' (Slaughter you) and a dying scream told the story. The jubilant duo trotted back towards the village, headdresses waving triumphantly in the late afternoon breeze and assegais warm and stained with Luyungi's blood.

The fate of the elderly men and women caught in the village was sealed. Thandie knew from eye witness accounts, told by the traumatised few who had been fortunate enough to survive the marauding Matabele that they quickly dispensed of the elderly and very young. They would murder the adolescent boys and take the younger boys old enough to walk, as potential future warriors. The young women were taken as sexual slaves and additional labour.

As the sun disappeared, and the chill of evening descended upon the river, Thandie could hear cruel taunting of the villagers by their captors, punctuated by the screams and pleas for mercy. Her inability to assist her people and the hopelessness of the situation caused the young women to writhe in this cauldron of distress. The Impis would have found the large reserves of maize beer and would drink, without restraint, thus exacting indescribable cruelty on their captives as a result.

Thandie, wore only a short leather skirt, the usual tribal dress for young women. Her upper torso was naked except for several strings of coloured beads worn neatly around her neck. She seemed unaware of the waves of mosquitoes that ravaged her face and body as she sat in the small cave. She wept silently for her family and friends. She decided that she would leave her sanctuary before first light and flee to the south along the river. She would risk death by wild animals rather than the humiliation and torture that she could expect as a slave to the a'Mandebele.

Thandie awoke suddenly from a fitful sleep. Instantly aware of her surroundings and situation, she heard a drunken conversation amongst a group of warriors, their voices carried clearly in the now quiet night. New fear gripped her as one warrior spoke out and was seemingly right at the entrance to the cave. The moon, now high in the sky, cast eerie shadows and silver light beyond the cave entrance. Thandie leaned forward slowly in order to peer out of the cave entrance. She felt a large stone under her foot. She lifted the rounded stone in her trembling fist and would not hesitate to strike if the opportunity arose. The warrior near the entrance spoke again, slurring in his speech. The girl squatted tense, trying to ascertain the purpose of the warrior near the cave entrance. The sound of running water reached her and she realised that he was urinating.

Unmoving, hardly breathing she waited for what seemed an eternity until finally the voices dulled as the party moved away from her cave and the river. She inched forward on cramped limbs towards the entrance of the cave. Sighting through the lower branches of the hook thorn towards the village she saw that there remained a dull glow, presumably from the remnants of the burning huts. She would wait until all was still before attempting to flee.

At the initial soft sounds of the waking turtle doves, before the first rays of light had touched the sky, Thandie left the cave. She moved with great stealth, listening and probing the darkened landscape before her. Fortunately, she knew the area well and had climbed to the top of the out crop on many occasions when younger. Maintaining her footing on granite surfaces she would leave very little evidence of her passing. She was sure that the Matabele would move northwards, whilst she would remain near the river and move southwards.

Thandie was young and strong, lithe in physique. She was nimble and moved through the bush with natural ability. She dropped down towards the river, always remaining within the tree line and twilight shadow. As she approached the river she was aware that the hippo would still be grazing on the banks, out of the water, where they were particularly dangerous and aggressive, especially when with young or if confronted suddenly. Though the hippo appeared cumbersome they would outrun a human with ease. This young African woman was more fearful of the human inhabitants of the land than she was of the many vicious bush predators.

An Ambush

Dries Pieterse arrived in Bulawayo both mentally and physically drained from witnessing the drastic impact of the plague sweeping south through east and Central Africa. He had met briefly with Dirk who had arrived the previous week and transmitted the urgent and distressing message from Courtney Selous to Cecil John Rhodes. This report described the plague-like disease decimating herds of cloven-footed beasts as witnessed by the delegation deployed north of the Zambezi River. The response from the Cape Government was prompt with a call for an immediate diagnosis. A Doctor of Veterinary Science was located in Vryburg working as a telegraph operator. He was dispatched to Bulawayo to identify the disease on behalf of the Cape government.

Dries Pieterse met with Dirk at the Zeederberg Depot in Bulawayo. Dries expressed his own thanks to Dirk and delivered a special word of gratitude wired from Cecil Rhodes for his courageous ride from the north and prompt delivery of the important message. The following day Dries boarded the Zeederberg coach bound for Mafeking.

Two days later Dirk departed Bulawayo for his long journey back to the railway camp. The British South Africa Police Officer at Essexville Police Post, situated twenty-five miles south of Bulawayo, informed Dirk and three other riders travelling south that the Police had received numerous reports of Matabele Impis moving towards Bulawayo leaving death and destruction in their wake. He warned the riders to take extra precautions and to report any attacks or unrest they may come across to their nearest Government post.

The members accompanying Dirk comprised one young Dutch farmer and two businessmen. The farmer was returning to Pretoria to collect his young wife and family in order to establish his farm in the New Rhodesia. Both businessmen had decided that there was opportunity and money to be made in Rhodesia and were returning to South Africa with a view to establishing outlets in the north.

Dirk noted that, of the group, only he and the young farmer had any real bush sense and were capable of efficient use of firearms, although both businessmen were well armed. Dirk suggested that he should lead the group and that the young farmer ride at the rear with the two businessmen in the middle. All agreed.

On the morning of the second day the small party crossed the Thuli River. They had passed several travellers heading towards Gubulawayo but, although there were rumours of unrest and the movement of Matabele Impis, none had been sighted.

Dirk was not comforted by this fact. He had lost his parents to the Zulu. A people he now despised for that fact, but he respected them at the same time. He often heard this African tribe being dismissed by ill-informed settlers as 'barbaric savages'. He knew that to be an inadequate and dangerous underestimation of a highly disciplined and determined race. Well organised and extremely brave in battle. He knew that, because elements hadn't been seen, it certainly did not mean they were not in the vicinity. These warriors could blend into their surroundings as effectively and naturally as a bush predator and could cover as much distance on foot in a day as a man on horseback. He remained vigilant and, repeatedly, encouraged the others to remain the same. The first indication of an ambush came from Dirk's horse as it balked suddenly. Dirk responded immediately, swinging his mount to the left, he pulled his rifle from its boot, whilst shouting a warning to those behind.

The warriors rose up from the grass on either side. Dirk barely had time to fire one shot as he urged his nervous horse forward. Charging directly at two attackers ahead of him, he swung his rifle at the head of the closest warrior. He missed, but it was enough to cause the attacker to duck down. The second warrior ran in and drove his assegai upwards into the broad back of the settler. Dirk initially thought he had got clear with only a tremendous blow to his back, but soon realised that something was terribly wrong. He spurred his horse forward, racing away as fast as possible. His left arm would not respond and hung limp at his side. He had dropped his rifle and was riding using his right hand. Dirk was unaware as to the welfare of his fellow travellers but he feared the worst.

Dirk urged his mount onwards but noted that he was slowing and struggling to maintain pace. He began to labour and slowed to a walk, then stopped. Struggling, Dirk slid from the saddle now in severe pain. He noted an assegai plunged deep into the right side of his horse. Dirk knew the horse was close to death and struggling for breath, but he had no weapon to end the suffering other than to remove the spear piercing the horse's lungs. Pink froth bubbled from the muzzle of the stricken animal. Dirk, now struggling to stand himself noted his own blood as it ran down from the wound below his shoulder onto his hip and leg discolouring his trousers. He took hold of the assegai shaft in his good hand and lunged backwards to remove it from the horse's side. The animal stumbled backwards two steps and immediately went down on its rump, as its rear legs buckled. Then the exhausted gelding went down on its side whilst blood bubbled and rasped from the savage wound in its side. Dirk went down on one knee, tears blurring his vision. He stroked the sweat drenched neck of his beloved horse as it breathed its last.

Wracked with pain now and gasping for breath himself he was unable to reach his terrible wound. Dirk was aware that he would need to stop the bleeding and attempt to clean the wound. He was also concerned that the Impi may follow his tracks to finish him off. He removed his water bottle from his dead horse and drank deeply, thirsty from loss of blood. He moved a short distance to a small thicket which offered some shade and concealment. Taking his bush knife he cut a square from his shirt front using his teeth to hold the cloth whilst cutting with his good hand. He then struggled out of his shirt. The garment was blood drenched and had a rent where the assegai had entered his back halfway down the left of his torso. The blade had travelled upwards along his rib cage and up under his shoulder blade and then been withdrawn.

Dirk, shaking now from the pain and shock, wrapped the clean square of cloth around the blade of his knife gripping the handle between his knees to achieve this. He then poured a small amount of his precious water onto the cloth.

Twisting his arm behind him he attempted to clean the wound. The young scout had to steady himself against a tree as the pain almost caused a loss of consciousness. After several passes over the wound area Dirk removed his belt. He wrapped the discarded shirt around the belt and, utilising the tree, he managed to manoeuvre the belt around his torso such that the shirt pad pulled up hard against the wound when he buckled the belt now just below his chest. He lowered himself down to grass covered ground maintaining his uninjured shoulder against the tree. He was now sweating profusely and panting from pain, shock and exertion. He remained in this position for some time whilst he recovered and attempted to gather his thoughts.

He realised he was in dire circumstances. He had half a bottle of water and a small bag of biltong packed in the saddle bag, which remained attached to his dead horse. He had an assegai, a knife, a bush jacket, and a blanket. Had he been healthy he would have a very good chance of survival but, wounded as he was and without assistance, he knew his chances were very slim. With a huge effort he forced himself to his feet. He returned to the horse and retrieved a few essential items. Dirk scanned the bush in the direction from whence he had come. There was no movement. There was nothing he could have done if he had been pursued in his current condition, he conceded. Dirk locked the fingers of his bad arm into the belt around his chest to ease the pain in his shoulder from the weight of his dangling limb. He draped his jacket across his shoulders such that it covered his wound, protecting it from the flies. He looked up and noted the sun was lower in the west. He swore at the pain, then hesitated and whispered a short prayer. Clenching his teeth he shuffled off slowly in a south-westerly direction.

Having to make frequent stops to rest, Dirk also fought a raging thirst. He stopped in the shade of an acacia tree with a lemon coloured bark. 'Fever Trees.' He must keep moving as malaria was known to be rife in the area of these trees. To the west was a range of hills. The injured man decided he needed to get up to higher ground and moved towards a saddle in the distant hill range. With the onset of twilight, Dirk had commenced his climb up into the granite hill range. He needed to find a situation that offered him some degree of protection up off the ground, but out of the wind. He was aware that he only had a mouthful of water remaining in his canteen and the pain from his shoulder was affecting his breathing. He needed to rest.

A huge wild fig tree had grown to encompass an assembly of large granite boulders, the largest of which had a natural shelf running under the canopy of the fig. The shelf was littered with leaves and old fruit. Dirk scraped the shelf clean with the assegai. He then shrugged into the jacket. With one arm he shuffled up onto the shelf, swinging his legs up onto the stone bench and placed the water bottle under his head. He lay on his good side, assegai at his side. Dirk lay awake as the darkness engulfed the hill and the night sounds grew about him. He heard rustling in the leaves below, but pain and exhaustion negated any interest and he fell into a fitful sleep. Several times he was awoken, during the night, to the sound of animal movement and, on each occasion, he eased his limbs which were cramping on the hard-stone surface.

When the first sounds of morning aroused him he found he was unable to move. His back felt as though it was on fire at the slightest of movements and the skin around the wound felt taught. His head ached and his thirst raged.

Weakly he sat up, dizzy with pain. A large lizard scurried from the shelf near his foot. He uncorked the water bottle and drank the remaining few sips. He struggled to think logically and began to shiver uncontrollably in the morning chill. With great effort he shuffled off the boulder and continued south-westwards, where he anticipated he would eventually cut across the trail coming up from Francis town.

The air was still and humid. Thunder rolled with authority over the dry African bush. Smoke rose in the distance from a veld fire ignited by lightning—nature's flint. Dirk was oblivious to these things. He was now delirious and close to death. Dehydrated and ravaged by the poisons that pumped through his fever-racked body. Despite his delirium, he knew that as soon as he ceased his pathetic shuffle and lay down it would be the end. With little sense of direction he had followed a slope in the ground which caused him to gravitate on to a steep river bank overlooking a dry river bed. A strong gust of wind brought the downpour of rain causing the stricken man to lose his footing on the wet slope. Unable to check his fall, Dirk fell headlong, landing on his injured shoulder. The explosion of pain sent him into oblivion. His unconscious body tumbled into the damp sand of the dry river.

The Witch Doctor

Thandie came upon a small village, comprising just two huts. There was no sign of inhabitants. She was nervous and extremely cautious. The young woman had been walking for three days, living on berries and grubs. She had left the river for fear of running into another Impi. Now she crept around the back of the largest hut, having entered the fence of thorn and cactus surrounding the huts. She found a small fireplace near the door of one of the huts with coals still smouldering and maize cobs, having been roasted, lying slightly aside from the heat. Her hunger caused her to salivate. She reached out to take a cob when a woman's voice, deep and controlled said, "Daughter, take and eat if you are hungry, but greet me first for that is my breakfast."

Thandie spun towards the voice. Already startled, she backed away when she was confronted by a small woman clothed in the pelts of many different animals. They did not hide her pinkish white face, arms and legs. The pale skin gave her an unearthly aura. Her features were African. Snow white hair tinged with orange escaped her strange feathered headdress in tight coiled tufts at her temples. Pink flesh surrounded half shut eyes which squinted continually in the morning light. Hanging within the tangle of pelts were several pouches.

"It is good that you are afraid, daughter, for I am the voice of many great spirits and I have the eye of the future and the past. You are not my enemy and, therefore, I will not harm you today," chided the same vibrant voice, followed by a hissing giggle.

Thandie knew at once that this was a Sangoma. She had heard stories of this woman who lived by herself, exiled from her tribe because she was born an

Albino. An outcast, she had been taken in by an elderly Sangoma who required an assistant and had, thus, trained this abandoned Albino in the use of herbs, potions and spiritual craft, with which to do both good and evil. She now resided by herself but was summoned, from time to time, by local chiefs and visited by those requiring spiritual assistance, divination, sorcery or healing.

The old woman limped towards a log bench situated near the door of the larger hut. She moved using a stick sheathed in a snake skin with a large knuckle bone protruding at its head, as a handle worn shiny with use. As she passed close to Thandie a pungent and offensive odour wafted past the girl. A hen with two chicks in tow came out from under the hut, probably seeking the corn. The woman shooed them away with her stick and said to the girl, "Come and sit. Eat the puti (maize) before I feed it to the chicken."

Thandie moved and sat on the swept earth floor near the fire. She took the cob and bit into it tentatively, not too sure what to expect from this woman. As she observed the old lady, she noted that she shook her head continuously, but only slightly. Her lips moved, silently, and she seemed ever engaged in some communication with an unknown source.

"I have been expecting you," said the woman suddenly. "My magic bones show your future life will not be as that of your fathers."

Thandie saw that the woman had several bones lying at her feet. She moved them with her toe...raised a white cottonwool like eyebrow and laughed a strange, cackling sound, revealing a mouth void of frontal teeth.

"You must eat and rest Daughter. There is water in the clay pot. You are safe here. All fear my power and will not come into my compound unless invited. Even the great Ndebele leave me alone. The lion and the leopard will not kill my goats and the hyena and the cobra only come when I call. You are quite safe."

The girl was tired and thirsty. She drank the cool water from the clay pot. The woman indicated a grass mat situated in a shady spot beneath a mango tree. Thandie lay down and was soon fast asleep as this was the first time she had let herself relax in the days and nights since the massacre.

She awoke with a start, to the sound of the old woman chopping wood, Thandie's face bore the evidence of tears released in her sleep. It was evening and she had slept since the morning. She sat up and the old woman called her.

"Come, Daughter. You are young and strong. You can chop wood for the fire then you can go to the stream and wash yourself before dark." Thandie did as she was directed and, as she gathered up the chopped wood, she realised that she had not said one word to this strange, but hospitable, woman since arriving that morning.

"Gogo, I wish to thank you for your hospitality. You have fed me and provided me with a safe place to rest when I was scared, hungry and exhausted."

"That is alright child. I was expecting you!"

"I will leave you first thing in the morning and travel towards my Uncle's Village."

"As you wish, Thombisaan (young girl), but I will see you again soon." The old lady began to swirl her upper body and force air between extended lips. She then commenced muttering in a deep and guttural voice causing Thandie to back away from her in fear. The Sangoma's eyes rolled backwards, leaving only the whites visible, her body began to tremble violently for a short time, then her eyes closed and she fell silent and still. She clapped her hands softly and uttered 'Nkosi, Nkosi'. Movement to her right caused the girl to tare her eyes from the entranced woman, only to observe a huge snake emerging from a caldron shaped clay vessel which lay on its side. Thandie wanted to run but was frozen in fear.

Stunned for words, she turned back to the woman who was watching her with a smile widening on her wrinkled, ash-painted face which erupted into a rattling laugh 'nYoka (snake) nYoka', she taunted the girl and hobbled away. The snake moved leisurely across the swept path between the huts with head slightly raised, its yellow and purple brown bands glistening in the sunshine as it disappeared into the surrounding bush. Thandie realised that the clay vessel was provided as a place of residence for the loathsome and deadly serpent.

Thandie slept fitfully on a grass mat, close to the door of the woman's hut. The presence of the snake and the woman's words had unsettled her intensely. She needed to leave this place as soon as she could. As the gentle sounds of morning entered the consciousness of the young woman, awakening her, she arose immediately. The old woman was nowhere to be seen, but a small basket of food and a gourd of sour milk had been placed beside the hut entrance. Thandie removed a string of coloured beads she had made herself and placed them on the upturned log where she had found the food as a payment.

The African girl took the basket gratefully and left. She followed a tributary of the river heading North East. The sun was filtering through just above the horizon in bright red and golden rays illuminating a thick layer of cloud, unusual for the time of year. Thandie had to be very cautious as this was a dangerous time of day to be alone on the veld.

As the rain eased, Thandie moved out from under a large denuded tree which had offered little protection from the rain. She was soaked through but exhilarated by the cool sensation of the wind against her wet, goose-bumped skin. Continuing along the path that followed the tributary she noted the small rivulets dropping down from the bank into the dry riverbed. The shower had barely dampened the thirsty land but would be enjoyed by all plants and creatures so dependent on every precious drop of this scarce, but essential, element.

The ground to her right began to rise steeply and was sparsely wooded with short dry grass. She stopped momentarily in the shadow of a thicket and scanned the open hillside looking for any sign of danger. As the sun moved out from behind one of the disappearing rain clouds, she observed an object glinting in the sun. She was intrigued, but also nervous. She was conscious of exposing herself to any danger lurking behind the tree line at the top of the hill. Moving out into the open to investigate was a risk as she would be visible for a significant distance. Thandie tarried…alert, listening and watching. Nothing moved apart from a flock of small birds which chattered and chirped contentedly. She stepped out into the open…nervous and moving swiftly uphill towards the item that had caught her attention. As she approached the reflective item, she realised that it was a metal container with a leather strap, obviously the property of a Settler, as she had not seen such a container used by a native before. She glanced down towards the river and noted another item in the grass. She retrieved the water bottle and moved towards a crumpled leather garment lying in the grass. A cloud of flies arose from the garment as she lifted it. Though dampened by the rain, streaks of dried and fresh blood covered the soft inner of the jacket, and an offensive odour emanated from the garment.

Thandie was now alert, quickened by the freshness of the blood. Whoever owned the jacket was close by and in a very serious condition, which would attract the attention of the scavengers soon, if not already. She scanned the area down towards the river. Just a few yards from her lay an assegai. She felt intense fear at the sight of the Matabele weapon and was tempted to run. She hesitated.

Matabele do not wear garments such as this, nor do they carry containers such as the one she had found, she reasoned.

From where she stood, she could not see the bed of the river so she lifted the assegai in one hand and carried the bloodied jacket in the other. She moved cautiously downhill towards the river.

He was lying face up with one leg flung outwards, the other bent. His left arm was flung in the same direction as his leg and his right arm lay at his side. A leather belt was strapped tightly around his chest holding a blood soiled and ripped shirt. His mouth was open and lips were cracked and dry. The Settler's body and clothes were damp from the rain and he had a sheen of sweat across his face surrounded by a halo of matted yellow hair. He was covered in flies.

She could not discern any wounds but as she came closer and lent over him, she could smell his rotting flesh. He must be dead she decided. She prodded him with the assegai, no response. Thandie took hold of his right hand, it was warm and supple. He was still alive! With some effort she managed to roll him over onto his stomach. Although the river sand clung to his back and trousers it could not disguise the huge, swollen and ulcerous, purple black, wound on his left side, which produced a foul discoloured discharge.

She knew he was close to death. She stood up looking down at the wretched white man. She was tempted to leave him and go on her way. The sun was regaining its intensity after the rain. Thandie walked a short distance to the river bank. She opened the cork on the Settler's water bottle and filled it from a trickle of remnant rainwater running down the bank. The young woman, feeling pity for the dying man, pulled him into the small patch of shade offered by the riverbank. She propped him up against the cool mud wall as best she could. She then took the water bottle now half-filled and poured a small amount into his mouth urging the muddied liquid through cracked and swollen lips. He coughed and swallowed weakly. His eyes flickered open for a moment, unseeing, and closed again. She was about to force the man to drink again when she was startled by the unmistakable bark of a domestic dog. Thandie glanced up over the top of the bank to see a dog running towards the river. She heard a shout and noted a small group of African tribesmen, S'swana by dress, accompanied by more dogs emerging from a tree line on the hill. Two of these men carried a pole on their shoulders and, slung beneath the pole, was a slain antelope. This was a hunting party.

Barking furiously at Thandie the whippet-like dog moved from left to right, maintaining his eyes on the girl who remained standing in the riverbed near the unconscious Settler.

As the party arrived at the bank of the river one of the older men picked up a stick and hurled it in the direction of the canine, which yelped and bolted to the rear of the group, with tail tucked under its sunken belly.

"What is this?" asked a well-muscled young warrior, obvious malice in his voice and stance, "A young Kalanga woman with a white settler!" He spat at his feet in disgust.

Thandie said nothing, but met his stare with contempt.

"What has happened here?" asked one of the older men.

Thandie turned her gaze towards the older man and unconsciously shifted the basket across her chest.

"I am not with the Settler. I was sent here by the Sangoma to collect him and you and your party were guided here to carry him back to her village."

The young warrior responded with a mocking and incredulous outburst, shaking his head he replied, "I think you are penga—as crazy as the old woman who sent you. I have a better idea of how I will spend my time with you." Grinning with undisguised lust the young man looked to others in the party for support to his lude suggestion. The older man stepped swiftly forward and struck the grinning warrior across the face with a resounding smack.

"You are a fool, Sepho. Do you not see the eye of the Great Sangoma on the girl's basket. It looks directly at us and she has heard your derogatory words and what you wish to do to her messenger. We are all in grave danger and must do as the young girl requests."

All eyes were now centred upon the basket, on the side of which was woven a large ochre red and black eye which stared directly at the group. Humiliated by the open-handed slap, the belligerent young warrior turned and strode a short distance from the group before turning and confronting the older warrior.

"I am not afraid of old woman, young girls or straw baskets. I do not have the time or inclination to carry the Settler anywhere. If you have any sense you will leave both the girl and her Settler for the lions and hyenas and they will be taken care of. I will take my dogs and the antelope and return to the village, where I will enjoy a meal and the company of my youngest wife."

No member of the group moved to follow or assist Sepho as he retrieved the dead antelope from the pole and slung it across his shoulder. The arrogant hunter turned once more and scowled at the group before departing at a brisk pace, whistling for his dogs to follow.

Imbada, the male leopard stretched languidly as the warm afternoon sun filtered through the leafy canopy of the large Marula tree. His tawny coat was covered in black spots which afforded him perfect camouflage in the mottled sunlight. The thick branch on which he lay was smooth from the many days he had rested here, high above the ground, safe from attack by lions and other predators. There were a few bones wedged in the higher branches where he had left portions of previous kills. When a lion had climbed the tree in pursuit of him in the recent past, he had simply climbed higher in the canopy where the lion was unable to follow due to its large size and lesser climbing ability.

The sun was still too high for him to hunt. He would rest for a few more hours and try to ignore the nagging hunger of his empty gut. Eyes wide open and ears erect, the leopard lifted his head, alerted by the high-pitched bark of a dog. The large cat altered its position by raising its hind legs which had, moments before, lazily straddled the tree branch. He now adopted a crouching posture, muscles bunched like a coiled spring, ready to launch the silent assassin from his concealed vantage to the ground below. As the whippet entered the shaded area of the massive tree the leopard launched itself, dropping onto its victim in a second. The dog released a dying yelp before its spine was crushed by the massive feline canines.

Sepho, hearing the commotion, shrugged the slain antelope from his shoulder. Raising his spear, he trotted cautiously through the waist high grass and undergrowth that obscured clear view of the area below the marula tree. He called nervously to his dog. A flash of movement in the shadows to his right, punctuated by a spitting snarl, was his only warning. The leopard, so magnificently designed for the ambush. Immensely powerful and agile, armed with inch long claws to hold onto its prey, it plunged its massive canine teeth into the victims neck, thus inflicting the instinctive death bite to the stricken human. Within a split second Sepho's brain registered the open jaws of the leopard, ears flattened against its head, fore paws up, claws extended. The impact threw him backwards off his feet as the massive teeth bit into his throat crushing his larynx and spine. His last conscious vision was the dark eye on a tawny background much like that on the basket.

The leopard stepped away from the human, panting heavily. It sniffed the air and trotted towards the slain antelope. The big cat took the antelope by the neck and dragged it with ease to the base of his tree. He leapt up the broad trunk of the tree in a series of practiced movements. Thrusting with powerful hind quarters and clutching with front legs and claws, retaining his stolen prize, he worked his way up higher until satisfied that he was safe and could enjoy his meal. Undisturbed, he wedged the buck in the branches. The remains of the dog and human would occupy his enemies, the hyena and jackals, when night came.

The Vows

Grace was decidedly unsettled, a new emotional turmoil within herself. This mixture of excitement and anticipation, tempered by nervousness for the future and the possibility of parting with Marty before she had the chance to really get to know him. She found it so difficult to concentrate on day-to-day tasks, continually looking out for the young scout. This total absorption with a man she hardly knew was so unlike her. From the moment she discovered that he, genuinely, suffered from a speech impediment similar to her own, her anger had melted to guilt and embarrassment. This then became empathy and, as she found herself finding excuses to be in his company, she realised she was falling in love with this young Dutchman. Grace took great delight in being party to the light-hearted banter, between Marty and Llewellin, in the evenings at the canteen and the mischievous antics the two youngsters would prepare for the ever-tolerant Cookie.

Marty's charming smile and good humour were infectious. He was popular with all members of the company and Grace could not ignore the twinges of jealousy she would feel if he spent time in conversation with any of the Sisters. Graces behaviour had not gone unnoticed by the Sisters. Hanna was deeply alarmed at these signs of attraction and had purposed to have a stern talk to the young lady.

One evening Hannah discovered Grace missing from her wagon. Hannah rushed down to the canteen and found Grace cutting Llewellin's hair under the scrutiny of Marty who informed his friend that he would not be able to remove his hat in public for many months since it now looked as though he had placed his head in a maize thresher to which he received a rebuke from both Llewellin and Grace.

Although Grace's actions appeared innocent, she had offered to cut Llewellin's hair only because she knew she would be in the company of Marty and this underlying motivation had not escaped Sister Hannah. The Senior Sister remained with the group in frosty silence, which stilted even the effervescent Marty. The grooming was completed in an embarrassed silence, at which time, Sister Hannah departed promptly with a humiliated and furious Grace in tow. When the sisters arrived at their wagon, Sister Hannah told Grace that they would discuss the situation in the morning since they were both too upset to think rationally and that they were likely to say something that may later be regretted.

Several times whilst cutting Llewellin's hair Grace had glanced in Marty's direction only to find him studying her. He wore a pensive, thoughtful expression which would transform into his charming smile and he would give her a conspiratorial wink. This caused her to blush and smile back in spite of the ominous presence of Sister Hannah. Marty studied this lovely Irish girl, scarlet hair, emerald eyes, strong beautiful limbs, and a fighting spirit. Just what a pioneering man needed as a life partner—a wife, mother of his children, but she was already a Sister of the Cloth. She was married to God. He felt his disappointment moving towards frustrated anger.

"That was the most painful haircut I've ever sat through," said Llewellin, as he brushed himself down with his hat.

"I felt your pain but was too scared to tell you," replied Marty! "Sister Hannah was extremely unhappy and I think your haircut is to be the source of discontent within the Nun's camp. I believe Grace is in for the high jump with the Sisters!"

As he made his way towards his wagon the young Scout decided he should perhaps get away from the camp for a while and clear his head regarding this forbidden romance? Where was Dirk? Surely he should have returned by now?

The following morning, after an extended time of Prayer, Sister Hannah summoned a calm but resolute Grace to accompany her. The morning was clear but chilly as the pair walked towards a deserted water tank. Sister Hannah approached the subject directly.

"I am forbidding you to meet with the men of this camp whilst you are on your own. You will always be accompanied by one of us sisters."

"With respect, Sister Hannah, I am now an adult and quite capable of deciding whom I shall see and when and in whose company."

Hannah regarded Grace with a shocked expression and blurted an emphatic response.

"Now, you listen to me young lady! I will remind you that you are under my authority and, as a Sister, you are bound by your Vows to Our Lord to remain in Poverty, Chaste and Obedient."

"Sister Hannah, The Lord knows I have been so blessed and privileged to have been adopted, welcomed even, by the Sisters into St Mary's Convent. Not only have I been clothed, fed and educated, but I have received genuine love. From as far back as I can remember this has been my home and my family, for which I am eternally grateful, and will never take my blessings for granted. But, Sister Hannah, I have never taken the Sacred Vows! I have served alongside the Sisters, not out of obligation, but because I have wanted to walk in the service of my fellow man and I have no doubt that I will always be motivated in this way. However, I have recently realised that I am destined to pursue a life outside of the Convent, although I will always treasure my precious Faith."

Initially Hannah was without words. Struck by her sincerity and maturity she realised suddenly that Grace was no longer a girl, but indeed a woman of fine quality, independent and capable. An asset wherever she should go.

"Dearest Grace, please be absolutely sure that you are not simply infatuated by this young man and that he has the same feelings as you. Please spend time in prayer before you make any rash decisions. Also be sensitive to the fact that you have been observed as a Sister and, although you did not make the vows, the impression will be that you have broken those vows. There needs to be a time of transition in order for respectability to be maintained."

Sister Hannah then tearfully, and unexpectedly, hugged Grace and apologised for her harsh behaviour of the previous evening. She said she would further apologise to Marty and Llewellin when the opportunity arose.

Once back in her wagon Grace decided she would ask Marty, challenge him directly, as to what his feelings towards her were, if any at all? She decided that if this handsome young man was of the same mind as she, then she was ready to become a married woman. Marty's woman.

The colonel Returns from Mafeking

The General requested that all the officers be seated. The room had been buzzing with anticipation and supposition as to the reason for the extra ordinary meeting of Staff Officers. The nature of information would be released by the General. The room quieted as the General looked around at the faces of his senior officers. He cleared his throat, before sipping from a glass of water.

"Gentlemen, what I am about to relate to you now is of the strictest confidence and please understand, that the consequences of these events are still unfolding. They will have far reaching effects on this region and, therefore, will impact us all. Two weeks ago British Colonial Statesman, Leander Starr Jameson in collusion with Cecil John Rhodes and his partner Alfred Beit, led an armed force of troops, comprising British South Africa Company Police and elements of the Bechuanaland Police to a point on the Rhodesia /Transvaal border. Pre-arranged communications between Jameson and Rhodes, broke down delaying the raiding party which eventually crossed the border into the Transvaal where defending Boer Commandos', having been pre-warned, were waiting in force to counter the insurgents.

It was intended by Rhodes and Beit that this ill-fated raid would trigger an uprising amongst the, primarily, British expatriate workers in the Transvaal but failed to do so. The Johannesburg conspirators were expected to recruit an army and prepare for an insurrection which did not eventuate. The column moved into Transvaal where, after several clashes with forewarned Boer forces, the raiding force was defeated and surrendered to the forces of the South African Republic. All raiders are in custody as I speak.

Co-owners of the British South Africa Company, namely, Cecil John Rhodes (the Governor of Cape Colony) and Mr Alfred Beit, were instrumental in the plotting of this infamous scheme which was intended to eliminate resistance from Mr Paul Kruger, who is President of the South African Republic. This debacle which is now dubbed the 'Jameson Raid' has caused such embarrassment to the British Government that we anticipate Cecil Rhodes will be removed as Governor of the Cape and Natal states forthwith.

More importantly, the very fragile peace that exists between the Boers and the British has been further damaged and I fear, what little trust that may have existed between the two Governments, is no more. War, I think, is imminent. The Boers are determined to hold onto their Republic and their Gold. President Kruger has received a letter of support and congratulations for his foiling of the plot from the Kaiser of Germany a strong ally of the South African Boers.

In a further development it is reported that, since Jameson's forces vacated the Bulawayo area, the Matabele nation have gone on the rampage and are killing white Settlers wherever isolated and vulnerable. We are presently assembling forces both from Bechuanaland and Mashonaland in order to relieve the situation in Bulawayo. In view of these developments, your regiments will remain on high alert until further notice. Orders will be dispatched shortly.

Four days after the General's Extra Ordinary meeting, Colonel Milton Smythe returned to the Survey Camp with a small troop of cavalry. Milton Smythe was not a generally a compassionate man and yet he felt an unusual obligation to William Brady perhaps because of the boyhood bond and William's connection to the colonel's home."

William was at his lodgings having a morning tea with Anna, when the Officer arrived.

Marty tapped on the wooden door and stepped back nervously as he heard Anna's melodic and happy voice announcing she was on her way to attend the door. Opening the door, partially at first, she smiled up at Marty who self-consciously stuttered out a greeting as he whipped the leather hat off his bushy blond head and enquired, politely if the B-B-Boss was in?

"Yes Marty. He is just finishing his tea. Would you like to join us for a cup perhaps?"

"N-no thank you, Miss Anna, my b-b-boots are full of horse… Ah, no thank you. The colonel is here to see M-Mr B-Brady."

"Oh, I see…William," Anna called, "Marty has come to tell you that the colonel is at the office and wishes to see you." William attended to Marty at the door and then requested Anna to accompany him to meet the colonel.

When Brady entered the office with Anna by his side the colonel rose immediately from the canvas chair within which he was seated. On seeing the lovely Anna, the colonel smiled and bowed slightly. He turned back towards William and shook his hand briefly.

Brady introduced Anna to the Cavalry officer, but had not missed the worried expression on the soldier's face as they had entered the room. Once the introductions were complete William hastily ushered Anna back to the quarters, citing the urgency of his meeting with the colonel. On his return to the office, Milton Smythe, grim-faced, retrieved a telegram from his top pocket which he held out to Brady. His face softened slightly and he said, "This is concerning news, not good I'm afraid."

William read the neat script which stated, "Small travelling party of four men attacked south of Figtree by Matabele Impi. Two travellers confirmed dead, one wounded—safe. One missing, presumed dead."

"I am informed that the man missing, presumed dead, is your Scout," The colonel said softly.

"Dirk?" enquired Brady incredulously.

The colonel nodded adding, "Unfortunately, William…due to the lack of available forces in the area, a search party has not been possible. You have my deepest sympathy."

The officer then proceeded to inform Brady that, due to unforeseen circumstances, he would be unable to assign any of his troops to the railway at present. For security reasons he was not in a position to explain why, however, the British Government were expecting some trouble in the Transvaal in the immediate future and that Brady and his Railway Guards should remain vigilant. He also advised that in the interest of their safety, Anna and the missionaries should postpone their northward journey until further notice.

William was struggling to pay attention to what the colonel was saying as his mind grappled with the news of Dirk's misfortune.

The colonel seemed impatient to be on his way and Brady, sensing his agitation said, "Thank you, Colonel Milton-Smythe, for delivering this information personally. I am sure you have other more important situations to attend to."

The colonel smiled briefly and replied, "When you are out here in this unsettled land, far from home, you realise family and friends are the most important possessions you have, Brady. But, as you say, I must leave at once." He turned back towards Brady, shook his hand and said, "I beseech you! Delay your lovely wife's journey north until you receive further notice from me, William."

Brady accompanied the pensive Colonel to his mount and bade him farewell. Whilst struggling to retain his composure, his mind was consumed by the impact this news would have on Marty, especially since he had already lost his parents to the spears of the Zulu!

The colonel and his squad rounded the small hillock in a skirt of grey dust and were lost from sight. William turned on his heel. He summoned one of the camp guards, instructing him to saddle his horse, and asked him to ensure that the camp scout, Marty, be ready to accompany him on a ride out to the survey party.

He would not deliver this dreadful news to Marty within the camp, but away where the young man could vent his emotion in the privacy of open bushland.

"D-Dirk? Dirk m-mis-missing. Presumed d-dead! N-n-no never! N-not, Dirk! H-he is too good, too s-strong! I don't believe this t-t-telegram, Mr Brady. Until I see h-h-his dead body I will not believe he is dead. I w-w-would know if he was dead! This is a m-m-mistake!"

"Marty. Marty…listen to me. Of course Dirk may be alive and that is our earnest hope, however, this report is accurate and you will need to prepare yourself for the worst. If he is alive then surely he should have arrived back by now or at least have made contact?"

The reality of William's words seemed to break through the tragic wall of denial protecting the heart of the young brother. In a husky, trembling voice, eyes brimming with grief and burning with anger, the young man requested immediate leave to go and search for his brother. William knew that regardless of his response Marty's mind was made up. Marty mounted his horse in one fluid and agile motion and rode off towards the camp. William let him go following in his dust at a slow walk, a heavy burden of sympathy causing him to shake his head in helplessness.

A tattoo of fast-moving horses wrenched William from his ponderings.

Sabotage

Sargent Deacon, galloping at the head of a small group of mounted Railway Police, rode towards William. He turned in a tight circle as they reined their mounts to an orderly halt a few yards from William.

'What now?' thought the Englishman.

Saluting smartly Deacon walked his horse forward.

"Mr Brady sir, Trooper Bartwell arrived at the camp shortly after your departure with an urgent dispatch from Mr Burns at Railway HQ." Deacon handed the dispatch to Brady.

"Thank you, Mr Deacon. I shall follow you shortly," said Brady accepting the sealed envelope.

William waited until the troopers had left before opening the despatch as he feared it may be confirmation of Dirk's death.

Classification: CONFIDENTIAL   17 January, 1896
To: All Cape Railway Construction Managers and Section Leaders
Priority: Urgent—Immediate
Subject: Sabotage

DUE TO DELIBRATE AND WILFUL DESTRUCTION OF CAPE RAILWAY BRIDGES AND RAILWAY EQUIPMENT AT TWO LOCATIONS WITHIN THE PAST WEEK ALL OPERATIONS ARE TO CEASE WITH IMMEDIATE EFFECT. CONSTRUCTION CAMP POLICE WILL SECURE EQUIPMENT AND RAILWAY PERSONNEL WILL REMAIN AT CAMP SITES UNTIL FURTHER NOTICE.

BY ORDER
J. BURNS
CONSTRUCTION MANAGER

William returned to camp at a brisk canter. On arrival he requested Deacon summon all personnel to return to camp for an urgent meeting at 1700 hrs.

All Railway employees attached to the Line Marking and Survey Team, apart from Marty, were assembled below the tarpaulins, which served as a sun-shaded area where meals and messing occurred.

Anna peered out from the small window located on the side of the wooden hut that served as William's living quarters. Squinting against the late afternoon sun she noted the gathering of rail personnel at the canteen, which was unusual for this time of day. William had his back to her, but appeared to be addressing the entire crew. Her curiosity was aroused but, underlying her need to know, was an uneasy sense that William was deeply troubled.

The frequent visits by the colonel, anxiety etched on his dark, sun-weathered features combined with the alert, nervous intensity surrounding him and his men, were obvious signs to Anna that all was not well. William had endeavoured to console her by insisting that the Senior Officer was just 'a very busy man' with much responsibility.

Just then Grace came into view she waved to Anna at the window, but turned her attention to the gathering, moving closer she listened to William's address.

William brought order to the assembly.

Good afternoon all.

It is no secret that there are troubled times ahead for all of us within this region.

I received a dispatch from Rail HQ earlier today informing myself and other Team Leaders that deliberate acts of sabotage have been carried out on newly constructed Cape Railway installations to the South.

Consequently, I am instructed to inform you all that normal operations will cease with immediate effect due to acts of aggression against the Cape Rail in the form of explosive devises detonated on the newly laid line to the south. All personnel will be confined to camp and Railway equipment and stock will be secured and placed under twenty-four hour guard until further notice.

This communique was hand delivered from Cape Rail HQ.

Immediately hands were raised to ask the many questions that were on the minds of the rail employees.

"I will answer your questions in a moment, but first I have sad news to share with you all." William hesitated, searching the assembly once more to see if Marty had joined the group in the interim. He had not.

"I received a report this morning informing me that Dirk Prinsloo and his party were attacked by Matabele Impis whilst on their return journey from Bulawayo. Dirk is missing, presumed dead." A deep murmur rolled out from the crowd.

"I have informed Marty of this terribly sad news and I realise also, that Dirk has been a comrade and close friend to many of you gathered here. You all know how resourceful and resilient he is and since he has not yet been found there is still hope that he is alive. Please keep both Dirk and Marty in your prayers at this difficult time. With regard to the cessation of normal operations there is little more that I can tell you at this time. I intend to travel to Mafikeng in the morning to gather further information. In the interim Mr Deacon will organise a twenty-four-hour sentry roster which will include all personnel apart from Cookie, and Marty, who is granted leave of absence forthwith. When not on sentry duty, all remaining personnel will be restricted to camp and remain on high alert. There is little reason for this camp to be attacked as we are Survey only, however, we will remain vigilant until further notice. Now are there any questions?"

The thoughtful assembly dissolved into small groups absorbed in hushed discussions.

Grace on hearing this news raced off in the direction of Marty's wagon where she found him packing personal items into a canvas saddle bag.

"Oh, M-M-Marty, I have just heard the news about Dirk!" she stammered as she reached up and gently touched his upper arm.

He studied her with red rimmed eyes and replied, "Sister Grace, I don't believe this r-r-report. If something h-h-had happened to Dirk I w-w-would know. I a-a-am going to find him."

"When are you l-l-leaving?"

"First thing in the m-m-morning," he replied.

"When will you come back?"

"When I h-h-have found Dirk."

"But, i-i-if you leave now I m-m-may not s-s-see you a-again!"

"S-S-Sister Grace, I m-must look for my brother!"

"Yes, you must, but then w-wh-what about us?"

Marty was struggling to grasp the significance behind her line of questioning.

"What about us, Sister G-Grace?" He said softly as he took a drink from his water bottle.

"Well, i-if I don't see you again h-h-how will we get married?"

On hearing these words, the young man almost choked on the water. He spun around looking at her with a shocked and confused expression.

"Me? M-M-M-Marry you? What about G-G-God?"

"Marty, I am not an ordained Nun. I simply ch-chose to travel with Sister H-Ha-Hannah as an aide and I have p-p-prayed and spoken to God and I have His B-B-Blessing-what about yo-you?"

"Oh, Yes Gracey, I-I-I-I have been-Y-Yes-"

"W-w-will you marry me...I mean, Y-y-y-yes, I will marry you, but first I must f-f-find Dirk."

He took her in his arms and they kissed. She smiled up at him and said, "I will s-s-stay with William and Anna and await your return. P-p-please be very careful and r-r-return to me safe."

Llewellin Jones approached William, pointing westwards along the sandy road that led towards the camp. A mounted troop of Railway Police accompanying a horse and trap had just come into view rounding the hillock that obscured the road further to the southwest.

William, squinting against the low afternoon sun shook his head slowly, 'I can't take much more bad news' he thought. Llewellin cleared his throat and without preamble he blurted out, "The Railway can go to Hell! I'm going with Marty to find his brother!"

William was a bit taken aback by the directness of the Welshman's approach, but, understanding the bond between these three young men he understood that Llew was emotionally charged and, therefore, he responded by saying,

"Good afternoon, Llew, how are you?" The Welshman dropped his gaze.

"I'm sorry, boss, but Marty is going to need support!"

"Let me deal with these visitors and then we will talk further, Llewellin," said William, patting the young man on the shoulder, as he turned towards the oncoming visitors.

A bespectacled, stooping and exhausted looking Mr Pervis alighted from the trap. Dusting himself down with a wide-brimmed hat.

"We will camp here overnight, Mr Foster. You can liaise with the camp Sergeant and he will assist you and your men. I am going to meet with Mr Brady. Please have Doyle see to my horse and erect my tent."

Meanwhile, Llewellin headed straight towards Marty's wagon and was almost bowled over by a departing Grace who seemed to be in a different world as she mumbled a breathless apology and moved off quickly towards her wagon. The Surveyor found Marty standing quite still, gazing sightlessly in his direction, wearing a bewildered look upon his face.

"Don't worry my friend, we will find Dirk. I have informed the Boss I will be going with you," said a concerned Llewellin, patting him on his shoulder.

"Thank you, Llew. Will you be my Best Man?"

"Your what? Hell, yes…I mean, definitely. Your pleasure, I mean, my pleasure, when?"

The Sangoma and the Settler

The hunting party had carried the comatose settler for a relatively short distance, when they were again joined by two of Sepho's dogs. All knew that this did not bode well for the belligerent hunter as he would never part with his dogs. One of the younger warriors blurted out that which was on everyone's mind.

"Surely something bad has happened to Sepho!"

"He is a victim of his own arrogance and disregard for the powers of the Sangoma," replied the older man.

This statement seemed to add vigour to the bearers and their pace increased. Although there were four bearers the limp body was difficult to carry and, after several trials, the tribesmen bound his legs together and arms to his sides and carried him on their shoulders like a supple log, alternating positions from time to time.

Dirk had begun to shiver and convulse. Thandie wiped the sweat from his eyes and felt the heat from his body. He was burning. She was quite sure that this exercise would be quite futile as surely the Settler would die. What would she tell the Sangoma? How would she explain the presence of the Settler in the first place? The old woman may well kill the Settler herself.

When the Party arrived at the Sangoma's village she was resting in the shade, whilst leaning on the twisted trunk of a Mopani tree. This formed a natural sanction for her thorned border fence. She had covered her face and hands with a white chalk-like substance which enhanced her transcendent image, portraying to the party of bearers that she had, indeed, been expecting them. She rose to her feet, though still bowed and leaning on her snake stick, she laughed and cajoled loudly at the group who halted in wide-eyed fear before her. The bearers placed the inert body hastily on the dusty path. The old woman shuffled over towards the Settler as the group backed away from her as one. She continued to babble and cackle whilst prodding Dirk with her stick. She waved for the girl to come and assist her, instructing her to roll him over onto his stomach. When Thandie struggled to achieve her bidding, the woman pushed her out of the way with her serpent wand and summoned the men, who sprang into action and rolled Dirk face down with little regard for his wellbeing. Kneeling down, the woman studied the foul, swollen and puss-weeping wound on the Settlers back. She turned and spat into the dust behind her. Rising painfully, she shuffled towards her huts mumbling to herself all the while. Turning, she instructed the bearers to carry the injured white man into the village where she placed him on a grass mat within her second hut. This hut was stacked with an array of herbs, plants, animal organs, bones and skins. Clay pots containing an assortment of vile smelling potions were placed adjacent to the curved mud wall of the hut. The odour from inside the hut was overwhelming and Thandie recognised the smell as that she had first noticed emanating from the old woman.

When the bearers had carried Dirk into the hut and placed him as she wanted him, the Sangoma told the men that they could drink water and then leave. The offer of the water was declined by all and the hunters left as quickly as they could, without showing disrespect.

The old woman wasted no time. She instructed Thandie to strip off Dirk's trousers and boots. Dirk was still in the grip of a high fever and his face and neck were flushed red, symptomatic of his high temperature. Whilst Thandie removed Dirk's clothing the old woman added a grey powder to a large clay pot of cold water. She proceeded to pour the contents onto his chest and upwards towards his head. She instructed Thandie to rub the liquid all over his upper body including head and neck. As she got to his neck, she pulled at a silver chain that was taut at the base of his throat. The chain swivelled around and dangling from the chain was a small, but ornate, silver cross.

At the sight of the cross the Sangoma screamed and staggered backwards, dropping the clay pot which shattered. The contents of which engulfed Dirk's face and head and he began to convulse once more. Thandie instinctively tried to pin Dirk's shoulders to the mat in order to reduce the intensity of his convulsions. This lasted only a short while after which Dirk went limp in her arms. She turned to find that the old woman was lying on her back groaning in the doorway of the hut. Thandie looked down at the item in her hand, whilst trying to analyse what had transpired. She saw that the delicate chain had parted during Dirk's convulsions and she held the cross in her hand. She leaped up and ran out of the hut, through the gate and well into the bush where she saw a large flat stone at the base of a small tree. She lifted the stone and placed the cross carefully beneath it, replacing the stone gently. Strangely she felt a bonding, a fascination for the necklace, a reluctance to part with it. Thandie ran back to the hut. The Sangoma was seated on the wooden bench outside her living hut. She seemed frail and afraid, shaken. She inquired of Thandie, "What have you done with the sign of the Spirit?"

"I have buried it, Gogo."

"There are some things that have power even when they are buried and there are some truths that are beyond the power of the Great Sangoma."

"Child, I will help you heal this Settler but his ways are not the ways of my people. As soon as he is well, you must take him and leave. You brought him here, you will take him away. It is of no advantage to me if this white man lives or dies. Perhaps my spirits would prefer that he dies. If you do not want to do as I say, let him die, and we will leave him for the animals."

Thandie was undecided. In her heart she wanted to go to the village of her uncle and continue her simple tribal life, but in her mind she knew that if she chose to leave, the Settler would die. She did not know why she felt any obligation to this man from another world. Perhaps she had witnessed the deaths of too many helpless souls in her short life.

"I will remove him from your village as soon as he is well enough, Gogo."

Continual bathing of the patient had reduced his temperature. The old woman positioned him with his wound uppermost. She took a razor-sharp flint and made several incisions, removing the rotting flesh and draining and washing away the foul pus. She cleansed the wound with an aloe vera plant extract and packed it with an herbal poultice containing sour fig, ghaukum and wild honey. She changed these dressings regularly, washing the wound with water within which she had boiled a tree root, turning the water into a cloudy white colour.

The wound had become a gaping hole in Dirk's back, but the flesh was healthy and responding to the treatment. Dirk was in and out of consciousness for the following two days, aware of the excruciating pain in his back whenever the old woman tended to the wound. There were detached images of the old woman dancing around him, covered in skins and chanting, whilst spraying him with the cold contents of a painted calabash accompanied by the acrid smell of burning hair. He was aware of another African woman, gentle and quiet, who did not exude the horrid odour that he associated with the terrible pain each time the rough handed person tended to his wound, whilst muttering unintelligible nonsense.

The warm gentle one was always there with food or water. When he shook with cold she covered him with his jacket. She spoke no English or Afrikaans only Zulu. Some of her soft spoken words he understood, some he did not. He was content to drift back under the comforting cloak of sleep where his muddled mind was free to wander away from the pain.

The ladies had fashioned a half cot which allowed for Dirk to lie on his back slightly suspended from the floor, such that his wound was free to drain. Thandie fed Dirk by taking a mixture of goats milk and water into her mouth and forcing it through a reed into the back of his throat forcing him to swallow. Initially this treatment seemed hopeless as Dirk would choke and vomit, but gradually, he seemed to respond.

Thandie slept near his cot at night and sat by his side during the day. Often she would awake after a fitful sleep and expect to find him cold and stiff in death and she would feel such relief when she saw his chest rise and fall.

On the morning of the third day, before dawn, Dirk awoke completely lucid and aware of his surroundings. The interior of the hut was almost pitch black apart from the illuminated rectangle of the hut entrance. All was quiet except for the steady breathing of a person lying in close proximity to him and the night noises from outside the hut. The heavy odour of rotting flesh and fermenting plant matter emanating from the many clay pots within the hut made him nauseous.

He was covered by his jacket and his lower body was naked under the cover of what felt like a soft cow skin. He needed to relieve himself. Turning away from the person on his left side, Dirk attempted to roll onto his knees. Pain exploded from his back as soon as he attempted to use his left arm, causing him to cry out involuntarily. Instantly Thandie awoke, she crawled over to him now on his knees and one good arm. They stared at one another in the darkness, the light from the doorway reflecting from her wide-open eyes, conveying both fear and concern. The Settler shook from the intense pain and effort. She spoke softly, coaxing him to lie down as she tried to ease him back into the makeshift cot. Dirk resisted her efforts and instead he placed his good hand on her shoulder and despite the agony stood up. First one foot, then the other. His head spun with the dizziness of a drunken man and he had to hold on to her, resting the majority of his body weight upon her. She managed to get to her feet despite his weight. The Settler staggered towards the hut entrance whilst the young woman struggled to assist him. As he bent his head to navigate the low doorway he fell forward, headlong through the opening onto the hard-packed earth outside the hut. The young woman struggled to lift him once more. He was panting heavily and a sheen of sweat covered his naked body. He vomited before losing consciousness once more, urinating where he lay. Dirk was, blissfully, unaware of this fact and of the good clean blood that now ran freely from his newly opened wound.

The girl placed a clean grass mat below the mango tree. She and the old woman dragged the settler onto the mat. Thandie washed his body with clean water from a clay pot. The Sangoma muttered and shook her head in her normal way as she treated his wound with little tenderness. Earlier she had heard the commotion and had emerged from her hut to investigate. Thandie had expected the witchdoctor to be annoyed with the situation, but instead she had commented that he was either recovering or he was to trying to kill himself. She had cackled in her high-pitched squeal, eerie and unsettling in the quiet of early morning twilight.

The sun had only just cleared the horizon and the streaks of sunlight ushered in the morning chill. Thandie covered Dirk with the cow hide. She had washed his trousers and under garments in the river the day before and she placed them close to him with the assegai and his knife. His shirt was beyond repair and she had used it to wipe him down, washing it after each usage. She placed his boots near his feet at the end of the grass mat anticipating his awaking and requiring all his clothes. She was unsure as to what reaction she could expect from the Settler once he awoke again. She sat a good distance away from him, grilling small fish on skewers above hot coals.

His dry cough alerted her to his awakening. She remained where she was and watched as he became aware of his surroundings. The Settler raised his head and shoulders and, unhurriedly, surveyed his immediate area. He discarded the hide blanket as the heat from the morning had long since dispersed the night frost. He smelled the roasted fish and turned to look in the direction of the young African woman. Their eyes locked for a moment. He sat up seeing his clothing in the neat pile beside his mat. Using one arm he dressed his lower body. He crawled forward to his boots and pulled them on. Panting now he took hold of the knife, placing it into his belt. He then took up the assegai and used it to lever himself onto his unsteady feet. Once upright he stood for a while gaining his breath and waiting for the dizziness to pass. Turning, he looked towards the girl who had not moved. His stare became intense…he altered his grip on the assegai. Breaking into a shambling run, he rushed towards her, assegai held aloft. She raised her hands above her head in fear and surprise as he drove downwards with the deadly spear with all his dwindling strength.

The razor-sharp tip of the spear entered the raised hood of the banded cobra driving its head backwards and pinning it to the hard clay path directly behind where the girl had sat. As the settler released the spear he had attempted to pull the girl clear of the deadly snake, but had fallen between her and the now writhing reptile. The girl had screamed thinking the white man was about to kill her. The impaled snake wrapped its brightly coloured body around the shaft of the assegai in its writhing dance of death, hissing its furious defiance. The girl lifted a length of fire wood and crushed the head of the snake, just inches from that of the Settler. Hearing the girl scream, the Sangoma came hobbling from her hut. A painted apparition clothed in several differing species of animal skin and face and arms white with ash and red ochre obscuring her human features.

Taking in the scene before her, the old woman first noted the girl with the log in her hand and the settler lying prone before her. Initially she reasoned that the girl had clubbed the white man, but movement caught her eye and she observed her precious and respected serpent writhing in its death throws and instantly, her look of mild concern altered to one of dread and alarm; she cried out, "Wenzeni, Baba wei-ubulele umzimba womoya!" ("What have you done? My lord, you have killed the body of the spirit!")

"Ayi cha ayi siyozwa ulaka lomoya. Kufanele uhambe kufanele uhambe nomfokazi wakho. hamba uphumehamba uphume No, No, Nooo." ("Now I will suffer the anger of the spirit. You must leave now and take your settler with you. Go, GET out. Leave this place!")

Thandie hastily pulled Dirk to his feet, whilst watching the trembling and shaking of the Sangoma. She wailed and remonstrated in a trance like fashion. Gaining his feet the Settler reached out grasping the assegai and wrenching it free. He flicked the body of the cobra from the bloodied blade. Dirk turned and stared at the distraught Sangoma, not fully understanding her distress at the death of the harmful snake. The girl propelled him from the compound collecting the water bottle and jacket as she went.

"Shesha, uhambe ngokushesha, kufanele siphume kule ndawo! (Hurry! Go quickly! We have to get out of this place!)"

"We have upset the spirit and must leave quickly." Thandie pushed him in a shambling trot along the path leading Southeast. Suddenly she turned and raced back towards the village. Darting off the path towards a small tree, she bent.

Lifting the flat stone at the base of the tree, she retrieved the chain and crucifix that she had buried days previously.

Dirk had stopped, leaning on the assegai. He watched unaware of what the young woman was up to. On reaching him she took his hand from the assegai and placed the precious necklace into his palm. He stared at the crucifix for a moment before pushing it back into her hands. She hesitated, holding it with both hands close to her chest. She looked up at him and he smiled. Before she could respond he began pushing forward once more urging her to proceed at pace. Weak and trembling with exhaustion, Dirk staggered, falling awkwardly to the ground. He crawled, crab-like, to the base of a shady tree against which he propped himself up, leaning on his good shoulder.

He had attempted to call out to the girl but his throat was dry and no sound came out. He was past caring at this point and the pain from the wound was again intense. He did not know her name. He slid slowly down the rough bark to the grass at the base of the tree and lay on the soft golden straw-coloured tufts. His mind wandered, influenced by the familiar scent of the bush about him. Strangely, he felt content, unconcerned, come what may. He awoke to the girl shaking him gently. There were two African men standing some distance behind her. One young and the other aged, toothless and wrinkled. The older man seemed annoyed and turned to walk away. The younger man pulled him gently back.

"Just leave me please, I want to sleep," croaked Dirk.

The girl produced his water flask and assisted him to drink. He sat up and the two men helped him to his feet. The younger man placed Dirk's good arm across his shoulder and grasping the Settler's belt from around his back, walked along side Dirk accommodating most of his body weight. The old man walked in front and the girl followed behind. The small party rested frequently with little conversation amongst the Africans. The Settler was aware that he was the reason for the tense atmosphere within this group. It was now late in the day, cooler and the trees cast long shadows. Dirk realised he must have slept for some time prior to the arrival of the girl and her two helpers.

The weakened white man was again at the point of collapse when the old African turned to his left and climbed a small hill, upon the crest of which was a hut constructed from sapling poles with a thatched roof. In the distance, Dirk could see a medium-sized village boarded by the white sand river-bed. This hill, though low in profile, offered an excellent view of the surrounding area. It was obvious that this was a lookout point for the village below.

The girl had disappeared with the old man and only the young man remained at the hut. He indicated that Dirk should enter the hut, but the Settler was content to sit against the poles in the cool twilight and regain his strength. The youth produced a clay pot within which was a maize cob, some maize porridge and strips of goat meat. Dirk ate a small portion aware that, perhaps, it was all the young man had. As the chill wind of the night descended, the Settler wearily, though gratefully, crawled into the shelter of the crude hut. He slept whilst the young warrior remained outdoors, ever vigilant, maintaining his watch.

The rains had been light the previous season and according to Chadawa, the youth who had carried Dirk, this season they had not come. The river which should be flowing now was a dry, white ribbon of sand within which the villagers would dig to access the precious water below. Chadawa made the effort to visit the Settler every day with a meal and a calabash of murky but cool water. He would call out 'Kutjena' (White-man) when some distance from the small hut and arrive with the provisions and always with a handshake and a huge smile. Dirk was warming to this young man who was a cousin to Thandie. With difficulty the young man had communicated to Dirk that his father was most annoyed with Thandie for having brought Dirk to the village. The village Chief on hearing the news of the White man's presence had summoned the old man and had made it clear that, should the White man enter the village without his express permission, he would be severely beaten, even killed.

His father had subsequently forbidden Thandie from visiting Dirk. It was Thandie that had secretly convinced Chadawa to deliver food and water to the settler until he was strong enough to fend for himself. Chadawa was enjoying the task and his new and interesting friendship with the first White man he had ever seen or met.

Dirk was filthy, apart from the area around his wound and his face and neck which he rinsed with a little water from the daily calabash supply. His trousers and leather jacket were in an appalling state. He inquired of Chadawa where about in the river he could bathe. Smiling, Chadawa agreed. Indeed he needed a bath, wrinkling the skin beside his broad nostrils. But there was no water near the village, the river was dry.

Noting Dirk's disappointment, the young man said he knew of a place, but it was half a day walk and he was not sure 'Kutjena Dirky' was strong enough.

Dirk assured him he was. Chadawa agreed to come and collect him before sunrise the following morning. That night Dirk recognised that, although slow and painful, he was regaining the use in his left arm. He also realised that he was missing the company of Thandie, which was extremely unsettling for many reasons and he tried, unsuccessfully, to push her from his mind.

A bright glow along the high ground to the east caused the trees to silhouette along the crest like warriors shoulder to shoulder, defending a mysterious land behind them. The fingers of light became stronger as the golden orb of the African sun announced the new day.

Chadawa and Dirk had been heading southwards for almost an hour, moving at a cautionary pace. Dirk followed fifteen paces behind his young guide. He held his assegai firmly in his right hand. Chadawa carried a long spear and a 'knob kerrie', or club, held by a throng around his waist.

A family of warthog burst out of a burrow close by and startled both men. The adult hog charged through the bush with three piglets in close pursuit, all with tails sticking straight upwards. Recovering instantly, Chadawa lunged, hurling his spear, but too late, the hogs disappeared unharmed into the morning twilight.

After a further two hours walk, the pair rested beneath the shade of a family of Baobab trees. Chadawa threw his club with practiced accuracy at the fruit of the baobabs…'Cream of tartar.' The pods fell to the ground and the young man cracked them open with his versatile club, exposing the white powdery seeds within. Dirk enjoyed the sour, but pleasant, taste and was exhilarated by the knowledge that he had been able to keep pace with Chadawa thus far.

Late morning heat from the scorching sun and the gradual incline that the two were now ascending was taking its toll on Dirk. The duo were in an area dominated by granite hills running along a small escarpment. Dirk paused with his shoulder against a tree. Chadawa, smiling as usual, urged him to continue as they were close to their destination. Dirk exhausted, lifted his assegai, nodded and pressed on. Finally they crested the summit of the wooded incline and Chadawa pointed with his spear down into a ravine to his right where the noonday sun reflected off the surface of a semi-circular pool. It was skirted by a golden beach on the near side and lapped against the rock face of a hill on the far side. This vista was so spectacular that Dirk no longer felt his exhaustion. There was a family of waterbuck standing up to their hocks in the water.

Dirk's bush instincts kicked in and he placed a hand on Chadawa's shoulder and they went down into a crouch. Dirk could see the water buck were attracted to something on the bank and, there drinking nervously, was a cheater. She was crouched down ever vigilant. Watching…ears twitching…listening. She then stood, stretched her neck to scan the bush behind her and, satisfied, she shook herself and trotted off into the grass and out of sight. This was a place of beauty, but also a place of peril for the unwary. Chadawa led the way down the small escarpment parallel to the water. A troop of baboon alerted all in the ravine to the human arrival with resounding barks which reverberated off the walls of the ravine.

When almost at the centre of the natural amphitheatre, Chadawa again began to ascend a short distance to a flat platform like rock which recessed backwards under an overhang. A series of ancient rock walls had been erected across the face of the overhang forming a fortress like enclosure. The walls had deteriorated over time but were essentially intact. Leaves and animal droppings were scattered across the floor. A strong odour of dassie or hyrax urine pervaded the area. Past human occupation, by way of smoke blackened rock face and long extinguished and scattered coals, were evident. The platform of natural granite in front of the overhang offered an unrestricted view of the majority of the pool, being approximately twenty yards above it in elevation. Dirk judged the distance to the pool to be one hundred and fifty yards. Shadows lengthened as the afternoon sun moved beyond the overhang and the paper trees rustled in the afternoon breeze. Chadawa was busy collecting fire wood which was in plentiful supply, naturally scattered all around the outcrop.

Dirk sat with his back against the cool rock, a feeling of contentment swept over him. The young Kalanga removed the small coal and tinder that he carried in a specially adapted calabash and lit a fire. He cooked a small and muddy tasting duck which he had speared late that afternoon. Warmth from the fire was reflected off the blackened rock face just as it had done for centuries before. The two men engaged in quiet conversation beneath a star clustered vault of infinitely clear sky.

Chadawa reported that Thandie and his father had left that day to go to the Mission from where it had been reported that several of the villagers, from Thandie's home, had escaped the Matabele and were seeking refuge at the settlement. The young man suggested that in the morning they should descend to the pool where Dirk could have his bath, but warned that the pool was guarded by a huge serpent and that Kutjena had better be careful and quick since the stories, told by tribal elders, spoke of many an unfortunate bather who had been taken by the huge Inyoka! But he, Chadawa, would stand guard nearby and watch over his white friend. The young man seemed anxious they should leave to return to the village immediately after Dirk's bath and, probably, before the return of Chadawa's father from the mission, reasoned Dirk.

Dirk awoke the following morning stiff and cold also sore after spending the night on the hard rock surface. A pheasant called close by and was answered immediately by another. The sun reached over the hill opposite lighting the pool and revealing a herd of impala interspersed with baboons, drinking at the pool edge.

Dirk had decided he would not return to the village, but would remain at the pool and regain his strength. After a few days he would make his way west towards the main route running north to south through Bechuanaland. He understood his vulnerability, especially with only partial function of his left arm, but food was plentiful in the area and he was gaining in strength every day.

A Time to Move Onwards

Seated within the bright yellow glow of a tilly lamp within William's office an exhausted and decidedly irritable Perky Perkin's rubbed his eyes with the heels of his bony hands. He blinked several times. Sighing deeply he regarded William, he shook his head slowly and remarked, "I'm afraid all is not well at the Railway HQ, Brady. In fact, all is not well in the whole region!" William noted the black rings that bordered the eyes of his visitor, accentuating his sunken eye sockets.

"I know very little about the present situation regionally, apart from what was contained within the orders I received today," replied William. Perkins sipped his coffee with pursed, unshaven lips. Wearily, he leaned backwards in his chair.

"William, I do not know all the facts, but what I do know is that Cecil John Rhodes was the author of a failed coup within the Boer Republic a few weeks ago and he has been removed from office as Governor of South Africa." William's shock at the news was obvious.

"Where does that leave the Railway," enquired William incredulously.

"Well, I'm unable to say at this time, since the impact of this treachery by Rhodes and Alfred Beit has further damaged the diplomatic relationship between Britain and the Boer Republic, which has been frail at best, of late. The attacks on the railway are a stark indication of the Boer dissatisfaction with the British. I believe that the German Kaiser has sent messages of support to Kruger, which has further inflamed the situation internationally. Mr Rhodes has the financial capacity to continue the Railway and the British South Africa Company remains intact. However, the stability of the region is much in the balance since the forces that were mobilised to de-stabilise the Witwatersrand were comprised of the British South Africa Police, from the Bulawayo area, and Units of the Bechuanaland Police, plus volunteers. There were some casualties resulting from the clashes between the Boers and invading forces. The Boers were prepared and waiting for the raiders and, thus, defeated them capturing the majority, including the leader, Leander Jameson. Trust between the Boers and the British Government is in tatters, William, and I feel a full confrontation between the Boers and the British seems very likely and in the near future."

"So, Mr Perkins, where do we go from here?"

"Jock Burns is in Cape Town as we speak. I am awaiting instruction. I have visited the major line camps along the construction corridor over the previous two weeks and they report several sightings of well-armed Boer patrols. The instruction to cease construction came yesterday, however, we were anticipating some reaction immediately after the failed coup."

William recalled the words of the colonel and now, much of what he had said, began to gel.

"You were the last in the line here at Payalape, Brady, and probably the least vulnerable due to the distance from here to the Boer Republic and, also, since there are no assets of strategic value here apart from the water tower."

"Is it likely that this cessation of works will be for an extended period?" asked William.

"I have no idea man, I cannot be sure. Certainly, high level diplomatic negotiation will be taking place between the Boers and the British Government as we speak, and no doubt extensive efforts are being made by the British to appease the Boers. The British government will be raking Rhodes over the coals and it is not yet clear whether Rhodes will continue to have the blessing of the Queen to progress development of territories to the north. We have also been advised that, since the raiding force left the Bulawayo area, Matabele Impis have gone on a rampage and have killed many white settlers. The whole region has gone mad!" Perkins was almost ranting, his voice rising an octave.

"Well sir, it seems we are in limbo. I have some pressing issues that I need to address, both personal and Company business, involving my key personnel."

"Oh…well, they better be important as I am tired and not in the mood for trivial matters!"

William proceeded to explain the situation regarding Dirk Prinsloo and Marty's determination to establish his brother's fate. In addition, Llewellin Jones had made it quite clear that he would be accompanying Marty to search for his brother.

"Well, I'm afraid that is out of the question, Brady. Jones can't just shoot off in the middle of a crisis. Surely you have denied him permission?"

"No not exactly. Dirk Prinsloo was attacked whilst on company business. The company has made no effort to assist Marty Prinsloo, his next of Kin and also an employee of this company, in locating his brother. I feel we have an obligation to do so." Perkins was irritated. He pondered the information for some time before clearing his throat. He rose stiffly from the canvas chair and placed his finger on the chart.

"This is the Bakalanga Mining Area and here is the Murchison Mine Area owned by the Tati Mining Company. It is located near the confluence of the Tati and Inshe rivers. A gentleman named Daniel Francis is the Director of the Company and has great influence in the area, having negotiated with Lobengula for the mining rights. Francis and his Board have laid out plans for a new town which is to be named 'Francis Town' for obvious reasons. The Board were pleased to grant the Cape Railway passage through the area, insisting, however, that the rail line run parallel to the main road which bisects the town. We will require a liaison with the Mine Board and Town Council in order to plan our line in relation to the existing and proposed infrastructure. I would suggest that the search party take advantage of this cessation, and, on return from the search, Llewellin Jones make contact with Tati Mining Board and survey this very specific section of line. For obvious reasons we cannot have an open ended 'leave of absence' for Mr Jones and thus I will need to agree a time restriction on the search period."

With a petulant stare, Perkins mumbled reluctantly, "I will agree to twenty-one days of company time allocated to Prinsloo and Jones, but not a day longer. Who else will accompany Mr Prinsloo?"

"Probably, Luka. I will enquire if he is willing to go, but it is of no consequence to the Railway, for as you know, I pay his wages."

"You mentioned personal considerations?"

"Yes. My wife Anna is due to give birth very soon and is presently with me, here in the camp. As you may be aware it was our intention to settle in the Matabeleland province of Rhodesia. Anna is in the company of a team of Missionaries on their way to Hope Fountain Mission near Bulawayo."

"You say your wife and other civilians…missionaries?" The word was said in a disapproving tone. "And they are resident here, on site?"

"Why yes sir. They were en-transit when I was cautioned by Colonel Milton Smythe to hold their passage north until further notice," replied William.

"Well, we can't have that sort of added responsibility at a time like this!"

"I beg your pardon, Mr Perkins?"

"Well, what if the camp were attacked, who will defend them? We will need every hand protecting Railway personnel and property. Besides Brady, this site is not a 'Halfway House' for persons travelling north!"

William stood to his feet, towering over his dishevelled and now cowering boss.

"I can't believe my ears, Perkins! This is not some obscure nomadic group. This is my wife we are talking about and your attitude towards your staff and their families is unacceptable. You would be very wise to understand that I have a life outside of this Railway and the welfare of my wife is my first concern. In view of your obvious disregard for our wellbeing you can have my immediate resignation!" With that William strode out of the office and into the cool, fresh night. Though enraged, he felt relief, as if a large weight had been lifted from his shoulders.

"Brady. Mr Brady," called Perkins as he appeared in the lighted doorway of the office, puppet-like…drowning in his crumpled clothes and arms flaying the night air.

"I earnestly apologise! I don't know what came over me. What was I thinking? Good Heavens. Please understand I have had a very unsettled couple of weeks!"

"It would be wise if we continue this discussion in the morning, Perkins, when I have had time to calm down but, little will have changed, me thinks," answered William over his shoulder, as he continued walking towards his hut and Anna.

When William arrived at his quarters he was surprised, and a little annoyed, to find Marty, Grace and Llewellin seated on a make shift bench all facing Anna who was also seated within a canvas chair which emphasised her pregnancy and obvious physical discomfort. On his entering the hut the two men rose to their feet, greeting him simultaneously.

"Sorry to bother you so late, Mr Brady, but I wanted to confirm arrangements for our departure in the morning."

Brady nodded in reply as he bent and kissed his wife on the top of her head. She smiled, looking up at him and said, "My dear, I know this has been a day of sad and disturbing news but there is an item of good news…"

"Well, I could certainly do with a bit of good news," replied William.

"Hello, Sister Grace," William smiled awkwardly not really knowing how to greet this godly young woman.

"William, Marty and Grace have agreed to be married. Isn't that wonderful?" said Anna with an affectionate glance at Grace. The news shocked William for a moment and he responded with, "But Grace is a Nun! What about God?"

"That is the second time I have heard that today, Mr Brady," said Grace, "but believe me all is in order with Our Lord."

"Well…Well, congratulations to you both," said William warmly, "my goodness, this is a surprise, but you do make a very handsome couple." The pair looked at one another, Grace blushing contentedly. William cleared his throat gently saying, "Excuse us please, ladies. Gents, shall we leave the ladies and go outdoors to discuss tomorrow?"

Anna and William talked late into the night discussing the regional situation as they understood it. William relied on Anna's sound counsel that was so balanced, abounding in common sense and tempered with faith and a love for her fellow man. With all situations considered, in particular Anna's condition, the couple agreed that William's resignation brought a semblance of peace and flexibility to their present situation. Thus, William resolved to formalise his resignation in the morning.

He had arranged to meet Marty and Llewellin at sunrise the following day, before which he would confer with Luka, and request that the tracker accompany the two men on their search.

He decided that he would confide his decision of resignation with Marty and Llewellin before they departed and that, since he was required to serve a notice period, he would not leave immediately but would make arrangements to meet them at Bakalanga Mines.

He anticipated that if a new town was about to be established then it was likely that there would be medical facilities available which would be reassuring for himself and Anna. In addition, the location of Francis Town was ideal for initiating travel into Matabeleland and north to Hope Fountain Mission located near Bulawayo.

Ncishana

Luka had named his pony Ncishana, or Short One. Needless to say the handsome and compact pony was the envy of many. The bushman and the bush pony had developed a close relationship which was quite evident, for as soon as Ncishana heard the clicking and clucking peculiar to the little bushman, he would whiney and come trotting, shaking his head affectionately to meet Luka. As soon as Luka came alongside the pony he would place an arm around the horse's neck and, speaking softly into its ear, launch into a flowery commentary. Explaining to the horse that both he and Luka were indeed beautiful, being almost the same colour, both small but of perfect shape. It seemed the bushman had an inexhaustible supply of wild cucumbers upon which he and the horse would munch contentedly together. Luka agreed to accompany Marty and Llewellin, but insisted that he would need to return in time for the birth of Anna's baby. In his tradition he was now an important member of the family and should be included in the birth celebrations. It took Luka all of twenty minutes to place his travel gear into a hessian sack. He folded a second sack in addition to his precious blanket across the back of his pony and was ready to ride.

Idle Hands

A vagrant whirlwind whipped the recently brushed hat from Father Davis head. With eyes clamped shut and lips compressed in a sealed grimace the Holy man almost swore in frustration avoiding the stinging dust clawing its way behind his spectacles.

He was annoyed, not so much at this flippant wind but more at the delay to his progress north. Four weeks his team had tarried. A full month! He understood that the situation northwards was unsettled and dangerous, but surely it was in these uncertain situations where he and his team could bring hope, peace and comfort and most importantly salvation. He understood Brady's reluctance to have Anna travel at this time, but the missionary team must have faith and unquestionable trust in their Lord. The Father was on his way to inform William that he and his team would leave the following day! On arrival at the Camp Office, Father Hamilton was greeted by the sound of William's voice resounding clearly through the unpainted doorway.

"I will not change my mind, Mr Perkins. Will you please have my entitlements ready at the Mafeking Office for this month-end?"

Perkins and William exited the Office together. Perkins was in front carrying a small bag. When they arrived at the carriage Perkins stuck out his hand, which William accepted. They shook hands briefly and without another word Perkins urged his horse forward with a slap of the reigns, and the small Railway Cavalry unit in close pursuit.

William walked back towards his office feeling relieved. Father Davis barred the entrance to his door.

"Bless you on this fine morning, William Brady."

"And morning to you, Father Davis ."

"I'm afraid we can wait no longer, William. Four weeks have gone by and here we are. No new converts and sitting idle whilst brother kills brother and the devil's hate rages just a short travel away. The people of this land thirst for the

Gospel. Due to the idle hands, my team of ladies are beginning to find their own reasons for rage. Thankfully, no violence yet!" he smiled, "But really, we must move on and answer the Lord's Calling."

"Father, I believe it is not God's will for you to travel knowingly into a land of unrest where you and the Sisters could be killed immediately you cross the border. Your party is extremely vulnerable and who knows what terrible fate could await the Sisters. Armed and capable men are being attacked. I know that you must trust The Lord, but there is no sense in throwing yourselves off the steeple!"

The Search Begins

Departing at sunrise, the trio were anxious to be on their way. Accepting advice from Brady, they took with them a pack mule that was lightly loaded in case they should require an additional mount. Marty took the lead with Luka in the middle and Llewellin bringing up the rear, with the mule in tow. Each was engrossed in their own thoughts, but alert to their surroundings. Grace had arrived at Marty's wagon early as he was saddling his horse. Her sudden appearance had startled him, as she was on his mind all the time at that moment. He turned at her voice and she came into his arms. They kissed intimately, naturally, as though their relationship was long established. Again, she had begged him to be careful and reiterated her plans to remain with Anna and William until his return.

He contemplated the events leading up to his present situation. Brady's news of his intended resignation was a bolt out of the blue and he, Marty, would not be too keen to remain once William had gone. Situations had altered rapidly and he was still working out his future priorities. He thought of Dirk and how proud he would be to formally introduce his lovely Grace and be able to tell him of his marriage plans. He clenched his jaw in a gesture of determination. He would find Dirk! He looked behind at the figure of Llewellin. A friend like no other! Llew' and Luka were loyal and dependable to a fault. Their presence inspired him with confidence and hope.

Before leaving Marty and Llewellin had agreed no fires after dark, cooking would need to be done during daylight on dry-wood fires to reduce smoke. The trio were advised to draw as little attention to their presence as possible as the situation regarding Matabele and Boers was unknown.

The first day of travel was uneventful. The trio had halted for a midday rest as the heat increased. They resumed travel at mid-afternoon for a further hour and a half and sought a suitable camp site for the night, which was a good distance off the main trail. They located a small wooded depression which suited their requirements. They tethered the horses to a rope stretched between two trees just above the depression. A large ant hill rose up behind the horses. Marty and Llew' placed their bedrolls just below the edge of the depression, whilst Luka found a spot closer to the horses. All being fatigued, they soon fell asleep.

Before dawn Marty was woken by Luka and was immediately aware of the sound of heavy beasts moving through the bush on either side of the depression.

"Inyati Nkosi," said Luka, before moving back to the uneasy horses. The bellows and moans above the thousands of hoof falls of the animals as they moved past had awoken Llewellin. Fortunately the anthill had formed a wedge parting the huge heard of buffalo as they moved past the trio and their horses. Marty and Llewellin joined Luka attempting to quieten the nervous horses. The cape buffalo paid them no attention as they moved on…a sea of animals on either side bringing with them a strong bovine smell and clouds of dust. Completely trapped, the small group had no choice but to remain where they were, keeping as still and quiet as possible, until this herd passed by and hope that none of these belligerent beasts decided to take an interest in them. After what seemed an eternity the last stragglers of the herd passed by as the sky was lightening to the east. Marty suggested they move quickly away as he was sure that large predators would be following the buffalo heard. Moving swiftly, but without panic, the trio packed up their camp, saddled their horses and headed back towards the northward trail. Reverting to the same order of march with Llewellin at the rear, leading a reluctant and nervous pack mule. Luka was in the middle with Marty in the lead.

The horses were agitated and not responding well. Marty removed his rifle from its boot. He dropped back, instructing Llewellin to go on ahead with Luka. He urged his horse onto a slight rise near another large anthill and scanned the bush along the path from which they had come. Suddenly, the morning quiet was shattered by an urgent shout from Llewellin, followed by the discharge of the shot gun. Marty, spurred his mount at full gallop towards Llewellin, who was now on foot, his horse and mule having bolted. A large lioness was spinning and leaping in a wild dance having taken the full blast of the shot to the side of her head. Marty assessed the situation in a moment. Pulling his horse to a stop, he leaped from the saddle rifle in hand. He aimed carefully at the wounded and wildly vaulting cat, and fired. His shot was followed immediately by another blast from the shotgun and the lioness lay twitching in death.

Llewellin ran the few yards separating him from his friend.

"Marty, Marty…these lions came from nowhere! There are two others!" said Llewellin, breathlessly scanning the bush as he talked excitedly. "This huge one leaped up onto the mule."

"Wh-where's your horse, M-man? How did you manage to sh-shoot th-this beast?"

"She was only yards away from me, Marty." I had dismounted to get the shot gun and shells from the mule, when you left. "Goodness! I had just loaded, Marty, when there she was! On the mules back…so close I could have touched her with the end of the shotgun. By God, I fired instinctively and, fortunately, I hit the beast. My goodness! I'm shaking like a leaf! Bloody hell! I think the other lions have run off, but be careful Marty." Marty's horse had bolted and Luka was nowhere to be seen.

The pair decided to follow Marty's horse. Both men were now alert in the extreme. With weapons ready, they tracked the horse, which was only a short distance away. Obviously it was nervous and unsettled, requiring that Marty make several patient attempts to coax the animal to remain still long enough for him to grab hold of the reigns. Once they had secured the nervous horse, they found a clearing close to where the lion was shot, anticipating that Luka would return to the area. A short time later Luka appeared on foot leading both horses and the mule. The mules halter rope was made off short and secured to Llewellin's saddle holding its head down and restricting it from bucking.

Luka joined the pair handing Llew' the reigns of his horse whilst hanging on to the mules halter. The animal was baulking and pulling to the side. It could smell its deceased attacker.

"Let us move from this area, Nkosi. The mule will not settle here and she is injured, but not badly," reported Luka.

"This dead lioness is the mother and the two following her are her young daughters, they will remain close by."

The trio walked a good distance with horses in tow whilst Luka coaxed the mule forward, constantly chatting in his soothing native tongue. After reaching the well-worn trail north the animals seemed to settle. Beneath the shade of a large tree the party rested whilst Marty inspected the mules injuries more closely. The canvas pack on the mules back had been ripped open on both sides by the claws on the lioness' forepaws. In several places the claws had slashed through the canvas and penetrated the hide of the mule. A paraffin lantern packed towards the top of the pack had been crushed by the jaws of the lioness. This would have been the spine crushing bite that would have ended the life of the mule. The pack and Llew's quick action had saved the mule.

Marty cleaned the wounds, sprinkling sulphur powder onto the exposed flesh. Llewellin suggested they name the mule Lucky. He laughed, repeating, "Llewellin, Luka and Lucky!"

"Marty, can you repeat after me? Long live Llewellin, Luka and Lucky!"

"Voetsak," was Marty's reply. (A forceful 'Go away'.)

Late in the afternoon of the fourth day of travel the trio arrived outside the growing settlement near Monarch Mine, which was destined to become Francis town. Both Marty and Llewellin were surprised at the volume of activity and the number of people mingling in the town centre.

"This is probably a result of the Matabele raids," said Llewellin.

Marty suggested that they fill the water containers on the mule and move to a less populated area on the northern outskirts of the town to which Llewellin agreed. However, he had sustained severe saddle rash on his inner thighs and was suffering much discomfort. He told Marty he would seek out some medical assistance and join him and Luka later. Could he or Luka return and collect him before dark.

A large red on white signboard mounted above the door of a newly erected tin structure announced 'General Store.' Several natives sat in the shade outside waiting in hope of work, loading or unloading in exchange for rations.

Llewellin climbed gingerly from his horse. The rash on his inner thighs was quite raw and, in addition, one on his left calf was now slightly infected. Llewellin stood for a moment gathering himself against the annoying pain and, peering into the gloom of the tin clad store, he squinted from below the brim of his bush hat, unsuccessfully, against the harsh glare of the afternoon sun. One of the natives came running up to him taking the bridle of the horse. Llewellin was reluctant to let go of his mount, but noted that there were two other horses in the care of the native group.

"Ok," he said to the bush valet, releasing the animal as he turned to walk into the store. The pain from the rash caused him to shuffle with his knees bent and legs outwards as if he was still in the saddle.

There were several men, all of whom were seated around a large, crudely made table, drinking from an assortment of mugs and bottles, all regarded the Welshman as he entered. Their conversation interrupted as they watched him, politely amused at his manner of locomotion. As his eyes adjusted to the dim interior Llew' acknowledged the storeman seated behind the raw plank counter and attempted, unsuccessfully, to walk more normally. He was startled by a deep voice with an unmistakeable Welsh lilt.

"Been in the saddle long, my friend?" asked a large dark bearded man at the table. Llew' spun around, taking in the group seated at the corner table. Blushing and self-conscious, he realised they would all have watched him shuffle into the store. All the men wore blue work overalls and mine boots and were covered with grease, grime and mud.

"That I have Gents, and I'm rubbed raw!"

"We noted that when you shuffled in like you had a watermelon between your knees," said one of the others. They all chuckled.

"Well, I have come in here to find a liniment or balm with which to treat my rash," said Llew', as he turned to the storeman who greeted him politely.

The big Welshman said, "I know an excellent cure for your ailment." Llewellin walked over to the table.

"Well," he said, "as you are a Countryman I would be pleased to hear your advice." He put out his hand, "Llewellin Jones," he said.

The big Welshman rose from his seat. Taking Llew's hand he introduced himself, "Adda Lewis from the South Valleys."

"I'm a Cardiff man, but always a pleasure to meet another Welshman, Mr Lewis." Adda proceeded to introduce others at the table, and then suggested that Llewellin get himself a drink and join them.

Llewellin hesitated. "Well that is very kind, but I am in rather a hurry and this rash is killing me. I must attend to it sooner than later."

"Well now. It is unlikely that you will find any ointment here in this store, but can I suggest a treatment that has worked for many in the past?"

"Really? Well I would be grateful to receive your advice," said Llewellin.

"Right. Good. Mr Roberts, the storeman, has a cask of good whiskey at the back and you will need two full bottles."

"Two bottles?"

"Purely medicinal, young Llewellin, of course!"

"You will also need five crepe bandages and one small towel."

"Very well," said Llew and requested the items from the storeman. The big Welshman turned to the party at the table and winked. Mr Roberts returned with two corked bottles, bandages and a small towel. The purchase came to four shillings and sixpence.

"That is very expensive, Mr Roberts," observed Llewellin.

"It's the price of the imported whiskey, sir. It is from Grants in England," he said proudly.

Behind him Adda smiled, rubbing his hands in anticipation. He came forward and requested that Mr Roberts be good enough to loan them a blanket. Assisted by one of the other miners, Adda took the blanket and tied it across the vacant corner. Llewellin placed the goods on the corner of the table. Adda leaned across and, taking a bottle, poured a generous amount of whiskey into a tin mug. Now you Llewellin. I suggest you have a good drink of that before we begin. Llewellin did as he was told and drained the mug with undisguised relish.

"Now, sir, if you would be good enough to go behind the blanket and remove your trousers." The tin mug was replenished and handed to Llewellin once he was behind the blanket which obscured his body to chest height.

"Drink up, Mr Jones," encouraged one of the other men. Llewellin did not have to be asked twice. He swallowed the fiery spirit in one gulp and proceeded to remove his trousers. In the meantime the second bottle had been opened and mugs around the table filled. When Llewellin had removed his trousers with painful care, he held them aloft and a chorus of applause came from the men at the table and they all gave a toast.

Now Adda poured a small amount of whiskey on to the towel and directed Llewellin to wipe a portion of the rash area. This Llewellin did and howled with ensuing pain to which another round of applause came from the group around the table and Llewellin's mug was refilled as another toast was enjoyed all round. This act was repeated several times with raucous applause and toasted recognition. Llewellin, although experiencing the stinging pain of the alcohol on the raw flesh, was enjoying himself falling further and further under the influence of the whiskey.

When all the areas of rash had been attended to, Adda handed each of the crape bandages to Llewellin instructing him to cover the affected areas with the bandage. Llewellin attempted to apply the second bandage but now, succumbing to the effects of the alcohol, he fell backwards, pulling the blanket down revealing his body. Huge applause erupted from the onlookers and the whiskey flowed, both bottles now empty. Reluctantly, Mr Roberts produced another bottle, but warned at the same time, that the store would close in half an hour. Mugs were topped up once more, bandages applied with assistance from unsteady hands. Llewellin Jones was quite inebriated by this time and stumbled around trying to pull on his trousers, his audience urging him on, when a shadow fell across the doorway.

Marty watched as Llewellin stumbled and fell several times. He laughed loudly with his trousers around his ankles, attempting all the while to contain the precious contents within his tin mug. His actions were like that of a deranged casualty having survived a horrendous calamity resulting in bandages all over his lower body. Despite his disappointment, Marty could not suppress his sense of humour and he chuckled, shaking his head at the comical scene before him, enhanced by the enthusiastic audience. Llewellin had not noticed the entry of his friend and continued to frolic about, whilst Marty approached the storeman and purchased a few items.

"Just in time," said Mr Roberts, "As I am about to close and it's time for this lot to go on to the miner's camp!"

As Marty walked across to Llewellin he was accosted by Adda who screened Llewellin protectively and was immediately joined by other miners. Llewellin pushed his head up unsteadily between the two and explained to Adda, in a slurred but proud voice, that this was his colleague and best friend, Marty!

Travel the following day was done in relative silence and there were no complaints about the rash, but several comments were made whenever Marty increased the pace to a head jarring trot! On the sixth night of their travel they had come across a recently prepared camp comprising a pair of ox wagons and several rough looking horsemen.

The horsemen were well armed and regarded the trio suspiciously. The wagons had been placed parallel to each other with a ten yard gap between them. In the centre was a cooking fire. Saddles had been removed from the horses and placed either end of the clearing forming a box between the two wagons. The oxen and horses had been tethered just outside the camp. A well organised defensive camp.

After an exchange of greetings Marty had dismounted and approached a dark sunburned man who appeared to be the leader of the group. They spoke in Afrikaans. Marty noted the strong and unmistakeable stench of rotting flesh emanating from the wagons. Marty explained that he was heading north to find his brother, reported missing after a Matabele attack near Fig Tree. The Boer's agreed they had heard of the attack. The Boer then explained that they were ivory hunters operating south of Fig tree and returning with ivory for shipment to Europe.

Marty asked for information from the north. The Hunter did not have much to tell other than they cut short their trip due to the Matabele unrest. They had not witnessed any atrocities but had heard reports of a fort called Fort Adams that had been set up near Empandeni Mission due to attacks on civilian miners in the area. They had talked to a trader who had recently left Fort Mangwe near Fig tree and he had informed them of the attack on four travellers. The trader said that the sole survivor was injured and under treatment at Fort Mangwe. This was valuable information and, if this was in fact Dirk's group, then the survivor could give Marty the exact locations. He reported that water was scarce in the area which had made their task much easier since the elephants had to restrict their wanderings to the few available watering holes. But the drought was causing starvation for some of the local tribesmen, adding to the unrest in the area. Armed with this new information, Marty thanked the hunter and the trio moved on for a half mile and set up their own camp.

As the night wore on, the weary travellers were disturbed several times by gun shots fired from the hunter's camp. Marty was unconcerned as the chilling laughter like calls of the hyena penetrated the cold night and he knew that the attraction was in the wagons and these calls would summon other scavenger clans. No doubt the courage of hyena and jackal would have been enhanced by the tantalising stench of the rotting flesh on the stack of ivory. These dangerous predators would make determined attempts to gain access to the hunter's camp throughout the night, and no doubt the hunters would now be regretting the fact that they had not cleaned their macabre bounty with more care.

With water reserves desperately low the trio arrived at a crowded Empandeni Mission. Groups of Africans sat under the sparse shade offered by the marula and stunted acacia trees. Matabele attacks, drought and starvation had driven hordes of desperate souls to the mission in search of food and water. At the end of a short avenue of pomegranate trees stood a stone church with an impressive bell tower and tall arched windows. Not a blade of grass was visible around the church, only bare sun scorched earth.

There were lines of cultivated vegetable beds, all empty of produce. It was clear to Marty that the Jesuit Priests would be overwhelmed by the number of displaced and starving natives. Tension amongst the desperate people was tangible. Mistrust and suspicion in eyes that followed the progress of the three horsemen as a gaggle of small naked children followed behind baying for food.

"I have a very uneasy feeling in this place, Marty!" called Llewellin softly from behind.

"Ja! There are too many people without food. We will need to be wide awake or we will be robbed blind. I think we will fill our water containers and gather what information is available from the Priests, then move on before sunset." Luka was happy with this suggestion as he and his pony were now attracting too much attention.

Once at the Church Yard, Marty dismounted, took his weapon and went in search of a church official. Luka led the horses and the mule to the stone walled water trough whilst Llewellin removed the two water casks from the mule's pack and attempted the laborious task of drawing water from the well by use of the hand pump, mounted above the dry water trough. The long pump handle was chained to the pump with a large steel padlock.

Llewellin swore and, looking up, realised that the growing crowd of natives were waiting for water to flow into the trough. As he rose to go and locate the key, Marty appeared pushing through the people. He had the key in his hand and, as he placed it into the lock, a series of scuffles broke out amongst the thirsty crowd and Luka and the horses were being pushed to one side by the pressing mob. A rifle shot rang out and brought instant order to the melee.

Llewellin looked menacing with rifle in hand, he called to Luka to tell the crowd to move back such that the riders could take the water they required and when this was accomplished the water remaining in the trough would be left for the thirsty onlookers.

Luka conveyed the message which was received with murmurings from a thirsty crowd that, reluctantly, gave way to Luka and the horses, pushing their way back to the trough. Marty proceeded to unlock the pump and began pumping. The horses drank greedily and initially the pump struggled to keep up with their demand. Llewellin finally completed the filling of the casks whilst Marty continued pumping into the trough which was a little over half fill when the pump began to suck air. The Priest had warned him that the water level in the well was dropping and remarked that the supply had been quite adequate for Mission use, but was unable to cater for the additional load of visitors and, therefore, had been locked to allow it to refill.

Marty motioned for the crowd to come forward and drink whilst he secured the pump arm once more. They came as one, scooping frantically for the water from the trough, pushing and shoving…Desperate! Marty was conscious of the value of the key he held in his hand and he considered that if the throng of displaced people grew at the mission, the key would have to be placed under armed guard. When he returned the key to the French Priest, Marty expressed his fears to the cleric, who calmly said, "The Lord will provide."

Llewellin and Luka were mounted and ready to leave the mission yard, anxious to find a suitable camp site for the night after the long hot day. The Jesuit Priest, Father Peter, had informed Marty that since the armed patrol had moved into Fort Adams there had been no further atrocities in the immediate area, but there was a large contingent of Matabele that were expected to attack Fort Mangwe.

As Marty left the church he was accosted by an elderly tribesman who carried a short stick with a long haired tussle at the end. The warrior pointed the stick at Marty and, shouting loudly, asked, "Why have you followed me here? You have brought curses on my village and you bring disgrace upon our daughters. You are not welcome in this land! Leave us alone or you will have to deal with the consequences. He spat, turned and sauntered off. He turned once more and, with his stick he gestured towards the road leading out of the Mission gardens shouting, "Hamba, hamba weyna!" (Go, Go, you") Stunned by the aggressive verbal attack, the gist of which he only partially grasped, Marty immediately asked Luka to interpret all the elderly warrior had said!

"Well, the elderly f-f-fellow must be a bit p-p-p-penga (crazy), Luka," Retorted Marty, as he climbed up onto his horse, "I have no Idea w-w-wwhat he is o-o-on about!"

"Yes, the sooner we get away from this place the better," said Llewellin, "It's a powder keg!"

"The Priest informed me that there is a small citrus orchid half a mile north where we can camp. There is no fruit and no water at the site so we should be left alone and, as it will be dark very soon, let's move."

The elderly tribesman being Thandie's uncle stormed off toward his niece his anger evident in his agitated stride.

"Your White Settler continues to cause us trouble. What possessed you to get involved with him, I cannot understand. You have brought shame on me and my family."

The old man's eyes were wide open, his anger glowed in the twilight and his whole body was shaking. He lifted his tasselled stick and struck Thandie across the face.

"I will not take you back to the village with me you can remain here at the Mission or follow your Settler," he struck her again.

Tears of frustration ran freely down the young woman's face. She took hold of the tassels, as he attempted to strike her once more, and ripped the stick from his hand.

"What are you talking about, uncle?" she shouted at him.

"I'm talking about your Settler friend. I have just spoken to him at the Church. I warned him to stay away! That if he continued to follow us he would be sorry!"

"That is impossible you…you old fool. The settler was injured and in no condition to follow us."

"I may be old but there is nothing wrong with my eyesight and there cannot be another settler with the same curly yellow hair. The only difference was he had a new shirt and was with two others. Another Settler and a Hottentot," he spat into the dust once more.

"Where is he now?"

"They rode their horses towards the gate and good riddance. Now give me my stick and get out of my sight."

Humiliated and confused, her few surviving tribespeople watched on, as she picked up her meagre possessions and walked out into the gathering darkness.

Thandie would not spend another minute in the company of her uncle who had bullied and harangued her from the day she arrived at the village asking for his assistance. He had never shown her the slightest bit of compassion for her losses in the raid. He had put her to work immediately and, this trip to the Mission was in the hope that he would be able to leave her with one of the male survivors in an arranged marriage and, thus, receive 'Labola'. A payment for Thandie. He had also accused her of having slept with the Settler leaving her spoiled and of little value. She wept silently as she followed the track out of the mission. Without much forethought she followed the road north out of the Mission yard. She had no plan, she simply needed to put distance between her and her despicable uncle.

She had gone some distance when she saw the glow of a small campfire, some distance off the road, amongst some cultivated trees. She turned off the road and crept slowly towards the campfire. Two white men were seated near the fire in quiet conversation. From where she was situated, she could not see them clearly so, fearful and trembling, she moved slowly to her right until she was looking directly at them. She crept closer. The man on the left removed his hat and she almost exclaimed aloud. Her uncle was correct! The Settler, Dirk, was looking directly at her. She held her breath in dismay.

Thandie felt the cold tip of a spear at the base of her neck and froze. Luka asked her politely what she was doing. She was unable to answer in her fright. He ushered her towards the campfire. As they approached the fire the two men stood with rifles at the ready.

"What the…who is this Luka?" enquired Llewellin.

Marty, realising it was a native woman, asked, "What does she want, Luka?"

"She was watching us, Nkosi."

Seeing Marty close up and hearing the way he spoke, as well as noting the sound condition of his left arm, Thandie knew it was not Dirk, but the likeness was startling. Marty was about to speak directly to the girl when her necklace glinted in the firelight catching Marty's attention. He instantly recognised the crucifix about her neck. His hand shot out and he grasped her roughly by the shoulder. "Where did you get the crucifix?" he demanded.

"Dirk gave it to me," she replied in a quivering voice. The mention of Dirk's name stunned Marty for an instant.

"No way," said Marty as he grabbed it and ripped it from her neck. "Dirk w-w-would never give th-this away. It b-b-b-belonged to our m-mother. Wh-Where is Dirk? Is he d-d-d-dead? Did you kill h-h-him?" Marty was struggling to get his words out in his agitation and the girl was answering in Kalanga. Llewellin pulled Marty away and calmed him down.

"Listen Marty, if he was dead how would she know Dirk's name? She must know where Dirk is. Let Luka find out if he is still alive."

"Luka, ask her if Dirk is alive?"

"He was alive when we left him near the village."

"Was he hurt?"

"Yes, he had a bad wound in his back that is still healing."

"Who is looking after him?"

"My cousin Chadawa is taking him food and water."

"Can you take us to him?"

"Yes."

"Luka is she sure? If she is lying, I will kill her myself!"

"She is sure Nkosi!"

Missionaries on the M[...]

The afternoon wind caused the canvas canopy to flap lo[...] conversation. The preacher was hanging onto his hat as [...] side of the wagon to avoid the dry, gusting wind. Willia[...] burdened with the news he must now impart to the frustrated Missionary.

"Father, you may have already heard that I have resigned from the Railway."

"So I hear William, So I hear!"

"Father, once I have completed my period of notice, a further two weeks hence myself and Anna, in the company of Sister…I mean, Miss Grace, will leave going northwards to a small settlement town established near the Murchison Mine Site which is situated close the Border of Rhodesia. This same town is soon to be renamed Francistown after the Director/Founder of the Mine, who negotiated the mining rights for the area with Chief Lobengula. The settlement is growing rapidly being a focal point for local mining and prospecting, but also an ideal transit point for travellers going north into Matabeleland. I will remain there with Anna whilst she has our child. We will then travel on to Bulawayo once things have settled in the region and Anna and baby are fit enough to travel north to Bulawayo."

The usually mild and smiling cleric removed his spectacles hastily with shaking hands and his ruddy complexion seemed to grow a shade darker.

"Are you telling me sir, that I have delayed here for more than a month for no reason? Goodness Man, had I known a month ago that Anna would travel with you we could have moved on and been at our destination by now. God Help us William?" Father Davis' pale blue eyes burned with anger and his thin bony hands shook with frustration.

"Father, this delay has surely saved your lives and it grieves me to inform you that Good Hope Mission was attacked last week and totally destroyed by the Matabele." Brady passed a copy of the message received from Colonel Milton Smythe earlier that day:

'Forty eight men of the Matabeleland Relief Force had been deployed to Hope Fountain Mission, where they were fiercely attacked by Matabele Warriors. Over the space of three hours they managed to beat off their attackers. Regrettably, prior to the arrival of the relief force, two of the local caretaking staff were murdered in the initial attack. In addition the Mission Church and dwellings were destroyed. Gutted by fire.'

The colonel had said in his communication that the Matabele Rebellion had basically been broken, however mopping up operations for small marauding bands continued.

Father Davis, having replaced his spectacles, read the message several times. Only the trembling of his chin revealed his emotion.

"It grieves me to bring this news, Father, but at the same time I see God's hand in having delayed your progress. According to the colonel a section of British South Africa militia have erected a fort at Hope Fountain Mission and he believes the Mission will be rebuilt once the rebellion is crushed. The murder of two of the local caretakers has prompted those native families living at the Mission to abscond in fear for their lives. So, the area is presently devoid of Parishioners."

"The Lord Have Mercy, William. Please forgive my rantings. Your news, though tragic, is an answer to prayer. Immediately after our last discussion I beseeched the Lord to give me a definite sign as to when we should travel. I have been so disappointed with the delays and have questioned God. Once again our Gracious Father has confirmed that 'all things work together for good for those that seek after Him and His righteousness'."

"Well, Father, Cookie and I will travel to Martins Drift tomorrow. The Driver of the grocer's supply wagon, that comes through from Martins Drift once every two weeks, is a good friend to Cookie and tells him that the Innkeeper on the Boer side of Martins Drift is selling a wagon and a complete team of oxen on behalf of a local farmer. If it is still available and if in reasonable condition then I will purchase the unit for Anna and I to travel to Bulawayo in." Handing the message back to William, and seemingly lost for words, the Pastor shook his head slowly from side to side and let out a weary sigh.

"So much hate in this world, William."

"Father, it seems to me that there is now no urgency for you to reach the Mission considering the present situation and I wish to make it quite clear that you and the Sisters will be most welcome to travel to Francistown in convoy with us. I believe that from there you will be able to communicate with the Missionary Society and also gain up to date information as to the security situation in and around Bulawayo."

Anna was now in her seventh month and much larger than she had been when carrying Elizabeth. She was in a positive state of mind and far more relaxed with the advent of the new arrangements. Having William travel with her was an answer to prayer and now Sister Hanna would be with them until they arrived at Francistown. Much of her time and effort had been expended in comforting Grace, who was in constant worry for the wellbeing of Marty. Ten days had passed since her husband-to-be had departed to locate Dirk and, although she knew that it was most unlikely she would hear any news until Marty actually returned, she asked for news from any and every stranger that passed through from the north.

William and Cookie left before sunrise on horseback with two mules in tow. The trip to the Boer Border would take a day and a half each way and so William informed Anna to expect him back on the morning of the fourth day. The trail took them directly due east towards the Limpopo River, which also formed the border between the Boer Republic and Bechuanaland. According to the Grocer there was a fairly large force of Boer Soldiers camped on the Republic side of the bridge. William concluded that this was obviously a result of the recent 'Jameson Raid' into the Republic by forces from the British South Africa company. This being the case, William realised that his presence in the Republic as an Englishman, and working on the Cape Railway, would not be met with much favour.

He and cookie discussed the situation whilst traveling the first day and decided that William would find a secure spot in which to wait on the Bechuanaland side of the Border, whilst Cookie, being fluent in Afrikaans, would cross over the border and locate the Grocer where he would purchase his supplies and inspect the wagon and oxen. If satisfied, Cookie would pay for the wagon and drive the unit back, collecting William on his way.

The pair made good time and their only delay was due to a large herd of elephant cows and calves that blocked the trail on the morning of the second day. The two men were happy to stand and observe the great beasts for a period of time as they pulled down great branches from considerable height with apparent ease, manoeuvring their muscular trunks with practised dexterity, leaving a trail of destruction behind them.

Just before midday the riders trail began to drop towards the river. The vegetation thickened as they neared the great Limpopo River. A lone outcrop came into view beyond which they could make out the causeway crossing and settlement beyond. A small Block House was situated just off the road above the River crossing. There were a series of rifle ports facing towards the crossing. Stationed well back from the border post was a group of rondavels, accommodation for the Cape Mounted Police manning the post. A section of six post guards were in attendance, their horses were held within a poled enclosure adjacent to the Block House.

Cookie went into the Reception Office at the rear of the building to complete clearance out of Bechuanaland. One official accompanied Cookie out to the horses. He made a cursory inspection of the mules and pack plus empty backpacks and then signalled Cookie to proceed. Looking across the river William could see two manned field guns pointing directly at him. This visual picture accentuated the reality of the instability of the region.

"Cookie, please...At the slightest sign of trouble, double back here! If the wagon is going to attract too much attention leave it behind."

"Don't worry, Baas. We coloured folk get away with murder by pretending we just don't understand." Smiled Cookie. Brady wished Cookie good luck and added that he would expect him back before night fall.

William led Max back up the road until he found a small trail that appeared to go down to the river. He took this and wandered down to the bank of the river. The Limpopo was almost dry. No water was flowing, but water was dispersed in pools of differing sizes, exposing islands of polished rock and sand. Upon the surface of some of the rock islands were dry tufts of water lilies and grass, evidence of wetter seasons in the past.

William, leaving Max in the shade of a large native tree, shuffled down to the riverbed, a drop of ten feet. He estimated the distance to the far side to be approximately two hundred yards but he could not see beyond the bank which was obscured by a line of trees. He was tempted to walk across but had no doubt that, already, he was being watched by the ever-vigilant Boers. He climbed the steep bank and settled down in the cool shade of the tree facing the opposite bank.

No sooner had he sat down when a column of riders appeared further down the river crossing from the Boer side. All were armed and complete with bed rolls behind their saddles. Obviously, this was a patrol crossing the border in broad daylight less than a mile from the manned border post. Brady was astonished as there was no evidence of stealth. They were brazen in their actions. Twelve horsemen made up the group.

The hours passed slowly as the afternoon sun dropped in the west. It was almost twilight when a wagon and a span of oxen came lumbering across the bridge with horse and mules in tow. Cookie had bartered with the storeman and had eventually arrived at a price which seemed fair. The wagon body had been well maintained and was in good condition, but the canvas had several rents and was rotten in places, mainly due to sun damage.

In an open area behind the block house the pair set up camp, tethering all the animals to the wagon. Cookie made his bed in the wagon whilst William placed his bedroll beneath the wagon.

Having departed at first light the next morning and anxious to get back to the Railway camp, the pair ate a meagre breakfast on the move. It was their intention to reach the Rail Camp by midmorning the following day, however, the oxen were ponderously slow. William contemplated leaving Cookie and returning on his own, but it would be against his better judgement. They had not come upon any other traffic for the entire day and had stopped to camp beneath the shade of a family of flat-topped acacia. Cookie was not too happy as elephants were attracted to the pods when in season, but as William pointed out, there were no pods visible.

The sun disappeared in its usual fiery magnificence and the evening sounds of the crickets and the nightjar accompanied the cool night breeze. Both men were hungry and tired after the long hot day. Cookie produced an excellent camp stew which they washed down with several generous tots of rum in their battered tin mugs. There was little conversation as each man rested in the comfort of his own contemplation, gazing into the campfire. The sky was clear, sprayed with millions of stars and the horses chomped peacefully on the scrub grass whilst Cookie sucked on his pipe. William loved this land. He thought of Anna and hoped they would reach Palapye by tomorrow evening.

Brady awoke suddenly to the sound of horses milling about, and a guttural command from the darkness behind him. With a taste of dust in his mouth he sprang to his feet, rifle in hand.

"How many, Nikko?"

"Only two, sir!"

Cookie called out, "Whose there?"

"Don't worry about who we are. Put your weapons down. There are twelve of us surrounding your camp."

"You had better lower you rifle, Baas William. There are twelve persons surrounding us and they want to know who we are."

William could just make out the intruder closest to him. He had dismounted and was squatting down alongside his horse.

"Tell them we are travellers heading for Palapye," answered William.

"I can speak English. What is your business in Palapye?"

"We are Surveyors!"

"What do you have in the Wagon?"

"A few supplies."

"Why would you have a few supplies in the wagon and two empty mules."

"We have just purchased the wagon and oxen from Groblersbrug."

"The two of you move slowly to the rear of the wagon, but leave your weapons where they are."

Cookie stood, slowly removing his pipe and followed William to the Wagon. Three armed men walked in from the darkness proceeding to search the wagon with a lantern hanging above the tailgate.

"No weapons are in here, sir," was the report after a few minutes.

A short stout man walked his horse forward into the dull glow of the campfire now only coals. He looked down at William and said, "I think you are a spy. I think you travelled into Groblersbrug to ascertain the size of the force stationed there."

"I can assure you, that is not true."

"Danie, Raabie bring a small piece of rope. We will tie them up and take them back to Groblersbrug, sir."

"William, they are taking us back to the Border," whispered Cookie.

"Not without a struggle," replied William.

Two men came forward with ropes as the eastern sky was beginning to glow with the promise of the morning sun. The taller of the two men instructed William to turn and face away from him with hands behind his back, William went to comply, but instead of turning only one hundred and eighty degrees he spun around completely catching the fellow with his elbow in the temple. The man dropped to his knee trying to steady himself by grasping at William's torso, but William simply brushed him aside and lunged at the man behind him. As he and the second man came face to face in the bear like embrace recognition was instant. As they hit the ground, a winded voice called, "William Brady!"

"Raabie? Raabie, is that you?"

Brady's words were cut short as Cookie, seizing the moment, attempted to dash into the darkness. A thunderous pistol shot rang out and Cookie dropped like a stone, spread-eagled and face down.

"Don't shoot, Uncle Joseph…don't shoot!"

"Good God, Cookie," cried William as he launched himself onto his stricken friend and in an instant turned him over onto his back. Already a large dark stain had developed on the right-hand chest area.

"Bring a lantern. Hurry!" demanded William.

By this time they were surrounded by others of the Boer party all with rifles on William. Cookie was wide-eyed but breathing fast and shallow. William's efforts to reassure him seemed empty.

"Van, get your first aid bag and see to this man," ordered Joseph. The medic sped off to get his bag.

"Raabie. You know this Englishman?" asked the leader.

"Yes, Uncle Joseph. This is the Englishman who shot the lion and nearly killed me."

"Bliksom, are you sure?"

"Yes Uncle!"

The medic was beside William in seconds. He jostled Raabie out of his way, then removed a large pair of scissors from his bag. He cut the Jacket and shirt away from Cookies ample chest revealing the bloodied wound area which was large, but miraculously not deep. The Medic had no problem in removing the flattened slug as well as a series of wooden splinters. He pulled the section of cut-away garment up and into the light. Out of the bloodied pocket area, he dug out the remnants of a shattered pipe.

"You will be fine my friend. Your wound is not life threatening provided it is kept clean. Your smoking habit has saved you?" With that the medic disinfected the wound area with alcohol and stitched the flesh together with rough stiches.

Several men assisted in getting Cookie settled comfortably into the wagon.

The leader pulled William aside.

"Mr Brady, please understand we are within a heightened state of emergency after the attempted coup a few weeks ago, we trust no-one. Events here this morning are most regrettable, but we have our orders and will protect our borders and our way of life most jealously, especially from the British."

"I think it is extremely fortunate that Raabie recognised you when he did!"

"I understand and can assure you we are in no way involved in any acts of war or destabilisation. We are simply collecting a wagon and oxen within which to travel further north."

"I accept your word and now I know who you are it is a pleasure to meet you. I have heard the story of how your quick actions saved the life of my nephew many times. Each time a little more incredible, but it is a pleasure to meet you! I am Raabie's uncle on his mother's side…er…Joseph Mostert." He put out his hand which William took.

Raabie approached William awkwardly, shaking his hand and attempting to lighten the moment.

"So William much water has passed under the bridge since we last met."

"That it has, Raabie. How are you and your father?"

"Very well, under the circumstances, thank you William. I run the farm now. That is when not called up by the Commando Leader of Operations.

Unfortunately, I hardly see father these days. He is very involved in the Politics of the Transvaal. But tell me William, did you marry the lovely Anna?"

"Ah yes. Anna is now my wife and very pregnant at present."

"That is good to hear, William. You have found treasure in Anna, there's no doubt about that."

Raabie and William exchanged hurried pleasantries and promised each other that greetings would be passed on to family members on their respective returns.

As the sun came flooding over the horizon the troop of soldiers were disappearing behind a veil of shimmering dust. This had been a bitter-sweet event for him, but had once again revealed to William how the power of friendship can positively influence situations even within the tensions of war and regardless of affiliations. We were still our brother's keeper!

William placed a half mug of rum into Cookie's huge and now steadying hand and told him 'to get that into his system' whilst he, William, prepared them for travel. No sooner had William crossed to his bed roll when the morning peace was broken by the sound of small arms fire. The firing intensified and then became sporadic until it ceased. The sound of the conflict had lasted for no more than fifteen minutes. Obviously the illegal Boer patrol had come into contact with a British patrol. Brady was inquisitive, as was Cookie, but William knew that there would be little benefit in investigating and, besides, he needed to get Cookie back to the Railway camp where Anna could attend to his wound. He wondered about the wellbeing of Raabie and prayed that his friend had survived the recent engagement. He wondered who had opened fire on whom?

The creaking and rattling of the Wagon as it moved along behind the ponderously slow oxen was almost hypnotic, coupled with the luxurious warmth of the morning sun. William yawned indulgently. Cookie was snoring and grunting in a restless sleep on the wagon bed behind him. Two mules and two horses followed in tandem behind the wagon. William looked out on the semi-arid savannah bushland when a pair of ostrich came into view causing him to smile. He wondered on the wellbeing of Marty, Llewellin and Luka and whether they had found any trace of poor Dirk.

The Mopane tree leaves were painted in rich autumn colours, in defiance of the dry dusty earth. He wondered how his lovely wife was managing in his absence and in her present condition. He took comfort in the fact that Sister Hannah and Grace were with her. With him being a day late already, he knew she would be anxious and fretting for his return.

A large Native tree showing signs of elephant damage provided a perfect shaded area within which to stop and rest as the midday heat began to cause shimmering mirages in the distance. William climbed into the wagon to see to Cookie, who had pulled himself up into a sitting position and was looking back towards the trail from where they had come. William noted that he was breathing normally and, although pale, seemed to be stable. After creating a small fire William set about warming a kettle of water for coffee. Glancing upwards, Cookie noted a plume of dust moving above the trees towards them.

"William, we will have company shortly." William rose from his position next to the small cooking fire, handing Cookie his rifle, he loaded a round into the breach of his own weapon.

"This is more than likely the Bechuanaland Mounted Police, who were probably involved in the skirmish we heard earlier today."

A complement of mounted cavalry came into view as the two sipped their coffee in contemplation and awaited the troops arrival. Recognition was simultaneous as the colonel gave the order to halt! Dismounting the colonel approached William who had left the wagon and was already striding towards him with hat off and arm extended. The two men greeted each other warmly. William explained they were returning after having purchased the team of oxen and wagon. The colonel nodded towards Cookie and his bandaged chest. Reluctantly, William related the events of the early morning visit by Boer Patrol.

"Well, we had running battle with that same patrol and, unfortunately, lost two good men and three wounded. Casualties on the Boers side are unknown, but we have one wounded—captured, whose horse was shot out from beneath him." The colonel pointed out the man, now dismounted, easily identified by his khaki camouflaged dress and securely chained hands.

"Raabie!"

"You know this man, Brady?"

"Yes, yes Colonel. He is a good friend."

"Well, he was in the country illegally, carrying and indeed operating, weapons of war. Your man, Cookie, and my two dead and three wounded are evidence of acts of terrorism against the peoples of Bechuanaland. This man is now a prisoner of the Government, of British Protectorate of Bechuanaland and will face serious charges."

"Colonel, the man you have in custody is Raabie Maritz, the son of Rooi Maritz. A Boer Leader of huge influence and following within the Boer Republic. Rooi Maritz has a deep resentment towards the British, which is understandable when one hears how he was mistreated by the British Administration. I think it would be in the best interests of all parties to ensure that this prisoner be treated with due consideration."

"Brady, this prisoner will be treated no better and no worse than any other prisoner under my command," stated the colonel with a flinty look that was both a warning and a reprimand.

"I apologise Colonel. That statement was definitely not a slight at the manner in which you would treat your prisoners, but rather an appeal for leniency for this individual, as it will certainly affect the response from the Boers."

"William, the man's fate will be determined by the Governing Justice Department and he will be delivered over to our HQ for processing immediately on our return. I don't like his chances and would not be surprised if he were sentenced to hang! Our field medic has attended to his leg wound and he will be fed and watered as well as any of my troopers. I have one badly wounded soldier who would do better to travel with your man in your wagon. We will organise to retrieve him from your camp at a later date."

Next the colonel summoned the Lieutenant giving instruction for the wounded man to be assisted from his horse and placed into the wagon. The injured soldier had taken a bullet just below his right collar bone and it had exited at the back of his neck causing damage to his spine for he had lost the ability to talk and his left arm and leg were useless. The medic handed a roll of bandages and carbolic lineament to a second wounded trooper instructing him to ensure his comrade's injury, and his own, receive a fresh dressing later that afternoon.

"I will leave Trooper Giles with you to assist with Trooper MacDermot. Giles is a good man and has suffered a minor flesh wound in his lower leg."

With that the colonel bade him a cool farewell and the troop left at an impatient trot. Raabie held William's gaze for a short distance…a nod in acknowledgment of William's wave and then the prisoner turned away, concealing his forlorn look of pale-faced fear. William felt sick, heartsore and helpless, a spectator in this bizarre situation. He struck out at an annoying fly and missed! William was wrenched from his deep contemplation by the unusual voice of Mr Giles.

"We are ready to depart, sir."

"Thank you Mr Giles, lead on." Giles urged his horse out ahead of the wagon. The oxen moved off at the crack of a whip with eager gait and the wagon followed. The wounded soldier lay with a tortured expression behind sightless eyes.

Time to Leave the Railway

The envelope was travel-soiled and had several over-marks of re-direction, but Johan's neat handwriting was unmistakeable beneath the jumble of addresses. Anna could hardly contain her excitement and emotion on receiving this precious letter from her beloved brother. The mood of the letter was light-hearted and entertaining and had been written three months previously.

Johan revealed he had fallen in love with the lady whom he had employed to assist him in his surgery. Helga Smit was the widow to a senior government official who had succumbed to malaria resulting from a trip into the African interior. After her husband's death she had intended to return to Dusseldorf, but their only daughter had married an extremely successful commercial fisherman based in Luderitz. Helga had then decided to remain in Africa where she would assist with her daughter's first child, due in the month of his writing. Helga was slightly older than Johan, but attractive and energetic. She possessed a charming and mischievous humour which delighted Johan. Working closely together exposed a peaceful set of common values, but most endearing to Johann, was Helga's real interest in the Missionary works linked to his surgery. Johann was convinced that Helga held similar feelings towards him and decided he would wait until a year had passed before proposing to Mrs Smit.

Luderitz had grown substantially since Anna and William had left. In particular, the Naval facilities at the port had been greatly enhanced to accommodate the ever increasing naval activity which was hardly surprising in these tense days of international sabre rattling.

Johan also reported that Fritz Grueber had become chronically ill and mentally unstable. Sadly, Grueber had been forcibly restrained, sedated and escorted by his younger brother to a Clinic in Germany for Specialist treatment. Johann was not optimistic with the Trader's prognosis, since the years of promiscuity and Grueber's insatiable lust for ladies of the night had taken its toll resulting in his present condition. The Doctor expressed his thankfulness, once again, that Anna had departed with William when she had. He asked after Luka, saying he missed having the little yellow man around as hunting had become a chore for him. Johann was utilising Zeus for his general transport and the horse was responding favourably, but was no Max. Johann ended his letter with the news of his intention to travel to Germany to visit their parents during the European Summer. Anna wept quietly as she placed the letter into a small material covered box where all things precious were kept. How she missed her family and God only knew if she would ever see them again?

Where was William? He was now two days late? It seemed to Anna that she spent her life waiting! Waiting for the baby, waiting for William, waiting to leave Palapye, waiting for news of Marty and Dirk. She prayed silently for strength and then went to find Grace. As Anna left the hut she saw the wagon in the distance and called anxiously to Grace. The two ladies stood in the shade of a thorned acacia tree as the wagon came ponderously onwards.

Cookie had recovered enough to sit up front with William whilst the wounded soldier lay in the wagon tray, and was in a bad way. He had lost consciousness earlier in the day and Mr Giles had climbed into the wagon to attend him, but couldn't do much other than keep him cool with damp towels. William mounted Max and rode on ahead of the wagon to prepare a suitable bed for the soldier. He dismounted when reaching the ladies. He hugged and kissed his wife tenderly and acknowledged Grace.

"No news from Marty I take it," he said. Grace shook her head with chin trembling.

William explained the situation with the soldier and Grace suggested that they place him in Llewellin's wagon as it was closest to the Kitchen and living area.

William summoned Mr Deacon, who appeared, magically, and took control of the wagon and the wounded soldier. Sister Hannah came over and joined the assembly. Cookie climbed down from the wagon and shuffled off towards his beloved kitchen, but not before a full interrogation by Anna as to his wellbeing and insistence that his dressing be changed immediately. Sister Hannah rushed off to gather her medical bag and rally the Sisters to assist with taking care of the wounded.

William took this opportunity to thank Cookie for his most valued assistance. Although he had sat for hours in the wagon William was exhausted and collapsed into a chair in his hut with Anna sitting by his side. He related all that had transpired and expressed his fears for young Raabie. Anna listened with deep concern. She had been impressed by the young Dutchman and now found it hard to imagine him as a threat to any nation. "And now? To go to the gallows? How awful!"

Wagon and oxen had performed well and William suggested that he and Anna begin loading into the wagon the following day. William's period of notice was now complete, however, he was finding difficulty in extracting himself from duties at the rail camp. To make matters worse, Cookie had decided his days working on the railway had come to an end. He had decided to resign and travel to the new settlement of Francistown and seek employment on the mine.

Four days after William's return from the purchase of his wagon a replacement Camp Boss arrived. William was happy to hand over, which he completed in less than a day. The new Boss, Gordon Fitzgerald, was not happy at discovering that Llewellin and Marty were absent, but due back in six days.

Father Davis was rearing to get on the road. He had all the Sisters aboard and yelled as much to William who was doing his final checks to the oxen drawing his wagon. Anna and Grace were finally aboard and William waved goodbye to Cookie as the wagon moved slowly past the kitchen.

The Reunion

Two giraffe stood statue-like, coloured light grey in the twilight hues, etched with gold against the eastern sky. They stood magnificent sentinels holding silent vigil from their high platform already alert before the waking of the Mission settlement as it belched forth its human sounds, polluting the serenity of the veld. The party consisting three horses and one mule silently skirted the waking Church and headed east towards the streaks of gold heralding the warm sunshine and Marty's lost brother.

The girl said the trip to her village would take a full day walking. As they were mounted Marty hoped they could cut that time in half, although she had also warned that water was extremely scarce.

Llewellin had overcome his saddle sores and was now quite comfortable and eager to locate his friend. The trail they followed was easily defined and the party made good time. Wildlife was in abundance and increased as the group neared the village and the river. Thandi led the party to the south of the village and up onto the hill where Dirk had convalesced in the crude look out hut. There was no sign of Dirk and a quick inspection of the area by Luka confirmed that the hut had not been used for some time. Luka conversed with the young woman who was obviously upset that there was no sign of the settler. She asked the three men to remain at the hut whilst she went down to the village to find her cousin who had been providing food and water for Dirk and would know his whereabouts. Marty agreed. Luka completed a search of the area around the hut.

"Dirk has been here," he stated after completing his search. He held in his hand a couple of long blond strands of human hair.

Llewellin exclaimed excitedly, "This hair has to belong to Dirk. It is too much of a coincidence. The local people do not have the same type of hair and the presence of the necklace, surely having come from Dirk, tells us he must have been here!"

Marty was trying earnestly to contain his excitement and relief, but the girl had told Luka that Dirk had been badly injured. He would only rejoice once he could see his brother face to face. Even as he sat staring at the hair he realised that they were in a vulnerable position. The girl could be raising the alarm and an attack force could be on its way.

"Llewellin, take the mule further up the hill to the tree line. Luka can you follow the girls trail and watch to see if any warriors are on their way to attack us. I will take your pony and wait with Llewellin. If you are seen or attacked we will be in the tree line above the hut."

"The woman can be trusted, Nkosi. It is she who has nursed Dirk."

"Perhaps Luka, but let us not take any chances."

Marty and Llewellin had tethered the animals and concealed themselves behind a clutch of stunted trees. They had an unrestricted view of the hut, the village and river a mile away.

After a tense and seemingly endless wait, Luka and two other persons appeared on the trail just below the hut, the girl and a young warrior. Marty could not hide his disappointment in not seeing his brother among them.

"Who a-a-am I to t-t-trust, Llewellin?" complained Marty.

"I think we should trust Luka's judgement. He seems to think the girl is honest and I am leaning that way because, if she was not we would have all the warriors of her village chasing us by now.!"

Marty asked Llewellin to remain with the animals, whilst he ascertained what had happened to Dirk.

When Marty arrived at the hut Chadawa was visibly shocked at his likeness to Dirk and he said as much to Luka. Luka explained to Marty that Dirk had wanted to move away from the village where he was not welcome and had asked to be near a good water source.

Chadawa had taken him to the Ichibi Lenyoka, Lake of the Snake, where he had left him in the care of the spirits. Chadawa was ready to escort the party to the lake, but daylight was almost gone and, therefore, suggested it may be beneficial to travel in the morning.

Marty was unhappy with remaining near the village until morning for several reasons. The first and foremost being, that their presence would surely have been compromised by now and an attack by villagers was possible. Secondly, if they left immediately the chance of an ambush was less likely as they would be on horseback and should cover more distance during the daylight remaining than the villagers on foot. In addition the young woman refused to go back to the village and she explained that, because she had assisted Dirk, the Village Chief and her family would no longer accept her.

Chadawa and the woman rode on the mule, behind Marty and Luka, whilst Llewellin remained at the rear. The party made good time avoiding wildlife wherever and whenever possible, reaching the base of the granite hill range that skirted the lake on its north eastern side by late afternoon.

Chadawa explained that they could climb down from the small escarpment on foot to reach the lake on the other side of the range or travel around the base of the granite hills on horseback which would take longer, but gave them the advantage of keeping the horses.

Marty considered this information and decided that their best option would be to find a good defensible campsite where the horses could be secured for the night. He was anxious to find Dirk but, at the same time, he knew those around him would be as exhausted as himself. Marty had a quiet discussion with Llewellin and Luka explaining his decision. All agreed. Luka took the last of the water from the mule and, having made sure that all the humans had filled their bottles, gave the horses water to drink.

Evening came quickly. The group had chosen a small river re-entry, which pushed into the hill side, as their campsite. The livestock were tethered towards the back of the small alcove formed by the dry river which came from further uphill.

Marty and Llewellin placed their bedrolls on one side of the small river on the incoming trail whilst Thandie and Chadawa selected a position on the northern side of the small dry river twenty yards further round. Luka would find a spot very close to the horses.

Thandie shared with Chadawa what had transpired at the Mission and how the old man had treated her. This was a difficult conversation for her, since the elderly man was not only Chadawa's father, but he was also a brother to the chief. If Thandie was expelled from the village, then she would be homeless.

Chadawa agreed that his father was becoming more difficult to deal with in his old age, but the old man could be excused in thinking the two brothers were one and the same as their likeness was unusual. The young warrior promised he would speak with his father on his return, but was not optimistic since the chief had been upset that Thandie had brought the Settler to the village. He was silent for a while and then he said, "Perhaps the Settler will want you to go with him. He asked after you when you left for the Mission?" She did not answer.

Luka revived the fire with bellows like gusts of air from his powerful lungs. The coals burnt bright red with a bluish aura igniting the twigs and additional brush wood he had placed onto the once dying fire. Chadawa placed several sweet potatoes on the coals. This would be their breakfast before the sun rose. Marty was seeing to his horse. He gave the animal the last of the water in his water bottle, pouring the precious liquid carefully into his bush hat which the horse sucked away at instantly. He was anxious to get under way. Llewellin was the last to finish his potato, complaining that it was far too hot to eat directly off the fire!

The order of march remained the same as the previous day and visibility was excellent, although the party travelled in silence with odd words of direction coming from Chadawa from time to time.

After a few miles the ground, extending away from the base of the hill range, began to level out. And, as they rounded the next hill there was a wide gap between it and the next hill of at least a mile. This formed the gateway to an arrow-shaped valley at the end of which was a sparkling lake with high-sided granite hills.

The view was breath-taking! The drought-affected landscape seemed to guard the oasis of water and greenery jealously within its granite cradle. The party sat their mounts in silence and awe. They could see the different herds of game scattered around the valley from their high entry point.

"Ichibi Lenyoka," said Chadawa.

"What is that?" enquired Llewellin.

"It means L-L-Lake of the Snake," answered Marty. "A w-w-w-warning in a n-name!"

The previous day when the sun was just at its zenith, Dirk had climbed up onto the rock ledge from which he had dived into the lake earlier. Dirk had sat watching the area of water with deep concentration for an hour, at least, before entering the water. From where he sat he could see down to the bed of the lake through the clear water. The cliff edge on which he sat formed the edge of the lake for thirty yards to the ever-expanding beach where a myriad of animals came to drink. A family of hippo had formed an island of pinkish brown bodies clustered together with heads and bulbous sides and backs exposed from time to time accompanied by both content and irritated grunts. They were attended by parasite eating oxpeckers. He was sure that there would be a crocodile presence in this water, but he could see no evidence. He lay enjoying the hot sun as it dried his naked body, not totally relaxed. He was ever aware of the seen and hidden dangers that existed all around him. Suddenly the pleasant sounds of the veld were shattered by the urgent barks and screams of the baboons higher up on the rocky face. Vervet monkeys that had been playing in the branches of a giant creeper nearby screamed their fear and disgust. Dirk lifted his assegai and stood. He climbed up onto a bolder and froze. Movement on rocks above the ledge and away to his right caught his attention. The phenomenon seemed to disappear and then reappear shadowed and shining, continuing for some time and then disappearing. Gigantic, moving lazily down the hillside was an African rock python the size of which was beyond belief. The creature moved purposefully down onto the ledge. The arrow-shaped head seemed small when measured against the huge muscled coils. It was a never-ending mosaic of black, silver and bronze. The serpent turned away from where Dirk stood. It continued along the ledge to a point where the water almost lapped the rock, where the giant snake slipped silently into the water, disappearing as it made its way towards the beach and an unsuspecting meal. Dirk shivered despite the hot sun on his back.

Watching on intently, Dirk tried to locate the serpent, but it was impossible with distance and also he could not be sure where along the beach it had gone, although there were several species of antelope as well as a troop of baboons drinking at the water edge.

The python, comfortable in the water and so well designed for the ambush, moved slowly in the shallow water. With just the tip of its nose and its eyes on the surface it selected its prey and moved slowly forward positioning for a lightning strike. The hugely powerful coils settled onto the lake bed shallows. The male baboon was more interested in the females about him in the shallows than looking out for danger. He waded a little deeper on all fours. He lowered his head to drink. The pythons head shot from the water, jaws open. The rows of hook-like fangs latched onto the baboon's shoulder. The momentum of the strike rolled the baboon onto its side. No sooner had the ape gone over when two massive coils of the snake's body had wrapped around the stricken animal. The baboon released a feeble cry as it was forced below the surface and the constricting coils crushed life from the baboon.

Dirk watched on as the giant predator moved slowly onto the beach with the baboon still wrapped in its coils. The serpent proceeded to devour its prey. The great jaws unhinged and slowly ingested, first the head and then the entire body. Slow, muscular swallowing movements in the snake's upper body forced the animal down into its throat cavity where the shape of the ape could be seen as it was sucked and digested deeper into the reptile's body. Satisfied, the serpent moved lazily up onto the side of an anthill to sunbathe and regain the energy it had expended in its hunt.

As Dirk climbed back up to the ledge where he had camped for the past week, he wondered when he could expect Chadawa to return. Food had been no problem in the few days that Dirk had remained at the lake. He had fashioned a conical fish net from cane grass which grew in abundance at the water edge. By casting the cone into the water and drawing it slowly to himself several times, he caught scores of small silver bream which he skewered onto several green branches and roasted whole on the fire. The sweet potatoes that Chadawa had left with him had been consumed by the third day. Wild figs were plentiful and, whilst scavenging around the rocky outcrops, Dirk had found a Mahobohobo, or wild plumtree, full of fruit which the baboons and vervet monkeys were already enjoying. A fallen tree, dry and brittle had fallen years past and was now infested with wood boring slugs known as mopani worms. They were as thick as a man's finger and just as long and, when cooked on the open coals, were an excellent form of protein and nourishment.

Dirk did not keep any food items in his immediate living area as the attraction to animals and insects could be deadly. Firewood, his sleeping mat and a gourd of water were all that were stored. Dirk and Chadawa had placed a thick barrier of thorn bush and scrub bordering the overhang, leaving a narrow entrance to an area no more than six square yards. Dirk ensured that the fire at the base of the overhanging rock burned continuously. At night the fire burned between Dirk and the narrow entry and light from the flames illuminated the entry. Dirk used strips he had cut from his leather belt to lace the assegai to a longer shaft providing him with a long spear which he could use to defend the opening of his den. Thus far a visit by an inquisitive serval cat had been his only visitor, although there was continuous movement beyond the entrance every night. Dirk's main fear was hyena. He was surprised that he had not attracted any, but reasoned that the abundance of game in the area and the fire combined to make his scent less attractive.

Dirk added wood to the fire. He shivered in the cool night air and adjusted his position on the hard granite surface. In the morning he would collect more reeds to add more cushion to his mat. He spread his leather jacket more evenly over his torso and grasped the shaft of his spear, which gave him comfort and he fell asleep once more.

The recking jaws of the animal were inches from his head! He screamed an oath, jerking his body backwards. He thrust the spear into the shadow standing over him as hard as he could. He felt the impact of steel upon bone and jumped to his feet at the same instant. The beast had the leather jacket in its jaws, and released an evil laughing squeal. He lunged again and again scoring a hit on each thrust. The animal had the shaft in its jaws and crushed the wood as if it were paper, but the blade was imbedded deep in its chest. Dirk, realising the spear head was gone, used the shaft to parry the hyena away from him. The animal was bleeding profusely and sat back on it haunches into the coals of the fire, it tried to rise, Dirk plunged the shattered end of the spear shaft into its screaming throat. The beast fell to the floor convulsing in its death throes.

Coals from the fire had been dispersed throughout the den and into the thorn scrub. Small fires were igniting. Dirk was in a state of shock though adrenaline was coursing through his veins. He scooped up the discarded jacket and the water gourd and climbed the side of the overhang. A few yards from the edge was a substantial paper tree which he had climbed previously. Climbing as high as he could before the tree limbs became too small to hold him, he rested. With one foot in a tree fork, he balanced himself. Dirk could hear the chilling calls of other hyena, but they were out of sight. He noted that the fires were petering out as the heavy dew laid a wet blanket over the landscape. Slowly the shaking of his leg ceased and was replaced by a cramp as he awaited the light of day.

A cold clear twilight with yellow-gold hues in the eastern sky was a great relief to Dirk, now stiff and cold, clinging to his perch in the tree. As the veil of dark lifted and he could see his surroundings he descended slowly from the tree. Once on the ground he made his way cautiously to the edge of the overhang and peered into the den. The Hyena lay as he had left her. There was no sign of any other animals, only the soft sounds of the birds as they heralded a new day. He was surprised that the other hyena had not consumed their deceased comrade, but perhaps the hyena do not eat members of their own clan?

Dirk shivered. He looked at the puncture marks and a long rent in his jacket and realised it was the jacket that had saved his life. He was encouraged that he had, under the circumstances, utilised his left hand and felt none the worse. Scanning the area once more Dirk was satisfied that it was safe for him to descend into the den. He was anxious to retrieve the spear head buried deep within the chest of the dead hyena.

The mid-morning heat was building when the party arrived at the base of the granite hill range on which Chadawa had left Dirk. The lake stretched out to their right and game was in abundance. Luka was anxious to get the horses into an open area where any predators would easily be seen before they attacked. Chadawa suggested they dismount and walk their mounts up into the kopje as there was a clear area slightly higher up. Marty agreed, and after a short climb they came to a level open area with plenty of shade for the horses.

Marty asked Llewellin to remain behind to protect the horses. The girl remained with the Welshman, whilst he and the two natives went to locate Dirk.

Dirk had no problem retrieving the spear head from the body of the female hyena. He noted that she had been pregnant which probably indicated that she was the Matriarch of her particular clan. In addition, it was more than likely the reason why she had not been devoured by the rest of the clan.

Although the hyena was now in a state of rigor mortis with fore legs stretched out in front and bone crushing jaws ajar its presence was still menacing. Dirk took hold of the fore legs and dragged the beast out of the den letting it fall to the ledge below.

In order to find a suitable replacement shaft for his assegai Dirk climbed higher towards the summit of the small escarpment, where in the woodland above, was a greater selection of trees.

Two hours after disposing of the hyena, Marty, Luka and Chadawa arrived at the den.

Blood stained the floor within the den, where large blue-green flies settled on the congealed blood, and bold bloodied drag marks could be seen leading in the direction of the opening. The broken assegai shaft was lying on top of the bloodied sleeping mat. Shocked and speechless, Marty stared at Chadawa, as if blaming him for what seemed to have been the brutal demise of his brother.

"Hou! Hou!" was the only exclamation to come from an equally shocked Chadawa!

The weight of grief and disappointment caused Marty to sink to his knees. Luka had said nothing. The little yellow man was reading the signs carefully. He scooped a trace of the congealed blood and sniffed at it several times, whilst clicking to himself and shaking his head. He then began following the drag marks which eventually lead to the point from which the hyena had fallen onto a ledge below. The bushman climbed down onto the ledge below and discovered the dead hyena within the bushes. Marty waited up above and when Luka pulled the Hyena out into the open it took him a few seconds to realise that the blood had come from the hyena, not his brother. The relief caused him to weep with relief.

Dirk moved cautiously. He was sure the sound he had heard was that of a horse. He climbed over a large bolder and, looking downwards, he could see the rear of a bush hat. Resting over the shoulder, beneath the leather hat, was a double barrelled shotgun. Dirk did not want to get shot and, naked as he was apart from the groin strap, would give the white man the impression that he was a native. He retraced his steps off the boulder and moved around the level area slightly higher up the hill. He then moved, cautiously, downwards such that he would be almost opposite the armed man he had seen. He was moving slowly forward when movement off to the left caught his eye. He stopped. Looking straight at him was Thandie. She did not acknowledge him, but moved such that she was between Dirk and Llewellin, where she stopped and said to Llewellin, "Look, Nkosi."

Llewellin looked in the direction directly behind Thandie, where the sun filtered through the trees and a silhouetted figure, Greek god like, Dirk stood almost naked. Sun-bronzed, with curly blond hair, holding a sceptre like spear. Stunned for a second, Llewellin raised the shotgun.

"Don't shoot, Llewellin. It's me, Dirk!"

Llewellin fired two shots into the air which he knew would bring the others post-haste.

Dirk came forward. He stopped in front of Thandie and placed a hand on her shoulder. He greeted her in Zulu.

"Sawubona Thandie, uyaphila, ngikukhambuleg." (How are you, Thandie? I have missed you.)

The young woman bent her knees slightly in a sign of respect. She answered him and took his hand in a handshake grasping her forearm with her free hand.

"Yebo sawubona Nkosi." (I have seen you, sir.)

"Sikonya, Siyabonga nina ninjani." (I am well, thank you.)

He then stepped towards Llewellin who embraced him in a brotherly hug. His hand touching the scabbed scar on Dirk's back.

"It is so good to see you alive and well," said Llewellin. "We thought the worst."

"Well, I should have died!" said Dirk.

Just then, Marty, followed closely by Luka and Chadawa appeared cautiously from behind a small rise at the edge of the clearing. As soon as Marty saw his brother, he ran forward, slinging his rifle over his shoulder, and shouted, "Thank y-y-you, God. B-B-But I knew you were alive, you o-o-old bush j-jackal!" Marty embraced his brother, almost bowling him over. "I should sh-shoot you now after all the t-t-t-trouble and w-w-w-worry you have caused."

The brothers laughed and joked together with Llewellin remarking on Dirk's manner of dress.

Dirk then stepped away and greeted Luka and Chadawa. Luka beamed his best smile showing all his magnificent teeth and shook hands with his friend. Dirk then turned to Marty and Llewellin and with a more serious tone, which became quite emotionally charged, shaking slightly in intensity, he said, "I would surely have died if it wasn't for Thandie who literally pulled me from the jaws of death and nursed me for days. And now, for her troubles, she has been banished from her own people because of her commitment to me."

All eyes fell on the young woman as she stood quietly in the background.

The Party Returns

Tired and saddle weary the group arrived in Francis town. They found a comfortable Inn which offered lodgings, meals, hot baths, and camping areas as well as livery for horses and oxen. The men decided to camp, but utilise the ablutions and provision of meals.

Two days after arriving in Francistown, Llewellin, having made contact with the Mine Town Planners, had all the documentation and plans on where the Rail line should enter the Town and where it would exit. He had also been offered a position with the Mine, which he had accepted in essence. However, he had asked for this to be put on hold until he had formally cleared it with the Cape Railway.

The group had parted ways with Chadawa two days previously. Dirk was particularly sad as he had become fond of the ever-smiling and helpful young man. They shook hands and Dirk bade him farewell. Chadawa responded with the words, "I will see you again."

Thandie was tearful at the parting with her cousin. Dirk had insisted that she accompany the group on their return journey to Palapye as she had no place to go. Marty accepted the request as fair, considering her taking such good and sacrificial care of his brother, but he had no idea as to the depth of their relationship.

Dirk and Marty had used this time to discuss all that had transpired since they were last together. There were many aspects that would affect their individual futures.

Marty shared his news about Grace and Dirk was genuinely excited at the prospect of his little brother getting married. Dirk, like everyone else, questioned Graces commitment to the cloth. Marty explained how Grace had been raised in the convent, but had not taken the vows to become a Nun.

The previous evening, whilst seated around their campfire, Dirk described the horror of the disease that was travelling southwards and how it was decimating clove-hooved domestic and game populations on a massive scale. He could not describe in words the magnitude of the problem, but he warned that it would reach South Africa eventually.

"It is like a curse from the Biblical times," he told his colleagues. "A never-ending nightmare!"

When Dirk explained, and described, the disease to Luka, the little man was overwhelmed and went into a trance like state stamping his foot and shaking his head as if he were engaged in an intense argument with some unseen being.

Thandie just seemed to hover in the background, spending time cooking and generally assisting. Mostly she positioned herself some distance from the men, chatting to Luka from time to time. Marty noted his brother in quiet conversation with Thandie on several occasions and considered it natural in view of their recent trials.

Dirk, having loaned money from his brother, purchased a complete set of clothes for himself and several blankets. He inquired of the storeman if there was a lady who could assist a native woman in the buying of clothes. The storeman sent for a coloured woman that lived with him. When the lady arrived, Dirk paid the storeman an agreed sum after explaining that Thandie would require two sets of working clothes and one Sunday outfit, including basic toiletries.

Thandie followed Dirk into the store. She took in the shelves packed with every kind of merchandise with childlike fascination. Dirk left her with the lady assistant. An hour and a half later Thandie emerged from the store wearing a modest blue frock and sandals. She carried a large carpet bag. A group of Kalanga women seated in the shade of an acacia tree called out ululating and clapping as Thandie tried to exit the store unseen. Dirk did not recognise her initially and he had to take a second glance, but was obviously pleased with the result, as Thandie walked towards him self-consciously, head lowered, but smiling.

When Dirk returned to the camp site with Thandie in her western dress Marty had the first thoughts that his brother may be developing a relationship with this Kalanga Woman.

That night Dirk asked Thandie what she had done with the crucifix he had given her. She said she no longer had it and that Marty had taken it from her at the Mission. Later, when the two men were together alone, Dirk asked Marty if he could have the crucifix. Marty was reluctant to return it to Dirk and he said as much, stating that it was a family heirloom and should be worn by a family member.

Dirk turned to face Marty and with a very quiet, but emphatic tone, he said, "Marty, I don't expect you to understand. I don't understand myself, but I owe my life to Thandie and not out of debt, but more of profound respect and fondness, she is family to me. You know how I have felt regarding Africans since the Zulus murdered our parents. Well, Thandie has paid that debt. She could have abandoned me on many occasions, but stood by me, even to her own detriment and for no reward. Her parents too were murdered by the Zulus."

Marty wore a shocked expression. He replied angrily, "W-w-w-what does this m-m-mean, Dirk? Are y-y-y-you going to take her for a w-w-wife? D-D-Do you realise how you will be sh-sh-shunned by society, b-b-both black and w-w-white, and what about your o-o-off-spring? Where do they fit into society? P-P-Please my brother, consider m-m-most carefully your f-f-future actions?"

"And, what about you, Marty? Will you shun me? Will you turn your back on my children in the future?"

"I d-d-don't know, D-D-Dirk. I need time to consider w-w-w-what you have t-t-told me."

"Well, give me the cross as we agreed it was mine many years ago."

Marty took the chain from his pocket and said, "It is broken and needs repair."

"Chains can be repaired when broken, but family relations when broken are sometimes irreparable, Marty," replied Dirk.

The following morning Dirk went to see the storekeeper and negotiated board and lodging for Thandie. The storeman agreed to Thandie working for her food and lodgings by assisting with housekeeping in his rest house. Dirk explained that he would return in one month.

Initially Thandie had insisted that she accompany Dirk to Palapye. But Dirk explained that it would be impossible for him to find lodgings for her within the Railway Camp. She had no idea of how the white man's world worked and did not understand why he needed to travel south. Or what a railway was, but he said he would return after a period of time so she agreed to remain with the store keeper until his return. He would also resign from the Railway and return to Francistown in one month. This would give him and Thandie a chance to consider their future. Llewellin and Marty were anxious to return to the railway where, they too, intended to resign.

By mid-morning, the four men were ready to depart. Dirk had purchased a rather worn saddle for the mule and soon became used to the short gait of the willing animal. Late in the afternoon of the second day Llewellin complained of aching joints and a severe headache. The Welshman crawled into his bed roll before the sun had gone down shivering uncontrollably. Dirk and Marty gave each other a knowing glance. The dreaded Malaria!

That night the brothers took turns in nursing their friend. Heaping on blankets when he shivered and cooling him with a wet towel when his fever burned. Luka had gone off on his little pony to forage for roots and bark that only he knew. 'Muti' as it was called. He returned later that night and boiled a concoction of his remedy. Marty forced Llewellin to swallow a mouthful or two but his patient vomited shortly afterwards.

Early the following morning the men shifted their camp to a treed hillock which offered more shade. The patient was too weak to walk unaided and it took both Luka and Marty to move him to the preferred location, which also gave an unrestricted view of the main trail. Dirk had departed before sunup on Llewellin's mount in order to return to the mining town in search of Quinine.

About midmorning Llewellin was alternating between sleep and wakeful delirium. Luka came running, smiling and clicking and clucking, whilst pointing in the direction of the trail. Marty was irritated and deeply concerned for Llewellin. He almost ignored the little yellow man, but stood and looked in the direction of the trail where two ox wagons moved ponderously northwards towards Francistown.

Luka persisted, "Villem Nkosi, Villem."

Immediately, Marty realised what Luka was saying and he sped to his unsaddled horse; leaping on the surprised animal's back, he galloped to intercept the wagons.

A Bittersweet Reunion

Llewellin passed away in the arms of his friend in the early hours of the morning. How tragic he should die in the arms of the very man he came to find. Only moments before, he had awoken from a fitful sleep and quite lucidly stated, "You will be best man now, Dirk," and shortly after, he breathed his last.

Dirk had arrived exhausted the evening before, with a bottle of Quinine he had bought from a British soldier. Sister Hanna and Anna had tried desperately to dose Llewellin, but the Welshman simply vomited up all attempts. He had taken very little water in the past two days and his urine was black.

When Anna saw the colour of the urine, she had known immediately that Llewellin had Blackwater fever and his chances of recovery were slim indeed. She had told Brady, but not the brothers. Marty and Grace had sat beside Llew most of the day and, after returning with the Quinine, Dirk had insisted he would nurse his friend.

Llewellin was buried on the side of the shady knoll not far from where he died, overlooking the trail to the north and, later, the Railway he loved so much. At the burial service Father Davis spoke of the wonderful character of the Welshman and related some of the antics that he and others had witnessed. He spoke of his readiness to laugh and sing, but most of all, his loyal friendships and how he gave his 'all' for his friend. There were no dry eyes, but within the bitter sadness, these memories held a divine warmth that brought comfort and peace borne of one man's love and goodwill for his fellow man.

As Anna reflected later, Llewellin Jones had been another 'bright candle 'in the African wind.'

William had written a report on the death of Llewellin Jones, addressed to Mr Burns directly. He described Llewellin's bravery and willingness to go beyond the call of duty that resulted in the successful search for the missing Railway worker.

He requested that all monies owed to the brave young man be forwarded to his family in Wales with recognition of his contribution to the building of the Railway and dedication to duty.

Dirk and Marty had departed at sunrise the day following Llewellin's burial. The brothers had always been inseparable and their travelling back to Palapye together with the same intention seemed quite normal. However, they had made up their minds independently and this was probably the first time that each man had taken a decision regardless of the plans of the other. The passing of Llewellin had affected the brothers deeply and, in the recent past Marty would have leaned on Dirk for emotional support. On this occasion Marty had drawn emotional strength within the loving arms of Grace. A new tender but mutual support satisfying in strength and genuine completeness. Of course, having the Big Brother influence was a comfort, but in a completely different dynamic.

Dirk on the other hand had formed a plan in his mind to remain in Francistown once he had terminated his contract with the Cape Railway. He had saved more than a year's earnings, which should purchase a property outside the new town where he could settle and provide a home for Thandie and himself. He would seek work on the mine, and his small property, at the same time.

When the Prinsloo brothers arrived back at the Railway site at Palapye, there was a notable increase in construction workers and sense of urgency. The Survey team was ready to move on to their next camp, but were awaiting a surveyor from Cape Town. Dirk explained the circumstances regarding the death of Llewellin Jones and surrendered his personal affects to the Railway Manager. He also requested the letter from William be forwarded to Mr Burns.

The new Manager was polite, but business like. His attempts to convince the brothers to remain with the Railway for a further three months were unsuccessful. They would remain at the Railway for a full week and assist with the move of the survey camp, after which time their severance entitlements would be paid.

The Railway was progressing at a mile a day and was due to reach Bulawayo in October 1897.

Francis

A cluster of white-washed, thatched-roofed, rondavel mud huts formed the Tati Mine Medical centre where a young English Doctor by the name of Ernest Blackie was only too happy to accommodate William Brady and his entourage of Father Davis and helpful Nuns. No sooner had Brady and Luka outspanned the weary oxen when Sister Hannah and her team of Nuns were assisting a grateful Dr Blackie, in his small and under equipped hospital. An underground blasting accident two days previously had left two dead and four men injured. The doctor had been awake for the previous twenty four hours and the arrival of the Sisters was a God send.

Anna had found it more comfortable to walk on occasions during the trek from Palapye to Francistown. The constant bouncing and jerking of the wagon took its toll and translated into backache. She hated to complain but found relief in walking which tended to slow the wagons. The young doctor had insisted that William and Anna inhabit one of the smaller rondavels, rather than Anna having to climb up into and down out of the wagon in her expectant condition. She was so thankful and relieved to be out of the wagon and able to sleep in an uncluttered space. Now in her eighth month she was more than ready for the baby to come. The interior of the hut was cool and comfortable after William and Luka had added some basic necessities. On the third day after their arrival the Doctor had given her a thorough examination and was pleased with her condition. Doctor Blackie was offended when William insisted on paying for lodging and medical attendance to Anna.

"In the past two days you and your lovely Nuns have transformed this centre into a spotless and orderly hospital," were his words to William.

Brady and Luka repaired several wooden beds and a hot water boiler, which pleased the Doctor no end.

One evening when Anna and Grace were preparing dinner on an open fire Anna complained of contraction like pains in her lower back and Grace suggested she go and lie down. No sooner had she reached the rondavel when her waters broke. She called for Grace who immediately summoned Sister Hannah whilst one of the other Sisters went for the Doctor.

Francis Johann Brady came quickly into the world with little fuss and was ready to suckle almost immediately. William beamed with pride and protective importance. He hovered lovingly over his wife and son, continually petting and reassuring Anna that he was at her service and that all was well.

William was so conscious of that debilitating fear of losing another child that he engaged Anna in conversation at every opportunity. The bond between Anna and Grace had strengthened immeasurably since Grace and Marty had agreed to marry. Now, after the birth of Francis, Grace tended to her every need. Although nothing was said all members, including Luka, understood that for the wellbeing of William and Anna, little Francis must survive!

Father Davis was enjoying himself as he visited and prayed over little Francis and Anna as well as visiting those in Hospital and taking every opportunity to share the word of God. With permission from Dr Blackie, he held a Sunday Service within the courtyard formed by the cluster of Hospital rondavels.

It soon became apparent that the best source of information regarding regions from the north was to be found at the Public house attached to the main General Store. William was informed, by a recent traveller, that unrest and rebellion had now arisen to the north in Mashonaland. Troops had been dispatched northwards since the Matabele rebellion had been crushed in the South. The Rinderpest had devastated the country, wiping out huge herds of cattle and cloven-footed livestock. In order to contain the disease a 'No Go' area, named the Tuli Circle, had been established in the South West of Matabeleland to ensure that no diseased animals or meat could travel south across the Shashi river into Bechuanaland or South Africa. As the main means of transport in the region had been the ox wagon for pioneers and general goods, trade had been significantly affected as the teams of oxen had succumbed to the dreadful disease.

Dirk's description of the plague, which was moving inextricably south, had appalled the group and when Dirk suggested that William and Father Davis replace their trusty oxen for mules, sooner than later, he was offering good advice. William commenced his search for mules to replace his condemned oxen in earnest. Brady paid elevated prices for six mules and an agreement to utilise a further team of eight mules which the Mule Trader was to deliver to Bulawayo. Brady paid the Trader for the eight mules and, in turn, would receive payment for them once delivered to the customer in Bulawayo. The price had already been agreed with the Bulawayo customer and Brady was incensed at the price he was paying for the team of six. The Mule Trader's attitude was 'demand and supply' dictated the price.

Brady sold his and Father Davis' oxen for a reasonable price considering that they could only be used locally or for drawing wagons returning south.

Dirk had spoken briefly of his ambush experience, and subsequent rescue and nursing by the Kalanga girl. He requested that Sister Hannah check on her welfare at the General Store on reaching Francistown.

Grace, Sister Hannah and Luka walked two miles from the hospital to the General store in Francistown. Sister Hannah explained to the Storekeeper that they were close friends of Dirk Prinsloo and were there to meet with Thandie, the young Kalanga Girl that Dirk had left in his employ.

The Storekeeper seemed extremely nervous and stated that it was impossible since it was Thandie's day off and she had gone to meet with relatives. He said that he would pass on the information to Thandie that her friends could be located at the hospital when she returned, making a hasty retreat into the back of the store.

Neither Grace nor Hannah were convinced by this story since Dirk had said she had been shunned by her family. The ladies purchase two chickens and a sack of sweet potatoes and returned to the hospital. Some hours had passed when Sister Hannah was told that Luka was outside with a patient. When Hannah reached Luka, he was standing with a black woman dressed in a plain frock. Her face was badly swollen on one side, forcing her right eye to be closed completely. Her lips were also swollen.

"This is Thandie," said Luka. "She has been beaten!" Thandie was taken into the clinic where her wounds were bathed and treated. Doctor Blackie gave her a thorough examination. Apart from the bruising to her face, Thandie was in reasonable health. Sister Hannah put her into a cot and told her to sleep. The girl was nervous in case the Storekeeper's wife came looking for her. Hannah assured her she was quite safe.

The girl slept for a full twelve hours and upon awakening the swelling around her eye had eased affording her partial vison, albeit through a weepy eye. She was hungry and thirsty. With the assistance of a Ward Aid, acting as an interpreter, Grace and Sister Hannah were able to glean that the Storekeeper's wife ran a string of prostitutes that were available to the travellers staying at the storekeepers Hotel. Thandie had refused to be incorporated into the "House" and was beaten several times. The Madam saw her as an ideal target as she did not have family, friends or any alternate refuge. The Settler who dropped her off was unlikely to return. She had witnessed this on several occasions. Once the girl became a burden, she was simply abandoned with a handful of empty promises. Thandie was informed that the beatings would continue until she agreed to sell herself to the travellers. She was told that she was a fool to believe the Settler would return for her.

When Anna related to William all that had happened to the young African girl he was furious and inclined to go down to the Store and confront the keeper and his wife. It was decided that the issue would be discussed with Dr Blackie, William and Father Davis, who decided to meet the following morning.

"I have been aware of the brothel run by the Storekeeper's wife for some time now as I have treated some of the ladies who work there. I have reported the fact to the Police Constable of the Bechuanaland Police who visits this area on a fortnightly basis. There has been little he can do since there are no witnesses and I am bound by patient confidentiality not to release names. There is also a strong contingent of workers employed by the Mine, and other entities in the settlement that wish the establishment to continue, William. I think you may be taking on more than you realise if you tackle this the wrong way," stated Dr Blackie. "It seems to me the way forward, in order to gain a result, will be for Thandie to lay an assault charge against the Storekeeper's wife. The Doctor can substantiate the wounds that support Thandie's testimony. What is needed is a witness," said Father Davis.

"Well," said William, "There are a few practical items to consider! We need to decide what we will do with Thandie. Obviously she cannot return to her previous situation. Dirk is a man of his word and he will return for her, of that I have no doubt. I do not know the context of their relationship, but, as a good friend of Dirk's, I must ensure that she is looked after until his return."

Dr Blackie said, "We are requiring some assistance within the Laundry at present. When Thandie is well enough, which should be in a day or so, we can see if she would be happy to assist there. This will give her lodging and a very small wage.

"That is very kind Doctor. The additional issue is the collection of her belongings. Can I suggest that Father Davis, Sister Hannah and myself escort Thandie and call on the Store-keeper to collect her belongings?"

Thandie was reluctant to retrieve her belongings at first, but when she heard that the two men and the Sister would accompany her, she was more at ease.

The new team of mules drew the wagon to the General store. Thandie and her escorts followed in after her. The storeman took one look at Thandie and knew this was not going to be a pleasant encounter. Father Davis took the lead.

"I believe that this young lady is in your employ? She has just been released from the hospital where she was treated for injuries sustained whilst under you care?"

"I ere…have no idea aa…"

William leaned over the counter, towering over the aproned man, and said, "Have a good look at the girl's face for you won't see her again until she has healed and the legal proceedings take place. Now we wish to collect her belongings and any monies she may be entitled to." The storeman stared at William as he comprehended the threat.

"Now!" said William, slamming his huge fist on the counter.

The storeman scuttled out of the store calling for Miriam. A solidly built coloured lady appeared, and was obviously slightly shaken to see Thandie in the company of Father Davis, Sister Hannah, and William. However, she quickly gathered herself and moved towards Thandie with hands out stretched, she said, "Where have you been, my poor child. I have been worried about you and, what happened to your face?" Thandie moved away from the advance and William stepped in between them.

"What we require from you are Thandie's belongings and her wages. We aren't fooled by your gracious talk as we know the truth!" The woman looked beyond William and shouted threatening remarks at Thandie in Kalanga.

"That's enough of that," said William to the Storekeeper, "and I suggest you take control of this situation immediately."

The storekeeper, obviously fearful of his aggressive wife, responded timidly, "Miriam, please. The police are now involved. We must assist and follow the request of these people. We cannot afford this type of trouble."

Scowling now with a look of disgust, she turned towards the Storekeeper.

"You act like a beaten dog with your tail between your legs, my husband. The girl knows where to find her belongings and she has been absent from work for three days. I have employed others to complete her work and, therefore, she is owed nothing."

With that she turned on her heel, whilst muttering a stream of obscenities.

She disappeared into one of the rondavel rooms, rudely dismissing the group.

Sister Hannah and Thandie followed the Storekeeper to her lodgings where she retrieved her few belongings. Father Davis and William stood in the shade awaiting the return of the ladies. The Storekeeper approached Father Davis.

"I am deeply sorry for this trouble, Father. Obviously, there has been a misunderstanding!"

"My dear man. There is no misunderstanding about the beating the young lady has received. We have no doubt who was responsible, and we also know the ungodly reason for the beating."

"Father, please. There must be some way that we can settle this business without involving the law?"

"That decision is not mine to make. You will need to appeal to the person laying the charge. The ladies had boarded the wagon." Father Davis climbed up next to William and, looking down at the Storekeeper, he said, "The wages of sin is death. You would do well to consider the manner in which you and your wife earn your wages!" With that, the mule wagon moved off towards the Mine Hospital.

Thandie had no understanding of the white man's laws. She had no idea that she would be able to report the brutal beating she had received from the Storekeeper's wife, to the police. A 'body' that she could expect to investigate the reported crime and the perpetrator to be penalised accordingly. She was grateful for the support and care that she had received from these Nuns and the Settler men. How they knew Dirk she did not exactly understand, but she knew it was in connection with this Railway to which Dirk had returned.

Released

After surrendering all their Railway equipment, the two Prinsloo brothers were reduced to a few personal items, but most importantly, their money belts were full. Both men had been offered jobs by Burns himself if ever they wished to join the Railway again. They were anxious to return to Francistown. Since their weapons had been handed back to Cape Railway they remained with their Martini Henri and the old Shotgun. Dirk took hold of the rifle and handed the shotgun to Marty. Instantly Marty thought of Llewellin and the lioness. He smiled and related the story to Dirk, who chuckled when Marty described how Llewellin couldn't stop talking and shaking at the same time!

"Oh M-M-Man, how I miss h-h-his humour and l-l-l-lopsided smile," said Marty.

Dirk nodded, as he patted his brother on the shoulder and said, "We had better get going, Broer."

The brothers had purchased a horse to replace Dirk's and two mules to carry extra water and their few belongings. The two men made good time, stopping before the heat of day and then proceeding late afternoon for a couple of hours before setting up camp for the night.

On the third morning, which was cool and dry, the brothers were following the trail, which dipped gradually down towards a dry riverbed. Suddenly a mother warthog, followed by three hoglets, came shooting out of the scrub and down the trail in front of them. Following immediately behind was the largest leopard Dirk had ever seen. The huge ginger and black spotted cat caught up with the rear piglet and simply swatted it on its hind quarter, causing it to spiral to one side, where the leopard scooped it up into its crushing jaws, hardly hesitating as it loped off into the scrub leaving the warthog mother with one less dependent! The incident had taken seconds and a life was taken. Africa certainly was a place of the quick and the dead thought Dirk.

Grace had been selfishly fearful regarding Marty's safety when he had taken leave to find Dirk. She knew that he and Dirk were inseparable and that her future husband would not rest until he had found his brother. This new love that she and Marty had found was wonderful, yet unbearable at the same time. She had prayed in earnest and on so many occasions over the twenty days that he had been away. She had pestered William for news when he was about, but he would always respond by saying 'no news is good news, Grace, be patient.'

When he suddenly appeared galloping on his horse 'bare back' alongside the wagon she was unable to talk. She simply sobbed with relief, and only after the wagons had turned and pulled up near the ailing Llewellin was she able to control the convulsive weeping.

Marty and Grace had no long-term plans, as they really hadn't had the chance to discuss the future. Marty had simply said that Grace should remain with Anna and William until they were married. It was fortunate that Grace and Anna had found such a strong friendship and so easily.

William was preparing for the travel to Matabeleland. He and Luka had hunted two Kudu, both of which were showing the effects of the drought. Luka assisted William to hang the heavy carcases from the branch of a large tree ready for skinning. The little yellow man spoke continuously to the dead Kudu explaining that their meat was extremely important and would be enjoyed by many. The kudu was by far William's favourite antelope, although smaller than the eland, Africa's largest of the antelope, the kudu males stand up to sixty inches tall, and weigh about six hundred pounds. They may vary in colour from reddish brown to a blueish grey with vertical white striped markings along their torso. They have a short spinal crest, and a nose chevron. The males have a beard which darkens with age, but their most distinguishing features are a set of tubular, twisting horns which are the longest of any antelope, up to 70 inches long. A truly beautifully-marked and adorned animal.

After skinning, the men carefully butchered the antelope wasting nothing. The good cuts were cut into thick strips and placed within several large baths ready to be treated with a combination of spices. Biltong was originally created by Dutch pioneers in South Africa…"Voortrekkers", who needed reliable food sources on their long treks across the continent. The method and spice mix hasn't changed much in hundreds of years, and comprises as follows: Brown vinegar, salt, brown sugar, black pepper and coriander. The strips of meat are coated with this mix of spices, then allowed to stand in a cool dry place for a day to soak.

The strips are then hung in a cool dry place for 10 to 14 days in order to cure and dry. This meat, once cured, will last for extensive periods if stored in a cool dry environment. The venison has a mild, wild game type flavour, which is enjoyed by most people. William was interested to learn that the word 'Biltong' came from the Dutch language where 'bil' meant hind-quarter and the word 'tong' means strips.

Father Davis was becoming more involved in the Tati Mining community by the day. He had received correspondence from the Missionary Society confirming that the Hope Fountain Mission near Bulawayo had been destroyed and that he and the three Sisters should travel to Inyati Mission. This Mission was planted by Robert Moffat in 1859, having received permission from Lobengula. The mission was situated sixty miles north of Bulawayo.

Rev Davis was in no hurry to move on now, as he saw the needs in the new Francistown, which was experiencing all the excitement and pain of a 'Gold Rush' with prospectors and fortune seekers arriving daily. Many who had spent their last penny were now broke and starving, desperate for work and lodgings.

Grace, when not attending Anna and little Francis, worked alongside Thandie in the Hospital laundry. This was hard physical labour and the two young women enjoyed the challenge. Whilst working together they had developed a language that enabled them to communicate surprisingly well. One afternoon the ladies were taking a rest break after hanging heavy sheets and blankets out to dry when Grace noticed the cross that hung around Thandie's neck. She was amazed since she was quite sure that Thandie was not a Christian. She asked Thandie why she wore the cross and she noted that Thandie became shy, self-conscious, as she covered the cross with her hand. She was quiet for a moment then turned to Grace and said 'Dirk'.

Unfortunately, Grace reacted with a surprised look and said, "You and Dirk?" in a moment of disbelief. At which Thandie dropped her head and began to weep, before turning and running from Grace's side. Immediately filled with a sense of guilt, Grace called after her, but she had disappeared from sight. The following morning Thandie arrived at the hospital dressed in her tribal attire and announced she intended to return to her uncle.

The August sun was dropping towards the horizon pulling the golden heat like a warm blanket from the darkening world. Marty pulled his jacket from his carpet bag.

"We should stop and camp for the night," he called to Dirk who was slightly ahead of him.

"Ja, Broer, (brother) but we are just a few miles from Tati."

"Dirk, s-s-s-soon it will be pitch d-d-dark and we w-will be asking f-f-f-f-for trouble!"

Silence from the older brother.

"D-Dirk!"

"Ok, ok…let's move off the trail and look for a good spot."

The brothers were extremely efficient setting themselves up for the night. Each had a mosquito net which they hung from the same tree to cover their canvas bed rolls. They built a small fire and placed sweet potatoes in the coals. These were eaten with hard biscuit and biltong. Marty loved his coffee with a touch of brandy at the end of the day. The chill of the night encouraged the pair into their blankets. Dirk's horse was uneasy, snorting and stamping, pulling against her tether.

"Don't be concerned," said Dirk, "It's just the mosquito net blowing in the wind, she is not used to it yet."

Marty's horse and the mules joined the restless snorting and stamping in concert with Dirk's mare. Marty rolled out of bed noiselessly. He instinctively grabbed the shot gun next to his bed roll and crept towards the horses. The moon was bright and visibility good, but initially he could not locate the cause of the horse's anxiety. He eased over to a small anthill and watched with nerves taught and shotgun at the ready. For a moment the animals seemed to quieten, when all of a sudden a small figure appeared, standing up right, it appeared to have a large head and wore a cape, it moved over to the mule packs, which were on the ground behind the horses, again causing them to stir. Marty shivered with fright. He immediately thought of the Tokoloshe, of which the Zulus often referred. This was a half-human spirit-creature, small in stature, but extremely evil.

From this angle, if Marty should fire the shot gun he was sure to injure one or more of the horses. He moved slowly closer whilst the creature endeavoured to open the pack. Just ten yards away and trembling, Marty carefully placed the shotgun on the ground. With a burst of speed he ran, diving headlong, he tackled the 'Tokoloshe', which let out a high-pitched scream. Marty screamed as well!

"D-D-D Dirk, Dirk! Help, H-H-H-Help!" The small figure fought like a demon! Wildly kicking and scratching and, my goodness, did it smell bad! Immediately Dirk was there and pulled the creature from beneath Marty. The two men manhandled their struggling and evil-smelling captive to the fire side and lit the lamp. What the light revealed, much to Marty's relief, was a very dirty European child, about ten years old. He wore a knitted jersey that was many sizes too large and hung down to his lower legs. The sleeves were missing and frayed. Baggy trousers peeped out from beneath the filthy oversized jersey. Upon his feet were a pair of worn wellington boots, also more than a few sizes too large. He had a bush of curly brown hair that would be admired if it was not so dirty and matted.

Marty had regained control of himself.

"He's just a child," said Dirk, raising his eyebrow at his younger brother as he did when he expected an explanation?

"G-goodness Dirk, in the d-darkness he looked like a T-Tok-Tokoloshe!"

"Really," said Dirk, "and what exactly does a Tokoloshe look like?"

They turned their attention back to the child who stared back at them with large and fearful brown eyes. Dirk addressed the captive, "Who are you and where are you from?" No response, only the stare. Dirk repeated the question in Afrikaans and Zulu to no response. Marty was still hanging on to his captive's arm, which he had twisted round behind him. Looking down he noted how thin the boy was. Immediately he began to feel pity for the child. Perhaps, thinking of his own childhood, although he had always had Dirk to look after him.

Marty let him go and walked over to the fire side. He pulled a sweet potato out of the warm coals and gave it to the boy. The child took his eyes off Dirk for a moment and almost swallowed the potato whole!

"Well," said Dirk, "What should we do with him?"

"Not su-sure," said Marty. "I'll give him a bag of f-f-food and let him g-g-g-go his way." With that Marty rummaged about giving the boy a food bag. The boy received the bag without a sound and remained standing where he was. The brothers told him several times that he was free to leave. They eventually doused the lantern and climbed into their bed rolls. Strangely, the boy simply stood where he was. After a time Marty pulled out a blanket. He made sure he placed it down wind and indicated that their young guest lie down on the blanket. Marty returned to his bed roll and watched as, slowly, the child laydown and wrapped himself in the warm cover.

Morning arrived with the visitor still wrapped in the blanket and asleep, although there was evidence that he had attacked the food bag. The brother's rose, washed and made a hasty breakfast of biscuits and coffee.

The boy woke with the two men watching him. He walked off a distance to relieve himself, then returned. Marty offered him coffee and biscuits which he took without a sound. Dirk insisted that the boy wash his hands before he ate, pouring water from a hessian waterbag over the claw like hands with dirty black finger nails. Dirk found the smell of the boy nauseating. After breakfast the brothers loaded the mules and saddled the horses. The boy watched.

"Dirk, w-w-we can't leave h-h-him here! It's o-o-o-obvious he has n-n-nowhere to go."

"Yes, you are right, but he's not riding with me. You found him!"

"I'll put him on Molly." (One of the mules.)

Marty took the boy by the arm, leading him to the mule he patted the bony spine of the mule and the boy climbed up without a word, still holding tightly to the blanket and food bag as one of his oversized boots fell from his dirt encrusted foot. The trio set off. Dirk and Marty were both anticipating their individual reunions on arriving back at Francistown. However, their guests' thoughts were locked behind his large brown eyes.

Dirk's Final Decision

The arrival of the brothers caused great excitement at the hospital. Grace clung to Marty as though she would never again let him out of her sight. There were hugs and handshakes all round with a great deal of excited chatter, with Luka dancing and skipping as was his custom when greeting friends. Anna paraded little Francis and, as usual, the little fellow smiled at everyone as if he knew them well. This trait really tickled his father, and he laughed with proud delight at his son. When Anna saw the young boy standing quietly, forgotten near the mules, still clutching the food bag and blanket, she enquired of Dirk, "Who is this young man?"

"We don't know, Miss Anna. He came scavenging at our camp, obviously alone and staving."

"Oh, the poor child," said Anna. "What is his name and where did he come from?"

"We don't know, Miss Anna. He doesn't talk. Careful," said Dirk, "He is filthy dirty and really ripe!"

"Ripe?"

"Yes, he stinks, Miss Anna."

Instantly, she was filled with compassion for the child as he watched the happy reunion within which he could not share. Anna passed Francis to his father, then she approached the child slowly. She halted a yard away from him and said, "Hello, my name is Anna!" The boy stared at her.

She smiled and simply held out her hand. The boy hesitated for a moment then reached out and took her hand. She led him to William who was still holding little Francis. Anna introduced him as "Mr William Brady, who is my husband, and this is little Francis."

Brady said, "Pleased to meet you young man." Baby Francis looked at the boy and gave his charming smile. A flicker of a smile crossed the young boys face and was gone.

"I'm sure you are thirsty and would like a drink," said Anna. She led the boy into the rondavel and poured the boy a mug of cool milk, which he devoured.

Brady lifted Francis and sniffed at his nappy, but it was clean. Brady realised the unpleasant odour came from the boy! Dirk was about to proceed to the General Store, anxious to see Thandie. Grace had watched him intently since the brothers had arrived back. She wondered if William had related to Dirk all that had transpired. She was acutely aware that it was her reaction to Thandie's intimation, that she was in a relationship with Dirk, that had caused the girl to leave. However, Anna had counselled her saying that Thandie was obviously having doubts herself and Grace should not blame herself solely for the episode. Just at that moment William came walking out of the rondavel, and called out to Dirk.

"Hold on a minute Dirk, I must speak with you." Dirk waited patiently for Brady to come alongside himself.

"What is it William. Is this concerning Thandie?"

"Yes Dirk. How did you know?"

"I just had a feeling."

"Well Dirk the wife of the storeman, who is not a likeable woman, physically beat Thandie because she would not join her clutch of prostitutes that service her husband's Hotel." Dirk stiffened at the news.

"We only discovered this because you had requested Sister Hannah to visit her and ensure she was well, which the good Sister did the day after we arrived at the Hospital. She was told that she could not see Thandie as it was her day off and she had gone to visit family. The Ladies knew that this information was not correct because you had told us that Thandie had no family to go to. Well, little Luka found her and led her to the hospital where the Doctor treated her wounds. We kept her here whilst she recovered for a couple of days and then Father Davis, Sister Hannah, myself and Thandie returned and confronted the storeman and his wife after having lodged an assault charge against his wife with the Police." Dirk was becoming more agitated as William continued.

"So where is Thandie now, William?"

"We don't know, Dirk. She worked here at the hospital in the laundry for two weeks and all was well, then this morning she arrived in her native dress and said she was returning to her Uncle. The ladies tried to convince her to stay but she said she did not understand the Settlers ways and was better off with her own kind. Luka may know more since he was the last to talk to her this morning."

Dirk walked towards his horse with deep anger and disappointment. Luka was assisting Marty to remove the packs from the mules.

"She goes to the Mission, 'Nkosi" (Empandeni).

Marty then said, "That will take her days on foot. Some of her Villagers who had survived the burning of their settlement were at the Mission. Dirk, we found her at the Mission before she led us to find you. But that was a good six weeks ago!"

Luka said, "I can find her, Nkosi, if we go now."

"Please get your horse, Luka, and we will go CheChe." The two cantered off within a cloud of grey dust. Marty stared after them with a look of concern on his face.

Brady was extremely happy to be reunited with his former Scouts. He had hoped that they would join him and Anna on their journey to Bulawayo. Nothing had been confirmed, but then again, situations had altered so rapidly, reasoned Brady. The three men had not had the opportunity to sit down and have a constructive conversation.

Grace had spoken to Father Davis about a Marriage Service on Marty's return to which he had smiled and answered, "Just name the day, My Dear, and it will be my pleasure!" So, Brady assumed the marriage would happen very soon, which was good because he was anxious to move northwards. Dirk's situation was a bit of an anomaly. Brady realised now that there may be a stronger relationship between Dirk and the native girl than mere friendship. Brady being anxious to leave was methodically ensuring all his preparations were complete, whilst Francis grew stronger and larger every day.

The following morning Brady could stand the smell of the boy no more. He filled the copper bath with warm water. He endeavoured to explain to the boy he needed to bathe. There was no response. He walked the boy to the bath and the child bolted. William chased him around the hospital yard causing some hilarity amongst the onlookers. Eventually, exhausted, he cornered the boy. In desperation he called Anna who simply walked over to the wide-eyed child, took his trembling hand and led him calmly to the bath. William lifted the lad, ragged clothes and all into the warm soapy water. The boy was crying softly now but had relented, accepting his fate. William coaxed him to remove all his filthy clothing and he scrubbed him with carbolic soap. In some areas on the boys emaciated body the dirt was ingrained and would take several baths to remove. William, who was now completely soaked himself, lifted the boy from the tub and towelled him dry. Anna had located a set of small men's pyjamas into which the boy was placed temporarily. William lifted the wet discarded clothes with a stick and placed them into the boiler fire which hissed and spluttered as if in disgust. Anna hugged the boy comforting him, cloaking his embarrassment. She and Grace spent a good deal of the morning cutting the child's matted bush of hair. Washed and groomed the boy sat next to a window basking in a warm shaft of silvery sunlight as he overcame his bathing ordeal. When Brady walked into the room, he was struck by how handsome, almost angelic, the boy looked within his silvery halo of light and spotless hospital pyjamas.

William and Marty had sat down and discussed the future over a coffee and buttermilk rusks. When William suggested that Marty and Grace join him and Anna on their journey to Bulawayo Marty agreed readily, saying that he and Grace had hoped that they would receive an invitation to accompany the Brady's!

Brady asked about Dirk's future intentions, to which Marty replied.

"I'm unsure William. I received a message from Dirk last evening saying that he had located Thandie, and he would make contact with us in a few days. The message was delivered by Luka after he returned from finding Thandie. I have a feeling that Dirk and Thandie will end up together!"

Dirk Confronts the Storeman

The second Dirk entered the General Store, the Storekeeper looked up toward him and recognition was instant, he dropped slightly, holding onto the counter cowering, with intense fear. Dirk wore his leather vest and held his rifle across his bulging chest, his hair had been blown backward by the wind creating a tangled main, he looked like a wild man, surely this vision would have intimidated even an innocent man.

"I believe you owe me an explanation you lying, thieving, vulture." Demanded Dirk as he held the quivering man by the front of his dirty apron, twisting the cloth such that the string tightened around his throat.

Yes, yes, please Mr Prinsloo, don't hurt me, the police have already been and charges have been laid, I am sorry, my wife cared for the girls I had no idea.

"Just like Adam blaming Eve hey? You have no excuse my agreement was made with you!"

"Please, sir my wife and I have separated after all this trouble, sir. Please…I am very sorry for the manner in which your Black Girl was treated!" Whined the storeman pathetically.

"She is not my 'Black Girl', she is my wife!"

"Oh yes, sorry— forgive me, yes of course. Well sir, I have your wife's wages for the work she completed, and I have included an extra five pounds in compensation for all the trouble she experienced."

"I will pass on your apology and these wages, but let me tell you that my wife and I intend to settle and live hereabouts and my presence will be a constant reminder that you can never be trusted and although I will not exact my revenge on you now, believe me, if you give me the slightest excuse, in the future I will destroy you and your business. Now where does one go to purchase land in this area?"

"I will make it up to you Mr Prinsloo I have learned my lesson, the Tati Mine Commission would be your best bet, sir." He wheezed.

"Where can I find them?" asked Dirk releasing the red faced but very relieved man.

They have their offices at the Mine. I will gladly take you there, sir, no trouble at all.

Dirk, accompanied by the Mine Land Representative, rode ten miles southeast of the Mine to a tributary of the Shashi River, where several fifty acre lots were up for sale. Dirk selected the Lot with the most trees and several pools of stagnant green water, which still remained in the riverbed during the height of the drought season. He was extremely pleased with the property he had chosen and purchased.

"You have bought at a perfect time and for a reasonable price, Mr Prinsloo. With the present gold-rush the value will only increase," the Land Representative said as they shook hands in parting.

"Your 'Deed of Sale' will be ready within one week."

Dirk and Thandie had camped on the outskirts of the town within a wooded area. After purchasing the land, Dirk had returned to the Hospital. There he explained to Marty his intentions to build up a poultry farm to feed the new town and Mining community. The men were joined by William who was excited when told of Dirk's plan and very interested in the land purchase. Dirk told the men that he would take Thandie as his wife.

Marty was silent but only for a moment, and then he said, "If being with Thandie brings you happiness, Dirk, then you have mine and Grace's blessing." Marty stood and hugged his brother. The release of tension from Dirk was visible. William had sensed the 'pent up' emotion in Marty and realised he must have done a huge amount of soul searching to respond the way he had. William shook Dirk's hand, wished him well and asked if he and Marty might come and view the land he had purchased? The following morning the trio rode out to the plot of land. Dirk chose the site of his future dwelling after having much discussion with Marty and William. That evening when the men arrived back at the hospital Thandie was there with the ladies in her western frock.

The ladies prepared a 'braaivleis' on an open fire. A canvas ground sheet was laid near the warm fire on which the boy and young Francis sat together. Glasses were filled and even Father Davis indulged in a weak whisky and water! After a good feast all were tired and the night had set in. The Doctor rose from his seat and said, "Well, I have examined the boy and can find no fault with him apart from the fact that he is a little undernourished and has endured immense mental anguish recently. So…I have something that I think will prove to be the best medicine for him at this time."

The Doctor walked off to his Rondavel and returned with a bundle in his arms that wriggled about. The doctor bent down and handed a golden coloured Staffordshire puppy to the boy, whose face lit up immediately. The little dog stretched up and licked the boy's face repeatedly, all the while, wriggling its rubber-like body with its tail wagging wildly from side to side. The boy began to giggle whilst attempting to sit up upright, but the puppy's eager energy pushed him over onto his back, and the dog bounced onto the boy's chest. His laughter was infectious and an enormous relief to Anna. From that time onwards, the dog and the boy were inseparable!

That night the dog slept on an empty maize sack next to the boy. William, when checking on the boy much later in the night, heard whispering in a strange language. He was astonished when realising it was the boy. He had lifted the puppy into his blankets and was consoling it. The following morning William informed Father Davis of his discovery. Father Davis smiled and suggested that the puppy would induce the boy to talk to it and William and Anna needed to listen for obvious words like 'no' and 'sit' and the name the boy would give to his new 'best' friend.

As Father Davis had anticipated the boy spoke to the pup in his own language and Anna recognised it as Polish. 'Nie' and 'dol', were the first two Polish words the boy uttered in Anna's presence, meaning 'no' and 'down'.

William, through the mine administration, located a Polish Fitter. Filip Adamik. William explained to him about the boy and requested that he come and talk to the youngster so that they might find out his name, where he came from and so on. Filip agreed and they set a time. Filip arrived at the Hospital the following evening as agreed. Anna, William, Francis, the boy and Filip sat at the table for dinner. Anna insisted that the boy put the puppy in the kennel outside whilst they ate and wash his hands. This was done mainly with hand signals, confirmed in English, to which the boy had been responding well. The bond between him and Anna was becoming stronger and more obvious on a daily basis. When all were seated and grace had been said by William, the meal was served and small talk was initiated.

Filip turned to the boy and introduced himself in Polish. He asked the boy his name, to which the boy responded shyly, "Gabriel Bosko, sir."

"That is a good strong name, Gabriel, and where do you come from?"

To this question the boy dropped his head. For some time he was silent and then still with head down, he said quietly, "I don't know. From a mine which my father worked but the mine collapsed and he was covered completely, only his legs were visible. I tried to dig him out, but the rocks were too big for me to move. His legs did not move and I think he was dead. After three days I buried his legs with stones. I waited for many days for help to arrive but no one came and when my food ran out, I decided it was best to leave. We lived under a canvas awning against the hill and we had very little. So I took what I could carry and left."

"I am so sorry to hear about your father, Gabriel," said Filip. "How did you arrive here with Mr and Mrs Brady?"

"I followed a path for two days and on the night of the second day I saw the campfire of Mr Marty and Mr Dirk. I waited until they were asleep and then went into their camp to find food. They brought me here."

Filip reached out and placed a hand on his shoulder and said, "Thank you for telling me your story. You can eat now and I will tell Mr William and Mrs Anna your story."

The sun rose, peeping over the wooded hill to the east. Cold and still the horses waited, saddled and ready to go. Luka ate a banana and tossed the skin into a rubbish pit nearby. Marty and William were inside with Anna.

"No, William, the boy…ah…Gabriel, has been through enough. I don't think he will gain anything by going back."

"Alright. Well, Marty and Luka, you will have to track the boy's movements from your old camp?"

The three men set off up the road. Marty had no trouble finding his and Dirk's camp site where they had captured the boy. Luka studied the tracks. He identified the Wellington boots and located where the boy had crossed the trail to get to the camp. Once on the trail he began to move quite swiftly. He was able to read the trail from the back of his pony. Gabriel had stuck to paths wherever possible, making tracking simple for Luka and Marty. They located where the boy had spent the night, showing good survival skill by climbing up into a Mopane tree. There were several implements which had been discarded along the trail which had obviously been too heavy for the boy to carry. A short time before midday the three men came to a small working. The dwelling area, adjacent to the mine comprised a canvas tarpaulin secured to the hillside then stretched over a timber frame. The canvas was held down along the base at the foot of the frame by large rocks. In the centre of the room created by the canvas was a 'T' shaped beam which prevented the canvas from sagging in the middle. Two sides of the room remained open which kept the room relatively cool. The contents of the room were meagre, including a wooden crate which served as a table and a bed covered with cardboard, which acted as a mattress. Two canvas chairs leaned against the wooden crate.

A portal, or entry, to the mine was cut into the hillside. Marty entered the darkened passage and hesitated for a short while for his eyes to adjust. There was a faint odour of death. A hand cart was half filled with ore just inside the entrance, a few feet beyond the catastrophic rock fall. Marty backed out telling William that it was extremely unstable. No shoring of the mine 'backs' or roofing had been done and he could see daylight through the cracks between large granite boulders above. He had also seen where the poor young man had buried the legs of his father.

"It is no wonder the child never spoke when we found him! How do you explain a tragedy and an existence like this?" said Marty shaking his head sadly.

William agreed. Luka foraged in the dwelling to see if there was anything of value that might be collected for Gabriel. He found a small leather bag which contained personal papers and a bag of salt. There were no other items of value. Very, very sad thought William. The papers were all in Polish—he would hand them over to the authorities. When William returned to the Hospital, he informed the Doctor of what they had found. The Doctor took charge of the papers and agreed to complete the formalities.

Father Davis and the Nuns alternated in providing English lessons for Gabriel. The boy was flourishing. He had named his puppy Zloto (Gold), and the two did everything together.

Anna, in her loving manner, set strict rules for Gabriel and Zloto and the boy always did his very best to abide by these rules. The bond between Gabriel and Anna was quite remarkable. He did not remember his mother and, obviously, Anna was an ideal substitute. He would sit with little Francis and practice his English on both Francis and Zloto, which was extremely comical at times.

His ability to communicate grew daily and William found he enjoyed having the boy's company. He realised that the child must have laboured for his late father, as he was quite mature, capable and responsible when allocated a task.

Gabriel took a particular liking to one of the mules, because it was not fussed by the puppy and he was able to ride it with the dog perched in front of his saddle. This opened the door for him to accompany the men and Luka, who loved imparting his bush knowledge to the boy.

There was great excitement about the Hospital. Grace looked lovely in her wedding dress. The ladies all crowded around her in last minute preparations. The men waited patiently for the bride, whilst Anna stood ready with her piano-organ to play the Bridal March. Father Davis had donned his habit and collar and Dirk stood shoulder to shoulder with his brother. From the rear it was difficult to tell who was who?

All the ladies appeared and took their seats. Anna began to play. Grace was on William's arm as they walked between the chairs, followed by Sister Hannah, holding a lovely bouquet of flowers. William 'gave Grace away' to be married and Dirk produced the ring. Marty struggled with the oaths, but Grace was fluent. It was a beautiful wedding with happy tears from Sister Hannah.

Dirk and Thandie left the small reception in a state of peace, especially in the knowledge that their marriage was one of mutual agreement and, although without a ceremony, their commitment was just as sacred and strong.

Into Rhodesia and New Horizons

Everything was packed into the Wagons. Two of the Nuns were to remain with Doctor Blackie until their final destination was confirmed. Father Davis and Sister Hannah would travel on to Inyati Mission, beyond Bulawayo. William and Marty and their families would remain together for the immediate future and seek a place to settle once in Bulawayo. Luka had been away from Luderitz for almost three years, and he explained to William that he must return home soon. He told William that he would not be comfortable living in the land of the n'Mandebele for his life would always be in danger. William understood and told his friend that, if and when, he needed to leave he would pay him his accumulated monies and he could leave immediately. Luka replied that he wished to see where William, Gabriel and Francis settled so that in the future he might bring his sons to visit.

William and Anna had heard nothing from the authorities regarding Gabriel and when asked if he wished to remain with the Doctor or travel with William and Anna, he immediately said he wanted to remain with the Brady family. As if to ensure his wish, he moved up next to Anna who placed an arm of comfort around the boy's shoulder.

The Doctor agreed with the decision and informed William that, should there be any recourse, he would correspond with him on the matter. He felt sure the authorities would be happy with the arrangement under the circumstances. The boy had found stability and, no doubt, would receive a sound education once settled in Bulawayo.

A small gathering of 'well-wishers' congregated at the Hospital on the evening of the day before the travellers were due to leave. Anna had put together drinks and snacks for their family and friends. Although Marty and Grace were excited about the next chapter in their lives as a married couple, there was sadness at having to leave Dirk and Thandie. Dirk had brought Thandie in from his newly purchased property to be a part of the farewells.

"Bulawayo is only a few days ride from here, Marty, and you know you will always be welcome," said Dirk, unable to keep the emotion from his voice.

"I'm going to miss you, my brother, but I can assure you that, if things do not work out then we will return. I can always apply to Mr Burns for a job on the Railway," promised Marty.

"Marty, understand that people here in Bechuanaland will accept a mixed marriage, but I do not know the circumstances in Bulawayo. It is time for Thandie and I to settle. Please understand that under different circumstances I would accompany you to Bulawayo." Marty nodded and patted his brother on the shoulder.

The Doctor and Father Davis completed discussions around the future of the Nuns, and once again, the Doctor thanked Father Davis and the Nuns for their selfless care and commitment.

When saying farewell to William and Anna the Doctor became quite emotional and promised to visit once the couple had settled in Bulawayo. He lent down and spoke kindly to Gabriel, petting the puppy and encouraging the boy to look after Zloto.

Two wagons, each with a team of eight mules trundled out of the Hospital yard following two riders. William and Marty rode abreast ahead of Anna and Grace's wagon followed by Father Davis and Hannah in their wagon. Bringing up the rear was Luka on his pony riding alongside Gabriel who felt very grown up riding his mule and perched in front of him was Zloto his dog. An additional mule had been purchased by Marty, at an inflated price, to replace the one now ridden by Gabriel. Anna had not been happy about the boy riding on the mule but had relented eventually, insisting that at the first sign of trouble the boy was to climb into the wagon with her. Gabriel had to promise that he would, in no way, have any involvement in skirmishes or scrapes with other travellers or wild animals. Luka assured Anna that he would be responsible for the boy's safety. Two-hundred-pound sacks of feed had been included on each wagon to feed the mules who would not survive on grazing alone.

Traffic along the trail to Bulawayo, both to and from, was constant but not heavy. The travellers had a distance of fifty-two miles to cover in order to reach Plumtree, which was approximately halfway from Tati Mine area to Bulawayo. Most disconcerting were the number of wagons travelling south that had been abandoned and some with dead oxen still within the traces. These poor beasts had been struck down by the terribly contagious cattle disease that attacked oxen, cattle, buffalo, wildebeest, and warthog.

After four days of travel the group reached a stage post at Ramokgwebana Village situated on the river of the same name. This river formed part of the North Eastern Border of Bechuanaland where traffic crossed to enter Rhodesia.

Anna was exhausted and wished to stop for a few days to rest. Gabriel, had suffered after the first day of riding and had rested in the wagon the second day, but had climbed back into the saddle on the third day. He seemed to have mastered the aches and pains thereafter.

On the morning of the fourth day, four young elephant bulls caused an interruption to travel. They were feeding on acacia pods on the trail, jostling each other from time to time and were obviously flexing their teenage muscles. The largest of the four, a magnificent animal, made several mock charges towards the wagons. Anna and Grace turned their wagon off the road and were attempting to return the way they had come when Marty intervened and assured them that the elephants were simply posturing. Father Davis drove his wagon straight towards the enormous beasts calling out to them, telling them to move on in God's name. The three smaller bulls, being confronted by the oncoming wagon, trotted off the road and into the bush, but the lager bull remained facing the encroaching vehicle. His huge ears were out like sails and his massive trunk swayed from side to side as he faced this impertinent challenge. He pulled up his trunk and charged towards the wagon, only a short distance, then veered off to one side and trumpeted his disgust as he trotted off after his cohorts.

Sister Hannah cried out in fright as the wagon passed the departing bull, now only yards away from the wagon. She then let Father Davis know in a torrent of angry words how she felt about his lack of consideration for her safety. When she had settled down, he simply said, "Bless you, Sister Hannah. I trust you remain as strong in body as you are in or spirit." The red glow on her face was answer enough! The group regathered itself and Zloto continued to bark and growl after the departing elephants!

When the group arrived at the staging post at Ramokgwebana they outspanned and set up camp on the bank of the dry river near a water hole that had been dug into the riverbed. There were large shady trees on the bank and the situation was quite comfortable.

Father Davis, as was his usual practice, went off on his search for lost souls. He visited other travellers camped in the vicinity and sought to preach the 'Good News of the Gospel'.

The following day he returned to the camp with a gentleman of Dutch descent named Gert Strydom. Father Davis introduced Gert to William and Marty and added, "I believe it would be beneficial for us all to hear Gert's story and perhaps we can assist him and his family in some way."

The Afrikaner related how he and his unfortunate family had narrowly escaped being murdered on their farm near Fulabuzi, which was situated just south east of Bulawayo. They were visiting a neighbour when a marauding band had arrived at their homestead. The Matabele Impi had slaughtered every animal they could find, including their dogs. They had burned the homestead and out buildings to the ground. Just a month beforehand the Rinderpest had already decimated their small cattle herd.

After the destruction of their farmstead the family had ended up with very little money as they had invested their every penny in this venture. Gert's wife, Maria, had become ill from the pressures of life in Rhodesia and, like others they had decided to return to family in the Freestate, South Africa. One of the abandoned wagons the group had seen on their trip north had belonged to the Strydoms. Their oxen had died in their traces from the disease which they had obviously contracted before commencing the trip south. The family had remained with the wagon for two days. A pride of lion had arrived at the wagon on the second night and devoured one of the oxen causing the family to seek refuge within the wagon. Once the lion were bloated and disinterested in Gert's family he escorted them away from the wagons to a secure kopje (hill) further south along the road. Fortunately, early the following morning they were uplifted by a freight trader, coming north who transported Gert and his young family back along the trail to Ramokgewbana.

Maria Strydom was suffering from depression and anxiety. Gert was sure that her disposition would not change for the better until she reached the refuge of her parent's home. She had witnessed so much death and destruction and lost all her worldly possessions when her house was burned to the ground. Tales of war bridled in racial hate abounded. Her husband's ex-employer had led the 'Failed Raid' into South Africa, her country of birth, and had been captured. Who were enemies and who were friends? All of these situations had conspired together resulting in her present instability. The couple and their two young children needed help.

Conversations with fellow travellers revolved around the Rinderpest, the Native Rebellion, Jameson's Raid, War between the Boers and the English, availability of food and Rhodes and his Railway. After listening to Gert, William offered to return and collect the Strydom's wagon with his mules the following day. Marty agreed and the men made plans to leave at first light. Gert Strydom was extremely embarrassed as he told William he would not be able to pay him for the service. Father Davis smiled and said, "The Lord will pay them in other ways."

When William related the Strydom's situation to Anna she was filled with empathy for the family. She called Grace and Hannah and the three ladies visited Maria. Maria looked unwell. She had huge black rings about her sunken eyes and she was just skin and bone. Initially, she informed her husband that she did not want company when the ladies arrived, but Gert invited the ladies into the tent and took the small girls out into the sunshine.

The ladies remained with Maria for some time and eventually the broken soul began to share her fears and loses. Her tears flowed as the ladies listened. There was little they could offer in comfort other than to say that the men intended to retrieve the wagon the following day. When the ladies returned later, Zloto was busy dragging baby Francis backwards in the sand by his oversized nappy!

"Gabriel," Anna called, "look what your puppy is doing to my son!" The boy came running, arms full of firewood.

"Zloto, Zloto, no!" he shouted.

Francis was enjoying the tussle, but desperately trying to crawl in the opposite direction. William stuck his head around the wagon and observed the scene. He said to Anna, "Leave the dog. He is teaching Francis to craw in reverse."

Anna bent and scooped the dust covered baby into her arms. She smothered him with kisses and said, "Don't listen to your father!"

Later that evening the two couples sat after supper and spoke quietly about the situation confronting the Strydoms. Maria had told the ladies that she and her husband had left in a hurry. They had not sold their property as many people were leaving or thinking of leaving. The rebellion was continuing in

Mashonaland, with Settlers and Prospectors in remote areas still being murdered. Anna suggested to William that if the property was worth buying, then perhaps they should make an offer as it would solve two problems at once. The Strydoms would have ready cash to purchase their mules and the two couples would have a place to call home.

"But we would be buying without seeing the property, and how do we know we can trust Gert? We hardly know him?" countered William.

"William, Gert strikes me as a good upright person. It is only due to his wife's illness that he is leaving. He told me he wanted to remain and start again, but he was placing his wife's health and wellbeing first," said Marty.

Grace said, "If they own the land there should be a 'Deed of Sale' similar to the one that Dirk received from Tati Administration?"

"That is correct, Grace. If he is willing to sell, then we will definitely have to have that document and the receipt of payment. Talking about payment how much cash can we raise?"

William's question was met with an embarrassed silence.

"Well?"

"William let us all sleep on this and give some thought to what we can afford. If you and Marty can find out more about the property and whether it will suit our needs, then you can propose the sale. If he is in agreement, we can make a combined offer!" suggested Anna.

"That s-s-sounds g-g-g-good to u-us," agreed Marty.

Early the following morning Gert joined William and Marty. The men drove a complete team of eight mules, with a full set of harnesses and draft gear southwards to collect the abandoned wagon. Gabriel had agreed to the loan of his mule to Gert for the trip. Luka remained in the camp to watch over Gabriel and the ladies, although Father Davis was always close at hand. The men made good time and reached the wagon by late morning. The wagon had been ransacked and there were no items of value left. Gert pointed out that there had been very little in the wagon apart from practical items purchased with the last of their money prior to leaving. They completed the gruesome task of moving the ox carcases from the wagon. The stench from the partially eaten and maggot infested remains was most offensive and definitely affected the temperament of men and mules, as they dragged the decomposed bodies away.

Whilst the men worked on the wagon, converting it to accept the team of mules William approached the subject of Gert's abandoned farm. Gert had obtained the land by chance some years before whilst in the employ of Leander Jameson. Members of the Pioneer column were promised a gratuity of three thousand acres. One parcel of land had been allocated to a Pioneer who had died in a shooting accident only months after acquisition. The land was reclaimed and administered by Leander Jameson, who split the parcel of land into two blocks of 1500 acres each and placed them onto a restricted market. Most of the land in and around Bulawayo was already owned by Cecil Rhodes and was extremely hard to obtain. Gert Strydom, on hearing about the land, and being a favoured employee of Jameson's made application and was allocated the right to purchase the land at a reasonable price. The farm was located in the Filabusi area, sixty miles southeast of Bulawayo. The land was considered savannah woodland. Gert had built the now destroyed homestead on a tributary of the Umzingwane river. Marty asked Gert what would happen to the farm now that he had left it, to which he replied that very few people knew he and his family had left. He supposed that when Jameson returned from Britain it would go on the market as 'Abandoned land.'

Marty and William moved away to the mules and discussed what they had heard from Strydom. William stated that he and Anna were able to put £150.00 towards the price thanks to Anna's Dowry. Marty and Grace could raise a further £50.00. The men agreed that they would make Gert the offer of £200.00 for the land which equalled 32p per acre.

Gert's response was quite unexpected. The big, burly, bearded man burst into tears as if a great burden had suddenly been removed from his shoulders. He was so grateful he never questioned the price and he assured William that he had the Deed for the property, though a little browned. It had survived the fire with other papers, within his locked cast iron safe.

All was quiet apart from a barking dog, when the men arrived back at the camp. Anna and Grace came out to meet the men. Luka took charge of the weary horses and mules. Gert walked across to where the ladies stood in the bright moon light, he removed his hat and said, "Thank you for visiting Maria yesterday. It is the first time she has been able to speak to other ladies and explain her pain. This morning she said she felt better before I left her."

Turning to the two men, he said, "William and Marty, how can I thank you for today? Perhaps the farm sale will bring blessing to your families. Goodnight and God bless you all."

Three days after the retrieval of the Strydom wagon, William and the rest of the party were ready to move on. The purchase of the farm had been concluded the previous day. Two hundred pounds had been paid to Mr Gert Paulus Strydom for the property Lot 27A, "Soet Gras Vlei" Filabusi, Matopo District. A receipt was drawn up and witnessed by Rev George Arthur Davis, and signed by all parties. Gert drew a descriptive and intricate map of the trail leading to the farm from a Stage Station named 'Balabala,' which is the 'nDebele name for the Kudu antelope. Attached to the map was a letter which Gert had written to his neighbour, Maj. Graham Campbell. The letter explained what had transpired, and that he, Gert, had sold his farm to William Brady and Martinus Prinsloo, the bearers of his letter. He requested that Campbell offer any assistance to the new owners and that they might require an introduction to young, Mr Foster the Assistant District Commissioner.

"Well said Marty, there is no turning back now. We have paid our money and must now commit to the challenge."

William, Anna, Marty and Grace were determined not to become disheartened by the news they were hearing and, indeed, the alarming sights and devastation left behind by the Rinderpest and the rebellion by the Matabele. Whole families had been slaughtered by the marauding Impis, who were convinced that the Settlers had planted the cattle sickness in order to starve them out of the area. In the north, Mashonaland area, the rebellion continued and, although the combined forces had quelled most of the unrest, small bands of natives continued to murder Settlers in remote areas.

Father Davis likened the groups experience to that of the Israelites, who sent spies to explore the Land of Canaan with instruction to report back after forty days. The spies returned acknowledging the beauty and potential of the land, but spread doubt among the nation stating the land could not be taken because they had seen giants and they were but grasshoppers in comparison!

"Have faith," said Father Davis, "don't see the 'Giants'. See only the tremendous opportunity before you and inhabit the land."

William encouraged his fellow travellers saying, "There is no doubt that the challenges of 1896 will have long lasting effects on the growth of the fledgling nation, but, the arrival of the Railway will have immediate and positive outcomes."

Four days travel brought the group to Plumtree in Rhodesia. Plumtree was a busy little centre with a General store and a BSA Police station. The name Plumtree was adopted for the location due to the abundance of Marula trees or Wild Plum trees in the area. The fruit is the size of a plum and turns from green to yellow when ripe. The soft flesh inside the thin, rubber-like skin is a dull white and has a wild, sweet, very peculiar taste. The hard stone within the fruit contains a nutty kernel which abounds in protein and is sought after by humans and animals alike. Many Africans had turned to this source of food in desperation.

William was able to purchase a recent copy of the Bulawayo Chronicle at the General Store. He was amazed at the number of Bulawayo businesses advertising within its informative pages. Some news spoke of the successes against the marauding bands of Shona rebels in the Mashonaland area. 'Locusts' management was to be introduced in the form of a fungus imported from the Cape Colony which was effective in destroying the pests.

Bulawayo was busy forming a Municipal Council. Electrification of Bulawayo was well under way and would mean that the town would enjoy electricity before London, which was still operating on gas. The optimism within the Chronicle was uplifting but the number of natives languishing in and around the centre of the small village of Plumtree, mainly woman and children, was alarming. After the Matabele rebellion, resettling of the native population had become a major problem, especially since the aftermath of the drought and confiscation of cattle. This had forced the women and children to seek assistance within the settlements as the rinderpest, war and drought, had robbed the region of food.

Later that day William and Marty were returning from a threshing floor with two sacks of feed for their mules, which had cost them twice as much as it should have, when a wagon-load of bagged maize came trundling towards them. One of the sacks on the wagon was leaking maize corns leaving a trail of seed on the sandy trail. A throng of native children (Picanins) followed, frantically retrieving the raw maize pips and consuming the dusty seeds as they came to hand. This pitiful sight left the two men silent in their contemplation!

An atmosphere of mistrust seemed to prevail in the centre, with everyone busy watching everyone else. Those expectant pioneers excitedly arriving in the country and those poor defeated souls that were leaving and, of course, the displaced Matabele all were watching!

Anna was uncomfortable in Plumtree as was Luka and she requested to move on as soon as possible! The group travelled on to Figtree, a small village which is located near a large fig tree, at which visitors to the Matabele and Matopo area would have to wait to receive permission to enter in the days of Lobengula.

The map drawn by Gert Strydom indicated a trail that headed east from Figtree skirting the largest Matopo Hills to the north and passing twenty odd miles south of Bulawayo Town. The route travelled eastwards connecting with the Balabala road just south of the Filabusi turn off. He stated that taking this route would reduce travel to the farm by three days at least.

After discussion with Father Davis, it was decided that the Rev and Sister Hannah would continue north to Bulawayo, by themselves, and then on to Inyati Mission thereafter. The Reverend would have twenty-three miles to travel to Bulawayo from Figtree.

William, Marty and their families would take the eastern route to their farm. With this decided William would endeavour to see Reverend Davis and Sister Hannah in Bulawayo, if not at Inyati Mission.

Tearful goodbyes were said well before the sun rose the following morning. All were ready to travel. Gabriel and Luka had mules and horses in harness and saddled before a quick coffee and rusks were consumed by all. Grace was extremely saddened at saying farewell to Sister Hannah who had been a mother figure to her for many years.

"I will see you again soon enough," promised Sister Hannah. "As soon as the Hope Fountain Mission is rebuilt we will be just down the road from you, according to Mr Strydom."

The wagons parted ways just as streaks of golden light peeped over the Matopo ranges to the Northeast. The landscape changed from open savannah to patches of savannah amongst wooded granite outcrops, magnificently sculptured and balanced rocks that seemed to defy gravity. Gabriel was fascinated as were William and Marty. Out of earshot of the ladies William informed Marty that he was a little anxious about the route they were taking since, although the Matabele had been crushed, he was sure that there would be dissatisfied elements possibly seeking retribution. The nature of the countryside provided excellent ambush positions and the massive outcrops offered extensive lookout positions which, since the area was the 'Matabele Stronghold', they would know intimately. He advised Marty that he and Luka should ride ahead as scouts whilst he, William, rode with the wagon and Gabriel.

Late morning the travellers crossed a sandy river bed. Whilst climbing the bank on the far side of the river the left side front wheel began to squeal loudly. Grace drove the team of mules up the incline until the wagon was on level ground, then stopped beneath a large leafy tree. William examined the wheel.

"Ok. I think we will stop here for a while and have bite to eat while I take a look at this wheel."

By this time Marty and Luka had returned to the wagon. Anna and Grace were quite practised now at producing a cup of tea and a small meal for all in very little time. Gabriel had Francis on a small ground sheet within a wooden framed pen, whilst Zloto was tied to the wagon with a length of hemp rope. The ladies produced a cold stew with maize porridge. Once the meal had been consumed Gabriel indicated the granite outcrop next to the trail and asked if he could climb the rocks and explore.

William's first inclination was 'No' but then he asked Luka if he would go with Gabriel to which the little man readily agreed. He said, "There will be leopards, baboons and snakes in these rocks, but I will teach the young man how to avoid them." The pair left together leaving Zloto, who whined and pulled against his rope. Anna looked on anxiously. William and Marty regreased the wheel hub and retightened all the wheels just for good measure. They waited whilst the ladies repacked the wagon. No sign of Luka and Gabriel.

William picked up his rifle and went off in the direction that Luka and Gabriel had taken up the sloping granite rock. At the summit of the rock the granite broke up into various channels and small gorges. The smell of Hyrax, or Rock Rabbit urine, was strong. Baboons barked a warning from another hill to the west. William called out loudly to Gabriel, who replied almost immediately from a location off to William's left. He scaled the rock between him and Gabriel's voice. He could see the entrance to a cave which began as an overhang. From the entrance to the overhang, looking west was a breath-taking vista that had unrestricted views of the river they had just crossed and the bushland on either side. Gabriel stood at the entrance to the cave looking lost. As William came closer, he could hear Luka's voice sounding as if he were in conversation with someone.

William entered the cave which opened into a large vault. Sunlight reflected off outside walls into the cave. On the granite walls were a myriad of ancient paintings, orange in colour and of individuals and animals of every kind. The people figures carried spears and bows. Some of the figures were male, some female and some children.

Luka was chatting in his Khoisan 'click-click' language to the different figures. He was completely oblivious of William and Gabriel's presence. Trance like, but in absolute reverence, he squatted down and related to the paintings, shaking his head as he chatted. Smiling from time to time, weeping at other times. William took Gabriel by the hand and led him back to the wagon where the group remained for several hours.

Eventually, Luka appeared, tears running down his stubble covered cheeks. He came to William and squatted down on his haunches. He looked up at the white man and said, "This is the place of my ancestors. This is where my people come from. I have seen their stories. I have spoken to them and told them that I have come from a distant land where there is much sand, a few trees and very little water, but we look after the animals and hunt them only to eat in the same way as they did in their time here. I have told them how we have moved away from here because of the Matabele. I have told them of my sons, and my wives. It is now time for me to return home, Nkosi. It was good for me to come here, to meet with my ancestors, and to see where my fathers have come from. But now I must go home. I am pleased...my spirit is happy. I have seen that your home and that of Gabriel and Francis will be in the land of my ancestors."

William explained that there was an additional two days of travel to his new home, and that he, Luka, was due money for the time of work since they had left the railway which would need to be settled. All Luka's accumulated monies prior to William leaving the Cape Railway had been wired to Johann, in Luderitz. Johann had agreed to forward the monies to Lukas's women and sons.

"I will need a small amount for travel with Nichana (short one) and I need very little." Since Luka could not be encouraged to remain, the travellers scraped together £15.10s. Luka trotted off on his little pony. He halted some distance away, turned and gave a final wave before disappearing around a small outcrop. His total possessions included two blankets, a small food pouch, a water skin, a quiver of five arrows, his small bow and an assegai. He had a small shoulder bag within which he carried his money and a letter confirming his ownership of his horse.

Anna, Marty and William were deeply saddened by Luka leaving and William was doubtful that he would see the little yellow man again, or that he would reach Lüderitz alive. He would need to travel a distance of some 1,300 miles through some extremely hostile country. William had learned so much from this humble and disciplined man. Remarkably, he had not a stroke of western education, yet he was able to impart such a purity of wisdom and friendship whilst in an attitude of servitude. William felt as though there were a huge weight on his chest, as he fought the impulse to sob. The whole family would feel the loss of Luka.

William insisted that Gabriel ride in the wagon for the following two days. He and Marty took turns in scouting the route up ahead. They saw groups of Matabele women, children and the elderly foraging for food along the trail, but no warriors were seen. The granite outcrops diminished as they travelled east. On the third day after the departure of Luka, they reached Wier's Store at Fulabusi with great relief.

The store had been renovated after the recent rebellion and was attended by Mr Gerald Young, who was well acquainted with both Gert Strydom and Graham Campbell. Mr Young was sorry to hear that the Strydoms had decided to leave the country, but he was not surprised since he had witnessed the decline in Mrs Maria Strydoms health since the Filabusi murders were committed during the rebellion.

Mr Young encouraged the travellers by informing them that the uprising had settled and that they had purchased a fine piece of land. He warned that labour was not easily attracted, but that it was improving. He said that the farmers were now salting their cattle against the rinderpest, whereby, the cattle were fed the bile of infected animals and this was preventing the healthy cattle from contracting the disease. William and Marty spent some time with Mr Young, ensuring they had the correct direction to Strydom's farm. The travellers remained camped at the store for that night ready to leave for the farm the following morning.

Pilgrims Rest

20 September 1897
My Dearest Johann,

I trust this letter will find you well and in good spirits.

I am seated fifty meters from a picturesque African riverbank, in the cool beneath a magnificent wild Fig tree. On the blanket next to me is Francis, who is fast asleep which allows me to write to you uninterrupted. Near at hand is a small shotgun.

So much has transpired since my last letter. God has blessed us abundantly over the past months. The bank on which I sit is on the Ingwenya River, which translates to Crocodile River, and is on our farm which we have recently purchased. We have named the property 'Pilgrims Rest' for obvious reasons. The river is dry at present, but the elephants dug down into the riverbed last night and exposed a good source of water. The area teams with game of every description. Just entering the river, less than 100 yards from me, is a herd of Impala antelope. I can hear the twittering of guineafowl somewhere to my left and earlier this morning we heard the haunting cry of a fish eagle. Later in the morning we saw a family of warthog chewing at overgrown lawn which was laid by the previous owner. We have purchased this land in conjunction with Marty and Grace, the young couple that were married in Francistown just three short months ago. The farm comprises 1,507 acres. There are no existing buildings as these were destroyed during the Matabele Rebellion just over a year ago. William and Marty are frantically building mud-walled, grass thatch-roofed huts for us to inhabit before the rains set in, which are due at the end of next month. Helping William and Marty is Gabriel Bosko Brady. This is my wonderful adopted son, just 11 years old. He was orphaned and wandered into Dirk and Marty's camp one night. He is Polish and is now learning to speak English. He is such a blessing, a very bright and sensitive boy. He has fitted perfectly into the family and we love him like our own.

We have contracted an African builder, recommended by our neighbour, to assist in building our rondavels. His name is Inyoni and he is extremely skilled. Unfortunately, though understandably, Luka left us three weeks ago to travel back to Lüderitz. We miss him so and fear for his safety on his long journey home. We have prayed earnestly for God's protection over him and hopefully he will meet up with one of Franz De Jong's caravans. Please let us know if and when Luka returns. I so wish you were here to see this beautiful place we now call home. We have much work ahead of us in establishing a living, but I have great faith in William and Marty's ability to make the right decisions.

We are approximately 60 miles from Bulawayo. Once the houses are built, we will take a trip to Bulawayo, which we are told is growing by the day. We hear also that the Cape Railway will arrive into Bulawayo in November this year. This will have huge economic impact on this area.

I am sure your travel to Germany has gone well and I trust our parents are keeping fit. I will write to them shortly to give them all my news.

I wish you all God's blessings.

your loving sister,
Anna and family
PS: I am intrigued to find out how your relationship with Helga is developing?

Llewellin's Map of Southern Africa (1896)

Synopsis

Rhodesia, Rogues, Rebellion, Rinderpest, Railways, Jameson Raid, Rattling Sabres and Romance.

This is a saga of the lives of a group of common people from different nations and ethnic backgrounds whose lives are inextricably intertwined and shaped by the colonial expanse of the 1890s within the rich but dangerous interior of Southern Africa.

The sabres rattled amongst nations, including Britain, Germany, South African Boer Republic, Rhodesia, Bechuanaland and the Great Matabele and Shona Tribes.

A humble prisoner, deported from England, in the bond of a military Colonel, grasps his opportunities in Africa, and through enthralling adventures, faith and unlikely friendships, woos a beautiful wife.

Cecil John Rhodes, Prime Minister of the Cape and Natal Provinces, will stop at nothing to expand the British influence and lay claim to the wealth and riches within the region. His vision is to push his railway north into Rhodesia and onwards to Cairo.

The Pioneers, moving North from South Africa into Rhodesia, encountered a series of tragic trials and challenges within the years of 1896 and 1897, including drought, a terrifying disease, the Rinderpest, which killed hundreds of thousands of cloven-footed beasts—both wild and domestic. Tensions between the South African Boer army and the British armies was heightened when a humiliating and badly planned attempt at instigating a coup on the gold rich Rand in Johannesburg failed at the hands of Cecil John Rhodes and his colleague, Leander Jameson. These events also inspired the Matabele and Mashona rebellions in Rhodesia.

This is a fictional story built around factual historical events and situations at a tumultuous time in the establishment of Rhodesia.